Linda Castillo  selling Kate

"GRIPPING."   —*People*

"CHILLING."   —*USA Today*

"EXCELLENT."   —*Publishers Weekly*

"STUNNING."   —Lisa Scottoline

"MASTERFUL."   —*Booklist*

"FASCINATING."   —*RT Book Reviews*

ALSO BY LINDA CASTILLO

A GATHERING
OF SECRETS

A KATE BURKHOLDER NOVEL

Linda Castillo

St. Martin's Paperbacks

This is a work of fiction. All of the characters, organizations, and events portrayed in this novel are either products of the author's imagination or are used fictitiously.

A GATHERING OF SECRETS

Copyright © 2018 by Linda Castillo.
Excerpt from *Shamed* copyright © 2019 by Linda Castillo.

All rights reserved.

For information address St. Martin's Press, 175 Fifth Avenue, New York, NY 10010.

Library of Congress Catalog Card Number: 2018004425

ISBN: 978-1-250-12132-5

Our books may be purchased in bulk for promotional, educational, or business use. Please contact your local bookseller or the Macmillan Corporate and Premium Sales Department at 1-800-221-7945, ext. 5442, or by e-mail at MacmillanSpecialMarkets@macmillan.com.

Printed in the United States of America

Minotaur Books hardcover edition / July 2018
St. Martin's Paperbacks edition / June 2019

10 9 8 7 6 5 4 3 2 1

This book is dedicated to my dear friend, the late Margaret Burris. She enriched my life with her friendship, her wisdom, her strength, her sense of humor—and all the fun, trials, and tribulations we shared at One Galleria Tower and beyond. She will be deeply and profoundly missed by everyone who knew her.

Acknowledgments

They always say what doesn't kill you makes you stronger. Some novels are more challenging to write than others, and this one fell somewhere between difficult and impossible. I owe tremendous thanks to my editor, Charles Spicer, and my agent, Nancy Yost, who guided me through several drafts and revisions and offered up their usual brilliance and unfettered open-mindedness. I'd also like to thank the entire publishing team at Minotaur Books: Sally Richardson, Andrew Martin, Jennifer Enderlin, Sarah Melnyk, Kerry Nordling, Paul Hochman, Kelley Ragland, Marta Ficke, April Osborn, David Rotstein, Martin Quinn, Joseph Brosnan, Allison Ziegler, and Lisa Davis. You guys are the best of the best, and I'm so happy to be part of your publishing family. Many thanks to my critique group pals—Jennifer Archer, Anita Howard, Marcy McKay, and April Redmon—for all the terrific ideas and support along the way. I also wish to thank my good friend and super librarian, Denise Campbell-Johnson, who always makes time for me when I'm in Ohio—and who's always ready for the next big adventure.

There is some soul of goodness in things evil,
Would men observingly distil it out.

— Shakespeare, *Henry V*

PROLOGUE

She didn't sleep. Hadn't slept through the night in a long time. There was too much darkness, not the kind that was restful. At dawn, when her *mamm* peeked into her bedroom and told her it was time to feed the animals and get ready for worship, she was already awake, waiting. Ready.

Ever the obedient daughter, she pulled on her dress, tugged her hair into a bun, and covered her head with her *kapp*. Stepping into her winter tights and sneakers, she left her room and took the steps down to the living room. She avoided the kitchen, where she could hear her *mamm* clanging breakfast dishes and frying sausage, and went out through the side door and into the cold. The morning was wet and gray, drizzle floating down from a sky the color of iron. Once in the barn, she tossed hay to the horses, filled their water buckets, dumped scratch into the chicken feeder, and gathered six brown eggs.

She'd never lied to her parents. Not once in all of her seventeen years. But when Mamm told her to get cleaned up for worship, she complained that she'd been sick and throwing up half the night. Mamm wasn't pleased that she would miss such an important day. But what could she say?

Morning chores complete, she went back to her room and lay down on her bed. She stared at the ceiling and listened to the sounds of the house. The voices of her younger siblings. The scrape of silverware against plates. The silence while the *gebet nach dem essen* or prayer after meal was recited. The slamming of the door when her *datt* went out to harness the buggy horse. The pound of feet on the wood floor when the little ones went out to help.

Oh, how she would miss them.

At half past seven the back door slammed. A few minutes later, she heard the clip-clop of the old Standardbred's hooves against the ground. Rising, she went to the window and parted the curtains to see the buggy moving down the lane toward the road.

Time to go.

It was a cold morning, well below freezing outside, but she didn't bother with a coat. Pushing open her bedroom door, she stepped into the hall. The lingering aromas of toast and coffee and kerosene from the kitchen heater comforted her as she descended the steps. She thought about her little brothers and sisters, and the pang of melancholy that assailed her nearly sent her to her knees. She'd known this would be difficult, but she also knew it was the only way. She'd asked God for guidance, after all, and He'd sent her a sign. Unlike her, He never, ever lied.

At the base of the stairs, she went left, through the kitchen, trying not to notice the still-warm cup of tea and dry toast her *mamm* had left. The sight of it made her smile. Dry toast and tea were her *mamm*'s cure-all for everything that ailed the world. If only life were that simple.

I'm sorry.

The words echoed inside her head as she crossed through the mudroom, pushed open the back door and stepped into the early-morning drizzle. She didn't feel the cold or wet as she ran down the stone path to the barn. Shoving open the big sliding door, she walked into the dimly lit interior. The aroma of her *datt*'s pipe tobacco mingled with the earthy smells of horses, alfalfa, and damp earth. The hay wagon was parked against the wall to her right, her *datt*'s pitchfork leaning against the side. Ahead, the old plow horse stuck its head over the stall door and whinnied. If the circumstances had been different, she might've taken a minute to stroke its muzzle. This morning, there was no time to spare.

The stairs to the hayloft were to her left. Not giving herself time to debate or dawdle, she took them to the second level. There were only two windows in the loft. Not much light penetrated the grimy glass. But even in the semidarkness she knew the place by heart. It was her refuge when things got bad. This morning, she knew exactly where to find what she needed.

Her sneakers padded softly against the wood plank floor as she crossed to the mound of loose hay beneath the window. Kneeling, she raked it aside with her fingers, uncovering the coil of rope she'd hidden yesterday.

Datt had bought it last summer when he'd made the swing for the boys. He'd had a few extra feet left over and stowed it in the shed for some future project.

She didn't let herself think about her family or what this would do to them as she uncoiled the rope. They wouldn't understand, and that would hurt them. But there was no recourse. God had spoken to her, and she had listened. This was the only way she could keep her secret.

The coil consisted of about ten feet of rope. It was about half an inch in diameter. She thought it might be cotton, but she couldn't be sure. Not that it mattered. She carried the rope to the place where the floor opened and the rafters were visible. Below, she could see the wagon and pitchfork and the horse in its stall.

Lying down on her belly, she looped the rope around the nearest rafter and tied a triple knot. She yanked it a couple of times, testing it, deemed it strong enough to hold. Sitting up, she studied the other end, not exactly sure how to fashion it. Her fingers shook as she formed it into a loop and tied another triple knot. A couple of quick yanks told her it would do.

Taking a deep, calming breath, she slipped the loop over her head, careful not to skew her *kapp*. The rope felt stiff and rough against her skin. At some point, she'd begun to cry. But she thought they were tears of happiness, of relief. Mamm had always told her that death was part of God's divine plan. This morning, she believed that with all her heart. She knew the Lord would welcome her with open arms. He would see her through this. Her family would just have to have faith in His wisdom. Someday, they would join her, and they would all be together again.

Still, she trembled as she rose, trying not to notice the quiver in her stomach, or that her legs weren't quite steady. She didn't think about what came next, but prayed it would be over quickly enough. Once it was done, she would be free.

"I forgive you," she whispered.

Closing her eyes, she stepped forward and fell into space.

CHAPTER 1

Six months later

He dressed in his English clothes. Blue jeans. Plain white T-shirt. The cowboy boots he'd laid down a boatload of money for at the Western store in Berlin.

Anticipation sizzled inside him as he left his bedroom and stepped into the darkened hall. He didn't like this secret thing he'd become. The part of him he barely recognized these days. But there was no stopping it. He'd learned to live with it. Some small part of him had learned to embrace it.

His parents' bedroom door stood ajar; he could hear his *datt* snoring from within. The door to the room where his sisters slept was open halfway. He thought he could smell their sweet little-girl scents, and he smiled as he slid past. The door to his other sister's room was closed. She'd been doing that for about a year now. Growing up, he supposed. Girls kept secrets, too.

He wasn't unduly worried about getting caught as he started down the stairs. He was on *Rumspringa,* after all. For the last few months he'd pretty much done as he pleased; his parents pretended not to notice. He'd tasted whiskey for the first time. Bought his first car. Experienced his first hangover. Smoked his first Marlboro. He'd been staying out late and coming home at all hours. Of course, Mamm and Datt didn't like it, but they held their tongues. They made excuses to his sisters. *Your brother's working a lot,* they would say. But they prayed for his soul. It was all part of growing up Amish. Maybe the best part.

Around him, the house was silent and dark, the only light filtering in through the windows in the living room, twin gray rectangles set into infinite blackness. The aromas of lamp oil and the remnants of the fried bologna sandwiches they'd had for dinner mingled with the cool breeze seeping in through the screens. He pulled the note from his pocket as he entered the kitchen. Pausing at the table, he plucked the tiny flashlight from his rear pocket, shined the beam on the paper, and read it for the dozenth time.

Meet me in the barn at midnight. I'll make it worth your while. ☺

She'd written the words in purple ink. There were hearts over the "i"s and frilly little curlicues on the tails of the "y" and the "g." The smiley face made him grin. He almost couldn't believe she'd finally come around. After weeks of cajoling, and a hundred sleepless nights filled with the longing that came often and with unexpected urgency now, he would finally have her.

No time to waste.

He was wishing he'd thought to brush his teeth as he

let himself out through the back door. Around him, the night was humid and breezy, the sky lit with a thousand stars. A yellow sliver of moon rested against the tree-tops to the east. Ahead, he could just make out the hulking silhouette of the barn sixty yards away. His feet crunched over gravel as he traversed the driveway and went up the ramp. The big sliding door stood open about a foot. Datt always closed it to keep the foxes and coyotes away from the chickens. *She's here,* he thought, and an electric thrill raced through him with such force that his legs went jittery, his stride faltering.

He went through the door, the smells of horses and fresh-cut hay greeting him. The interior was pitch-black, but he knew every inch of the barn, and though he couldn't see his hand in front of his face, he knew exactly where to find the lantern, on its hook hanging from the overhead beam. He reached for it, felt around, but for some reason it wasn't there.

"Shit," he muttered, and pulled the flashlight from his rear pocket, flicked it on. The shadows retreated to the corners, the beam revealing a floating universe of silver dust motes.

"Hello?" he called out. "You there?"

He listened, but there was no reply.

Puzzled, he walked past the wagon mounded with the hay he and Datt had cut last month. Next to it stood the old manure spreader with the broken wheel he'd promised to repair a week ago. In the back of his mind he wondered why the two buggy horses didn't greet him from their stalls. No matter the hour, they were always ready for a snack and never shy about asking for it. He crossed the dirt floor, reached the step-up to the raised wood decking where they stored the burlap bags of oats and corn and chicken scratch. He stopped, sweeping the beam right and left. A grin spread across his face when he spotted the sliver of light beneath the door of the tack room.

"Come out, come out, wherever you are!" Lowering the beam, he started down the aisle.

At first, he thought it odd that she would choose the tack room. But on second thought the small space was clean, with a hardwood floor that was swept daily, and smelled of leather and saddle soap. It was the place where they stored the horse blankets, halters, and harnesses. More important, the door had a lock. Datt had installed it after a halter, a saddle, and two leather harnesses were stolen a couple months ago. He knew it was the *Englischer* down the road who'd done it. Probably sold them at horse auction in Millersburg for some quick cash. The guy was a thief and a boozer, to boot.

He hadn't even laid eyes on her yet, but already he could feel his body responding as he drew closer to the tack room. His *datt* called it *lusht* and warned him to beware of its power. But what did an old man remember about lust? What did he remember about being eighteen years old? If God had put it into the hearts of men, how could it be bad?

Reaching the tack room, he twisted the knob and opened the door. Golden light filled the small space. The smells of freshly oiled leather and kerosene and the lingering redolence of her perfume filled the air. Two horse blankets had been spread out on the floor. Atop the old fifty-gallon drum, a candle on a little white dish flickered. She'd even brought a bottle of wine. Two plastic glasses, the kind with stems. His smile grew into a laugh as he stepped inside.

"The only thing missing is the girl," he said, knowing she was within earshot, listening. "I wonder where she is."

Keenly aware of his surroundings, knowing she had to be close, he flicked off his flashlight and walked over to the blankets. The wine bottle was already open. Setting the flashlight on the drum, he sat down cross-legged, resting his hands on his knees.

"If she doesn't show up soon, I'm going to have to drink this wine all by myself," he said, louder now, expecting her to sweep into the room at any moment, giggling and ready. He'd already gone hard down there, a heated pulse he could no more control than his own breathing. He could imagine the soft warmth of her body against his, the firm rise of her breasts, and he couldn't believe he would finally have all of her tonight.

Reaching for the bottle, he poured, anticipating the sweet tang of red wine against his tongue. He was thinking about all the things they would do when the tack room door creaked. A quick jump of anticipation, then the door slammed hard enough to jangle the halters hanging on the wall.

Startled, he set down the bottle and rose.

The sound of the lock snicking into place sent him to the door. "What are you doing, babes?" He tried the knob, found it locked.

"Hey!" he called out. "Baby, you are so going to pay for this!"

Sounds outside the door drew his attention. Something being dragged across the floor. Heavy things thumping against the door. Perplexed, he jiggled the knob and forced a laugh. "What are you up to?" He'd intended for the words to come out playfully, but there was an edge in his voice now. He wasn't in the mood for this kind of game. Not tonight.

"Come on, babes!" he snapped. "Enough playing around! Come on in here and keep me company!"

The sounds outside the door ceased. Curious, he set his ear against the wood, listened. Nothing.

"If I have to break this door down, you're going to be sorry!" He tried to keep his voice light, add a playful note, but his patience was wearing thin. "You hear me?"

He waited a beat. Thought he heard footsteps. Wood scraping against wood. What the hell was she up to?

"All right, baby. Have it your way." He jiggled the knob again, tamped down a rise of irritation. "I'm just going to pour myself a glass of wine and drink it without you."

No response.

Moving away slightly, he braced his shoulder and shoved against the wood, testing its strength. The door shuddered, but held. Frowning, he jiggled the knob again. "Come on, baby, let me out. Whatever I did, I'll make it up to you."

When no reply came, his anger surged. Using his shoulder, he rammed the door. Another satisfying shudder. He was gearing up to do it again when the smell of smoke registered. Not from the candles or lantern. Not from a cigarette. Something was burning.

Cursing beneath his breath, he looked down and was shocked to see tendrils of smoke rising from beneath the door. Something definitely burning. Wood and hay. Kerosene maybe. What the hell?

All semblance of playfulness left him. He slapped his open palms against the door. "Open up!" he shouted, anger resonating in his voice. "You're going to burn the damn place down, baby. Come on. This isn't funny!"

Backing up, he got a running start and slammed his shoulder against the door. Wood creaked, but it didn't give way. He set his hand against it, realized the surface was warm to the touch. What the hell was this? Some kind of joke? What could she possibly be thinking?

"This is a dangerous thing you're doing!" he shouted. "Stop screwing around and open the damn door. Now!"

He listened, heard the crackle of what sounded like fire. Fingers of alarm jabbed into the back of his neck, sharp claws sinking in deep and curling around his spine. He stood back and landed a kick against the wood, next to the knob. Another satisfying crack. Raising his leg, he kicked it again. Part of the wood jamb split. He could see the brass of the dead bolt now. At some point he'd begun to cough. Smoke was pouring in from beneath the door, black and choking and thick.

"*Come on!*" he screamed. "Are you fucking nuts? Open the door!"

Coughing, he stepped back and lunged forward, his shoulder crashing against the door. Pain zinged across his collarbone, but he didn't care. The door opened an inch. He shoved it with the heels of his hands. There was something in the way. Something outside the door. Too heavy to move. Through the gap, flames and smoke and heat rushed in, scorching his face and hands, stinging his eyes. He smelled singed hair and the cotton fabric of his shirt. He stumbled back, stunned by the scope of the fire, disbelieving that she would be so irresponsible. That this could be happening at all.

"Hey! Go get help!" Looking around wildly, he grabbed the bottle of wine, the only source of liquid, and thrust the open end toward the blaze. Wine splashed onto the fire and door, but it wasn't enough to douse the flames. The fire seemed to drink it in and ask for more.

Heat sent him back another step. Smoke poured through the gap, hot black ropes twisting and rising, taunting him, reaching for him. Yellow flames licked at the wood, growing and moving closer. Raising the crook of his arm to his face, he rushed the door, slammed his body against it. Heat seared his shoulder, the side of his face, his ear, but he didn't feel the pain. The lock had given way; he'd gained another inch. Hope leapt in his chest. But within seconds the opening ushered in a tidal wave of ferocious flames, hungry for fuel, gobbling up the dry wood, eating up the floor.

"Help me!" he screamed. "Fuck! *Help!*"

Smoke and fire streamed in through the gap. The heat scorched his face, set his lungs ablaze, stole all the air in the room. He could hear himself panting and gasping, every inhale like a hot poker shoved down his throat. Choking, he looked around, seeking something, anything, he could use to pound his way to freedom.

Through the thick smoke, he spotted the homemade saddle rack—dual two-by-fours formed into an inverted V and nailed to the wall. He shoved the saddle to the floor, raised his foot, and slammed his boot down on the boards. Nails screeched as they pulled from the wall, the rack slanting down. He stomped it again and the boards gave way, clattered to the floor. Another dizzying leap of hope as he snatched up one of the two-by-fours. Rushing the door, he swung the section of wood like a bat, slammed it against the door. Once. Twice.

On the third swing, the board tore through the wood. An instant of hope, and then fire burst through the hole, a roaring beast with flames tall enough to lick the ceiling.

Panic tore through him. The blaze was burning out of control. There were thirty bales of hay in the loft, dry as tinder and waiting to explode. If the fire reached that hay, he wouldn't make it out.

Choking and cursing, he stumbled back. Too much heat now. Too much smoke to breathe. Ripping off his T-shirt, he dropped to his knees and set the fabric over his nose and mouth. Lowering himself to the floor, he rolled onto his back, raised both legs and rammed his booted feet against the door. Once. Twice.

The door gave way. Wood and ash and sparks rained down on him, embers burning his bare chest and arms and face. A rush of superheated air washed over him. Acrid smoke in his mouth. In his eyes. Through the haze he saw glowing cinders on his jeans, the fabric smoldering, the searing pain of a dozen burns. He brushed frantically at the tiny coals, but there were too many. Too much heat. Not enough air to breathe. Dear God . . .

Fire burst into the room, a rabid, roaring beast that came down on top of him, tore into him with white-hot teeth. Smoke seared his face and neck and chest. The full force of his predicament slammed into him. He screamed, twisted on the floor, rolling and flailing, trying to get away from the pain, but there was no place to go.

His lungs were on fire, burning his lips, his teeth, his tongue. Air too hot to draw a breath. Blinded by smoke and heat. Eyes sizzling in their sockets. The smell of burning flesh in his nostrils. *I'm dying,* he thought, and he was incredulous that this could happen.

"Datt! *Datt!*" But the words were little more than muffled cries. He rolled, clawing at the flames crawling over his body, but he hit the wall, no place else to go. No escape.

He tried to scream, but his spit seemed to boil in his mouth, his tongue clogging it like a piece of cooked meat.

With a final hideous roar, the fire swept over him. Red-hot teeth tearing into him, chewing him up, grinding flesh and bone into a molten ooze, and sucking him into its belly.

CHAPTER 2

When you're the chief of police in a small town, a call at four A.M. is never a good thing. As I roll over and reach for my cell, I'm anticipating news of a fatality accident or, God forbid, bad news about one of my officers or my family.

"Burkholder," I rasp.

"Sorry to wake you, Chief," comes the voice of my graveyard-shift dispatcher, Mona Kurtz. "I just took a call for a barn fire out at the Gingerich place. Thought you'd want to know."

I'm familiar with the Gingerich family. Miriam and Gideon are Amish and live on a small farm a couple miles out of Painters Mill. I don't know them well. They're a nice family and lead quiet lives. Last I heard, they still have four kids at home.

Getting my elbows beneath me, I scoot up to a sitting position. "Anyone hurt?"

"Not sure yet. I talked to one of the volunteer firefighters and he told me the family hasn't been able to account for their son, Danny."

A sense of dread sweeps over me as I throw off the quilt and set my feet on the floor. "Anyone mention the cause?"

"No one knows anything yet."

"I'm on my way."

I hit END as I rise and head to the closet for my uniform.

"What's up, Chief?"

In the light slanting out from my closet, I see my significant other, John Tomasetti, sit up and squint at the clock. His hair is mussed. Even in the dim light, I can see the overnight stubble on his jaw, concern sharp in his eyes.

"There's a fire out at the Gingerich farm," I tell him, shrugging into my shirt. "I got it covered. Go back to sleep."

"Everyone okay?"

It's always the first question asked by law enforcement. Property can be replaced. A life cannot. Grabbing my trousers, I walk over to the bed and step into them. "Teenage son is unaccounted for."

"Well, shit." He sits up, throws off the covers. "You want some company?"

"Or you could stay here and grab another couple hours of sleep."

"I don't have to be at the office until nine."

Tomasetti is an agent for the Ohio Bureau of Criminal Investigation and works out of the Richfield office, half an hour to the north. Painters Mill falls within his jurisdiction, so it wouldn't be unusual for him to show up at a barn fire, especially with someone missing. I know one of these days our relationship—our living arrangement—will be discovered. This morning, with a teenage boy's whereabouts unknown, Tomasetti will be an invaluable resource.

Grabbing my equipment belt and .38 from the drawer, I round the foot of the bed, buckling it as I reach him. "Anyone ever tell you you're a glutton for punishment?"

"Anyone ever tell you how good you look in that thirty-eight?"

"Just you."

Rising, he lays a quick kiss on me, his mouth lingering a beat too long, but I like it.

"Do you know the family?" he asks.

"Not well, but I've met them. They're Amish. Well thought of."

Stepping around me, he goes to the closet, yanks a shirt off a hanger. "Let's hope Junior shows up before we get there."

I turn in to the lane of the Gingerich farm to find one side of their massive bank barn engulfed in flames. The fire is so large, I could see the orange glow above the treetops from half a mile away, and I knew even before seeing it that the structure had sustained major damage.

A tanker from the Holmes County Fire District rattles past as I park out of the way on the grassy shoulder. Tomasetti's Tahoe pulls up behind me as I'm getting out of my city-issue Explorer. A hundred yards away, yellow flames shoot forty feet into the air, licking at the night sky like a thousand fiery tongues.

Embers and ash swirl like snow all around. The

stench of smoke, burning wood, and a myriad of other burning materials mingle with the smells of diesel fuel and exhaust. Four fire trucks from two districts are parked haphazardly in the gravel between the house and barn, engines rumbling. Closer to the structure, several firefighters man hoses, water trained on the flames.

I'm midway to the house when Tomasetti catches up with me. As we cross the side yard, I hear a *whoosh!* and the crack of breaking timber as part of the roof caves in. Sparks fly into the night sky.

"I hope they got the livestock out," I say as we take the steps to the porch.

The door flies open before I can knock. An Amish woman rushes out, soot and panic on her face. Her *kapp* is askew; a cardigan she didn't bother buttoning is thrown over the shoulders of her dress. She looks at me, her entire body shaking. "We can't find Danny," she blurts.

"Is everyone else accounted for?" I ask.

"Yes, but Danny should be here, too. In his room. I can't find him anywhere." She turns and goes back inside, leaving the door open.

Tomasetti and I follow. The living room smells of candle wax and a hint of smoke that's wafted inside through the open windows. A lantern flickers from atop a homemade end table. The Amish woman leads us to the kitchen, where a second lantern casts a dome of yellow light on a big table surrounded by six chairs. The glimmer from the fire outside slants in through the window above the sink.

Without speaking, the woman goes to the back door, which is standing open, and steps onto the porch to stare at the burning barn. Beyond, an ocean of emergency vehicles, flashing lights, and firefighters clad in protective gear fill the space between the house and the barn.

"Danny is your son?" I ask.

"*Ja.*"

"How old is he?"

"Just turned eighteen." She turns to me, her arms wrapped tightly around her midsection, her face ravaged.

I feel Tomasetti's eyes on me as I cross to her. "When did you last see him?" I ask.

She blinks as if trying to kick-start a brain that's overloaded and misfiring. "Last night. He'd gone to bed. Early because he was out late the night before. He has to be at work this morning."

"You've searched the house?"

"That's the first thing we did. Looked all over for him." She can't seem to take her eyes off the barn, giving me only half of her attention. As if the sheer power of her stare will conjure her son.

"Is it possible he got up early and left without telling anyone?" I ask. "Maybe he went in for some overtime? Met a friend for breakfast?"

She shakes her head. "Danny has a car. An old thing he's been driving since he started *Rumspringa*. Gideon doesn't let him park it on the property, so Danny keeps it at the end of the lane. It's still there."

Vaguely, I recall seeing an old Chevy sedan parked

at the mouth of the lane, beneath a walnut tree when I pulled in. I didn't think much of it at the time; my attention had been on the fire. The revelation doesn't bode well for her son.

"Is it possible someone picked him up?" I ask. "A coworker? Or girlfriend?"

"I don't see why anyone would pick him up in the middle of the night. Not when he has a car and doesn't have to be at work until eight. Danny likes his sleep, especially with all the running around."

Expression anguished, she turns to look out the door. "Maybe they've found him by now. Maybe he's out there, helping the firemen put out that fire."

Tomasetti touches her arm. "I'll go check."

Hope leaps into the woman's eyes. A wild thing, barely contained. "My husband, Gideon, is out there, too. He's half crazy with worry, but the firemen won't let him get close to the barn."

"Hang tight." Giving us a final nod, Tomasetti goes through the door.

My radio screeches with dozens of calls, so I lower the volume. "Mrs. Gingerich, while we're waiting, why don't you and I check the house one more time? Just to make sure someone didn't miss something."

"*Mamm*?"

We turn to see a teenage girl come through the kitchen door. Her face is red and tear-streaked. She's wearing a sleep gown and socks, the soles soaked through with mud, a barn coat thrown on over the gown.

"Did you find Danny?" she asks.

"Not yet." The woman wrings her hands, paces from

the door to the girl and then back to the door. "I'm sure he's around somewhere."

I make eye contact with the girl. "Danny's your brother?" I ask.

"*Ja.*"

"When did you last see him?"

"Right before he went to bed. We had ice cream on the porch and then he went to his room."

"What time was that?"

"Ten o'clock or so."

"You checked his bedroom? Bathroom?"

The Amish woman turns to me. "Of course we did. I told you. We checked. He's not here."

I keep my attention on the girl. "Let's you and I check the house one more time, okay? Bathrooms. Closets. Just to make sure. Can you give me a hand with that?"

It doesn't take us long to ascertain that young Danny isn't in the house. Two little girls share a small bedroom and are sleeping peacefully in their beds.

I stop the girl in the upstairs hallway. "What's your name?" I ask.

"Fannie."

"I'm Kate." I offer my hand and she gives it a weak shake. "Does Danny have a cell phone?" I ask.

"Having a phone is against the *Ordnung,*" the girl says, referring to the unwritten rules of their church district.

I press her anyway. "He was on *Rumspringa,* right? Maybe he'd gotten a phone and didn't want your parents to know?"

Fannie shakes her head. "He wouldn't."

I nod, but I know better. More than likely, an eighteen-year-old Amish boy on *Rumspringa* does, indeed, have a phone.

"*Rumspringa*" is the *Deitsh* word for "running around." It's the time in a young Amish person's life when they have the opportunity to experience the world without all those Amish rules, usually right before they become baptized and join the church. It gives me hope that Danny simply slipped out in the middle of the night and didn't tell anyone.

I go to Danny's room next, open the door, and step inside. Fannie follows. Like most Amish bedrooms, this one doesn't have a closet. Clothes are hung on wooden dowels. Shoes are lined up against the wall. I notice immediately one of the dowels is bare. A single pair of work boots is tucked beneath the bed.

I motion toward the boots. "Does he have more than one pair of shoes?"

She tilts her head to look at the boots, and her face screws up. "His cowboy boots are gone." She begins to cry.

"Cowboy boots?"

She pulls a shredded tissue from her pocket and dabs at her eyes. "He bought them with his first paycheck from his job in town. He's crazy about them." She chokes out a sound that's part sob, part laugh. "Says they drive the girls wild. They're the ugliest things I ever saw, but he wears them everywhere."

I reach out and gently touch her arm. "Fannie, maybe he sneaked out to meet some friends or a girlfriend.

Don't give up hope just yet. We've barely begun to search."

The girl's expression brightens, but she doesn't look hopeful. "Luane's *mamm* and *datt* would never let her leave the house after dark, especially with a boy. Even a good boy like Danny."

"Luane is his girlfriend?"

"*Ja.*" She starts to cry again, but regains control quickly. "Her parents are Swartzentruber. Strict, you know. They love Danny like a son, but they still wouldn't allow such a thing."

"Where there's a will, there's a way." I mutter the words beneath my breath and motion toward the stairs. "Let's go talk to your *mamm.*"

A few minutes later, Miriam, Fannie, and I sit at the kitchen table, trying hard to ignore the cacophony of voices, engines, and sirens outside. Miriam made coffee and set a cup in front of me. No one drinks.

"Fannie tells me Daniel has a girlfriend," I begin.

The Amish woman nods. "Luane Raber. She's a sweet girl. Only sixteen years old. They're a good match. I suspect they'll get married. . . ."

"Do the Rabers have a phone?" I ask. "Maybe he went to see his girl."

"They're Swartzentruber and have no need for a phone."

I hit the lapel mike at my shoulder and hail my third-shift officer. "T.J.? What's your twenty?"

T.J. Banks is the youngest officer in my small department and the only rookie. Since he's got the least amount of seniority, he usually ends up on the grave-yard shift.

"I'm setting up traffic cones in front of the Gingerich place, Chief."

"I want you to run over to Mose and Sue Raber's place out on Dogleg Road. Tell them there's been a fire here at the Gingerich farm and we're trying to locate Daniel. See if he's there. Check any barns or outbuildings. And find out if their daughter, Luane, is there. Make sure you speak to her personally, just in case he decided to sneak over without her parents knowing."

"Got it."

I turn my attention back to Miriam. "I understand Daniel is on *Rumspringa*."

"It's true. He's at that age."

"Mrs. Gingerich, can you think of anywhere else he might've gone? Some place we might find him?" I look from Miriam to her daughter. "Any friends he might be visiting?"

Fannie shakes her head. "He would have taken the car."

"Unless someone picked him up," I put in.

Closing her eyes, the woman shakes her head. "None of his friends have a car, Chief Burkholder. Danny works hard. Saves his money. He bought the thing a few months ago and drives it every chance he gets."

A knock sounds on the back door. Before Miriam can get to her feet, it opens and Tomasetti enters the kitchen. He makes eye contact with me and I see the answer in his eyes before he speaks.

Miriam stands. "Did you find him?"

Tomasetti shakes his head. "We're still looking, ma'am."

I excuse myself and Tomasetti and I go outside. Standing on the small porch, we look out at the emergency vehicles and firefighters. The barn is still burning, but not as ferociously now. Smoke and steam pour into the night sky. The rafters are visible, much of the roof eaten away by the fire.

"Did they lose any livestock?" I ask.

"That's what I wanted to talk to you about."

I look at him, puzzled.

"I talked with Gideon Gingerich a few minutes ago. He told me at about eight P.M., he and Danny put their two buggy horses and four calves in the barn for the night."

I know what he's going to say next and a slow rise of dread wells in my chest.

"We found the two horses and calves out in the pasture behind the barn," he tells me.

"Someone released the livestock," I murmur.

"Looks like it."

"One of the firefighters? Maybe one of the first responders?"

"Gingerich told me that by the time the fire department got here, the barn was already engulfed. The livestock had already been let out."

"That's interesting."

"According to the fire chief, a little too interesting."

I wait.

"Kate, someone let those animals out. It wasn't Gideon Gingerich. And it wasn't a firefighter."

"Maybe it was Daniel," I say. "Maybe he woke up, smelled smoke. Got up to check it out and saw the fire."

"Or maybe he was pissed off about something or angry with his parents and decided to torch the barn. Maybe he couldn't bear the thought of killing those animals."

"If he took off, he would have taken his car."

"I agree." Tomasetti gives me a hard look. "We need to find him, Kate."

"For a lot of reasons."

"The fire chief called the fire marshal's office. They're going to take a hard look at this."

"He suspects arson?" I ask.

"He's suspicious enough so that he made the call." He slants a look at me. "Chances are the fire chief is just being thorough. More than likely, someone left a lantern burning. The globe overheated or a barn cat knocked it over."

"Or maybe Danny Gingerich started the fire by accident and panicked."

"That's a possibility. I mean, we're talking about a barn full of hay. Gingerich had thirty bales stored in the hayloft. They went up like kindling." He shrugs. "But with the kid missing and those animals released, he thought the situation warranted a thorough once-over."

I nod in agreement, but I'm troubled by the possibilities. "The kid's car is parked at the end of the lane."

"I saw it when we pulled in." His brows knit. "Why would he park it there?"

"His parents don't approve and don't allow him to bring it onto the property. I've seen it happen before."

"Any bad blood between Daniel and his parents?"

"No one has said anything, but I'll dig a little, see what I can find out."

My cell vibrates against my hip. I glance at the display, see T.J.'s name come up. "What do you have?" I ask.

"I'm out here at the Raber farm, Chief," he tells me. "Talked to both the parents as well as the daughter, Luane. Daniel Gingerich hasn't been here for a couple days."

"Thanks for checking."

"You bet."

"Can you do one more thing for me before you call it a day?"

"Name it."

"I want you to canvass the area around the Gingerich farm. Take a drive around the perimeter. Knock on some doors, talk to the neighbors to see if anyone has seen Daniel."

"You got it."

I end the call and look at Tomasetti. "If Daniel Gingerich took off, not only did he leave his car behind, but his girlfriend."

"Doesn't sound like something an eighteen-year-old boy would do." Tomasetti reaches for his phone, glances at the display, and then drops it into his pocket. "I've got to go. Keep me posted, will you, Chief?"

"Thanks for coming along."

"Any time." He glances left and right, but there are too many people around for him to risk kissing me. Instead, he offers up a grin. "See you later."

CHAPTER 3

It's noon by the time I arrive at the police station. Before leaving the scene I talked to the fire chief from Millersburg. I've met Fred Achin on several occasions over the years. He's a family man, a good chief, and an experienced firefighter. The interior of the structure was still too hot for them to make entry, but they laid down over five thousand gallons of water and Fred thought they'd be able to start sifting through the rubble this afternoon.

At first light I spent a couple of hours walking the property, but there was nothing there. No sign of a vehicle, no unusual footprints. Law enforcement doesn't get too excited right off the bat about an eighteen-year-old boy going missing, but in light of a suspicious fire and the passage of so much time without contact, we're actively looking for him. I also spent some time with Gideon and Miriam Gingerich. The Amish are generally stoic in the face of adversity. Even so, the couple was understandably distraught about their missing son. I sat down with them and they supplied me with a list of Danny's friends as well as places he might've gone. I promised them I would leave no stone unturned. Even if he had something to do with the fire—whether it was accidental or deliberate—locating him is job one.

My uniform reeks of smoke as I slide behind my desk and boot up my computer. I've just taken my first sip of coffee when my phone jangles. It's Fred Achin.

A wave of foreboding rolls over me at the sound of the fire chief's voice. In my heart of hearts, I know there's news—and it's not good.

"We got a body in the barn," he tells me.

"Shit." I get to my feet. "Are you sure?"

"We're sure."

My mind spins through the repercussions. "You got ID?"

"No."

"Has anyone talked to Gideon or Miriam Gingerich?"

"No. Look, the investigator just discovered the remains a few minutes ago. I knew you'd want to know right away."

"The fire marshal is on scene?"

"Investigator got here an hour ago." He pauses. "Look, we don't have anything official yet, but he thinks the fire is suspicious. There was an accelerant used. Gasoline."

"How do you know?"

"You can smell it."

That the fire may have been intentionally set casts an even darker shadow over an already terrible situation. "Have you called Doc Coblentz?" I ask, referring to the coroner of Holmes County.

"That's my next call."

"Fred, can you hold off a few minutes?" I pick up my keys. "I'm ten minutes away. Even though we don't have a positive ID on the body, the family needs to know about the remains." I struggle to find the right words. "I think it would be best if I was there to explain the situation to them before they see the coroner's vehicle arrive."

"Shit, Chief, I don't envy you that chore." He heaves another sigh. "I'll hold off a few minutes, but you'd better get over here quick."

I run my lights, blow the stoplight at Main Street, and make it to the Gingerich farm in record time. I take the lane too fast, gravel pinging inside my wheel wells, tires raising a cloud of dust. A single fire truck from the Painters Mill volunteer fire department is parked thirty feet from the burned-out shell of the barn, probably in case a hot spot flares. There's a black SUV I don't recognize. A red Suburban. A red and white van with STATE FIRE MARSHAL emblazoned on the side. Fred Achin and two men I don't know are standing next to Fred's vehicle, talking. A nice-looking bay gelding hitched to a buggy stands tied to a post a few yards from the house. There's no sign of the coroner's van, and I'm relieved Fred kept his word.

I park behind the buggy and head toward the back door. I'm midway down the sidewalk when the door opens. Gideon Gingerich steps onto the porch, his eyes fastened to mine, his expression beseeching.

"You bring word of my son?" he asks.

His wife Miriam stands in the doorway, looking at

me as if she's about to wrench information from me by the sheer force of her stare. "Did you find him?"

I reach them, dividing my attention between them. "Can we go inside and sit down for a few minutes?" I motion toward the door. "Please."

Without speaking, Gideon pushes open the door and ushers me inside.

A cop never knows how someone is going to react to that initial punch of grief. All I can do at this juncture is relay the facts and emphasize the point that we have no definitive proof the body is their son.

I nod at the middle-aged Amish couple sitting at the kitchen table. I suspect they're the Gingeriches' neighbors. They're solemn-faced and wearing their best clothes. Here to support the family, I think, but then that's the Amish for you.

"Mr. and Mrs. Gingerich," I begin, "may I speak with you privately?"

"This is my brother and sister-in-law." Gideon sends a nod toward the couple. "Whatever news you've come to relay, Chief Burkholder, they can hear it."

I nod at the couple, and turn my attention back to the Gingeriches. "Let me preface by saying I do not have definitive news about your son." I pause, giving the statement time to sink in. "But you need to know that the fire chief discovered a body inside the barn."

Miriam Gingerich makes a noise that sounds like some small animal being slowly crushed to death. Raising her hand as if to stop me from saying anything more, she bends slightly and backs away from the table. "No. *No.*"

"We do not know that it's Daniel," I say firmly. "There's been no positive ID. But I wanted you to know that human remains were found and the coroner is on his way. Once the body is recovered, we'll begin the identification process."

Gideon opens his mouth as if to speak, his lips quivering, but he doesn't make a sound.

The visiting couple lowers their gazes to the tabletop. They don't speak. They don't move.

"An investigator from the fire marshal's office is here now. He'll be investigating the fire and will hopefully be able to find the origin and the cause."

"The . . . dead person in the barn . . ." The Amish man's words come out as a hoarse whisper. "You think it's Daniel?"

"I don't know," I say honestly. "I wish I could give you a better answer. We just don't know yet."

"Who else would it be?" Miriam chokes out the words. "Our sweet Danny. I can't believe it."

The Amish woman at the table rises, goes to her, and sets her hands on Miriam's arms. "*Du moosht ohheicha net da Deivel.*" You must not listen to the devil. "Believe the best until you know for sure."

Movement from the doorway snags my attention. Fannie Gingerich is standing in the hall just outside the kitchen, her hands on the shoulders of her two little sisters, about four or five years of age. Three sets of eyes flick from me to their parents and back to me.

"What happened?" the girl asks.

When no one answers, she begins to cry. The little

girls look up at her and, seeing their older sibling's face, begin to cry as well.

"Hush now." Miriam opens her arms to the two little ones, who rush to her and bury their faces against her bosom. "You just shush now. You hear? All of this is in the hands of the Lord and we trust Him to show us the light."

I turn my attention to Gideon. "Can I speak with you outside for a moment?"

He nods and follows me onto the back porch. I give him a moment to collect himself and we look out across the driveway where two men in protective suits are already inside the blackened remains of the barn. Doc Coblentz has arrived on scene. His Escalade is parked just outside the caution tape.

"Mr. Gingerich," I begin, "according to the arson investigator, there may have been an accelerant used to start the fire. He thinks it was gasoline."

The Amish man looks at me, misery boiling in his expression. "Are you saying someone *did* this thing? They burned our barn on purpose?" He looks down at the ground, raises his hand to his face, and scrubs it over his eyes as if all of this is too much for him to take in. "*Mein Gott.*" My God. "*Danny . . .*"

I ask gently, "Do you keep gas in the barn? Do you store it anywhere on your property?"

He shakes his head. "The *Ordnung* forbids the use of gasoline. We use only diesel for the generator."

"Can you think of anyone who might have done this? Either intentionally or accidentally?"

He shakes his head adamantly. "No."

"Have you had any disagreements with anyone? Any problems with neighbors or acquaintances? Strangers? Family members?"

"No."

"Has anyone been angry with you or any of your family members?"

Another shake. "We get along with our neighbors just fine."

"What about business associates? English? Amish? Anyone?"

"No. *No.*"

I choose my next words carefully, knowing they will not be received well. "Mr. Gingerich, have you had any problems or disagreements with Daniel?"

"*Danny?*" He looks at me as if I've just admitted to pouring the gasoline and striking a match myself. "Never," he says, his mouth trembling. "He's a good boy."

"Has Danny—"

"No!" he says abruptly, the word as much a cry as a warning. "No more questions."

"Mr. Gingerich, please—"

"Enough!" He cuts me off and then turns away, opens the door. "If you want to help us, Chief Burkholder, I suggest you get out there and find my son."

Casting a final look over his shoulder, he goes into the house, letting the door slam behind him.

Ten minutes later I'm standing outside the yellow caution tape surrounding the barn, watching two investigators wade through ash and debris. Most of the exterior walls are still standing, but some of the rafters have collapsed, bringing down a segment of the roof.

"Good thing the fire department got here when they did or this place would have burned clean to the ground."

I glance over to see Ludwig Coblentz toddle toward me, a suitcase-size medical bag at his side. He's a portly man prone to bad fashion choices and the occasional fedora, and has a well-known weakness for fast food. He's one of six doctors in Painters Mill; he's been coroner for nearly twelve years.

"Hi, Doc." I cross to him and we shake hands. "Thanks for getting here so quickly."

He sends a pointed look toward the barn. "I understand we have an as-of-yet-unidentified body."

"The homeowner's son is missing."

His expression darkens. "A child?"

"Teenager. Daniel just turned eighteen."

"Chief Burkholder?"

We turn to see one of the investigators approach, peeling off his gloves, his head covering, and the outer layer of protective clothes as he crosses the remaining distance between us.

"Bob Schoening, Department of Commerce." He sticks out his hand and we shake. "I'm the investigator for the state fire marshal's office."

"Any idea what happened here?" I ask.

"I just completed my initial walk-through. We've got one body. Badly burned but intact, so we'll probably be able to extract DNA, if necessary."

"Any ID on the body?" I ask.

"I don't believe any type of plastic ID, like a driver's license or credit card, could have survived the temps of that fire. That said, if the victim was wearing metal jewelry that can be identified by family members or some type of metal medical ID bracelet, we might be able to get an unofficial ID."

He shrugs. "I got a pretty good look at those remains and I didn't see any jewelry. But I need to get in there, thoroughly document the scene, and take my samples before I release the scene to the coroner."

I nod. "How long?"

He glances at his watch. "A few hours."

I sense there's more coming. "Look, this is all preliminary," he tells me, "but just so you know . . . I found intense localized burning outside what looks to be a tack room."

"Tack room?" I ask.

"There was a leather horse saddle, some halters, and other equipment that's still recognizable. That's where the body is located."

"I understand there was an accelerant present."

"Plenty of it. So much that I could *smell* it the instant I entered the scene and you know how fallible the human nose is. I'll know more once I get in there with the hydrocarbon sniffer." He produces a small electronic device about the size of an old-fashioned telephone handset. "It can sniff out even trace amounts of ILRs."

"ILRs?"

"Ignitable liquid residues." He pockets the device and leans close. "Let me tell you—there's nothing trace about any of this. I got a pour pattern right outside the tack room door. Worse, the door appears to have been locked and barricaded with some kind of debris. Hay maybe. It burned, of course, but the baling wire was left behind."

"So the victim was in the tack room and had possibly been trying to keep someone out?" I ask. "Some threat maybe?"

His laugh is a humorless sound, like the scrape of dry wood against stone. "Preliminarily speaking? It looks to me like someone locked that poor son of a bitch in the tack room, barricaded it with hay, some cinder blocks, and a wheelbarrow. Then they soaked all of it with gasoline, including the door, and set it on fire."

It takes a moment for the horror of the scenario to sink into a brain that doesn't want to believe. "Is there any way it could have been some kind of . . . freak accident?" I hear myself ask. "Or a prank gone wrong?"

"I suppose it could have been a prank that went south, but who would do something so dangerous and stupid?"

"Could it have been accidental? I mean, the Amish do use lanterns."

He looks around, raises an arm to blot sweat from his forehead. "Look, all I'm saying at this juncture is that either one of those scenarios is a stretch. I mean, the door was locked. It was *barricaded*. That's not to mention the presence of an accelerant. That's all I got to go on."

We fall silent, our minds working that over. "I know you're still in the preliminary stages of your investigation, but was there any physical evidence left behind?"

I ask. "Footwear impressions? A gas can? Anything that might have fingerprints on it?"

"Not that I've seen, but it's a mess in there. Hayloft burned and all that hay came down. I got debris everywhere. Still got a few hot spots, too. Once we get everything photographed, I'm going to do some digging around, see if there's anything left that needs to be preserved and taken back to the lab. We'll check everything for fingerprints—"

"Can prints survive a fire like that?" I ask.

"Interestingly, latents can survive temps up to a hundred degrees Celsius. For a few hours anyway. It's premature to know if we'll get anything at this point, but we'll do our best."

He glances at his watch again. "Look, I'm going to get back to it. Once I get my samples, photograph everything, video the scene, and collect any evidence, I'll turn the body over to the coroner." He nods at Doc Coblentz. "I'm probably not going to have a final ruling on any of this for several days, maybe a week. That said, I'm telling you now, unofficially, that there's enough evidence here now for me to tell you this was no accident."

CHAPTER 4

Nothing happens quickly in the course of investigating a crime scene. Any evidence left behind must be painstakingly collected, preserved, and documented, especially if there's a fatality involved. It takes a tremendous amount of time, expertise, and patience. Any cop will tell you: Waiting for results is the bane of their existence. Fingerprints. DNA. Footwear impressions. Tire tread imprints.

Doc Coblentz and I wait for more than four hours while Schoening collects samples, utilizes the hydrocarbon sniffer, photographs and videotapes the entire scene, both the interior and exterior. In the meantime, Doc's technician unloads a gurney upon which a body bag and tarp have been unfolded. As soon as the scene is turned over to the coroner, the victim will be transported to the morgue at Pomerene Hospital, where the official identification process will begin.

While we're waiting, Gideon Gingerich emerges from the house twice. The first time, he walks over to us, looks at the gurney, doubles over as if he's going to be sick, then turns and goes back inside without saying a word. The second time, he stops next to me and asks, "Is it him?"

"We haven't been able to get in there yet," I tell him. "I'm sorry. I know the waiting is difficult."

The Amish man can't seem to stop staring at the wrecked barn or the two biohazard-gear-clad men tromping around inside it. He makes a sound, a whimper, and for the first time I see tears. He returns to the house without saying anything else.

At just before five P.M., Bob Schoening walks over to me, his expression grim. "We're done here for now, Chief Burkholder. Everything's been documented. Samples taken. We've bagged a few items. I've marked the location of the body with flags." He motions toward several small white flags that are about a foot tall; the kind a utility company might use to demark underground electric or gas lines, the small squares of vinyl flapping in the breeze. "The coroner is free to take control of the scene and retrieve the body."

"Are you still confident this was arson?" I ask.

He nods. "I believe the evidence will support that." He passes me his card. "If you need anything else or have any questions, give me a call."

After pulling on biohazard gear, Doc Coblentz and his technician wade into the ash and debris, toward the flags demarking the location of the victim.

Not for the first time I wonder how he does it. How a man committed to healing the sick can look death in the face so often and still remain such an upbeat and optimistic person. But when the dead are brought to him, he doesn't see the victim as they'd been in life; he doesn't mourn their passing or get caught up in the tragedy of their death. He sees a puzzle that must be solved—and sometimes an injustice that must be remedied. I once asked him if this part of his job ever bothered him. His answer was straightforward and far too easy to understand. When it's a kid, he'd said.

I stand outside the caution tape and watch as the technician photographs the remains. When he's finished, he and Doc Coblentz carry the stretcher to the flagged area and set it down among the debris. I don't have biohazard gear, and I'm vastly relieved they don't need my help. I'm not squeamish; I've seen my share of death from traffic fatalities, farming accidents, natural causes, even murder. While blood and decomposition are bad enough, there's something particularly disturbing about the remains of a burned human being.

Extreme heat causes the skin to shrink, which can bring about splitting. The dehydrating effects of heat also cause the muscles to contract, producing the "pugilistic attitude" of many burn fatalities. Novice investigators have been known to attribute the pose to a defensive position, the splitting to blunt-force trauma. I'm reassured that Doc Coblentz is a veteran.

I watch from my place at the perimeter of the scene as the two men gently heft the body onto the stretcher and drape it with a blue sheet. Gideon Gingerich has been walking over to us every twenty minutes or so. The last thing any of us want to do is expose him to the charred body of what may be his son.

When the two men emerge from the ashes, I pull

aside the caution tape. After they pass through, I replace the tape and follow them to the van. All the while I keep an eye on the back door of the house, but no one comes out. I wonder if Gideon is distracting his wife and children long enough for us to get the body into the van and out of sight.

"Are the clothes intact, Doc?" I ask.

Doc Coblentz shakes his head. "The only thing that's recognizable is the shoes. Boots, actually, and only then because they're leather and withstood the heat."

Something quickens inside me at the mention of leather boots. Daniel's sister had mentioned cowboy boots . . .

I glance at the technician. "May I take a look at the shoes?"

Since I'm not wearing gloves, he lifts the bottom corner of the sheet. I brace, my eyes quickly taking in the black, vaguely human form. Arms curled across the chest. Legs bent. The exterior is charred black and covered with gray-white ash. I hold my breath because I know the smell of burned flesh will follow me home and haunt me through the night.

For an instant, I'm not exactly sure what I'm looking at; then I see the shape of a foot. The pointed toe and slanted heel of a Western boot. The stitching has burned, the sole separating from the leather upper. But I can still make out the distinctive silhouette of a classic cowboy boot.

"Danny Gingerich's sister told me her brother's cowboy boots are missing from his room," I say. "According to her, he wears them all the time."

"Good to know, Kate, but at this point, I believe everyone suspects this is likely Daniel Gingerich," Doc Coblentz responds in a low voice. "That said, shoes can be put on or taken off after someone is deceased. And so we must be certain and go about the identification process, starting with dental or medical records if there are any. Once we confirm the identity, we'll move on to determine cause and manner of death."

"I'll check with the parents to see if Danny had any dental work or X-rays done," I say.

"That would be helpful," he tells me, and replaces the sheet.

The coroner's van is pulling away as I take the sidewalk to the back porch. The door swings open before I can knock, and Gideon comes through it. His eyes are red, his mouth drawn into a grim, hard line. I see wet spots on the front of his shirt, and I realize he's been crying.

"I'm sorry to bother you again," I say, wishing there were something I could do to alleviate his pain. "Mr. Gingerich, I need to ask you a few questions about Daniel."

He nods.

"Do you know if your son has had any dental work done? Did he ever have a broken bone? Any X-rays taken?"

Closing his eyes briefly, he nods. "He was kicked in the face by one of the cows when he was thirteen. Broke two teeth. We took him to the dentist in town. Dr. Gray, I think."

"Did Dr. Gray take X-rays?"

"I think so."

I nod. "Did Daniel ever have any broken bones?"

The Amish man's face twists into a mask of agony, but he fights the wave of emotion and recovers. "When he was seven. Fell out of the hayloft and broke his arm."

"Do you recall which doctor he saw?"

"We took him to the emergency room at Pomerene." His mouth quivers again. "I know why you're asking these questions. I cannot . . ."

Unable to finish the sentence, he lowers his face into his hands, emits a sob fraught with unbearable sadness.

I reach out and set my hand on his arm. "I'll come see you the moment I know anything, good or bad."

Raising his head, he nods, then walks into the house without a word.

The Mercantile was usually silent at nine P.M. The shop closed at six o'clock sharp six days a week, and that schedule hadn't altered since the place opened a year ago. Tonight, however, Shania Twain belted out a song, proclaiming to the world she felt like a woman. The industrial lighting that lent so much character to the old barn, with its ancient beams and concrete floor, buzzed with electricity. The aromas of apple cider and cinnamon filled the air with the essences of autumn.

Neva Lambright would never tell anyone, especially her *mamm,* but this was her favorite time of day. After hours, when the customers, with all their stupid questions and nitpicky complaints, were gone, the music was blasting something that would make her *datt* frown, and it was just her and her friends, Ina Yoder and Viola Stutzman.

The three girls had been best friends for so long, Neva couldn't even remember when they met. They'd grown up together, attended school together, shared the trials and tribulations of becoming young women together. And so last year, when Neva's *mamm* and *datt* opened their Amish tourist shop, Ina and Viola were the natural choices for employees.

Tonight, the three of them were at the front of the store, working on the two display windows for *Alle-lieweziel,* or Halloween, which was a month away. Viola, the most creative of the three, had come up with the idea of displaying a few of their trick-or-treat costumes for the little ones, everything from pirates to Superman to cute Amish outfits replete with dresses and *kapps* for girls, and trousers with suspenders and straw hats for boys.

The second window had been fashioned to look like a *spuk haus,* or haunted house. They'd borrowed one of the boxed electric fireplaces from the housewares department. Viola added the skull lantern with its grinning mouth and backlit eyes. Ina had kiddingly suggested adding a skeleton, but Neva had run with it. They'd dragged a chair from the café, put Mr. Skeleton in the chair, and given him Edgar Allan Poe's "The Raven" to read.

"Some of the Amish aren't going to like all this spooky stuff," Ina pointed out.

From her place inside the display window, Viola

sprayed cobwebs onto the chair. "The *Englischers* are going to love it."

"Especially the little ones." Neva stood just off the front window, studying the display with a critical eye. "It's perfect."

"Oh, you Beachy Amish," Ina said teasingly. "Always pushing the limit of what's acceptable."

Neva took the gibe in stride. The Beachy Amish are a progressive group that allows its members to drive cars and the limited use of technology like phones and computers. Some of the Old Order don't even consider them Amish. But Neva never felt lesser in any way, especially when it came to her friends.

"Car comes in handy when it's ten below or raining," Neva said breezily.

"I'll second that." Viola cleared her throat. "Car aside, if it's all the same to you two, I'd like to finish sometime before midnight." Brushing the spray-can cobwebs from her dress, she stepped out of the window display. "Let's see how all of this looks from the outside."

Exchanging grins, the girls headed toward the door. The evening was crisp and breezy. Neva smelled burning leaves and she knew the English boys down the road had spent the afternoon raking Mr. Groves's yard.

"It's the best we've ever done," Viola said.

"Better than any of the other shops." Ina rubbed her chin. "What if we add some of those little lights?"

"Too cheerful," Neva replied. "We want this to be scary."

"As long as we don't frighten the little ones," Viola said.

"Little pansies need not apply," Neva said, and the three of them broke into laughter.

Ina sighed. "I can't wait for your *mamm* to see it."

"We still have to do the pumpkin display," Viola pointed out.

Ina looked from girl to girl. "Are we carving them?"

"Definitely carving and using those tea lights for the inside," Neva said. "Tomorrow, though. I've been here since seven A.M. and I'm beat."

"Says the slave driver," Ina muttered.

Viola elbowed her. "Let's clean up and get out of here."

While Viola and Ina stowed the stepladder and gathered the trash they'd amassed in the course of their work, Neva went to the café. She dumped the remaining cider into the sink and rinsed the pot. She'd just finished wiping the table where they'd sat and drawn out their plans earlier, when the lights went out. The radio fell silent. The darkness that followed was so complete, Neva couldn't see her hand in front of her face.

"Not funny!" she called out.

"I didn't do anything," came Viola's voice.

Ina countered with, "Maybe your *mamm* forgot to pay the electric bill."

Slowly, Neva's eyes adjusted to the darkness. She could barely make out the front windows from where she stood. Gray light seeping in.

"What do we do now?" Viola asked.

"I think there's some kind of electrical box out back."

Neva left the café and stopped just outside the rail. "There's a flashlight in Mamm's office," she called out. "I'll be right back."

Carefully, she made her way through the darkness and went into the office. Inside, she felt around for the desk, found the flashlight in the second drawer. Relief slipped through her when she flipped it on and a cone of yellow light filled the room.

She was on her way to the front of the shop when a crash sounded. It was like breaking glass and was followed by a yelp.

Holding the flashlight beam in front of her, she ran toward her friends. "What happened?"

"The window," came Ina's voice. "It just . . . shattered."

"*What?*" Neva shifted the beam. Her friends stood near the display window, looking startled. Glass sparkled on the floor. She jerked the beam to the window. Sure enough, there was a hole the size of a basketball in the center.

"We were just standing here, waiting for you to come back with the flashlight, when the window just . . . exploded," Viola said.

"I think someone threw something," Ina added.

An instant of silence ensued. It was so quiet Neva could hear the wind rushing through the trees outside.

"What's that?" Ina motioned toward an object the size of a soccer ball lying on the floor.

Neva shifted the beam. Recognition flashed, followed by a stab of disbelief, of revulsion. "*Mein Gott.*"

The cone of light illuminated the severed head of a

hog. It was white with a pink snout. Cloudy eyes. Mouth open. Tongue hanging out. The smear of blood on the floor gleamed black in the semidarkness.

Gasping, Viola set her hand against her chest and stepped back. "It's . . . a butchered hog."

"Someone pitched it through the window," Ina said.

"Why would someone do such a thing?" Viola whispered.

The silence that followed sent a shiver through Neva. She hadn't told her friends what was going on. Hadn't told anyone. Now, she wondered if she should have. If she should have done something about it.

"It's a stupid Halloween prank is all," she said.

"It's creepy," Viola whispered.

"What do we do?" Ina asked.

Another exchange of looks, thoughtful this time, and frightened.

Neva swept the beam over the macabre scene, felt cold fingers of dread clamp over the back of her neck. She'd hoped it would stop. The threats. The intimidation. The hatred. It was the only secret she'd ever kept from her friends. She'd prayed he would find the strength to move on. To let *her* move on and forget about what she'd done. The mistake she'd made.

"Should we call the police?" Ina asks.

Doing her best to look unaffected, Neva shook her head. "I'll call Mamm."

Ina and Viola exchanged looks.

"She'll know what to do," Neva said. "She always does."

CHAPTER 5

After leaving the Gingerich farm yesterday afternoon, I went to see Dr. Charles Gray—the dentist who'd X-rayed Daniel Gingerich's teeth when he was thirteen years old. I let him know that Doc Coblentz would be forwarding him a set of dental X-rays for comparison and, as usual, we're anxious for results.

It's eight A.M. now, and I'm in my office, thinking about a third cup of coffee, when the call finally comes. I glance down at the display to see BRIGHT SMILE DENTISTRY, and I brace.

It's Dr. Gray.

"I just compared the X-rays from my archive with the films Dr. Coblentz sent over," he tells me. "They match. The victim in that barn is, indeed, Daniel Gingerich."

"Damn," I mutter.

"Sorry to be the bearer of bad news. I figured you'd want to let the family know as soon as possible."

Grabbing my keys, I head for reception, catch my first-shift dispatcher just as she's finishing up a call. Lois Monroe is in her mid-fifties, a mother and grandmother, and a much-appreciated fixture in the department. She's coolheaded and candid; I've seen her take more than one overly cocky young cop down a notch or two.

"Lois, I need you to dig up everything you can find on Daniel Gingerich. Check for warrants. Run him through LEADS. Family members, too. Parents, Gideon and Miriam. Girlfriend, Luane Raber. He's got a teen-aged sister, too. Fannie." LEADS is the acronym for the Law Enforcement Automated Data System, which is a statewide criminal justice database administered by the Ohio State Highway Patrol.

"You got it." Scribbling, she cocks her head. "I take it you confirmed the victim was him?"

I reach the door, turn to face her, and nod. "We don't have manner or cause yet, but we're treating his death as a homicide. I need you to get a tip line set up. We're offering a five-hundred-dollar reward for information leading to the arrest and conviction of the person responsible. Get that out to all media outlets." I have no idea how I'll come up with the money, but I'll figure something out.

"You got it."

"I'm going to see the family. If you get any media inquiries about the fire or investigation, tell them we'll be sending out a press release end of day."

I call Sheriff Mike Rasmussen on my way to the Gingerich farm. "I suspect Doc Coblentz is going to rule the manner of death as a homicide."

"Considering there was an accelerant present, I suspect that'll jibe with the fire marshal's report, too." He pauses. "Kate, is there any way this was some kind of practical joke that got out of control?"

"I thought of that, Mike. Teenagers aren't exactly the smartest of God's creations. But I don't think that was the case here, especially with the presence of gas." I choose my next words with care. "Interestingly, the Amish church district here in Painters Mill doesn't allow gasoline for their generators, just diesel fuel."

"So whoever did this wasn't Amish?"

"Gideon Gingerich told me he doesn't keep gas anywhere on the farm. Whoever set the fire went to some trouble and brought the gas with them."

"Sounds pretty goddamn premeditated." He sighs. "Someone made sure that kid couldn't get out, too. Kate, who the hell does something like that?"

The image of a young man trapped in a small room while smoke filled his lungs and fire slowly consumed him flashes unbidden through my brain, and I have to suppress a shiver. "Look, I'm on my way to talk to the family. I'll run through some questions with them while I'm there and let you know if anything pops."

I arrive at the Gingerich farm to find the investigator with the fire marshal's office poking around inside the remains of the barn. I park behind a buggy and offer a wave as I head toward the house.

Gideon Gingerich comes to the door as I'm about to knock. Desperate for news, but dreading it. A sleepless night piled atop another. I see all of those things in his beleaguered expression, and my heart gives a quick, hard twist.

"Is it him?" he asks.

I nod. "I'm sorry. I'm afraid so. The dental records from Dr. Gray match the X-rays taken by the coroner. I'm very sorry."

Miriam Gingerich has come up behind him, dish towel in hand, her eyes seeking mine. Evidently, she overheard the tail end of my response, because she puts her hands over her mouth and turns away.

Steeling myself against their grief, I train my attention on Gideon. "May I come inside?"

He sags as if he's suddenly too exhausted to remain standing. But he straightens, opens the door wider, and trudges inside.

Miriam is standing at the sink, her hands against the counter, leaning heavily, looking out the window. She's started coffee, but somehow ended up with spilled grounds all over the counter. The dish towel lies on the floor at her feet. She doesn't seem to notice either. The weight of their grief is tangible.

Gideon pulls out a chair and sinks into it. His face is pale, his eyes blank. "Our boy is with God." He addresses his wife without looking at her.

The Amish woman bends to pick up the dishcloth and then stares down at it as if wondering how it got into her hands. "God always has a plan." She whispers the words but her voice lacks conviction. "Sometimes we just don't know what it is."

Gideon turns his attention to me and motions to the table. "Sit down, Chief Burkholder."

I take the nearest chair. "Mr. Gingerich, the fire marshal believes the fire was arson."

"I don't understand why anyone would do such a thing."

Once again, I ask if he uses or stores gasoline anywhere on his property. I have to, because I know some Amish try to skirt the rules of the church district—to save money or for the sake of convenience—and hope they don't get caught. "Maybe you stored it for someone else? One of your neighbors maybe?"

"No." He shakes his head. "The *Ordnung* allows only diesel fuel. That's all we use."

"Did you keep small square bales of hay near the tack room?"

He cocks his head, his expression puzzled. "I keep a few bales down by the stalls for the horses. Makes it easier for Fannie when she feeds in the mornings."

"What about a wheelbarrow?"

"We keep it for mucking stalls. I usually push it against the wall, next to the stall doors, out of the way so we have room to bring the horses into the aisle when we need to." His eyes narrow. "Why are you asking me these things? What does it have to do with . . . Danny?"

I hesitate, knowing the details surrounding his son's death will undoubtedly upset him and his wife. But sooner or later, the details will get out.

"Mr. Gingerich, the investigation isn't complete, but the fire marshal believes Danny somehow became trapped or was locked inside the tack room. He believes some of those items—the wheelbarrow, cinder blocks, and bales of hay—may have been used to barricade the door."

I watch him carefully as I relay the information. His

eyes widen as he realizes what I'm telling him. Vaguely, I'm aware of Miriam rushing from the room. I don't take my eyes off of Gideon. He's begun to shake. His mouth quivers. A tremor overtakes his hand when he reaches up to wipe his eyes.

"Locked?" He utters the word as if it's a foreign language. "I don't see how that can be true. The door can only be locked with a key. The investigator must be mistaken."

"The lock was engaged," I tell him.

"But . . ." Grief flashes, but he pushes on. "Chief Burkholder, it was a double-cylinder dead-bolt lock. The only way to lock it is with a key. That can be done from the inside or the outside. There's no way he could have locked himself in the tack room by accident."

Which can only mean the door was locked from the outside. . . . "Do you have the key?" I ask.

"No. There are two. I keep them in the barn, tied together with a string, and hang them on a peg across the aisle. We figured if some thief came in at night, they wouldn't be able to find the keys, yet the keys would still be handy when we locked up."

"You keep the tack room locked at night?"

"Usually."

I nod. "Mr. Gingerich, can you think of anyone who was angry with Danny? Someone who may have wanted to harm him?"

He looks straight ahead, unseeing. I see abject horror in the depths of his eyes and I know his mind has gone to a place he is loath to venture. "No," he whispers. "Danny was a good boy. Hardworking. Well liked."

"Can you think of any reason why he would've gone into that tack room at night?"

"I don't know why he would do that."

I'm still thinking about the keys, wondering if they're buried in all that debris—or if the person who locked that door took them when they left. "Who knows about the keys?"

"Just me and Danny. My wife and daughter. The little ones probably, but they don't go out there much."

"Is there anyone who might be angry or upset with you or your wife? A relative? Neighbor? Extended family? Business associate?"

"We are *Amisch*." He says the words as if that somehow explains everything. "There is no one," he tells me. "*No one*."

I pull out my notebook, glance down at my notes. "What can you tell me about Luane Raber?"

"She's a good girl. Quiet. *Demut*." Humble. "She never got caught up in all the *Rumspringa* goings-on." He looks down at the tabletop, his fingertips shaking against the surface. He raises his eyes to mine. "Danny was going to marry her."

"Her family approved of the relationship?"

"Of course they did."

"Who else was Danny close to?"

"His best friend is Milo Hershberger. He lives up to Millersburg now. Trains horses for the *Englischers*. He and Danny were good friends. Practically grew up together. Don't see him much anymore. But Milo is a good man and Danny thought the world of him. They worked together down to the farm store in Painters Mill for a spell."

We fall silent, our minds working over everything that's been said. "Mr. Gingerich, is there anything else you can tell me that might be important?"

"We had some things stolen from the barn a few months ago. A saddle. A couple of harnesses." He shrugs. "That's when we started locking the tack room door."

I don't recall a burglary report, but I'm not surprised. More often than not, the Amish prefer to deal with problems on their own, without involving the police. In the back of my mind, I'm wondering why he didn't mention it sooner. "Do you have any idea who might've done it?"

"I know who did it. The neighbor, Chris Martino. Lives down the road in that trashy old house."

I'm familiar with Chris Martino. He's a convicted felon and did two years in Mansfield for possession with intent to sell. He rents the farmhouse next door to the Gingerich family. The owner of the property still farms the thirty or so acres surrounding it. Martino is forty years old, unemployed, divorced—and has a mean streak as wide as Lake Erie. He spends his days drinking and most weekends hawking goods at the local flea market or Amish horse auction. Two years ago, I pulled him over for running a stop sign and ended up arresting him on a DUI charge. He became so combative, I had to call for backup.

"Did Daniel ever have any run-ins with Martino? An argument? Harsh words?"

"They had words over the stolen tack. Martino got mad when Danny asked him if he took it."

He raises his head, his gaze locking with mine. "Do you think Chris Martino did this thing?"

"I don't think anything at this point. I'm just gathering information, Mr. Gingerich." When he doesn't elaborate on the altercation between Daniel and Martino, I press on. "Did they argue?" I ask.

"I didn't see it, but Danny told me they had words." He shrugs, shaking his head. "We knew Chris done it, but what could we do?"

Call the police, I think, but I don't say it. "Did Chris Martino make any threats? Anything like that?"

"I don't think so, but it don't take much to set him off."

I pause, shift gears. "How was Daniel in the last week or so? Was he acting normally? Happy? Sad?"

His eyes soften, his mouth relaxes, and I know he's remembering his son. "He was the same as always. Helpful. Conscientious. Danny worked hard. He loved God. Loved his family."

"Had he experienced any problems in his life? With friends? His girlfriend, maybe?"

He shakes his head. "He was looking forward to getting baptized." He closes his eyes against tears, squeezes them away. "Getting married. Starting a family."

"Mr. Gingerich, do you mind if I take a quick look around Danny's room?"

"Why on earth do you need to do that?"

"Maybe Danny left something behind that might be helpful in some way. I don't know. A note or something."

He doesn't look happy about the request; his wounds are too fresh, bleeding. But he's too immersed in grief to voice the reservations I see on his face. "You can look if you want." He motions toward the stairs. "It's the second door on the right."

"Thank you. I won't be long." I start toward the stairs, but he calls out my name. I turn and look at him.

"He was a good young man, Chief Burkholder. Humble and kind and generous. Had his whole life ahead of him. I don't know who could have done this horrible thing. I just don't know."

Lowering his face into his hands, he begins to cry.

Daniel Gingerich's bedroom is typical of a room belonging to a young Amish man. Clean, but untidy. Sparsely furnished. Practical. It's a small room with a single window that's about halfway open. A dark blue curtain is swept to one side and held in place with a length of string. A twin-size bed with an oak headboard is draped with a well-worn navy quilt. Next to it is a night table with three drawers. A floating shelf is mounted on the wall above the bed. On the opposite wall a rustic length of wood with six dowels holds a jacket, a straw hat, and trousers with the suspenders still attached. From where I'm standing I see a pair of wadded-up socks under the bed, and it reminds me that just days ago, an eighteen-year-old boy called this small, modest space home.

Ever aware that his grieving parents are downstairs and in need of privacy, I set to work, starting with the night table. The first drawer contains a white, unscented candle that's melted onto a saucer. A plastic flashlight. A tin of cough drops. A half-eaten bag of potato chips.

I go to the next drawer and discover that Daniel was a reader. On top is the *Es Nei Teshtament,* which is a Pennsylvania Dutch–English edition of the New Testament. Beneath it is a tattered *Field & Stream* magazine. An ancient-looking library book about hunting game in Ohio. The third drawer is a mishmash of junk. A screwdriver. A box of screws. A set of baseball cards. A tape measure.

Rising, I turn to the mattress, kneel and run my hands beneath it. Daniel Gingerich wasn't very creative when it came to hiding things from his parents. First thing I feel is a pack of cigarettes. I pull it out, flip the top. There's a lighter and two cigarettes inside. I replace the pack and my fingers slide over something else. I pull out a sandwich bag into which several photos are tucked.

The first is a picture of Daniel and a pretty Amish girl. I wonder if it's his girlfriend, Luane Raber. She's wearing a blue dress, a *kapp* with the ties dangling over her shoulders, and a huge smile. They're at some large body of water, blue with whitecaps in the distance, possibly Lake Erie. They look young and carefree and incredibly happy. The way young people ought to look.

I go to the next photo. It's a close-up of the girl. She's got a pretty face. A shy, sweet smile. Still wearing her *kapp*. Her hand is outstretched, as if she's trying to keep the photographer from snapping the shot. I suspect the photographer is Daniel. I see the same lake in the background. Blue water, a sandy beach, and a line of trees.

The last photo is of Daniel. He's shirtless with wet

hair and flexing his muscles. Grinning from ear to ear, he's pointing to a large brown spot on his torso, saying something. At first I think the spot is a leech he must have picked up while swimming, but upon closer inspection I realize it's a birthmark or mole. He's poking fun at himself, I realize. A typical teenager having a good time at the lake with his girlfriend. Staring at the photo, I feel a tug of something I shouldn't.

I pull a baggie from a compartment on my belt and slide the photos into it. Before leaving, I'll ask the parents if I can borrow them with the promise to return them. Since the Amish shun photos, chances are they won't want them. But with their son being gone . . .

I systematically search the rest of the room; I'd hoped to find a cell phone or journal, but there's nothing of interest. Certainly nothing that would explain his fate.

Daniel Gingerich was a son, a brother, a grandson, a boyfriend. According to everyone I've talked to, he was well-liked and happy, a typical Amish boy anxious to start his life as an adult. Who wanted him dead and why? What kind of monster would lock an eighteen-year-old boy inside a room and then set the barn on fire?

CHAPTER 6

Some people say murder is a senseless act. I don't agree. There's no doubt murder is a brutal act. It's a cruel act. An immoral act. It's wrong in the eyes of the law. A sin in the eyes of God. Murder is an unthinkable deed in the mind of any decent human being. But murder is rarely senseless.

As with any murder investigation, especially when there's no hint of a suspect, it's imperative to establish motive and develop a suspect as quickly as possible. Right now, information is the name of the game.

After leaving the Gingerich farm I swing by the station and pick up my first-shift officer. Rupert "Glock" Maddox has been with the department for about five years now. He's a former marine, a rock-solid cop with a steady personality and a boatload of common sense. He's charming and funny and easy to be around. I consider him not only an asset to the department but a friend.

"Where we headed?" he says as he slides into the passenger seat of my Explorer.

I fill him in on the turn of events surrounding the death of Daniel Gingerich. "I thought we might pay Chris Martino a visit."

"Ah. My favorite felon. Colorful guy." Then, he adds, "Martino's a mean son of a bitch and dumb as a box of rocks."

"Bad combination." I make the turn onto the county road that will take us to the Martino place.

"You check for warrants?" Glock asks.

"Yup." I slow for the lane, a narrow strip that's more weed than gravel, and turn in. "None currently."

"Maybe he's decided to keep his nose clean."

"And take up yoga."

We exchange grins.

The lane is a quarter mile long and wends right just as the old farmhouse looms into view. Martino rents the house from the owner, Owen Brice, who lives in Millersburg and stores his tractor and equipment in the barns and still farms the land.

The first thing I notice is the tall grass. It's hip high and chock-full of weeds, with bits of trash scattered throughout. I take the Explorer over a huge rut where someone drove through mud and let it dry jaggedly. The driveway is semicircular. In the middle of the circle is a rusty fifty-gallon drum someone shot up with a large-caliber firearm and used to burn trash. The drum is lying on its side, a waterlogged pizza box and several containers of auto oil spilling onto the ground.

We wade through a jungle of grass and nondescript bushes and take a broken sidewalk around to the front porch. The wood decking is warped, the gray paint peeling. A lawn chair lies on its side next to a hanging basket that's fallen and smashed to bits. Standing slightly to one side, I knock and wait.

I hear the thump of footsteps, and then the door swings open. Chris Martino is forty years old and wearing faded blue jeans and a plaid shirt he didn't bother buttoning. I try not to notice the smattering of silver hair on a fleshy white chest. He's holding a beer in his right hand, his eyes skating over me and my uniform and then moving to Glock.

"I was wondering when you guys were going to show up," he says.

I show him my badge. "Why is that?"

"When the shit hits the fan around here, who else you gonna hassle?"

"Mr. Martino, can we come in and talk to you for a second?"

He looks past me at Glock and frowns. "I reckon you ought to just stand right there and tell me what the hell this is all about."

I give him the basics of the barn fire. "Daniel Gingerich was inside. He didn't survive."

"Whoa. Man." He manages to look genuinely shocked. "I knew there was a fire. Saw all that smoke and the trucks. I didn't know the kid got burned up in it. *Damn.*"

"I understand you had words with Daniel over some horse tack."

He blinks at me. "Who told you that?"

I try a more direct approach. "Did you have an argument with Daniel Gingerich?"

"What are you insinuating exactly?"

"I'm not insinuating anything. I'm simply asking you if you argued with Daniel Gingerich."

"Well, if I know you cops, you're going to try and blame that fire on me 'cause you don't feel like looking for the real guy who done it. I didn't have nothing to do with it."

Glock sighs. "If you'd just answer the question, sir."

His eyes flit to Glock and back to me. "Lookit, that kid might be Amish and all that, but he ain't no fuckin' angel. In fact, he's a real asshole when he puts his mind to it."

"How so?" I ask.

"Well, he marched over here one day a couple months ago and accused me of stealing a bunch of shit from his barn. Like I got a use for a buggy harness."

"What happened?"

"I told him I got better things to do than steal crap outta his barn."

"You were angry with him?"

"Yeah, I was pissed. He was being a pushy little shit. Let me tell you something, when someone gets pushy with me I push back."

"How exactly did you push back?" I ask.

"I told him to hit the fuckin' road. I ain't going to let anyone accuse me of stealing. I don't care if he's Amish. That little snot-nosed shit accused me of taking it up to the auction in Millersburg and selling it." He huffs. "Like I got the time to do crap like that."

"Did you take the harness?" I ask.

He glares at me as if I'm being purposefully dense,

which I am. In reality I'm listening to him, watching his body language, trying to get a feel for his personality, what makes him tick.

"What did I just tell you, lady?"

Glock cuts in. "That's Chief, dude."

Martino looks at him as if he's spoken a language he doesn't quite understand. "Well, I didn't take a damn thing outta that barn. I done told you that twice now."

"Did the argument get physical?" I ask.

"No, it was just a bunch of mouth flapping mostly."

"Did you threaten Daniel?"

"I told him if he didn't leave I'd pick him up and throw him off my property. That wadn't no threat; it was a promise and I'da made good on it, too."

"Where were you two nights ago?" I ask.

"Are you fucking kidding me?" He gapes at me. "You going to try to hang that fire on me just because we had a little argument? Or because I got a record?"

Glock steps up beside me. "Why don't you just calm down and answer the question."

Martino's eyes flash black and go mean. Itching for a fight. No thought past the next thirty seconds and an impulse that has his hands clenching into fists.

"I didn't do shit to that little punk-ass bitch," the felon spits.

Glock has faced down worse than the likes of Chris Martino. He doesn't talk about the things he saw in Afghanistan, the things he did. But there's been a few times in the years I've known him that I've seen it in his eyes. I think on some instinctive level, he knows we're kindred souls.

"You better think real hard before you make a move," Glock says quietly.

"Chris." I say his name firmly.

Martino blinks, seems to snap out of it.

"Come on," I say. "I have to ask the same questions of everyone who knew or had contact with Daniel. If only to eliminate them from my list of suspects."

The statement isn't exactly true, but it's enough to break him out of street-fighter mode. Martino's brows knit and he seems to think about it. "I went bowling with my ex–old lady, then we went down to the Brass Rail."

The Brass Rail is a bar just outside Painters Mill. There's a live band every weekend. Beer by the pitcher. Dollar shots on Wednesday. Fights in the parking lot. Drugs sold out of the men's room. One-stop shopping for any knucklehead looking for a good time or trouble or both.

I pull out my notebook. "What time did you leave the Brass Rail?"

"We stayed till close. Two or so. Bunch of people saw us. You can ask."

"Did you go straight home?"

"Yeah."

"Alone?"

He sighs and for the first time looks inexplicably embarrassed. "My old lady was with me."

"She stay all night?"

"Yup."

"Ex–old lady got a name?" Glock asks.

"Trisha. Last name's still Martino."

I jot it down and then look at him. "Thank you for your time, Mr. Martino."

Glock and I turn away and start toward the Explorer. As we get in, Glock makes eye contact with me. "That guy has killed a lot of brain cells in his time."

"Drugs and alcohol have a tendency to do that." I start the engine.

"You think he did it?"

"I think he's capable." I ease the Explorer through high grass, hoping I don't run over anything that might puncture a tire. "He doesn't seem like much of a planner."

"More like a punch-first, think-later kind of guy."

We smile at each other.

"When we get back I want you to go talk to the ex-wife," I tell him. "See if she can corroborate Prince Charming's alibi."

"So we're going to keep him on the list for now."

"For now," I say.

Daniel Gingerich's girlfriend, Luane, is just sixteen years old. She lives with her parents, Mose and Sue Raber, and six siblings on a farm seven miles south of Painters Mill. The Rabers are Swartzentruber Amish, one of the Old Order sects that maintains a vise grip on the long-standing traditions. Untrimmed beards for the men. Black bonnets for the women. Windowless buggies. They refuse many modern conveniences used by other Amish. Things like indoor plumbing, milk machines, and linoleum floors. Unfortunately for me, they're also known to maintain the so-called wall of silence when it comes to dealing with outsiders, a practice that promises to make the extraction of information an exercise in frustration.

The use of gravel for their lanes is another convenience the Swartzentruber Amish choose not to make use of. The Raber lane is a quarter-mile track of pitted dirt with potholes large enough to swallow a tire. By the time I pull up to the house, the Explorer has developed a rattle. I park behind three buggies, the horses still hitched. Two young hostlers with dirty bare feet and flat-brimmed straw hats eye me suspiciously.

"*Wie geth's alleweil?*" I say to them. How goes it now?

The boys exchange looks as if I've just spoken to them in Swahili.

Despite my mission, I'm smiling as I take the sidewalk to the front door, cross the porch, and knock. A pretty girl not yet into her teens pushes open the screen, her young face solemn.

"*Sinn du eldra haymet?*" I ask. Are your parents home?

Without responding, she calls out over her shoulder, "*Mir henn Englischer bsuch ghadde!*" We have a non-Amish visitor!

Before I can say anything else, she turns and runs back into the house.

They don't keep me waiting. A heavyset Amish woman in a gray dress walks cautiously to the door and gives me a once-over. "Can I help you?"

I have my badge at the ready. "Sue Raber?"

"*Ja.*"

"I'm looking into the fire at the Gingerich place," I tell her. "I'd like to ask you and your husband a few questions." I glance past her and see four girls standing in the shadows of the hall behind her, eyes wide, watching the exchange with curiosity. "Luane, too, if that's all right."

The woman lowers her gaze to the floor with a great deal of solemnity. There's no surprise in her expression; she'd known about the fire, and I'm reminded how quickly word travels among the Amish.

"We heard about the fire," she says quietly. "Sweet Danny, too. Such a terrible thing." Her eyes flick to the girls and she motions in the general direction of the next room. "*Gay kinner hiede misse.*" Go mind the children.

"Mrs. Raber," I begin, "I'm talking to everyone who knew or had contact with Daniel in the days before he died. I've been told Daniel and Luane were close. That they were planning to get married." When she only raises her gaze to mine and stares, I add, "May I come in?"

A few minutes later, I'm seated at the big table in the kitchen with Mose and Sue Raber. It's a somber assemblage. There's no offer of coffee or iced tea. They are polite, but one thing is clear: I'm an outsider and the sooner I leave, the better.

From all indications the Rabers thought the world of young Daniel. They liked him as a person as well as a prospective son-in-law. They approved of his relationship with their daughter. In fact, when I asked them about the engagement they seemed anxious to marry her off. Whether they're looking forward to grandchildren or simply one less mouth to feed, there's no doubt they believed the two were destined for marriage.

"Would it be possible for me to speak with Luane?" I ask.

The couple exchanges a look.

"She's been . . . *umshmeisa*," Sue tells me. Upset.

"*Ich fashtay*," I tell her. I understand. "I won't keep her long."

Mose looks at his wife and shrugs. "*Ich hab nix dagege*." I don't object.

The Amish woman rises and disappears into the living room. A minute later she returns with one of the Amish girls who'd been watching us when I first arrived. Now that she's closer, I recognize her as the girl in the photo I found beneath Daniel's mattress. She'd looked a lot happier back then.

"This is Chief Burkholder with the police," Sue tells her daughter in *Deitsh*. "They're looking into the fire over to the Gingerich place and she wants to ask you some questions."

Luane visibly winces at the mention of the Gingerich name. Clasping her hands in front of her, she fastens her gaze to the floor. She's a pretty thing with flawless skin and cheeks prone to flushing. Her almond-shaped eyes are the color of faded denim and fringed with lashes so long and perfect, they look fake. Like her *mamm,* she's slightly overweight, but even in the homemade blue dress she's wearing, her curves are appealing.

Generally speaking, the Amish are stoic when it comes to displays of emotion, and that includes grief. They believe that death is part of God's plan. But sixteen-year-old girls—whether they're Amish or English—are not predisposed to emotional self-control, and Luane Raber looks as if she's spent the last two days crying. Her eyes are puffy. Her cheeks are red. And her nose looks as if it's been blown enough times to chafe skin.

"I know this is a difficult time for you," I begin. "When's the last time you saw Daniel?"

"Four days ago. He helped Datt cut corn and then stayed for supper."

"He was courting you, right?"

Luane blushes prettily, looks down at her hands where she's slowly shredding a tissue that's long since served its purpose. "*Ja.*"

"How long have you known him?" I ask.

"Since I was nine or ten."

"You've been friends most of your lives then?"

"*Ja.*" A smile touches her mouth. "Once he stopped picking on me, anyway."

"Tell me about him," I say, hoping to get a feel for what kind of relationship they had.

Her smile expands and for the first time she looks animated. The way a girl her age should look. "He was . . . *goot-maynich.*" Kind. "Funny, too. Always making people laugh. We were going to get married." She closes her eyes and another round of tears squeezes between her lashes and rolls over her cheeks. "Next fall. After harvest."

Realizing his daughter is in distress, Mose steps in. "Daniel was a hard worker. Put in ten hours on the farm with his *datt* and then went to his regular job down to the farm store in town."

"He's been like a son to us for years," Sue adds.

"Ate like a horse," Mose puts in with a smile.

Luane doesn't bother wiping the tears that have begun to roll down her cheeks; she doesn't look at me. Her misery is palpable, her grief all-encompassing. "I don't know what I'm going to do without him. He was . . . everything."

"*Gott immah havva en planen,*" her mother says quietly. God always has a plan.

"Did Daniel have any disagreements with anyone recently?" I ask. "With any of his friends? Or family? A customer at the farm store? Anything like that?"

The three people exchange looks, their expressions perplexed and searching. Finally, Mose answers, "He wasn't the kind of young man to have an argument with anyone."

"He was easygoing," Sue adds. "Even if he disagreed with something, he wouldn't say."

"Too polite, probably," Mose puts in.

Interestingly, Luane has remained silent. I turn my attention to her. "Luane?"

My question seems to jolt her. She lifts her gaze to mine. "Everyone loved Danny." Her eyes fill. "*Everyone.*"

Someone didn't, a little voice whispers.

I wait, but no one attempts to fill the silence. "Luane, did any of the other boys want to court you before Daniel came along?"

Mose makes a sound of disapproval, letting me know he doesn't like the question. I don't look at him. I don't take my eyes off his daughter.

"Daniel was always the one," Sue cuts in. "Always."

I maintain my focus on the girl. She can't seem to make eye contact with me. I can't tell if she's shy or uncomfortable or too upset to answer, or if there's something there she doesn't want to discuss with me—or in the presence of her parents.

I rephrase the question. "Were any of the other young men jealous of your relationship with Daniel?"

"I don't think so," she mumbles.

"What about the girls? Were any of them jealous?"

She shakes her head. "No."

Once again her mother interjects. "The *Amisch* aren't that way, Chief Burkholder."

I nod, keep my attention focused on Luane. "Is there anything else you want to tell me? Something that might be helpful in terms of figuring out who might've set the fire?"

No one speaks. Luane picks at a hangnail that's begun to bleed. Her mother fusses with the kitchen towel in her hand. Mose makes eye contact with me. Something in his expression tells me he wants to say something in private.

I rise. "Thank you for your time."

Mose walks me to the door and follows me outside. He doesn't speak until we reach the Explorer. "Daniel had an argument with his best friend," he begins.

"What's his name?" I ask.

"Milo Hershberger. Trains horses up in Millersburg now."

The name pings my memory. I recall Daniel's father mentioning Hershberger. He hadn't said anything about a quarrel. "What was the argument about?"

"What else are two young men going to argue about?" The Amish man's lips twist into an ironic smile. "A girl."

I can think of plenty of things that might set off a young male, but I know where this is going. "Luane?"

He tosses a glance over his shoulder, toward the house, and nods.

"Any idea why she didn't mention it?"

"I think it's an uncomfortable thing for her to talk about, especially with a stranger."

I nod. "How bad was the argument?"

"Bad enough. They were best friends since they were little. Practically grew up together. Neither boy ever uttered a cross word." Grimacing, he shakes his head. "But boys grow into men. And when there's a woman involved . . ." Shrugging, he lets the words trail. "They haven't spoken since it happened. I reckon if you want the details, you ought to talk to Milo about it."

I call my second-shift dispatcher, Jodie, on my way to Millersburg and have her run Milo Hershberger through the various databases. He comes back clean. Never been arrested. Not even a parking ticket.

It's nearly dusk when I pull into the gravel lane of the double-wide mobile home where he lives. It's a pleasant little ranch located in a rural area a few miles west of Millersburg. I park behind an older Ford F-250 to which a horse trailer is hitched. The property is well tended, the grass mowed, the trees trimmed. Behind the double-wide, I see a small raised garden with a dozen or so tomato cages and a couple rows of corn.

A horse barn with Dutch doors and a cupola with a weather vane on the roof is the focal point of the property. Both the front and back sliding doors are open and I can see the silhouette of a horse standing in cross ties. Two more horses stand inside steel pipe runs. The pound of hooves draws my attention to a large round pen comprised of stock panels. Within a cloud of dust, a young man in a cowboy hat is astride a rangy Appaloosa gelding. The animal lopes prettily, its nose tucked, body collected. Not a buggy horse . . .

I get out of the Explorer and walk over to the round pen, enjoying the evening as much as the sight of the horse. "He's gorgeous," I say by way of greeting.

The young man's hat slants toward me. "And don't he know it, too," he says in a deep voice. "Whoa."

The animal plants its hindquarters and stops on a dime. The man turns his attention to me. "He's a headstrong one, that's for sure."

"I'm looking for Milo Hershberger."

"You found him." He plucks sunglasses off his face and drops them into his shirt pocket, then gives me a thorough once-over. "You here about Danny?"

Milo Hershberger is nineteen years old and boy-next-door attractive. He's got a round face with brown puppy-dog eyes and a full mouth. His shoulder-length hair is pulled into a short ponytail, revealing a gold stud in his lobe. All of it accentuated by a scruffy beard stylish enough to give Tom Ford a run for his money.

I nod. "Do you have a few minutes?"

"Let me get him cooled off and I'm all yours."

I don't feel like waiting, so I follow Hershberger and his horse into the barn and watch while he untacks the animal and slips a sheet over its back. When he's finished he goes to the small refrigerator in a niche off the aisle and pulls out a cola.

"You want something to drink?" he asks. "Fresh out of beer, but I got pop."

I shake my head. "It's a nice place you've got here."

"Thanks. I'm training horses full-time now. I got two colts, a barrel horse, and a kid horse that ain't no kid horse." He dips his head and grins. "I got a rent-to-own deal with the owner. If all goes well, this place should be mine in about a year."

"Sounds like you're doing well."

He takes a long pull of the soda and then sobers. "But then you're not here to talk about me or my place, are you?"

"I'm afraid not."

I run my hand over the Appaloosa's shoulder as we make our way to the big door. Beyond, my Explorer sits in the waning light, ticking as the engine cools. We stop just outside the doorway.

"I heard Danny got killed in that barn fire. Is that true?" he asks.

"The coroner made positive ID yesterday."

"Shit." He looks out over the land. Anguish flashes on his face. "God, I hate that. Hard to believe he's gone."

I'm no schmuck when it comes to identifying phony emotions, but his seems genuine.

"I've known Danny since we were a couple of dumb Amish boys, six or seven years old. We were best friends once upon a time. I mean, he was like a brother to me. We basically grew up together."

"You were Amish?"

"I still am, really." But he looks down at his clothes and laughs. Dusty jeans. Denim shirt. Cowboy hat and boots. "On the inside, anyway."

"What happened?"

"Couldn't keep my nose clean. I pissed off my parents. Pissed off the bishop. I'm under the *bann* now. Haven't seen my family in almost three months."

"So you've been baptized."

"Ran around for a couple of years and got baptized last year."

It's an all-too-familiar scenario. I don't have to ask if he misses them; the pain of it is written all over his face. Every time I catch a glimpse of it, he's quick to cover it with a smile.

"Brothers and sisters?" I ask.

"Six of them. Younger. Three girls and three boys. God, I miss them something fierce."

"Why did they put you under the *bann*?"

Grinning, he motions toward the F-250. "She was the love of my life the instant I heard the purr of that engine. So they got me on the truck. We've got such an

entrepreneurial spirit, you know. I mean, the Amish. I
don't know how they expect me to haul all these horses
around without a truck."

"Wouldn't be easy. Unless maybe you have your cli-
ents bring them to you."

"I could, I guess." Smiling, he sighs. "Sure do like
that truck, though."

Despite the circumstances, I find myself liking Milo
Hershberger. He's soft-spoken with a boyish charm and
a quiet, kind demeanor.

He looks at me closely, narrows his eyes. "You that
cop used to be Amish?"

Now it's my turn to smile. "Guilty."

"Guess that makes two of us." He raises his can of
soda in a toast and takes another swig.

"Milo, what happened between you and Daniel?" I
ask.

"Girl got in the way, I guess." When I continue to
stare at him, he continues. "Luane Raber. Me and
Danny, we had it bad for her. I don't know if you've met
her, but she's pretty as a picture. I've known her most
of my life, too. I was always too shy to talk to her. But
we saw each other at worship. I'd see her in town every
so often. Then, during *Rumspringa,* the three of
us—me, Danny, and Luane—went to some parties.
Hung out."

I wait.

Frowning, not quite so comfortable now, he sighs. "I
thought she was . . . you know, interested. I mean, in me.
I knew she was sort of *with* Danny, but I figured girls
can change their minds, right?" He looks at me as if ex-

pecting me to confirm it, but I don't bite. "A guy can hope.

"Anyway, Luane and I went out a couple of times." He shrugs. "I liked her. A lot. I mean, seriously. I was really smitten with her. But I reckon the feeling wasn't mutual because when it was all said and done she chose Danny. End of story."

"How did all that affect your relationship with Danny?" I ask.

"How do you think? He didn't like it much. Neither did I."

"Did you argue about it?" I ask. "Fight?"

"Both." Another shrug. "To tell you the truth, I don't know which was worse, losing him as a friend, losing Luane as my girlfriend, or losing my family. Life's been pretty lonely without them."

"So, you and Daniel came to blows?" I ask.

"Yeah," he admits. "Couple times. Let me tell you something, Danny had a hell of a left hook." When I say nothing he flushes. "Look, it was a guy thing. We were both being a couple of shitheads. We were on *Rum-springa,* had a few too many beers, and for the first time in our lives we had a lot of freedom. We both . . . loved her. But no one got hurt. I mean, physically."

"When's the last time you saw Daniel?"

He blows out a breath, takes a moment to search his memory. "I honestly don't know. I saw him down at the farm store a couple weeks ago. Went in to buy some stuff for my truck and he was there. He works in the tire department part-time, you know."

"Did you speak?"

"I would have, but he just sort of looked away and went back to whatever he was doing."

"When's the last time you were at the Gingerich farm?"

"A few months. Maybe last fall. Used to go over all the time. I'd help Mr. Gingerich bale hay. Stayed for dinner a hundred times, probably. Then the shit hit the fan and I stopped going."

"When's the last time you saw Luane?"

"I went to worship when it was at her parents' farm a few weeks ago. She was with Danny, so . . ." He lets the words trail. "It was awkward. We didn't even speak. I don't think *anyone* spoke to me. Haven't been to worship since."

I nod, sensing there's something else there that he's not telling me, but I'm not sure how to get him to open up. "Where were you night before last?"

He frowns, letting me know he's not happy with the question, but he doesn't voice it. "I was here. All night. I rode until dark. I had a beer, hit the shower, and I was out like a light."

"Can anyone corroborate that?"

He grins. "That Appaloosa over there, but he ain't much on conversation." When I don't smile, he sobers. "Hey, I'm not a suspect or anything, am I?"

"At this point I'm talking to everyone who knew or had contact with Daniel."

"I reckon I'm the only one who punched him."

I say nothing.

"Look, me and Danny might've had a falling-out, but there's no way I'd ever hurt him, or anyone else for that matter."

"So what aren't you telling me?"

He stares at me as if I've reached into his brain with my fist and stolen his most private thoughts. "I don't know what you mean."

I hold my silence.

Looking left and right, he steps closer, and for the first time I realize he's a good-size young man. He's got big hands and strong shoulders. He smells of horses and dust and sweat.

"Keep your distance," I say.

Blinking, he takes a step back and lowers his voice. "Look, I may have that truck over there, and I might've done some things that ain't very Amish like. But I'm still one of them. I believe in God. I loved Danny like a brother and I was raised not to speak ill of the dead. But let me tell you something, Chief Burkholder. Everyone who thinks Danny was some kind of saint? Maybe they didn't know him as well as I do."

"What do you mean?"

"I mean, he treated Luane like shit and that ain't all." For the first time, his voice is bitter. "She didn't seem to mind, though, did she?"

"Milo, you need to explain that to me. Right now."

"Let's just say Danny wasn't always a nice guy and leave it at that." He glances toward the barn, where the horse is still tied and pawing at the ground. "Look, I gotta get back to work. We done here?"

"You can't make a statement like that without backing it up," I tell him.

"You want to know about Danny the Saint? I'd suggest you talk to Emma Miller." He starts to turn away and then stops as if thinking better of it. "But I reckon it's a little too late."

"What do you mean?" I ask. "Where do I find her?"

"Good luck, Chief Burkholder." Turning, he walks away without looking back.

CHAPTER 7

In Holmes County, the most common Amish surname name is Miller. After leaving Hershberger's place last night, I went directly to the station. My second-shift dispatcher, Jodie, and I spent two hours looking through the latest *Ohio Amish Directory for Holmes County and Vicinity,* an enormous tome published in nearby Walnut Creek that lists local Amish church districts, their bishops, and the names of all their members, including their children. By the time we found Emma Miller, it was nearly ten P.M.—too late to pay her a visit.

At eight A.M., I'm back in the Explorer just east of Charm and heading north on County Road 159. A few miles down the road I find the address I'm looking for. A hand-painted sign at the end of the lane reads: BIRD-HOUSES. FEEDERS. DOGHOUSES. NO SUNDAY SALE. I make the turn.

Sam and Esther Miller live on a well-kept farm that sits prettily atop a hill overlooking a picturesque valley. I pass by an old cinder-block milk house and continue on. The brick farmhouse was built at the highest point on the property and offers stunning views in every direction. The house is plain; there's no landscaping, no shutters or flowerpots, but the lack of ornamentation doesn't detract from its beauty. A massive pine tree dominates the front yard, which is enclosed by a split-rail fence and a row of lilac bushes. The sliding doors of the barn stand open. I see someone inside, so I pull up to the base of the ramp and get out.

I'm on my way to the door when I notice the bird feeders. Dozens of them are mounted on freestanding poles; others hang from the eaves of the barn. They're handmade artistry, fashioned to look like mini gazebos, log cabins, buggies, and the iconic Amish-country red barn. Sparrows and cardinals chatter and vie for millet and sunflower seed.

"Can I help you?"

I look up to see a middle-aged Amish woman in a dark blue dress approach. She's Swartzentruber—I can tell by the black bonnet and the style of her dress—but her expression is friendly and open.

"The bird feeders are lovely," I tell her. "Do you make them?"

"My husband does. I do the painting. We make everything here. Doghouses. Birdhouses. God gave us strong hands and strong backs, and we sure ain't afraid of a little work." She looks around and lowers her voice conspiratorially. "We don't usually open till ten, but if you got your eye on something, I can sell it to you."

"I'm afraid this is an official call." I show her my badge and introduce myself. "I'm looking into the death of Daniel Gingerich."

Her smile falters. She recognizes the name. Something else in her eyes I can't decipher. A quick dart of apprehension. "Heard about that," she says. "Awful for that poor family. A young man just starting his life." But she doesn't look too broken up about it.

"I'm looking for Emma Miller," I say. "Is she around?"

That shadow again. More pronounced this time. Something dark emerging from the shadows where she keeps it hidden away. "Emma was my daughter," she tells me. "Passed away six months ago."

Surprise ripples through me. I find myself wishing I'd done more homework before coming here. "I'm sorry."

"*Sis Gottes wille.*" It's God's will.

"She was just seventeen?"

The woman nods. "Left us all too soon." The smile that follows is sad. "She's with the Lord now, but I sure wish I'd had more time with her. She was our oldest and I miss her sweet soul every day."

I try to get a handle on the rise of tension, identify its source, but it hovers just out of reach. "Did your daughter know Daniel Gingerich, Mrs. Miller?"

"They met a few times. Daniel did some work here at the farm for my husband last summer. Painted that old milk house down the lane. Put up a cross fence for the calves."

It's a vague answer, and in the back of my mind I hear Milo Hershberger's parting words. *You want to know about Danny the Saint? I'd suggest you talk to Emma Miller.*

"Were Daniel and Emma friends?" I ask.

Something ugly peeks around the corner of its hidden spot. "Just to say hello."

Either she's being willfully evasive, or Milo Hershberger has sent me on a wild-goose chase. It wouldn't be the first time. Still, I sense this woman is keeping something cached away, just out of sight, so I push a little harder. "Are you certain about that, Mrs. Miller? I was told your daughter and Daniel Gingerich knew each other."

"Someone got their information wrong," the woman says.

"Maybe Emma and Daniel became friends and you didn't know about it."

"I knew everything about my daughter. Everything."

I try another tactic. "Did you or your husband have any problems with Daniel while he was working for you? Were there any disagreements? About his pay or his work? Anything like that?"

She shakes her head. "Danny was a good boy. A good worker. Did his job every day and we paid him a fair wage for his time."

"*Die zeit fer is nau.*" The time to go is now.

I turn at the sound of the deep male voice to see a middle-aged Amish man standing in the doorway of the barn, leaning on a pitchfork, watching us. He's wearing dark trousers. Blue work shirt. Suspenders and a wide-brimmed straw hat. His expression tells me he'd been standing there for a while, listening.

"Mr. Miller?" I start toward him and identify myself.

Taking his time, he meets me halfway, his eyes sweeping over my uniform. "What are all these questions about?"

"I'm investigating the death of Daniel Gingerich."

"Daniel Gingerich? We barely knew the boy. We don't know anything about him. I don't see how we could help you."

"Your wife was just telling me Daniel did some work for you." I pause. "I understand your daughter, Emma, was friends with him."

Something that resembles a shiver runs the length of his body. High emotion, I think. Anger? Grief? A mix of the two? Whatever the case, my question touched a nerve.

"All I know about Dan Gingerich is that he was *en faehicher schreiner*." An able carpenter.

"Mr. Miller, this is a death investigation. It's important for you to tell me everything you know about Daniel Gingerich. If your daughter was friends with him or had any dealings with him, I need to know about it."

The Amish man stares at me, saying nothing.

"Did you or your wife have any problems with Daniel while he was here?" I ask.

"There were no problems," he says.

"What about—"

"We've answered enough of your questions. Our business with you is finished. You should go now."

"Mr. Miller—"

"We don't know anything. We have nothing more to

say to you or anyone else." He motions toward the lane. "Go now. Just go."

My odd exchange with the Millers nags at me on the drive back to Painters Mill. There's no doubt in my mind they know more about Daniel Gingerich than they were willing to discuss; I'm even more certain that knowledge has something to do with their deceased daughter. But why are they so reluctant to discuss it? While it's true that many Swartzentruber Amish prefer to remain separate from the "English," I don't believe that's the case in this instance. The Millers are, after all, running a business and evidently dealing with tourists on a daily basis. So why are they so reluctant to speak openly with me?

It's after ten A.M. when I arrive back at the station. Lois is at the dispatch desk, squinting at some handwritten report, bright pink fingernails pecking at the keyboard. I'm not surprised to find my third-shift dispatcher, Mona Kurtz, occupied with busywork that could more than likely wait until her shift at midnight. I've talked to her about her penchant for "staying over" and my inability to pay overtime due to budget constraints. So far my concerns have fallen on deaf ears.

At twenty-four and a recent grad from the local community college with a degree in criminology, Mona is enamored with every facet of law enforcement. I decided a while back that when my most senior officer, Roland "Pickles" Shumaker, retires, I'm going to promote her.

Both sets of eyes land on me as I cross to the dispatch station. "Nice of you to stay late, Mona," I say easily.

She smiles a little guiltily. "Sorry, Chief. I was just helping Lois while she translates Skid's chicken scratch."

"Uh-huh." I pluck messages from my slot. "Since you're here, do you have an hour or so to spend on a special project for me?"

"Are you kidding?" She stands, catches herself, and jumps back into a more professional persona. "I mean, of course. What do you need?"

"I want you to dig up everything you can find on Emma Miller. Seventeen years old. Amish. Lived in Charm with her parents. Now deceased."

Her face lights up. "I'm all over it."

I can't help it; I grin.

I've just sat down at my desk with a dubious-looking cup of something I hope is coffee when my phone erupts. The display tells me it's Doc Coblentz.

"Hi, Doc," I begin, hoping for some preliminary information on Daniel Gingerich.

"I'm about to begin the autopsy on Daniel Gingerich. Sheriff Rasmussen is on his way. I thought you might want to be here as well."

There are two schools of thought when it comes to cops attending autopsies of a victim whose manner of death is likely a homicide. Some cops prefer to rely strictly on the autopsy report. I've found those reports as daunting to read as they are to decipher; they contain a virtual encyclopedia of medical and forensic jargon. For me, it's more helpful to see the body in a medical setting, with proper lighting, and a coroner present to answer questions. This is particularly true when there is foul play involved. The few times I've had to rely solely on the autopsy report, I ended up spending an undue amount of time on the phone with the coroner, asking for clarification or opinion or explanation.

Some of the old-timers harbor the unspoken belief that attending the autopsy is also a sort of homage or final respect the cop pays to the victim. That mind-set ventures a little too close to personal for me, though I'd be a hypocrite if I didn't admit I'm guilty of it, too.

"I'll be there in ten minutes." Grabbing my keys, I head toward the door.

I call Tomasetti on my way to Pomerene Hospital. "The coroner is about to begin the autopsy on Daniel Gingerich," I tell him.

"That was fast."

"We have less customers down here in Holmes County."

"They could use him up in Cuyahoga County."

"Can't have him, Tomasetti."

He sighs. "I'll be there as soon as I can."

Pomerene Hospital is a fifty-five-bed facility north of Millersburg off of Wooster Road. I nab a parking spot outside the Emergency entrance portico, cross the short span of asphalt, and push through the double glass doors.

I'm thinking about Daniel Gingerich as I take the elevator to the basement. From all appearances, and judging from what everyone has told me about him thus far, he'd been a typical young Amish man with a bright future ahead. He'd been loved by his parents. His girl-friend. According to his former best friend, he hadn't been perfect, but then who is? The death of Emma Miller remains a question. But I've learned nothing to indicate Daniel had taken a wrong turn somewhere along the way. So why did someone see fit to lock him in that tack room and set the barn on fire, knowing he would suffer a horrific death?

The elevator doors whoosh open and I step into a quiet, tiled hall. I walk past the yellow and black bio-hazard sign and a plaque that reads: MORGUE AUTHO-RIZED PERSONNEL. I go through a set of swinging doors and, at the end of the hall, enter the reception area. I discern the vaguest hint of odors I've grown to detest. The smells of death and chemicals despite a separate state-of-the-art HVAC system.

"Hey, Kate. Any sign of rain out there yet?" Carmen Anderson has been the receptionist at the morgue for several years now. She's bright, pleasant, and profes-sional, with a quirky sense of humor. It's probably not a good thing that we're on a first-name basis.

"Not yet," I tell her.

"That's the thing about working in a basement," she tells me. "I go all day without knowing if it's sunny or raining. A nuclear bomb could go off and Doc and I wouldn't notice."

She's wearing a floral skirt with a crisp white blouse and a pair of block-heeled sandals that look comfortable despite the height of the heel. I wonder if she has to wash her clothes every day to remove that hint of decay that permeates the air here in the basement.

"Not to rub it in or anything," I tell her, "but it's sixty-five degrees and sunny."

"Well, I'm glad I'm out there to enjoy it." Rolling her eyes, she motions toward the doors that will send me into the heart of the morgue. "He's expecting you."

I go through the swinging doors that take me to the medical side of the facility. The autopsy room is ahead, at the end of the hall. Right, there's an alcove where the biohazard supplies are stored. Doc Coblentz's windowed office is to my left. The door and blinds are open and I see that Sheriff Rasmussen and Tomasetti have already arrived.

"Hi, Doc." I step into the doorway of his office and extend my hand.

Doc Coblentz is clad in blue scrubs covered with a transparent green gown that resembles a low-budget raincoat. A surgeon's cap covers his head. A mask dangles at his neck. He's a portly man and when he's suited up like this he sort of resembles a glazed doughnut.

We shake and I turn my attention to the other two men. "Mike." I extend my hand first to the sheriff and then to Tomasetti. "Agent Tomasetti."

Tomasetti gives me his stone face, but I don't miss the slight twitch of his mouth. "Chief Burkholder."

Sheriff Rasmussen knows we're involved, though I don't believe he's aware that we're living together. Such a relationship would be frowned upon not only by the Ohio Bureau of Criminal Investigation but my own department as well. I'm pretty sure we'll be officially discovered at some point. When that happens, chances are

Tomasetti will be reassigned and working with him will come to an end.

Doc Coblentz is focused on the much grimmer cerebrations at hand. "There's not much left of this poor kid, Kate." Sighing, he motions toward the door. "Let's suit up and we'll get started."

The coroner leads us to the alcove off the main hall. There's a bench against the wall and a dozen or so shelves jammed with individually packaged gowns, masks, hair caps, latex gloves, and shoe covers. The three of us set to work tearing open packages and slipping into protective gear, and then Doc Coblentz ushers us toward the autopsy room.

The space is large and brightly lit, with gleaming gray subway tiles from floor to ceiling. The temperature is maintained at a chilly sixty-two degrees. The odors of formalin and other equally unpleasant aromas hover in the air. I see stainless-steel counters cluttered with plastic buckets, trays filled with tools of the trade, and two deep sinks with tall, arcing faucets. A scale that's far too similar to the kind you might find at the grocery for weighing produce hangs benignly above the counter to my left.

Stark fluorescent lighting rains down on a single stainless-steel gurney. I force my eyes to the vaguely human shape laid out atop it. The flesh is charred and black; the skin has cracked in places, exposing the red muscle beneath. The victim is in the typical pugilistic pose, with the arms and legs sharply angled. This occurs when intense heat triggers contractions of the tendons. The arms are bent. The hands have burned away, exposing the red and black jut of the ulna and radial bones. The legs are spread and bent at the knee. The feet are still intact. Doc Coblentz is right; there's not much left of Daniel Gingerich. Nothing recognizable, anyway.

"Poor son of a bitch." Mike Rasmussen removes a tube of Blistex from his pants pocket and smears a generous dollop under his nose. He offers it to Tomasetti, but he shakes his head. My stomach is already quivering uneasily at the smell of burned meat that's gone slightly bad, so I take the proffered tube and do the same.

"Daniel Gingerich. Eighteen years old." After double-checking the identifying toe tag, the coroner pulls up his face mask and lowers the protective glasses from atop his head. "As you can see, this victim is in the typical pugilistic attitude, a result of heat-related joint contractures. Total-body radiographs have been taken and the victim has been extensively photographed for all requisite documentation.

"One of the initial points of interest I noticed in the course of an X-ray of the skull is a fracture of the temporal bones here." Using a laser, he indicates the temple area of the skull.

"Skull fracture?" Looking a little too excited by the news, Rasmussen glances at Tomasetti, then back at the coroner. "Blunt-force trauma?"

Doc shakes his head. "Postmortem heat-related artifact."

Rasmussen raises his brows. "Come again?"

"An antemortem fracture—one that occurs when the individual is still alive—will most often terminate at the suture lines. This fracture crossed a suture line and also displays ragged edges. Both of those events indicate the fracture occurred postmortem."

"So the heat fractured his skull," the sheriff says.

The doctor looks at Rasmussen over the tops of his glasses. "If you'd like to see the film I'm happy to show you."

"I'll take your word for it," the sheriff says dryly.

"Were there any other injuries?" I ask. "Any signs he was in a struggle or fight? Anything like that?"

"There's no gunshot wound, sharp-force trauma, or blunt-force trauma indicated." He gives me his full attention. "Preliminarily speaking—and toxicology aside—in my opinion, this fire death was not the concealment of a homicide."

"He was alive when he was locked in the tack room?" I ask.

"There's soot deposition on tracheal mucosa and the dorsum of the tongue," the doctor replies, "which means he was breathing and alive at the time of the fire."

"Conscious?" Rasmussen asks.

"There's no way to know that for certain." The doctor sighs. "But there's no doubt this young man died a horrific death."

"Cause of death?" Tomasetti asks.

"I've more work to do here, of course. But preliminarily speaking, the decedent died of thermal injuries as well as smoke inhalation. Chances are, he fell unconscious due to the smoke and then he burned to death."

"Manner of death?" I ask the big-daddy question, the one all of us want and need to know.

"I'm still waiting for results on some of the tests I've run. More than likely I'm going to rule this one a homicide."

"Toxicology?" I ask.

"I sent six vials to the lab this morning," Doc Coblentz replies. "Going to be a week or so before results are in. Once they are, I'll make my official ruling."

When the final questions are asked, Tomasetti, Rasmussen, and I file from the room. We're in the alcove, peeling away our protective layers of clothing and stuffing them into the biohazard receptacle. Tomasetti is watching me with a little too much interest, making me nervous because Rasmussen is just a few feet away.

"I guess the question now is who did Daniel Gingerich piss off?" Tomasetti says as he sheds his shoe covers.

"Who the hell does something like that to an Amish kid?" Rasmussen mutters.

Tomasetti is still staring at me. "Any thoughts on that, Chief?"

I tell them about the falling-out between Daniel and his former best friend, Milo Hershberger.

"You think Hershberger did it?" Tomasetti asks.

"I'm still digging," I respond vaguely.

"You talk to the girlfriend?" Rasmussen asks.

I nod. "I'm basically talking to everyone who knew or came in contact with Daniel. From all indications everyone thought pretty highly of him."

"Except the sick fucker who locked him in the tack room and set the barn on fire," Rasmussen mutters.

CHAPTER 8

Daniel Gingerich not only worked on the farm full-time with his father, but also held down a job at the local farm store. Quality Implement and Farm Supply is located just across the railroad tracks on the industrial side of Painters Mill. I still smell the formalin clinging to my clothes as I park next to a handicap spot and head inside.

I enter through the double glass doors and am immediately greeted by a petite woman with brown hair and a red Quality Implement smock. She's standing at the customer service desk, jotting something on a form. I've been in this store plenty of times over the years, for everything from work boots to tires to potting soil, and I recognize her immediately.

"Morning, Dora," I say.

"You here about Danny?" she asks.

I nod, glance up toward the manager's office up on the second-level mezzanine. "Is Al around?"

"He's there." She lowers her voice. "His phone's been ringing off the hook since . . . it happened. A lot of our employees and customers are donating money for the Gingerich family. I mean, no one organized it or anything. Money just started pouring in."

"You knew him?" I ask.

"He was sort of a fixture around here. I saw him a few times a week. Nice kid." She shakes her head. "I still can't believe he's gone. He was such a sweetheart. Helpful. Funny. Good with the customers. One of the cashiers had to be sent home yesterday because she couldn't stop crying. We've even had some of our customers break down."

"Thanks, Dora." I set my hand on her shoulder, give it a squeeze, and then head up to the office.

Al Shields has been the manager here since I was a kid. When I was fifteen, he caught me swiping a candy bar. Instead of calling the cops or, God forbid, my parents, he walked me to the cash register, pulled a dollar out of his wallet, and paid for it. Somehow, that was worse. I never stole anything again.

I'm midway to the steps that will take me to the office when I see Al jogging down them. "Hey, Chief."

I smile and for a split second I know both of us are remembering that long-ago day that helped put me on the right track.

"Hell of a note about Danny Gingerich." He reaches for my hand and gives it a vigorous shake. "We're all kind of shell-shocked around here." He narrows his eyes on mine. "I heard it was arson. Is that true?"

I nod. "Do you have a few minutes? I need to ask you some questions."

"Sure." He motions toward the office from which he'd just emerged. "Come on up."

I follow him up the stairs and take the plastic chair across from his desk. "Had Danny been acting normally in the days and weeks before the fire?"

"I never noticed anything different. He was . . . the same. A solid worker. Always willing to lend a hand. Cheerful. Seemed to like his job here. I mean, he'd come in on the weekend if we needed him. Even on Sunday, after worship."

"Did Danny get along with his coworkers?"

"He got along with everyone, Kate, and that's no exaggeration. All of us . . . we really liked him. Sweet kid."

"What about customers? Any . . . arguments or disagreements?"

"Customers loved him, too. That kid could sell snow tires in July. I just can't figure someone doing that to such a fine young man."

I nod. "Anything odd or unusual happen in the days or weeks leading up to his death?"

"It was business as usual."

Al is a terrific manager. But I've had enough jobs in my lifetime to know there are things that happen among employees that the manager isn't always privy to. I also know that oftentimes an employee is more apt to talk if said manager isn't around.

"Where did Daniel work exactly?" I ask.

"TBA." He motions toward the rear of the store.

TBA is retailspeak for tire, battery, and auto. "Was he close to any of his coworkers?"

"He used to hang out with Ralph Baker. I'd say they were buddies."

"Do you mind if I talk to Ralph?"

"Sure. He's there now. Just go on back." He motions toward the stairs. "You do whatever you have to do, Kate. I'll be here if you need anything."

I find Ralph Baker talking to a customer about a set of radials. I hang out in the oil filter aisle for a few minutes. When the customer walks away, I approach Ralph. "Mr. Baker?"

He's a big guy. Six-three. Two hundred and fifty pounds. Mid-thirties with sandy blond hair, hazel eyes, and jaw in need of a shave. His eyes widen when he spots my uniform. "Ma'am?"

I show him my badge. "I'd like to talk to you about Daniel Gingerich if you have a minute."

"Danny. Oh, man." He blows out a whistle, looks down at the floor then back at me. "What a bad deal that was."

"Did you know him well?"

"Sure did. We worked together here for almost two years. He was a heck of a guy. A good worker. Fun. Great with customers. Knows his tires, too." He grins. "For an Amish kid."

"Did Daniel have any arguments or disputes with anyone that you know of?"

"Aw, I can't imagine Danny having a disagreement with anyone. He was real easygoing. Everyone liked him. He was the kind of guy didn't take things too personal."

I go through the usual litany of questions and I get

the same answers. "Is there anything else you can tell me that might help with the investigation?"

His brows knit and he seems to consider it for a moment. "Not really. I mean, he worked until noon the day before it happened. I don't even think I told him good-bye." His eyes mist. "Jeez, I didn't know that would be the last time I saw him."

I'm in my office poring over the preliminary autopsy report Doc Coblentz emailed earlier, when movement at the door draws me from my dark reading. I glance up to see Mona cross the threshold. Usually, she's a knocker, so she's excited about something. Judging from the file in her hands it has to do with the Gingerich case.

"That didn't take long," I say.

She makes a beeline for the visitor chair opposite my desk and drops into it. She's holding a purple folder in her left hand. A short stack of papers in her right. An expression that tells me her time and effort were fruitful.

"Did you know Emma Miller committed suicide?" she begins without preamble.

The news stops me cold. "No, but that's certainly an interesting development."

"She hanged herself in her parents' barn six months ago. Mother found her body when the family came home from worship."

"Any mention of suspected foul play?"

"No." She glances down, opens the file, rifles through the papers. "There was an autopsy. Girl died of cerebral hypoxia. Self-induced. Petechiae present." She flips the page. "Tox was ordered. Lab report says no drugs or alcohol were present."

"No wonder her parents didn't want to talk about it," I murmur.

"Oh my God."

That garners my full attention. Mona gapes at one of the papers in her hand, then looks up at me. "I'm just now seeing this, Chief. Says here Emma Miller was *pregnant*."

"Well, hell." Even as I feel that jump of cop's excitement, another part of me is saddened by the thought of a seventeen-year-old Amish girl believing death was a better alternative than life.

Mona passes me the file and papers.

"Her parents didn't mention either of those things when I talked to them." I look down at the autopsy report where the results of a pregnancy test stare back at me in stark black and white. "This explains why."

"Do you think any of this has something to do with what happened to Daniel Gingerich?" Mona asks.

"I think it opens a door worth looking into."

Even as I say the words, I recall Sam and Esther Miller's reluctance to talk to me. Is their reticence due to my being English and a police officer? Were they protecting their daughter's privacy? Her reputation? Or do they have something to hide?

You want to know about Danny the Saint? I'd suggest you talk to Emma Miller.

What's the connection between Daniel and Emma? It's an important question, because even if there was no foul play involved in her death, if young Emma had a relationship with Daniel, became pregnant, and ultimately committed suicide, her father may have a motive to commit murder.

"Nice work, Mona."

She dazzles me with a smile. "Thanks, Chief."

"One of these days you're going to make a damn good cop."

"That's the plan."

"You'll let me know if some other department tries to steal you away, won't you?"

"Count on it."

It takes me half an hour to get through the file Mona amassed on Emma Miller. I am impressed not only by her thoroughness, but by her creativity when it comes to mining information not necessarily found in law enforcement databases. As I read, I'm vaguely aware of Glock arriving to start his end-of-shift reports and my second-shift officer, Chuck "Skid" Skidmore, coming in early for some pre-shift bullshitting.

Mostly, I'm engaged in my reading, trying to find some connection between Daniel Gingerich and Emma Miller. There are a few parallels I can't ignore. Both were in their late teens. Their deaths occurred just six months apart. Both happened in Holmes County. And of course Daniel did some work for the Millers.

I go through the file again, this time looking for details about Emma Miller's life in the weeks and months before her suicide. There isn't much. Mona made a copy

of the obituary from *The Budget,* which, in typical
Amish fashion, is simple and short. I move on to the
next page to find a printout of a newspaper story from
The Daily Record titled "The Mercantile Is Charmed."
In the body of the second paragraph, Emma Miller's
name is highlighted in yellow.

I read the article with interest. It's a fluff piece written to let people know about the newest Amish-owned
business in Charm, Ohio, which is about twenty minutes from Painters Mill. It's a tourist shop that caters to
out-of-towners as well as locals, selling everything from
quilts and candles to housewares, chocolates, and teas.
According to the article, the owners, Edna and Isaac
Lambright, are also planning to open a café in the one-
hundred-year-old round barn located on the same property. Mona must have done a general Google search,
because Emma's name is mentioned only in passing. But
the story includes a photo of her along with three other
young Amish women who are featured in the story. Evidently, Emma was one of four part-time employees, all
of whom are Amish. According to the story, she was
working at The Mercantile up until the day she died.

I study the photo. Emma was a pretty girl with big
brown eyes behind wire-rimmed glasses, a milky complexion, and a serious expression despite the smile. Her
dress is dark gray. *Kapp* strings hanging down. I go to
the next photo, which is a group picture of four girls.
All look to be in their late teens or early twenties. All
of them are smiling. Arms linked. One of the girls has
her arm draped around Emma's shoulder. Her head is

thrown back in laughter. They look like a wholesome, carefree group of girls on the cusp of adulthood, their lives just beginning.

"What happened to you, Emma?" I whisper.

The only reply is silence.

The Mercantile is just down the road from the Keim Lumber Company, where Tomasetti and I spent many an afternoon while we were fixing up our farmhouse. Located in an old barn that's been completely refurbished, The Mercantile is chock-full of personality, with massive overhead beams, reclaimed wood on three walls, galvanized metal shingles on the other, and a concrete floor that's seen as many hooves as it has boots. It's a rustic-chic retail shop that beckons one to peruse—and buy.

A cowbell mounted on the antique door jingles cheerfully when I enter. To my right there's an attached silo that's been gutted and transformed into a candle-making shop that smells of patchouli and bergamot. To the left of the counter is a railing, and just beyond it is a small café with a scattering of bistro tables and chairs. An antique buffet has been transformed into a coffee station replete with flavored beans—hazelnut, vanilla, and Southern pecan—half a dozen teas, and a pewter tray piled high with pastries.

Outside the seating area, I spy a rack of straw hats, Western style as well as Amish. Beyond, the store is a jungle of items Amish-country tourists and locals can't live without. Gardening tools and fertilizer. An endcap display of handmade cards. Two rows are dedicated to

Amish-themed Halloween costumes. I see hot pads in the shape of dog paws and I find myself thinking about my sister's birthday.

"Can I help you find something?"

I turn to find myself looking at a pretty young Amish woman. Late teens. Raven hair. Peaches-and-cream complexion. Eyes the color of cognac. Not a stitch of makeup and she's cosmetic-commercial pretty. She's wearing a pastel pink dress with a white, organdy head covering that tells me she's Beachy Amish.

She's smiling at me, brows raised as if I've somehow amused her, waiting. "There's more stuff in the back," she tells me. "My *mamm* makes the soap. We've got lavender and rosemary this week. She puts olive oil in it for soft skin."

"Tempting, but I'm actually here on official business." I show her my badge and introduce myself. "I'm looking into the death of Daniel Gingerich."

"Oh." Her smile falters. "I heard about it. That awful barn fire over in Painters Mill. What a horrible thing. Mamm said a bunch of the men from the church district are going to rebuild the barn for the family. We're going to send pies. I can't imagine losing a loved one that way."

"That's one of the things I admire about the Amish," I tell her. "When tragedy strikes, you can always count—"

"Neva! Look! I finished! And it's so pretty!"

Female voices and the pound of footsteps against the floor snap my attention to the rear of the shop. Two young Amish women burst through a curtained door.

Moving fast, they dart between shelving units. I guess them to be in their late teens or early twenties. They're wearing conservative Amish dresses in different shades of blue. Off-brand sneakers. They're giggling, shoes sliding on concrete as they race around an endcap of pet supplies.

The girl in the lead draws up short at the sight of me. She's a tad shorter than the other two, blond and hazel eyed with a round face and twenty pounds of extra weight. Her eyes go wide upon spotting me. "Oh. Sorry."

The second girl literally runs into the first, grunting on impact. She's brown-haired with a widow's peak, blue eyes, and a smattering of freckles on a turned-up nose. Tall and thin of build, she has the gangly arms and legs of a girl who hasn't quite grown into them yet.

The girls are toting a large swath of fabric that looks like a quilt. It strikes me that these are the three girls in the photo taken with Emma Miller.

"I didn't realize you were with a customer," the brown-haired girl says softly.

The blonde is staring at my uniform. "Is everything okay?" she asks.

The Amish are generally low-key; they're not prone to loud verbal outbursts, particularly in public. Evidently, I've caught them at an unguarded moment, and I find myself charmed by their innocent fun.

The girl I'd been talking to sighs. She's trying hard to maintain her professional persona. She's not quite succeeding, because she's having a difficult time withholding a smile. "You finished the quilt?"

The blond girl glances at her sidekick and grins. "Just now."

"She cheated on stitches," says the brunette.

The blonde elbows her. "Did not."

"Go on back to the sewing room." The black-haired girl slants her eyes at me. "I'll be there in a minute and we'll take a look."

"*Ich will's sana,*" I say, looking at the quilt. I'd like to see it. "If you have a minute?"

They stare at me, as surprised that I know *Deitsh* as they are to see a uniformed police officer in their homey little shop. I introduce myself and show them my badge. "I'm looking into the death of Daniel Gingerich over in Painters Mill."

No one has anything to say about that.

I wait a beat and then ask, "What are your names?"

The black-haired woman—evidently the leader of the trio—sticks out her hand. "I'm Neva Lambright."

I take her hand and we shake. She's got small, delicate hands, but they're callused, telling me she spends much of her time working not only here at the store, but at home as well.

"I'm the manager here at The Mercantile," she tells me. "My parents own the place."

I turn my attention to the blond girl. She's several inches shorter than me, so I have to look down to meet her gaze.

"I'm Viola Stutzman." Mimicking the older girl, she sticks out her hand with great panache, but doesn't quite convey the same level of confidence. I don't hold it against her. Amish girls aren't exactly taught how to make acquaintance with the English police, and this girl seems to be the youngest of the group.

I turn my attention to the brunette. She's tall and gangly with intelligent, watchful eyes.

"Ina Yoder." She offers a good-natured smile. "We don't see too many police in here," she says as we shake.

"Evidently, they don't know what they're missing," I return. "Coffee, quilts, and pastries all under one roof."

"This old barn has been in the family for almost a hundred years," Neva tells me. "Took some doing to restore everything. Now Mamm wants to turn that old round barn out back into a café. That's going to be our next big project."

She motions toward the other two girls. "Viola and Ina work here part-time."

I let my eyes rest on Viola. "You're the quilter?"

Nodding, she offers the quilt. "It's my first."

"She's been working on it six months," Ina whispers.

"Five," Viola corrects.

Humility, or *demut,* is a core belief of the Amish. To exhibit *hochmut,* or pride, is frowned upon. I discern pride in the eyes of this young woman, but it's a good kind of pride I hope she holds on to.

Taking the quilt, I run my hands over the fabric. It's a sampler quilt, a mosaic of burgundy, cream, and brown. I see the requisite seven stitches per inch, straight and perfectly spaced. Again, I think of my sister's birthday, but these heirloom-quality quilts are a tad out of my price range.

"Is it for sale?" I ask.

The girl shakes her head. "I'm giving this one to my *grossmudder*. She taught me everything I know about stitching so I thought it only right. She's going to be seventy-two years old in November. Can't sew as much as she used to because of her rheumatism."

"I'm sure she'll treasure it." I pass the quilt back to her. "Not only because it's beautiful, but because her granddaughter made it."

"Thank you," she says quietly.

I take a moment to look around, giving them a moment to get used to me; then I glance at Neva. "Your parents did an amazing job with the place."

"They poured their hearts into it, especially Mamm," Neva replies. "But it was a labor of love."

"Who knew work could be so much fun," Ina says.

"And we get a discount on all the merchandise," Viola adds.

"One-stop shopping for Christmas." I shift the conversation back to the subject at hand. "I understand Emma Miller used to work here."

The mention of their deceased coworker dims what had been a buoyant mood. Glances are exchanged and then their eyes are lowered.

"Our sweet Emma," Neva says.

"Did you know her well?" I ask.

"We were best friends." She makes eye contact with the other two women, including them. "The four of us, I mean. We were like sisters. Practically grew up together. Went to school together."

"Emma worked here part-time," Viola says.

"She made the candles," Ina adds.

Neva shakes her head, smiling. "Emma and her candles."

"For the longest time after she died, I kept expecting to see her rush through the door, all excited to tell us about some new fragrance she'd concocted." This from Viola.

"She was so creative," Neva tells me. "A good girl and an even better friend."

"We all loved Emma," Ina says. "She was a gentle soul and . . ." Sighing, she looks around. "It's not the same around here without her, that's for sure. I miss her every day."

There's a sweetness inherent to teenage girls and young women. That innocence and incorruptibility seems to run even deeper in the Amish. In the back of my mind, I wonder if I was ever that young. If I was ever that innocent . . .

I press on. "I understand Emma knew Daniel Gingerich."

The silence that follows goes on a beat too long. Both Ina and Viola look to the slightly older Neva to answer. "If I remember correctly," Neva says, "I think he did some work for her parents on their farm."

"Were they friends?" I ask.

"I think she may have gone to a singing with him once," Viola says.

Ina wrinkles her nose. "I don't think she liked him that much."

"Why not?" I ask.

Viola gives a half smile. "Emma was all about Elam Schlabach."

"Elam was Emma's beau," Ina clarifies.

"Besides, Daniel already had a girlfriend," Neva tells me.

"Oh, I almost forgot about Ruth," Viola says.

"Her name is Luane," Neva corrects.

"I think he courted Ruth Beiler for a time," Ina says.

"Daniel and Ruth went to a singing once or twice," Viola puts in.

Neva firmly overrules them. "Luane Raber was his beau and has been for as long as I can remember."

It's the first I've heard the two names, and though they may not be important, I jot them in my notebook. "So Daniel and Emma weren't close?"

"They were more like acquaintances," Neva replies.

"Barely knew each other," Ina adds.

"What about while Daniel was working for her parents at the farm?" I ask. "Did they see each other then? Interact?"

Ina shrugs and looks at the other two girls. "I don't really know about that."

Neva shakes her head. "She never mentioned it."

"Did Emma ever have any disagreements or arguments with Daniel?" I ask.

Neva laughs. "Emma never said a cross word to anyone."

"She'd agree with you just to be polite," Ina adds.

I consider the dynamics of relationships among young men and women, all of those gnarly complexities, emotions that can be a little too intense, and, of course, hormones. It's far too easy for those early connections to become cumbersome, even among the Amish.

"So Emma and Elam Schlabach were tight?" I make eye contact with each of the girls.

Viola blushes, looks down at the floor.

Neva holds my gaze. "Emma was crazy about Elam. He loved her, too. But she was kind of shy. You know, quiet about such things."

Ina chuckles. "We had to practically pry things out of her and even then she didn't tell us much."

"Did Elam know Daniel and Emma went to a singing together?" I ask.

The girls exchange quick glances. Uncertain, I realize, and loyal to Emma even though she's gone. They're not sure where I'm going with this line of questioning, but they don't like the direction or the connotations.

Again, Viola and Ina look to Neva. "If he knew about it," she says, "I don't think it was a big deal for either of them. Daniel never really entered the picture."

"Is Elam the jealous type?" I ask.

"He's pretty laid-back, actually," Neva tells me.

"Were any other boys interested in Emma?"

"All the boys liked her," Viola responds.

"She was sweet and pretty." Ina sighs. "It's like you just fell in love with her the instant you met her. That's what kind of person she was."

Grief flashes in Neva's eyes, followed by a wistful smile. "She had way too much common sense to go out with most boys."

I didn't know Emma Miller, but I find myself liking her. "That's not such a bad thing."

Ina folds her arms across her chest. "Especially when

most of them her age were on *Rumspringa* and had the sense of a cow."

"Did Emma ever have any problems with any of the guys that liked her?" I pose the question to Neva. "Were any of them too forward? Anything like that?"

"If they were, she never said. But then she wasn't a complainer, either. To tell you the truth, I can't imagine her giving any of them anything to be jealous of. Emma was a good girl. She had no interest in running around. She wasn't boy crazy. Didn't go out. Never drank beer or anything like that."

Ina has been watching the exchange with interest. When we fall silent, she narrows her eyes on mine. "Chief Burkholder, do you think what happened to Daniel Gingerich has something to do with Emma?"

"I'm not sure," I say honestly. "I was just surprised to hear Daniel and Emma knew each other and now both of them are gone."

"The Amish community is a small one." Neva shrugs. "Everyone knows everyone. You know how it is."

I nod because I do. Still, I'm no fan of coincidence, and I don't think it's happenstance that these two innocent teenagers' paths crossed—they knew each other, spent time together—and now both of them are dead.

I look from girl to girl. "Was Emma upset about anything in particular in the days leading up to her passing? Some life event? Was there something going on in her life that led up to what happened to her?"

A heavy silence ensues, ticks on for a too-long span of time. Finally, Neva heaves a sigh that's fraught with emotion. "Her *mamm* said Emma always had a sad heart. Even when she was a little girl she had days when she was blue. You know, depression. Emma was . . ." Her voice trails and for the first time, tears well. "She was innocent and yet she had an old soul, if that makes sense. She felt things deeply. Too deeply, probably. She was thoughtful and incredibly kind. She couldn't bear the thought of hurting others, even if it was inadvertent."

"She was a worrywart, too," Viola says.

"The silly thing." Wiping at the tears, Ina chokes out a laugh. "She worried about everything and everyone."

The girls chuckle quietly, remembering, but they're edging closer to being overcome with emotion. For them to be experiencing this level of grief after six months is profound.

"Was she worried about anyone or anything in particular?" I ask.

Neva shakes her head. "I don't think it was any one thing. She was just . . . sad. And too quiet. I mean, when most people get upset about something, they talk and complain."

"Piss and moan," Ina inserts.

Viola chuckles.

Halfheartedly, Neva smacks her on the arm. "Not Emma. When things got bad or she was trying to work through some problem, she just sort of clammed up. She held things inside."

"Her *mamm* says that's what killed her," Ina whispers. "Her heart couldn't contain all the sadness," Neva says. "The only comfort she could find was with God."

CHAPTER 9

Before leaving The Mercantile, I purchase three individually wrapped rosemary and lemon soaps, a hand-dipped candle, and a tin of cinnamon tea for my sister. I call the station as I stow everything in the back of the Explorer.

"Hey, Chief, what can I do you for?" asks Lois.

"I need an address for Elam Schlabach." I spell the last name and glance down at the time. "Get me a work address, too, will you? Check for warrants. See if he's got a sheet."

"You got it." Computer keys click on the other end of the line. "Here we go. Schlabach, Elam." She taps a few more keys. "Home address is 4139 Hogpath Road."

"Work?"

Fingers snap against keys. "Last place of employment . . . Buckeye Woodworks and Cabinetry on Fourth Street in Painters Mill."

I know the place. It's an Amish-owned cabinet and woodworking shop that caters to local home builders, remodeling companies, and DIY homeowners, both Amish and English.

"You got a lead on the Gingerich case?" Lois asks.

"Probably just spinning my wheels."

"Well, if you're going to talk to Schlabach at work, you'd best hurry," she says. "I think they close at six."

Buckeye Woodworks and Cabinetry is a large establishment set up in a metal building that faces Fourth Street. The front of the structure is adorned with rustic wood siding and two Craftsmanesque windows replete with flower boxes overflowing with bright orange mums. Half a dozen Adirondack chairs span the length of a wide porch. I've been inside once or twice, when Tomasetti and I were looking to repair some of our water-damaged hardwood floors, and I know the owner employs some of the best woodworkers in the state.

All the parking spaces in front are occupied, so I pull around to the rear and park next to a loading dock and Dumpster. I get out, traverse the pitted asphalt, and take the concrete stairs to a big double door that stands open. A sign above the door reads GOTT SEGEN AMERIKA. God Bless America.

The roar of tools—saws and drills and the rumble of what sounds like a generator—increases as I approach. The smells of sawdust and wood stain fill the air as I go through the doors. I see several good-size workbenches with air hoses hanging down from steel arms mounted on the ceiling. Most of the tools are being operated by Amish men with full beards and wearing straw hats and work clothes—trousers with suspenders and blue shirts.

A couple of the guys have noticed me, but they don't stop what they're doing. I'm midway through the shop when a male voice rings out.

"Looking for work?"

I turn to see a white-haired Amish man approach. He's about my height with a silver beard and a friendly, open expression. He stops a few feet away and tilts his head back, looking at me through thick-lensed glasses that magnify rheumy brown eyes.

"Actually, I'm looking for Elam Schlabach," I say.

"Some people come in through the front door and ask for who they want to see." He says the words good-naturedly, but I've been effectively dressed down.

"I'll keep that in mind next time I visit," I reply.

His mouth twitches and he leads me to a workstation where a young Amish man pushes a saw blade through an intricately grained piece of walnut. He glances up, but takes the time to finish his cut before pushing his goggles onto his crown.

He's in his early twenties with sandy-colored hair and green eyes. His beard is of the barely-there variety, telling me he's a newlywed. He's got a keloid scar on his left cheekbone and I wonder if at some point he was injured in the course of his work. Judging from the way he's handling his tools, he's been at it since he was too young to get paid for his time, and he's good at what he does.

"Elam Schlabach?" I ask.

"Yup." His eyes flash over my uniform, more curious than worried. He reaches for a second piece of wood, lines it up for a cut. "Who wants to know?"

I have my badge at the ready and introduce myself. "I'm investigating the death of Daniel Gingerich."

"Heard about all that," Schlabach tells me. "Bad business."

I look at the partially finished table next to where he's standing. "That's a beautiful piece."

"Still gotta distress and stain it. I made the benches, too. There's going to be six of them." I see pride in his eyes as he runs his hand over the wood. "I'm making all the dining room tables for the new restaurant going up at the end of town."

"The Red Rooster?"

He almost smiles. "That's the one."

"I know you're busy, so I won't keep you." I slide my badge back into my pocket. "I understand you knew Emma Miller."

A quiver moves through his body. He doesn't look away from the saw and for an instant, I think he's going to make the cut. Instead, he straightens and switches off the saw, giving me his full attention. "I knew Emma."

"You were close?"

He takes his time responding. "What's that got to do with Dan Gingerich?"

"I was hoping you could tell me."

"I don't have anything to say about that." He turns back to his work, flips on the pneumatic saw. He lines up the board and makes the cut. I can't tell by his demeanor if I've hit on a nerve or if he's simply impatient and irritable by nature. The one thing that is obvious is that he doesn't want to talk to me. He's doing a little too good a job ignoring me, so I decide to push.

When he's finished with the cut, I round the bench and turn off the saw. "*Du sinn heiyahra nau.*" You're married now.

He gives me an annoyed look. "I reckon the *Deitsh* earns you points. You Amish or what?"

"Used to be. I left."

He's not impressed. "So what do you want with me?"

"I want to know why Emma Miller committed suicide."

Another quiver. More pronounced this time. His eyes flick away. Some of the attitude drains from his eyes. He looks longingly at the cutting bench; he'd rather be working. He wants to make that cut. Instead, he's standing here with me being forced to answer questions he doesn't want to answer.

"She's gone. Dan Gingerich is gone. I don't see why any of it matters now."

"It matters because I don't think Daniel Gingerich got locked in that tack room all by himself."

He stares at the wood he'd been cutting, refusing to look at me. Is he being stubborn? Or is there something in his eyes he doesn't want me to see?

I try another tack. "How long have you been married?"

"Three months."

"You're a newlywed."

"We got a baby on the way." He doesn't seem too happy about either of those things. One thing has become abundantly clear: Elam Schlabach is an angry and bitter young man.

"Congratulations." I wait a beat. "You and Emma were close."

He reaches for another board, lines it up for a cut. It's as if he can't control the impulse to keep moving. As if he'd rather be doing anything but partaking in the conversation at hand, including cutting off his own fingers.

"You could say that. I was going to ask her to marry me. Is that close enough for you?"

"What happened?"

"She hung herself." His voice breaks with the final word, but he covers it with a cough. "It was . . ." He lowers his voice. "A fucking mess."

I give him a moment. Let him make another cut. Save face. Maintain his dignity. When he's finished, I ask, "Why did she do it?"

"If I knew the answer to that, she'd still be here. I would have . . . I would have stopped her." He sets down the saw with a little too much force. "How does anyone even conceive something like that? I mean, if you were Amish, Chief Burkholder, then you know that to take your own life is a sin."

He's trying to play it cool, keep his emotions under control, put all of that energy into the anger. But it's evident that even after six months the death of Emma Miller affects him deeply.

"Sometimes people get caught up in a dark place and can't get out," I say. "Sometimes no matter how much we love them, we can't save them."

Tightening his mouth, he lifts the board and sets it atop the others he's already cut to size. "So you think someone murdered Dan Gingerich, or what?"

"I do."

"I hate to disappoint you, but I didn't know him very well."

"Did Emma?"

Instead of answering, he picks up another length of wood, sets it on the saw, and lines it up. "I wouldn't know."

"Are you sure about that, Elam?"

"Everyone says he was such a great guy." He spits out the words, a quick spew of venom. And hate. "He was *maulgrischt*." A pretend Christian.

"Why do you say that?"

He flips on the saw, cuts the board, tosses it with a good deal of vigor, and it clatters onto the stack.

"Elam." I say his name firmly. "Talk to me. Please. It's important."

He leans against the bench, and skewers me with a hard, uncomfortable look. "I guess you're pretty smart for putting two and two together."

My heart jumps, wondering if he's just made some sort of bizarre confession.

He sees my reaction and his mouth twists into an unpleasant caricature of a smile. "Wish I could make it easy for you, but . . . I didn't do it." He shrugs, a coiling of muscles beneath his shirt. "I didn't figure things out until . . . after."

"Figure what out? After what?"

"Why she did it," he says. "I blamed myself for a long time. I mean, she was . . . sensitive about things. I figured I'd done something wrong or hurt her in some way. I thought I'd put too much pressure on her." His face colors, another emotion he's not comfortable with, and he mutters a curse beneath his breath. "I wanted to . . . you know. She didn't. I mean, she wouldn't . . . until we were married. She was clear about it. And she was . . . pure. After she died, I thought I was the reason she did it. I mean, I'd wake up in a cold sweat in the middle of the night and I'd see her with that rope around her neck . . ."

I wait.

"My mind would just . . . run with it. Replaying all these things she'd said to me in the weeks before she died. It wouldn't stop." Shaking his head, he makes a sound I think is supposed to be a laugh, only it's not. At some point, he's begun to sweat—his forehead and upper lip; the keloid scar glows bright pink. He doesn't seem to notice. "It's like she was trying to tell me something from heaven. Or hell, maybe."

"Tell you what?"

He hesitates. "She never came right out and said it. So I'll never know for sure."

"Said what?"

"I think Gingerich . . . I don't know. I think he did something to her. Something she didn't want him to do."

I feel myself recoil, but I'm not sure if it's emotional or physical. I try to cover it, find myself hoping he didn't notice. I remind myself this case isn't about me or my past. Not even close. But I remember all too well what it was like to be a fourteen-year-old Amish girl. I remember all too well what it was like to be innocent and then feel that first brutal punch of shock when I learned that violence existed in my small, perfect, and safe world.

In the back of my mind I wonder if he knows Emma Miller was pregnant when she died.

"What did he do to her?" I ask.

For the first time he becomes aware of his surroundings. He looks around as if to make sure no one is listening. "Look, Dan Gingerich did some work for the Millers a few months before Emma died. He was over there all the time. It took me a while to figure it out, but that was about the time when I noticed . . . changes."

"What kind of changes?"

He shrugs, but his body language tells me he does, indeed, know. "Emma wasn't much of a talker. She was kind of shy. Liked to keep the private shit private. But she . . . stopped laughing. She stopped looking at me the way she had before. She just, I don't know, *changed*. I'd never heard her say anything bad about anyone, but she didn't like Dan Gingerich."

"Any idea why?"

He doesn't answer.

"Elam, you know Emma was *ime familye weg* when she died, don't you?" "In the family way" is the Amish term for "pregnant."

He sucks in a breath, looks away. "Yeah, I found out about that."

"She didn't tell you?"

He shakes his head. "I don't see how she could have."

"What do you mean?"

"She was innocent. I mean, I thought . . ." His gaze meets mine. This time I see something sharp and hard in his eyes. Even for an Amish man, an emotion that if unleashed could fester into something unpredictable and dangerous. "We never . . ." He looks away. "You know."

"Is it possible she was seeing someone else?"

His smile is bitter. "You know I'm going to say no. Dumb fucking guy always does, right?"

"What do you think happened between Emma and Daniel?" I ask.

He bends, picks up another board, and slams it down on the bench hard enough to draw the attention of the man standing at the next workstation. "I don't know."

Now it's my turn to look around. I lower my voice. "Do you think Daniel made advances toward her? Forced her to do something she didn't want to do?"

Bracing both hands against the board, he stares at the piece of wood as if it's his only salvation. "She wouldn't talk to me. She just wouldn't say."

"Did you ask?"

"Yeah, I did."

I wait, but he doesn't elaborate, doesn't even look at me.

"Where were you two nights ago?" When he glares at me, I add, "I have to ask."

"Home with my wife. You can ask her." He swings around to face me. "Don't expect me to be sorry about Dan Gingerich being dead. Far as I'm concerned, that son of a bitch got what he deserved, especially if he's burning in hell."

Certain cases take on a life of their own. They touch us in unexpected ways. Sometimes they touch us in ways we don't want to be touched. They take us to places we don't want to venture. Remind us of people we don't want to be reminded of. Cases are rarely limited to the victim or loved ones or the families. Cops get drawn in, too. They become involved with the people they come into contact with. While we do our best to keep a handle on all of those gnarly emotions and preconceived notions we keep tucked away in that back drawer, we don't always succeed.

When I walked into the Gingerich case, I saw Daniel as a victim. An innocent kid who'd been preyed upon and murdered brutally. But as in most cases, the deeper you dig, the more you learn—and sometimes you realize the people you're fighting for aren't who you think they are, and none of what happened is black and white.

If Emma Miller and Elam Schlabach were involved in a serious relationship and hadn't had yet had sex, how did she end up pregnant? Was she seeing Daniel behind his back? Did that relationship, her pregnancy, or her death have anything to do with Gingerich's murder? Is Elam Schlabach telling the truth about any of it?

The possibilities gnaw at me as I drive to the farm. I hate to call it a night when I have so many unanswered questions buzzing inside my head, but it's late; any answers are going to have to wait until morning.

It's dusk when I arrive home. I'm so preoccupied, I barely notice the way the sunlight slants through the trees at the back of our property or the mist rising from the pond. I glance at the dock where Tomasetti sometimes likes to fish, but he's not there. Two mallards glide through the smooth-as-glass water.

I'm midway to the old Victorian house we've shared for nearly two years when a pang of something I don't recognize stops me in my tracks. The chatter in my head grinds to a halt. Turning, I look out across our property, and for the first time in days, I see the simple beauty of my surroundings and I drink it in. Somehow I hadn't noticed that the foliage is abloom with fall color. I stand there, listening to the calls of the red-winged blackbirds that swoop and play among the willows by the pond. The whisper of the wind through the treetops. The bawling of Mr. Cline's cattle to the south. The tinkle of the wind chimes I bought on impulse at one of the Amish tourist shops in town. Autumn evenings in this part of Ohio are magical; they are a feast for the senses, balm for the soul of a troubled cop. And I've been missing all of it for so long I hadn't even noticed when it slipped away.

I'm about to open the back door to find Tomasetti and talk to him about my epiphany when I hear pounding coming from the barn. Setting my laptop case on the stoop, I turn and head that way. The structure is nearly as old as the house, in dire need of new shingles and a paint job, but it's chock-full of character. Tomasetti and I have done little in the way of barn renovation, and it's probably going to be our next big project.

The sliding door stands open, so I go up the ramp and walk inside. The sound of the pounding is louder. I move more deeply into the dimly lit interior. Someone is definitely hammering away on something.

"Tomasetti?"

"Back here!" comes his voice from somewhere outside at the rear.

The bank barn is an old German design that's built into a hillside. The front has two stories. The back has three stories due to the additional livestock stalls on the underside of the building. I head toward the rear, take the step-up to the wood floor, and cross to the window. I look out to see Tomasetti working on a good-size shed of some type.

"What are you doing?" I call out.

He looks up at me and grins. "I think the technical term for it is busting my ass."

I grin back. "You look good in that hammer."

"Why don't you come down here and show me?"

Laughing, I take the stairs to the lower level. I cross through the livestock stalls mounded with decades of manure that's long since composted to dirt. Tomasetti has set up shop ten feet from the barn. I see the orange snake of an extension cord. A handsaw lying in the dust. A toolbox full of his tools of the trade.

The structure he's working on is about ten feet square. It's not finished; there are only three walls and it's not yet too heavy for him to move. No windows or door yet. It looks like some sort of rustic, giant doghouse.

I don't want to ask what it is; I feel as if I should know. "Are we getting a dog?" I ask, though neither of us would ever consider leaving a dog in a doghouse.

Tomasetti removes a nail from his mouth, sets it against the wood, and drives it home with four blows of the hammer. "Two too many legs."

I think about that a moment, as amused as I am baffled. "We're getting a kid?"

When he's finished with the nail, he sets down the hammer and gives me his full attention. "How's the Gingerich case going?"

Only then do I realize that I don't want to talk about the case. I don't want the ugliness of it to intrude on this otherwise perfect moment. Still, I'm thankful he asked. Not only because he's a good sounding board, but because I'm floundering and making little headway.

"I don't think Daniel Gingerich was as sweet and innocent as everyone seems to think," I tell him.

"That can certainly change the dynamics of a case," he says. "Especially in terms of motive."

When I don't respond, he rises to his full height and crosses to me. He's wearing blue jeans and a plaid shirt that makes me smile. "I like your shirt."

"It's my farm shirt." He kisses me on the mouth, and a quiver of pleasure goes through me. He smells of this morning's aftershave and sawdust and man.

After a moment, he draws back and motions to his project. "Give up yet?"

"I'm stumped."

Taking my hand, he starts toward the barn. "In that case I'll show you."

We cross through the livestock stalls and clamber up the stairs. I can see our house through the big sliding door and I realize in that moment this is exactly where I want to be. Where I've always wanted to be. I hear the red-winged blackbirds and the frogs from their place on the muddy bank of the pond. And a burst of simple happiness engulfs me. I'm reminded of how lucky I am. How differently my life might've turned out if I hadn't met this man.

We approach a small homemade pen, something Tomasetti has thrown together with quarter-inch plywood and a few nails. I see a heat lamp clipped to a two-by-four set across the top. I hear the chirping before I see the chicks and I feel a catch in my chest.

"You didn't," I whisper.

We reach the pen. I look down to see a couple dozen fuzzy chicks chirping and milling about. They're a few days old and about the size of my fist. They've got tawny brown backs with butter-yellow undersides. Some have dark spots or a stripe on their heads. Tiny yellow beaks and feet. Tomasetti has placed a galvanized poultry drinker and matching chick feeder inside and laid a few inches of wood shavings on the floor. The temporary enclosure is about two feet square, giving the chicks plenty of room to move around, but there's enough heat coming off the lamp to keep them warm during the night.

"They're Buckeyes," he tells me.

I feel his gaze on me, trying to gauge my reaction, figure out if I'm pleased or put off because both of us work too much to care for such delicate little creatures.

"They're adorable," I say after a moment.

"Good layers, too. Brown eggs."

I look at him and I can't keep what is surely a stupid grin off my face. "I love the sound of a rooster in the morning."

"They're not sexed. The breeder said there are probably two in there."

One of the chicks chooses that moment to let out a loud, distressed-sounding chirp. Grinning, I reach for it. "Gotta be the rooster."

Tomasetti chuckles. "If the beak fits . . ."

The chick is tiny and warm and soft in my hand. I was raised around them, went through a period when it was my job to care for them. But I never appreciated them the way I do now.

"He's a cute little guy." Gently, I pass the chick to Tomasetti.

I can't take my eyes off him as he takes the chick and an unexpected surge of affection moves through me. I've seen this man at his worst. I've seen him beaten down by grief and haunted by the kinds of memories none of us should ever have to face. I know the part of him that is capable of violence. But I've seen him at his best, too, and I love him more than I've ever loved anyone else in my life. More than I ever believed possible.

"How long until the coop is finished?" I ask.

"A few days. I want to include a couple of roosts. Room for them to grow. I thought we might start looking for some of those galvanized laying boxes for eggs." He leans over and sets the chick back into the enclosure. "Or maybe something retro. Antique."

"We should hit some estate sales, garage sales."

"If we train them to come in and roost at night, we can free-range them during the day."

I nod, feeling like an idiot because I'm overcome with emotion. "I love them," I say.

He slants me a look. "I'm not going to end up being

jealous of these chickens or some nonsense like that, am I?"

Choking out a laugh, I elbow him. "Tomasetti, you are so full of shit."

He laughs. I love the sound of it. I want to stop this moment. Freeze it. Put it away. Save it for all of time, because both of us know how precious and rare this kind of happiness is.

"Chief?"

"Yup?"

"You're not crying, are you?"

"Something in my eye."

"You're full of surprises, aren't you?"

"You, too, evidently."

He reaches for my hands and pulls me around so that we're facing each other. The sound of the chicks fades to the background when I look into his eyes, and I know something is about to change. Something solid and good and forever.

"We haven't talked about making this arrangement of ours . . . official," he says.

"You mean getting married."

"You've been skittish."

When I don't respond, he looks away, then back at me. "How do you feel about setting a date?"

It's not easy to cry in front of Tomasetti. He's been through so much. We both have. More than our share, probably. For me to break at a moment like this seems . . . ridiculous.

"Hopefully, those are happy tears, if there is such a thing."

"There is." I let go of his hand and swipe them away. "Sorry."

"I kind of like it when women weep over me. It happens more often than you think. They just sort of line up and the floodgates open. . . ."

We're facing each other. Hands clasped. I look down at the chicks, then back at him. "The Amish marry after harvest, usually in November or December. Maybe January."

"It's almost October."

"I'm a practical woman. I thought we might . . . keep it simple."

"One of about a thousand things I love about you, Chief Burkholder."

"Only a thousand?"

"And counting." He puts his arm around my shoulders and pulls me closer, and, side by side, we start toward the door.

CHAPTER 10

I arrive at the station a little before eight A.M. to find Mona, Lois, and Pickles in the midst of relocating the coffee station to the corner by the window. Lois dons the dispatch system headset while Mona and Pickles heave and ho the old desk to its new home.

"Morning, Chief." Hands on her hips, Lois directs. "Move it to the right, guys. Six inches or so. It needs to be centered."

"Your six inches is my ten," Pickles grumbles.

Mona bursts out laughing. "Don't even go there."

"Well, it's not centered," Lois snaps, then looks at me. "We're almost finished here, Chief."

The coffee station is an old metal and laminate desk we inherited from a motel that closed back in the 1980s. It weighs close to a hundred pounds, and with Pickles being seventy-five years old, I question the wisdom of him moving it and I jump in to help.

When the desk is in place, all four of us stand back and look at it. "Looks great," Mona proclaims.

"I say we test it out by making some coffee," Pickles grumbles.

Lois snaps up the carafe and sets to work.

I'm midway to my office when it occurs to me Mona shouldn't be here. She's already worked her shift, which is midnight to eight A.M. At the door to my office I turn and look at her. "You're still here."

She gives me a deer-in-the-headlights look. "I was on my way out the door when—"

"I could probably muster a couple hours overtime for you this morning," I tell her. "If you're game."

She brightens. "Oh, I'm game. What you got?"

I pull out the small notebook I keep in my pocket. "See if you can come up with an address for Ruth Beiler." I spell the name. "She's Amish. I don't have a DOB, but she's approximately twenty years of age. Last known residence is Painters Mill."

"Coming right up." She starts for her computer.

"Mona?"

She stops and turns, her expression telling me she's afraid I'm going to lay into her for staying late yet again when I've asked her not to. "I was on my way out the door when you walked in, Chief. I couldn't let Lois and Pickles move that desk—"

"When you find her address, I thought you and I might go speak to her."

"Seriously?" Her eyes and mouth open wide; then she catches herself, grapples for cool. "I mean, that would be great. Experience."

"Good. Thanks."

I'm nearly to my office when I hear her let out a *whoop* loud enough to rattle the windows.

A few minutes later my phone buzzes. I glance down to see DEPT OF COMM pop up on the display. "Burkholder."

"Hi, Chief, it's Bob Schoening. I wanted to let you know about an interesting development on the Gingerich case."

I shove the file aside. "I could use some solid information about now."

"As you are aware, I collected a number of items from the scene. Among them were two mason jars located just outside the tack room door. We suspect whoever set that fire used the jars to transport gasoline to the scene."

"Are the jars intact?"

"Unfortunately they are not. In fact, there's nothing about them that makes them particularly unique. The most interesting item I've examined was a key. It was discovered with a metal detector a short distance from the tack room where the body was found."

"Is it the key to the tack room door?" I ask.

"It is. But, Chief Burkholder, what's significant about the key is that we processed it for latents and, amazingly, we got a good print off it."

"A fingerprint survived the fire?"

"The key was beneath some wood, lying against the dirt floor. It was somewhat protected from the fire and remained cool enough for the latents to show up when we tested it."

I sit up straighter. "Do you have a name to go with the print?"

"We submitted to BCI via LiveScan and they're running it through AFIS now."

AFIS is the acronym for the Automated Fingerprint Identification System. "Any idea how long that might take?"

"Twenty-four hours, give or take."

It's good news. Of course, the print could belong to one of the Gingerich family members. Even if it belongs to an unknown individual, like all law enforcement databases, AFIS is only as good as the information it contains. If the owner of those prints doesn't have a record or has never been fingerprinted, there won't be a match.

"Anything else?" I ask.

"I'm sending my report your way now." Papers rattle on the other end. "I do have a couple more notable items. A wine bottle was found inside the tack room. A ceramic plate. Residue from a candle."

"Latents?"

"No."

"That's an interesting combination of items."

"I thought so, too."

"Any chance the candle started that fire?"

"I've determined that the fire started outside the tack room. That, I'm sure of. It's possible there was a secondary fire, but I've not seen indication of that."

I rattle off my cell phone number. "Keep me posted on that latent, will you?"

"You bet."

* * *

Mona is a whiz when it comes to digging up information. Not only is she adept on the law enforcement databases—LEADS and Ohio's OHLEG—but she's also quite the sleuth when it comes to the search engine and venturing into some of the internet's best kept secrets.

"Would have found all this sooner, but Ruth Beiler is actually Ruth Petersheim now," Mona says from the doorway of my office. "Married Mark Petersheim about a year ago. They live up in Wilmot now. She works part-time at the Amish Door restaurant."

"Nice detective work." I grab my keys. "Want to run up there with me?"

Her grin is the only answer I need.

Wilmot is a pretty little village with a population of about three hundred souls thirty minutes northeast of Painters Mill. I plugged Ruth Petersheim's address into my GPS before leaving and head north on US 62. I stop for gas in Millersburg and continue on, passing a few buggies and driving by dozens of Amish farms. At the edge of Wilmot, we idle past the Amish Door Village and I smile. Two weeks ago, Tomasetti and I spent a rare Saturday morning together, pigging out on scrambled eggs and pancakes at their breakfast buffet.

As we approach the dogleg before Winesburg intersects with Main Street, the female voice instructs me to make a right on Milton.

Mona points. "There it is. Little house just past the church."

I park curbside in front of a small frame home with white paint and a crooked front porch. There are two vintage metal chairs painted a pretty shade of turquoise and a planter box full of yellow and lavender mums.

"Is Ruth Petersheim Amish?" Mona asks.

"She was at some point." I look at her, remind myself this is a learning experience for her. "The main thing to remember is that Petersheim is neither a suspect nor a witness at this point. We're basically on a fishing expedition. The more she talks, the more fruitful this visit will be."

"Got it."

"Mainly, I want to know if she knew or was friends with Daniel Gingerich. I'm interested in what kind of relationship they had. If they were close. That sort of thing. You never know where some seemingly insignificant piece of information might turn out to be important."

She stares at me, nodding, eyes wide, seeming to hang on my every word. "Right."

"I'll take the lead, but if you think of something important, jump in."

We leave the Explorer and take a narrow, buckled sidewalk to the porch. At the door, Mona looks at me. I give her a nod. Standing slightly aside, she knocks firmly.

The door opens and I find myself looking at a young Amish woman. Early twenties. Dishwater blond hair encased in a gauzy *kapp*. Light blue dress, apron, and discount-brand sneakers. I hear a baby gaggling somewhere in the house.

She looks taken aback by the sight of my uniform. "Has something happened?"

I show her my badge and introduce myself. "We're looking into the death of Daniel Gingerich," I tell her. "May we come inside for a few minutes to speak with you?"

"But . . . why?" Looking like a trapped animal that's just realized its life is in danger, she glances from me to Mona. "I don't know anything."

She's too polite to refuse my request and steps back, ostensibly allowing us entry.

"Thank you." I take the initiative and step inside. "We won't take up too much of your time."

I'm greeted by the smells of burned toast and fresh-brewed coffee. The house is slightly cramped and typically Amish. The living room contains an overstuffed sofa piled high with crocheted pillows. Two end tables, both adorned with kerosene lamps set on doilies. Two rocking chairs with homemade seat cushions. Through a wide entryway I see a decent-size kitchen. White cabinets. A wringer washer on the back porch. A baby crib is set against the wall between the kitchen and living room.

"I don't know why you're here." Petersheim crosses to the crib and looks down at the baby before turning to us. "I don't know anything about Daniel."

"I was told you were friends," I begin.

"I don't know who told you that, but we weren't friends. I knew him. I mean, when I lived in Painters

Mill with my parents. But that was a long time ago. I'm married now." She takes a breath as if she'd forgotten to breathe while speaking.

I puzzle over the level of her nervousness. Of course, anxiety isn't an indication of guilt; some people simply get nervous around cops. Or they don't like strangers. But even taking those things into consideration, Ruth Petersheim seems disproportionately affected by our presence.

"Is your husband home, Mrs. Petersheim?"

"He's working."

I pull out my notebook. "Where does he work?"

"Obermiller Construction. He's putting in the fence out to the Inn this week."

I jot it down, giving her a chance to calm down, and then try again. "I understand you went to a singing with Daniel Gingerich."

She looks at me as if the statement makes her nauseous. "Oh, that. It was an . . . informal thing. And there were lots of other Amish there. We weren't . . . together or alone. I mean, it wasn't just the two of us."

I'm not sure why any of those things matter, or why she felt the need to point them out, so I don't press her too hard. "So you were never close," I say easily.

"No."

Nodding, I offer a smile, but I sense the tension coming off her. She's wringing her hands and keeps looking at the baby, as if hoping the infant will cry so she can escape.

"Did Daniel ever have any arguments or disagreements with anyone that you know of?" I ask.

"No, but then I didn't know him very well. Hardly at all."

Her reply came too quickly. She's not thinking about the question before blurting out the answer she wants me to hear. The one that will bring this unpleasant exchange to an end and send us on our way. What the hell?

I try to engage her. "Are you sure, Ruth? Maybe he had a disagreement with someone over money? Something like that?"

"He never argued with anyone that I know of." She looks longingly at the door as if she wants us to make use of it.

Mona interjects. "Maybe it didn't seem like a big deal at the time?"

Petersheim blinks at her as if realizing it's now two against one. "No."

The baby begins to cry. Looking unduly grateful for the interruption, the Amish woman turns away and rushes to the crib. *"Ich bin om cooma."* I'm coming.

When her back is turned I look at Mona, and she shrugs.

Ignoring us completely, keeping her back to us, Petersheim scoops the baby into her arms. *"Wie geht's, mei lamm?"* How goes it, my little lamb?

I cross to the crib and, trying to find a way to put her at ease, I look down at the baby in her arms. *"Er is schnuck."* He's cute.

For the first time, she looks at me as if I'm a person, not some monster that's forced its way into her home, and a smile touches her mouth. *"Cannscht du Deitsh schwetze?"* Can you speak Dutch?

"I used to be Amish."

Her eyes shift to Mona. "You, too?"

"Oh no, ma'am. Not me." Mona raises both hands as if to fend off an attack. "I'm an *Englischer* through and through."

The three of us look down at the infant.

"What's his name?" I ask.

Smiling, she raises the baby's face to hers and rubs her nose against his. "William."

"How old is he?" Mona asks.

It's an innocent question, but Petersheim stiffens slightly. "Almost a year now."

The baby chooses that moment to spit up. Clabbered milk dribbles onto the front of his plain little onesie.

The Amish woman clucks her mouth. "Well, that's what I get for not burping you, isn't it?" she coos.

"Can I help?" I ask.

She sends me a grateful smile, but shakes her head. "I've had lots of practice. Happens every time he drinks too much milk and I don't burp him right away. Midwife says he'll grow out of it soon."

Little William is wearing a onesie with Amish-like suspenders over a white T-shirt. Mona and I watch as Petersheim deftly folds down the bib and slips the soiled T-shirt over his head.

"It's just a little bit of *schmierkees*," she mutters in a baby voice, referring to the Amish version of cottage cheese. She turns her attention back to the baby, covers his fat cheeks with a dozen smacking kisses. "Isn't that right, *mei lamm*?"

She leaves him for a moment to grab a fresh shirt

from a drawer beneath the changing table. That's when I notice the dark brown spot on the right side of the baby's tummy. It's large for such a little guy—about four inches in length and an inch wide. A birthmark, I realize, and I get the odd sense that I've seen it before. . . .

Petersheim returns and with deft hands, slips the fresh shirt over the baby's head, carefully pulling his little arms through the holes and then smoothing down his hair.

I wait until the baby is dressed before addressing her. "Ruth, can you tell me where you were Monday night?"

Her gaze jerks to mine, her eyes widen. "What? Why do you need to know that?"

"I have to ask everyone who knew or came in contact with Daniel Gingerich. You understand?" I offer a smile I hope will reassure her. "Just to eliminate you from the equation."

"I was here," she tells me. "Mothers with new babies can't just run off in the evening."

"Can your husband vouch for you?"

"Of course he can," she snaps. "He was here, too. Please, if you could just go now . . . I need to feed him."

"Of course." But I hesitate. "Is there anything else you can tell me about Daniel Gingerich that might help me with the investigation?" I ask.

"Like I said, I barely knew him." She motions toward the door. "That's all I've got to say."

A minute later Mona and I are back in the Explorer.

"That's got to be the most uptight Amish woman I've ever met," Mona says.

"No doubt." I pull away from the curb. "The question is why."

"You think she knows something about Daniel Gingerich?"

"I think she knows *something* she doesn't want to share."

I reach Winesburg Street and take a left. Ruth Petersheim had said her husband was working on a fence at the Amish Door Village. I don't recall seeing one on US 62 when we drove past, so I make a left on Lawnford. Sure enough, a quarter mile in, just past the dogleg, I see two Amish men working on a four-rail white fence.

Parked on the shoulder, an older Dodge pickup truck bakes in the sun. Its tailgate is down and in the bed I see a pile of tools—a shovel, a hammer, boxes of screws, a battery-powered screwdriver—and an insulated water cooler.

I pull up behind the truck and kill the engine. "Since we're here, I thought we might make contact and double-check Ruth's story about where she was the night Gingerich was killed."

We get out and start toward the men. The older guy is standing next to the fence, leaning on the shovel, a collapsible cup in hand, watching us approach. I guess him to be about forty years of age. He's got a full beard that's shot with gray. Blue work shirt. Dark trousers. Suspenders. A summer straw hat and sunglasses. The younger of the two is digging a post hole, a physically taxing chore, especially with the sun beating down. He's dressed much like the older man, but his shirt is soaked through with sweat beneath his arms and along the center of his back.

"*Hays genuk fa du?*" I say as I approach. Hot enough for you?

Grinning, the older man takes a sip of water and motions toward the man digging the post hole. "*Hays genuk fa eem fleicht.*" Hot enough for him maybe.

I introduce myself. "I'm looking for Mark Petersheim."

The young man glances over at me before ramming the digger back into the hole. He's blond-haired with a thick red beard and eyes the color of tea. "I'm Petersheim," he says.

"I'm investigating the death of Daniel Gingerich," I tell him. "Do you have a minute? I'd like to ask you a few questions."

The two Amish men exchange looks. Sighing, Petersheim tugs the post hole digger from the hole, sets the tip against the ground, and offers it to the other man. "*Alle daag rumhersitze mach tem faul,*" he says. Sitting all day makes one lazy.

Chuckling, the older man takes the handles and gets to work.

I watch as Petersheim crosses to the truck, snaps up a collapsible cup, fills it, and after removing his hat, dumps it over his head. He fills the cup a second time and drinks it down before returning to where Mona and I stand. He doesn't look pleased that we're here.

"I didn't know Gingerich," he says, wiping the water from his face with a kerchief.

"Did you ever meet him?" I ask.

"Nope."

"Do you know of him?"

"Heard about the fire. That kind of thing is big news, especially since he was Amish and all."

I nod. "I understand your wife knew him before you were married."

A brief hesitation. "I think they might've been in the same church district for a while. We're Beachy now, so . . ." He motions toward the truck and shrugs.

"Were Daniel and your wife friends?"

He looks away, watches the other man dig, then turns his attention back to me. "Don't think so."

"She never mentioned him?" I ask.

"Not that I recall."

"We just talked to Ruth a few minutes ago," I tell him.

"I reckon you should have asked her instead of me."

While he hasn't said or done anything overtly hostile, he's being rude and evasive. Resentment simmers beneath the surface of his otherwise calm facade. Since no one I've talked to today seems inclined to talk about Daniel Gingerich, I push, hoping to find out why.

"I understand your wife and Daniel went to a singing together."

"A lot of *Amisch* go to singings. That's what the young people do. So what?"

"Would you mind telling me where you were Monday night, Mr. Petersheim?"

"Same place I am every night." He doesn't blink, doesn't look away; he's not the least bit intimidated by me or my questions. "Home. With my wife and our baby." He glances over at the other Amish man, who has finished with the post hole, then turns his attention back to me. "You done? I gotta get back to work."

"I appreciate your time."

He walks away without looking back.

"He's a font of information," Mona says when we're back inside the Explorer.

"He knows more than he's letting on," I say as I buckle in and start the engine.

"Seems like no one wants to talk about Daniel Gingerich," Mona says. "I wonder why."

"Sooner or later all of these weird little secrets everyone is keeping are going to come to light." I put the vehicle in gear and pull onto the road. "When they do, we'll have our answer."

CHAPTER 11

It's after noon when I pull up to the police station and drop Mona. I'm thinking about Emma Miller and the possibility that her death was the result of some event linked to Daniel Gingerich in the days he worked for the Millers. Instead of going inside, I make a U-turn and I'm back on the road, heading north on County Road 159 toward the Miller farm.

The last time I spoke to Esther and Sam Miller, they made it clear they had no intention of opening up about their daughter. The case has evolved since then. Now that I know more about Daniel Gingerich—more about young Emma—I realize their silence may not be solely based on grief, but secrets.

I take the winding lane to the house on the hill. The barn door stands open, so I park in the gravel a few yards away and go inside. The interior is shadowy and smells of horses and hay and earthy things. But I also smell a hint of paint.

"Hello?" I call out. "Mr. Miller?"

I wander toward the rear of the barn, passing a workbench loaded with several unfinished birdhouses and feeders. I'm thinking about going up to the second-level loft when I hear footsteps behind me. I turn to find Esther Miller standing there in her black dress and bonnet, a gallon bucket of paint in her hand.

"Thought I heard someone out here." Watching me out of the corner of her eye, she crosses to the workbench and hefts the paint can onto a section of old newspaper. "You change your mind about buying one of those feeders?"

"I think I'll take the red one that looks like the Amish barn. For my sister. It's her birthday next week."

"That's a nice one." Her amicable tone belies the wariness in her eyes as she goes to the chosen feeder and sets it on the bench. "Would you like it wrapped? I use these old copies of *The Budget* and a bit of twine. Makes for a nice, rustic effect."

"I think she'd like that."

The Amish woman tugs a folded newspaper from a shelf beneath the bench, then pulls a length of twine from a roll affixed to big steel bolt that's welded to the wall. "Can't use corn in this one, unless it's the cracked kind. It'll clog up the holes there at the bottom and the millet won't come out."

"*Ich fashtay.*" I understand.

I watch as she sets the feeder on the newspaper and begins to wrap it. "I know Emma was *ime familye weg* when she died," I say.

The Amish woman winces as if I'd reached out and sliced her down the back with a knife. Among many of the Old Order and Swartzentruber sects of Amish society, pregnancy is not discussed. The word "pregnant" is never used. The Amish adore children and usually have a large brood. But when it comes to the mechanics of it—the birds-and-the-bees aspect—there's a certain level of squeamishness.

Among many of the Amish, there's an undeniable stigma attached to a woman who becomes pregnant out of wedlock. Oftentimes, the family of the mother-to-be will step in and urge her to marry, even if the prospective groom isn't the father of the baby.

When Esther doesn't respond, I cross to her and set my hand on the bird feeder. "I know you're still mourning your daughter, Mrs. Miller. I understand how painful it must be for you and your husband to speak of her. But I need your help."

Letting her hands fall away from the feeder, she turns and gives me her full attention. "I won't speak of her. Not to you. Not about that."

"Because she was with child?" I ask.

Tightening her mouth, she reaches for the length of string and wraps it around the newspaper covering the bird feeder, yanking it tightly to hold it in place.

"Or maybe you don't want to talk about her because of what happened to her."

Esther's gaze snaps to mine and narrows. "Nothing happened. I don't know what you're talking about."

"I think you do. I think Emma went through something awful. You and your husband are either in denial or you're lying to me because you're trying to protect her."

"I don't want to discuss this," she hisses. "I won't. It's not proper."

"Mrs. Miller, I need to know what happened between Emma and Daniel Gingerich. I promise I'll do my best to keep it confidential."

"My sweet Emma is in heaven now. She is with God. She's at peace, and I'll be with her one day. That's all that matters now. And that's all I've got to say about it."

She shoves the bird feeder at me. "Take it and go. Just . . . go and don't come back."

I don't move; I don't reach for my wallet or take the feeder. "I spoke with Elam Schlabach."

The Amish woman turns away, but not before I see the grief and shame in her eyes. "I won't discuss this."

I cross to her, set my hand on her arm. "He said Emma was innocent."

She turns back to me, blinks. "Of course she was."

"We both know that doesn't make sense. She loved Elam. She was saving herself until they were married and yet she became pregnant." I wait a beat. When she doesn't respond, I add, "What did Daniel do to her?"

She glances toward the barn door—watching for her husband, I think—and in that instant I know she's going to tell me something that's going to change everything. I've lanced the boil that's been festering inside her. For better or for worse, the poison is about to spill out.

"Emma wouldn't want anyone to know," she whispers. "She wouldn't."

"I'll do my best to keep this just between us." I'm not

sure I'll be able to uphold complete confidentiality, but I'll try.

"Sam and I thought he was such a sweet boy," she tells me. "Smart. From a good Amish family. Had a good work ethic on him. Daniel never gave us a reason to think otherwise."

I wait, willing her to continue, ignoring that small part of me that doesn't want to hear what's coming.

Pressing her hand against her stomach, she walks to the workbench, sets both hands against it, and leans. "I saw them one afternoon. Together. In the milk house. They were . . . on the floor by the stanchions. He was . . . on top of her . . . you know how they do. Her dress was . . ." Shaking her head, she doesn't finish. "She was down there in all that manure. Just lying there for all the world to see. Like *that,* you know. Muck all over her dress."

I choose my next words carefully. "Was it consensual?"

She squeezes her eyes closed. "At first I didn't know. I mean, Danny was a handsome young man. And Emma was nearly a grown woman. Both were of *Rumspringa* age. I thought . . ." She breaks off, puts her hand over her mouth as if to smother a cry.

"Did he coerce her?" Too late I try to remove the edge from my voice. "Force her?"

She straightens, seems to gather herself, pull her emotions together. "Emma came to me. Later that night. She said he'd . . . you know, done things to her. Things she didn't want him to do. She said they were . . . of one flesh."

"He raped her?" I ask.

Tears glitter in her eyes, and within their depths I see the truth she doesn't want to face. She doesn't let the tears fall. To do so would be to admit the unthinkable and she's not that strong. I watch her face as the pain gives way to denial. Even before she speaks I know she's going to shift back to the only lie that will save her from herself. From a life of self-loathing because neither she nor her husband had kept their daughter safe.

"I told her good girls don't do those kinds of things," she whispers. "I told her to pray harder. That she should have resisted him. Resisted herself. I told her God doesn't let things like that happen to good girls. She must've done something to tempt him and for that she should seek forgiveness."

Tension grips the back of my neck like a vise. I stare at her, a violent tide of disgust rising inside me.

This isn't the first time I've encountered that mindset among the Amish. It's one of the reasons I have a love-hate relationship with the community to which I was born. The part of me that is fourteen years old and shattered inside wants to strike out at her. Wants to snarl and scream, *Your daughter came to you and you blamed her? How in the name of God could you do that to a teenage girl who'd come to you for help?*

Sweat gathers beneath my arms, at the back of my neck, between my breasts. I look at her, wondering how she can live with herself. I want to ask her: If you'd listened to your daughter, if you'd protected her, would she still be alive?

"Did it happen more than once?" I ask.

"I don't know. She didn't speak of it again, but I think maybe it did." She shrugs. "It's such a private thing. You know, the things that happen between men and women. I thought they were, you know, beaus."

"Does your husband know what happened?"

"Enough so that he doesn't want to talk about it."

"What does that mean?" I snap. "Did you tell him? Did Emma tell him? Did he see something, too?"

"I told him."

Motive, a little voice whispers.

"How did he react?" I ask.

"He said they shouldn't tell the bishop. If the bishop found out he would be forced to excommunicate them for six weeks. We didn't want that to happen." She looks down at the ground and then levels her gaze on mine. "Chief Burkholder, I know how all of this must sound to you, what you must be thinking."

"I'm not thinking anything, Mrs. Miller."

"I was not a bad mother to Emma."

A hundred words tangle in my throat. None of them are kind, so I buckle it down and keep my mouth shut.

After a moment, she closes her eyes, presses her fingers to her lids as if to keep the dam from bursting. "If God were to give me another chance, I would have stopped Daniel."

"Thank you for your time, Mrs. Miller," I say, and I walk away.

God doesn't let things like that happen to good girls. She must've done something to tempt him . . .

I can't get the words out of my head. The thought of an Amish girl being abused in her own home is bad enough. But to know that girl went to her parents for help only to be blamed by them fills me with outrage. How could parents crush their daughter so completely, allow her to feel so hopeless, so betrayed, that she chose death over life?

The ugliness of the question drags me back to a time in my own life when I was that girl. The girl who still believed the world was a safe place and people were fundamentally good. The girl who had no concept of violence or the darkness that lurked in the depths of the human heart.

I was fourteen years old when Daniel Lapp walked into my *mamm*'s sunny farmhouse kitchen and destroyed everything I believed about the world and the people I knew. He stole my innocence, shredded any semblance of happiness, replacing both with shock and shame and numbing disbelief.

I don't dwell on the past or what happened to me; I don't let myself think about it and I damn sure don't let it define me. But there are times, when I'm tired or my guard is down, that all those old emotions come creeping back. Sometimes when I close my eyes I still see his face. I see the way he looked at me, as if I weren't there, just a piece of meat to be torn to bits, devoured, digested. I still feel the revulsion of his closeness, the stink of his breath, the pain of the violation. The sense of betrayal that followed.

No one came to help me that day. No one stepped in

to defend me. I was alone with a monster, and I did what I had to do to survive. An act that, according to my parents, was the darkest sin of all.

Furious, hating the parallels, I rap my hand hard against the steering wheel. "They swept it under the rug," I want to shout, not sure if I'm talking about what happened to Emma Miller or myself.

I'm northbound on Ohio 83 when suddenly I can't get enough oxygen into my lungs. I clutch the wheel, order myself to calm down, get a grip. It doesn't help.

My vision narrows and dims. I hit the brakes, pull onto the shoulder, stop hard enough to make the tires skid on gravel. For the span of a full minute, I hang on to the steering wheel so tightly my knuckles go white. The sound of buzzing fills my ears; I hear the pound of my heart beating out of control. I taste vomit at the back of my throat, grapple for the door handle, shove it open, spit.

"Goddamn you." I choke out the words, not sure if I'm cursing my own weakness, my hapless parents, or the son of a bitch who caused so much pain in my life.

After a few seconds, the vise around my chest loosens. The haze clears. I become aware of traffic passing me on the road. The sound of a lawnmower somewhere nearby. The smell of fresh-cut grass. The call of a blue jay from the treetops in the woods to my right.

"Officer?"

I glance left to see a red SUV roll up beside me. A young woman in the passenger seat has her window lowered and she's looking at me with concern. "Everything okay?"

"I'm fine." I muster a smile. "Lunch didn't agree with me."

"Just checking." She smiles back. "Have a good day."

Closing my door, I watch the vehicle pull back onto the highway. I lean against the seat back and close my eyes, taking deep, slow breaths, trying not think about what just happened.

Too close to home, a little voice whispers.

The logical side of my brain reminds me that emotion has no place in police work. This case isn't about me or my feelings. It isn't even about Emma Miller, despite what happened to her. This case is about the murder of Daniel Gingerich. My job is to find the person responsible and build a case against them. The rest is up to the courts.

But I'm human and as imperfect as the next guy and I know better than most that emotions rarely cooperate with intellect. Daniel Gingerich wasn't some innocent farm boy. If what I'm hearing is true, he was a rapist and a son of a bitch. I'd damn well better get used to it, because I've been charged with finding the person responsible for killing him despite the fact that some small, unacknowledged part of me believes he deserved his fate.

In terms of motive, the sexual assault and death of Emma Miller are important developments. If she was, indeed, raped, discovered she was pregnant, and committed suicide to escape the stigma and pain, those who loved her would have a pretty strong motive to seek vengeance on the perpetrator. That includes Elam Schlabach and Sam Miller. I think about her mother but dismiss the notion. Any woman who could blame her daughter for being raped possesses no sense of justice, not even the dark and twisted variety that leads to vigilantism.

CHAPTER 12

Life would be a hell of a lot easier if people just told you what they know the first time you talked to them, rather than stonewalling or lying or playing all those hide-and-seek games some folks are so damn fond of. No one understands better than I do the desire for privacy, particularly when there's a personal tragedy involved. I get that, and I go out of my way to protect reputations at risk.

In dealing with the Amish, I know that their avoiding me isn't necessarily an indicator of guilt, but a reflection of their "tenet of separation" from the rest of the world. Most Amish deal with "the English" on a daily basis with no problems. But some of the Old Order and Swartzentruber sects go to great lengths to avoid dealing with non-Amish individuals. I understand and respect their belief system. That said, I will not allow the mind-set to interfere with or hinder my investigation.

It's a little after four P.M. and I'm in my office, resisting the urge to beat my head against the desk, when Lois rushes in. "Tip just came in over the line we set up for the Gingerich thing."

Despite her enthusiasm, I don't get too excited. So far the tip line has been as fruitful as a dead tree and I'm too discouraged to get my hopes up. "Go ahead, make my day."

She slaps a notepad in front of me. "Female caller says Chris Martino, the neighbor, set the fire that killed Dan Gingerich. She claims there's proof in Martino's shed."

It's the last kind of information I expected. Even without hearing the details, I experience a precipitous rise of skepticism. "Did she say what kind of proof?"

"No."

"Did she leave her name? Contact info?"

"She said she was scared of him and wants to remain anonymous."

"Did you get a number?"

"The call came in from the Amish pay phone out on County Roads 407 and 58."

A phone anyone could have used to make the call. Still, despite my doubts about its validity, I'm obliged to follow up. At the very least I need to find out if there's any so-called evidence in Martino's shed.

"Call Judge Siebenthaler and tell him I'm on my way over," I say. "Tell him I need a warrant to search Chris Martino's home."

"You got it."

But I know all too well that any warrant based on an

anonymous tip is going to be a hard sell. Still, in light of the seriousness of the crime—and my lack of progress in producing a viable suspect—the judge might just bite.

Thinking about Martino and his temper, I ask, "Who's on duty, by the way?"

"Skid came on about an hour ago."

"Tell him to get over here. I'm going to put together a quick affidavit and head over to the judge's chambers."

Two hours later I'm armed with a warrant and on my way to the home of Chris Martino. Judge Siebenthaler wasn't thrilled about issuing a warrant based on an anonymous tip. As a result, he limited my search to the shed. I wasn't happy with it, but at this point I'll take what I can get.

Skid rides shotgun in the passenger seat. "Might've been beneficial to wait until happy hour before laying that affidavit on the judge." He grins. "Just sayin'."

I try not to smile. It's common knowledge that the judge spends most afternoons at the country club up in Millersburg and chases his usual nine holes of golf with a round or two of Woodford Reserve. "I don't know," I tell him. "This 'tip' seems a little convenient."

"Someone with an ax to grind against Martino?" He shrugs. "He's not exactly Mr. Charisma."

"Or someone who wants to divert us," I say. "It's noteworthy that the caller had no interest in the reward money."

"We do have one thing going for us, Chief."

I glance over at him and raise my brows.

"Chris Martino might just be dumb enough to have set that fire and then left the torch and gas can in his shed."

"You've rekindled my faith in mankind."

Afternoon is giving way to evening when I pull into the weed-riddled driveway of the Martino place. There's only one vehicle—Martino's old pickup truck—so I pull up behind it and park adjacent to the shed. It's a dilapidated building with a broken overhead door, siding that's gone to rot, and half a dozen shattered windowpanes. It's a relatively small building—about the size of a single-car garage.

Plucking the warrant from the console, I get out.

The air is hazy above the hip-high weeds and grass where insects swirl and crickets sing a raucous chorus. The windows of the house are open and chain saw rock blares from inside.

"Sounds like Martino's having a hell of a party," Skid says as he gets out.

"There's an image I don't want in my head." I'm hoping Martino isn't intoxicated.

We take the sidewalk to the house, go around to the front door, and ascend the steps to the porch. The door stands open about two feet. Through the screen, Neil Young proclaims that rock and roll will never die loud enough to rattle the windows. There's no sign of Martino or anyone else; no movement inside.

Since Martino is a felon, it's illegal for him to possess a firearm. That doesn't mean he's not armed. Worst case, he's drunk and armed and pissed off.

Standing slightly to one side, I knock firmly. "Mr. Martino?" I call out. "Painters Mill Police Department. Can you come out here and talk to us a moment?"

Skid's got a decent amount of experience under his belt. He's laid-back, likes a good laugh, especially at the expense of someone else, and he doesn't get too excited about much of anything. But I can tell he's as antsy about this as I am.

I wait half a minute and knock again, using the heel of my hand. "Chris Martino! Painters Mill PD. Can you come out and talk to us!"

A thump sounds from inside. I tense, step right. Skid moves left, sets his hand over his sidearm, leans over to peer inside.

Through the screen, I see someone approach. An instant later the interior door swings open and Chris Martino appears on the other side of the screen. I step back, keeping him at a prudent distance. Yanking open the screen door, he staggers halfway out and squints at me, holding the door open with his right hand. "The fuck you pounding on my door for?" I glance past him, check for other individuals, but he appears to be alone. "Mr. Martino, can you come out here and talk to us for a moment please?"

"What's this about?" The big man moves through the door, steps onto the porch, and lets the screen door slam behind him. His hair is mussed, standing up on one side. He's wearing a white T-shirt and blue jeans with flip-flops. Dirty feet. Dirty hair. He's impaired, but not unsteady on his feet. I can smell the alcohol on his breath from where I stand. His eyes are glassy and red, telling me he's likely on something else, too. Either a narcotic or prescription drug or all of the above.

"Okay, here I am. What do you want?"

"You alone this afternoon, Mr. Martino?" I ask.

"Just me and Jack Daniel's."

I hand him the neatly folded document. "This is a warrant, Chris. I suggest you read it carefully. We have permission to conduct a search."

"A *search*?" He stares down at the warrant as if I've handed him a live snake, but he doesn't unfold it; he doesn't read. Instead, he raises his gaze to mine. A weird smile overtakes his face. He's got a missing eyetooth. The rest are yellowed from tobacco. "Just out of curiosity, what the hell are you looking for?"

"Everything you need to know is in the warrant." I look past him, toward the interior of the house. "Do you mind if we come inside and take a look around?"

A search of the house isn't included in the warrant, but it never hurts to ask. If he grants us permission, we can lawfully conduct a search and use anything we find in whatever manner we see fit.

Martino unfolds the warrant. "If it ain't in the warrant, you ain't coming in."

Skid and I wait while he reads. After a full minute he looks up at me and smiles nastily. "Fuckin' Nazi cops."

"Thank you, Mr. Martino." I step back. "We're going to go ahead and take a look in that shed, then we'll get out of your hair."

"Knock your socks off," he says. "You ain't going to find shit unless you plant it."

Skid and I turn and start toward the shed. When we're out of earshot, Skid mutters, "That's one squirrely son of a bitch."

The overhead door is open about a foot, but has fallen off the track and hangs at a precarious angle. We go around to the side door. Skid tries to open it, but it jams and he has to put some muscle into it. Not for the first time I'm glad I brought him along.

"Holy cow," he mutters as we enter.

My heart sinks when I get my first look. The small space is jam-packed with every imaginable variety of junk. An old car of indiscernible origin is parked in the center of the mess. Both front fenders are missing. One tire is gone, the other is flat. The hood is raised about a foot. Every square inch of the rusted metal is covered with bird droppings. I look up and see half an inch of buildup on the rafters and I realize it's a pigeon roost.

Beyond the vehicle, a wheelbarrow lies on its side. An ancient bicycle is propped against the wall. Half a dozen clay pots sit on the concrete ledge of the footer. An old door that's being used as a workbench is covered with what looks like engine parts. Cinder-block-and-board shelving lines the far wall. The stink of bird droppings, dust, and moldering wood permeates the air.

"Doesn't look like anyone's been here in a while," Skid mutters as he circumvents the car and heads toward the workbench.

He's right. Dust and cobwebs coat every visible surface. Again, I wonder about the veracity of the tip. "You take the workbench. I'll start with the shelves and we'll work our way toward the door. Let's make it quick."

"You're not going to get an argument from me, Chief."

I pluck gloves from my pocket and jam my hands into them. Carefully, I step over a galvanized tub and make my way toward the shelves. Though the door is open and the single window is uncovered, there isn't much light, so I pull out my mini Maglite, flip it on.

I start with the top shelf, which is at about eye level. There's an old garden sprayer. A coiled hose. A box filled with oily rags. I work my way from top to bottom, checking each shelf as I go, finding nothing of interest.

Behind me, I hear Skid clanging around, muttering the occasional obscenity. "Anything?" I call out.

"Not finding shit, Chief."

I work my way over to the car. I'm entertaining the idea of calling it a day when I glance at the door handle—it's an old chrome thing with a thumb button—and I notice a smudge in the dust.

I look down; there's a mark on the concrete floor where the dust has been disturbed. A heel print, I realize; someone has been here. I glance through the windshield, but there's too much grime for me to see the interior. I reach for the handle. The hinges groan when I open it. The red vinyl seat has been torn to shreds by some animal intent on nesting. The steering wheel is missing. There's a hole in the dash where a radio had once been. Wires dangling. I shine my light on the floor and do a double take when I spot the mason jars. Two of them, shiny and clean and filled with clear amber liquid. They're lined up side by side like a couple of Mom's canned goods.

"Skid, I've got something."

I'm bent at the hip, shining the beam onto the backseat, when he rounds the hood and comes up behind me. I motion toward the two jars. "They haven't been here long."

"Looks like gas." He whistles. "Didn't the fire marshal find a couple of broken mason jars at the scene?"

"Yep." Squatting, I lean into the car, put my nose an inch from the jar lid, and sniff. "It's definitely gas."

"What's that sticking out from beneath the jar?"

I lean back on my haunches and shift the flashlight. Sure enough, the beam glints off of something metallic. Using my gloved hand, I push the jar aside. "It's a key."

"Looks new."

"The dead bolt on the tack room door over at the Gingerich place was only a couple of months old." I glance up at Skid. "There were two keys. One was found at the scene."

"Maybe this is the other one. State boys pick up latents?"

"They did. Haven't heard back on the ID yet," I tell him. "Should be any time."

"Easy enough to figure out if the key fits the lock."

I hear myself sigh as that uneasy sense of skepticism mushrooms into cold, hard suspicion. "Skid, why would someone who was questioned by the police about an arson hide something like this on his property?"

"That's a stretch even for Chris Martino."

I flip off my Maglite and look around, find Skid's eyes already on mine.

"You think someone planted it?" he asks.

I nod. "The big question is who."

He jabs a thumb in the general direction of the house. "What do we do with Prince Charming?"

"Let's see what he's got to say."

I glance toward the door to see Chris Martino standing in the doorway, looking in.

I lower my voice. "Call BCI and get a CSU out here. We need those mason jars and that key processed for latents."

"You got it."

"Set up a perimeter with tape, too, will you?"

"Sure thing."

We start toward the door. I hear Skid on the phone behind me as I slip through. Martino is standing a few feet away, one hand in his pocket, the other holding a beer. "Told you you weren't going to find anything."

I cross to him. "When's the last time you were in that shed?"

"Been so long I don't even remember. Two or three months, maybe."

"We found the mason jars," I say quietly, watching him.

"Mason jars? What? Do I look like I can tomatoes?"

I say nothing.

"Look," he says, "whatever crap's in that shed don't belong to me. That ain't my car. Ain't my junk. All of it belongs to the landlord."

I think about asking him about the key, decide to keep that bit of information to myself. "Do you keep gasoline here on your property?"

The nasty smile falters. "I got a gas can on the back porch for my lawnmower. Mower's broke and I think the can's empty." Some of his belligerence drops away, and for the first time, he looks worried. "What's this all about?"

"Has anyone been in that shed, Mr. Martino? Landlord? Neighbor?"

"No one," he tells me.

"Has anyone been on the property? Visitors?"

"No. I mean, not that I know of."

"Have you had any prowlers out here? Any unidentified persons on your property? Strange cars? Anything like that?"

He lifts the beer, takes a long pull, watching me carefully. "What did you find in there? A dead body?"

I glance over at Skid. He gives me a thumbs-up, letting me know the CSU from BCI is on the way. I turn my attention back to Martino. "Look, we're going to tape off this area. We've got a crime scene unit coming out here to take a closer look at the shed."

"Crime scene unit, huh?" He laughs. "You people better not be aiming to hang anything on me."

"The only way you're going to get anything hung on you is if your prints turn up on those mason jars," I tell him. "Do you understand?"

"Yeah, I got it."

"I may want to talk to you again, Mr. Martino, so if you have to leave town for any reason, you need to let me know."

"I ain't going anywhere." Taking a final, disgusted look at me, he sighs and heads back toward the house.

* * *

Shvetzah f'um da Deivel un du zayl da saund funn sei flikkels. Speak of the devil and you'll hear the flap of his wings. It was one of her *grossmudder*'s favorite sayings. It basically means if you spend too much time thinking about the Devil, he'll come your way. . . .

If Neva hadn't been so scared, she might've laughed. She'd known he would come after her. For weeks, she'd been driving the car to and from work. She'd been careful. No stops along the way. Not even for gas. She didn't take any chances. Didn't tempt fate. She rarely left the house after dark. When she did, she was never alone. Mamm thought she was such a good girl. So focused on her job at The Mercantile that she had no interest in the things some of the other Beachy Amish girls were doing. If she only knew . . .

He'd bided his time, waited for her to let down her guard, make a mistake. Of course, fate had obliged. His rage, the darkness inside him, was a fear she'd lived with for months now. He might be Plain, but he hadn't forgiven her. And he would never, ever forget.

Not that she'd done anything wrong. She hadn't. Had she? She'd made one wrong decision. *Just one.* Dear God in heaven she was sorry for it. She couldn't have known someone else would pay such a terrible price. By all accounts, it should have been her. If she could go back and change it, she would. If she could trade places, she would.

Too late now . . .

Earlier this afternoon, one of her little sisters had fallen out of a tree and broken her arm. Her parents had ridden to work together this morning, but Mamm had taken the car to the bank. Left without a vehicle, Datt took Neva's, leaving her at the shop with nothing more than a bike. Of course her *datt* had no way of knowing he'd placed her in danger. But he had. And now, here she was, alone, out in the middle of nowhere, and it was almost dark. She'd been peddling as fast as she could for miles; she was breathless and sweating, looking over her shoulder like some scared rabbit.

He'd driven past her slowly the first time, his face a pale oval as he stared at her through the window. As far as she could tell, he was alone. That was bad, because it meant there was no one to pull him back. No one to calm him down. Or stop him. No, she thought, he'd be back, and she still had three miles to go.

The hiss of tires against asphalt sounded behind her, made the hairs on the back of her neck stand on end. A glance over her shoulder revealed he was just twenty yards away, driving slowly, pacing her, watching her.

I didn't mean it, she thought. *Please leave me alone. . . .*

Easing the bike to the right, she pedaled faster, keeping the tire on the white line, giving him plenty of room. He didn't pass this time. He hovered, moving ever closer. Fifteen yards. Ten. The truck he drove was a big thing with a noisy engine that stank of exhaust. It was too close. A couple of yards behind her. Then it was crowding her.

Slowing, she ticked the handlebars right. Her front

tire slipped easily off the asphalt and onto the gravel shoulder.

"Go away," she whispered beneath her breath.

The engine groaned. She glanced left, saw the hood. The grille swerved. The fender hit her knee. The impact knocked the bike sideways. The handlebars jackknifed and were yanked from her hands. The bike careened into the ditch. Then she was falling. A yelp tore from her throat when she slammed into the ground.

Neva lay facedown, gasping, the breath knocked out of her. Dirt in her mouth. Tufts of grass scraping her cheek. She tasted blood on her lip, and spit dirt. She rolled, got to her hands and knees, looked toward the road to see him jog down the incline. Eyes on her, intent and filled with rage.

"Leave me alone!" She was scrambling to her feet when viselike hands clamped over her shoulders.

"Shut up," he snarled.

She was dizzy with fear as he dragged her up the incline toward his truck. She stumbled, tried to twist away, but he was too strong. At first she thought he was going to put her in the vehicle. Take her somewhere and kill her. But when they reached the pickup, he spun her around and shoved her against it hard enough to dent steel.

"I told you to keep your mouth shut, you fucking little whore!" Lips peeled back, teeth clenched, he grabbed her arms, fingers digging into her flesh. He shook her violently, and slammed her against the vehicle again.

"I didn't say anything," she choked.

"You talked to the fucking cops!"

"I didn't . . . I didn't . . ." She ran out of breath, couldn't find the words, couldn't think, couldn't breathe.

His face was so close she could feel the spit flying out of his mouth as he spoke. The wet stickiness of his sweat where his skin touched hers.

"I didn't do any—"

His hand snaked up. Viselike fingers found her throat, dug in, squeezed hard enough to cut off the blood to her head. "Shut up and listen."

She grabbed his wrists, tried to get him to loosen his grip, but his hands were like steel. Her vision went dim. Her knees buckled, but he held her up by her throat, shoving her against the truck.

Grinding his teeth, he loosened his grip slightly, yanked a folding knife from his pocket, snapped it open, and set it against her cheek. "If you open your mouth again, I will hunt you down and I will cut your throat. I'll cut off your fucking head and bleed you like a pig. I'll kill your friends. And I'll kill your fucking parents. Do you understand me?"

She stared at him, frozen in terror, certain he was about to slit her throat, and no one would ever know the truth . . .

"*Do you understand?*" he roared.

She jerked her head.

Lifting her off her feet, he swung her around, and shoved her into the ditch. Neva reeled backward, arms flailing, and she landed hard on her back. She rolled, struggled to get her knees under her, raised her head.

He pointed the knife at her. "Don't make me come back."

Giving her a final, scathing look, he put the knife away, turned, got into the truck, and left her in a shower of gravel and dust and the bitter taste of her own fear.

CHAPTER 13

The *graabhof* is located on the township road west of Painters Mill. It's nearly ten A.M. and, as I make the turn, I spot a convoy of black buggies headed toward the cemetery. Daniel Gingerich was well thought of among his brethren and they've shown up in force to pay their final respects. In the back of my mind I can't help but wonder: *How many of them know who he really was?*

The actual funeral was held earlier at the Gingerich home. I drove past on my way to the station and, judging from the number of buggies in the driveway, I'm betting there were a hundred people in attendance.

I contemplated stopping in, but decided not to. Because the service was in an Amish home, I wouldn't have been welcomed. Though they would have been too polite to ask me to leave, it would have been awkward. The family has been through enough.

Following that service, friends of the Gingeriches, other family members, and the hearse—which is a single-horse spring wagon—traveled to the *graabhof* where Daniel will be laid to rest. This is the rite I can attend without intruding.

At the intersection, I pull onto the gravel shoulder, shut down the engine, and get out. I've been to many Amish funerals over the years, not only as a family member or friend, but as a cop with concerns about traffic. Sometimes there are upward of fifty buggies and, invariably, some driver who's in a hurry.

I raise my hand in greeting as another buggy passes, and then I go to the rear of the Explorer, dig into my box of traffic flares. It's not a busy highway by any means, but there's enough traffic to warrant reminding drivers to slow down.

By the time I finish with the flares, most of the buggies have entered the grounds and parked with extraordinary neatness along the gravel lane. I drive through the gate and park in the shade of the old bois d'arc tree that's guarded this entrance since I was a kid. I try not to think of the other funerals I've attended here, my own parents' included.

While a funeral is always a somber occasion, the Amish generally view death as part of life's cycle and God's divine plan. They're accepting of death and often don't question its cause, however untimely or unfair. Most believe the dead are in a better place, with God, and are confident of, and comforted by, the knowledge that they will one day join them.

I respect the Amish ways. It's pretty futile to rage against something as inevitable as death. That said, I could never quite buy into the whole acceptance thing. I was always the one to rail against the unfairness of it, whether it was from natural causes or something a hell of a lot more malevolent.

Aside from keeping an eye on traffic, I've come to observe the mourners. Listen to them. In the course of a homicide investigation, attending the victim's funeral can be helpful. There are many ways in which guilt manifests itself. Undue crying. Excessive emotion. Making a scene. With the Amish, even the subtlest of reactions today could be telling.

My being here is also good PR for the department. Despite my efforts since I've been chief, there remains a level of distrust between the Amish and the English government. My being formerly Amish goes a long way toward bridging the gap, but a divide still exists. I want them to know I'm here to support them.

I hang back until the coffin is removed from the hearse. Leaving the Explorer, I enter the cemetery as the casket is carried by pallbearers using two stout hickory poles. I reach the crowd as the casket is placed over the open grave.

Miriam and Gideon Gingerich and their three children—Fannie and the two little girls—stand nearest the grave, heads bowed in silent prayer. Bishop Troyer with his long silver beard stands next to his wife a few feet away from them. Luane Raber, her siblings, and her parents are on the other side of the grave. Luane is leaning against her *mamm,* shoulders hunched, her face in her hands. I spot the three girls I met at The Mercantile yesterday, standing together instead of with their respective families. Neva Lambright makes eye contact with me, but looks away quickly. Even Milo

Hershberger has shown up, though I suspect he came more out of loneliness than to pay his final respects. There's no sign of Esther and Sam Miller.

Once the casket is in the grave, one of the Amish ministers reads a hymn. A silent prayer follows, and then the four pallbearers begin to shovel dirt into the grave.

"Chief Burkholder?"

I turn, surprised to see Ralph Baker, from the farm store, approach. "Hi, Mr. Baker."

He's wearing a navy JCPenney suit with a shirt still creased from its packaging. He draws up next to me, shoves his hands into the pockets of his slacks. "After talking with you the other day, I remembered something that might be important. About Danny."

Realizing we're standing too close to the mourners to discuss the case, I motion toward the Explorer. "Sure."

"Anyway," he says as we start that way, "I didn't think anything about it at the time, but the day before Danny was killed we took our supper break together, went out for burgers. He was all pumped up about some woman. Said she'd left him a note and he was going to hook up with her that night."

My interest jumps. "Did he mention a name?"

He shakes his head. "No. And to tell you the truth, I was kind of ticked off at him. I mean, I'd met that sweet Luane a couple of times." He gestures toward the crying girl. "I'd liked her. I told Danny I just couldn't see him two-timing her like that, right? But he was all hot under the collar about meeting this woman. Talked about it like he was going to . . . uh, you know, get lucky and he'd been wanting to hook up with her for some time."

I think about that a moment, try to make sense of the scenario. "Is it possible the note was from Luane? Maybe she was going to surprise him?"

"Seems like it was kind of an illicit thing, you know? Some kind of tryst."

"Did he say where they were meeting?"

"No, ma'am."

"Did he say when?"

"Well, he got the note the day before he was killed in that fire. I assumed it was that night," he tells me. "The night he was killed."

"Did you see the note, Mr. Baker?"

"Caught a glimpse of it. I mean, he was laughing and sort of waving it around. I kind of gave him the cold shoulder about it because I didn't think it was right."

"Do you remember anything specific about the note?" I ask. "The kind of paper? Was it handwritten?"

"I think it was just regular notebook paper." Brows knit, he rubs his chin. "I think it was colored ink. Pink or purple. Come to think of it, the writing was kind of girlish, with swirls and hearts and stuff like that."

I pull out my notebook and write it down. "Any idea what happened to the note?"

He shakes his head. "Never saw it again. Me and Al went through Danny's locker at the store, but there wasn't anything in there. Just an old cap and his work gloves."

"Had he ever mentioned this mystery woman before?"

"Well, you know, he wasn't an alley cat or anything like that. But he was a young guy. He liked . . . you know . . . girls." Ralph Baker ducks his head. "Talked about 'getting some' all the time. I figured he was lying, like the rest of us. Now, I'm not so sure."

Arson is a particularly difficult crime to solve. Mainly because much of the evidence left at the scene, DNA, fingerprints, or footwear impressions—the structure itself—is often destroyed by the intense heat or by the efforts of the firefighters. Tomasetti informed me that in the state of Ohio only about twenty-six percent of arson cases result in an arrest. Unless you have a witness, a confession, or a damn good security camera positioned in just the right place, chances are it will go unsolved.

Despite my growing suspicions about Daniel Gingerich, the notion of someone getting away with such an insidious crime doesn't sit well. I know from experience that once someone crosses the line and commits a violent crime, they're a hell of a lot more likely to do it again. That's one of the reasons I've focused on motive.

I recall my conversation with Ralph Baker and his assertion that Daniel had received a note from an unidentified woman. I believe Baker is telling the truth. But I learned a long time ago never to take anything at face value. Just because Daniel was waving some note around doesn't mean it came from a woman. Anyone could have used such a tactic to lure him into that barn. But who? And why?

Pulling out a legal pad, I go to a fresh page and write down the things I know about the case so far.

Note? Unknown individual lured Daniel Gingerich to the barn. A woman?

I underscore the word "unknown."

Premeditated? Definitely.

Suspects: The neighbor, Chris Martino. Felon. Ex-con. Argument over stolen horse tack. Temper.

Early on, Martino was a viable suspect, but no more. Now, the question foremost in my mind is who left the mason jars and key in his shed—and why.

Milo Hershberger. Jealousy over Luane Raber?

Emma Miller's parents, Sam and Esther Miller. Daughter was pregnant. Had she been raped by Daniel Gingerich? Was he indirectly responsible for her suicide?

Elam Schlabach. Did he find out something happened between Daniel and his girlfriend and decide to mete out a little revenge?

Luane Raber? Did she know her husband-to-be was cheating on her?

Did Mose and Sue Raber know their daughter was planning to marry a serial seducer—or worse? Did they murder Daniel to prevent her from making a mistake?

What about Ruth Petersheim? Nervous. Evasive. Mark Petersheim? Connection?

Frustrated by my lack of progress, I toss the pen aside and go back to the file, page through it. I come across the photos I found in Daniel's bedroom and something pricks at my memory. Something about the photo . . .

Reaching into my desk drawer, I snatch up my reading glasses and study the picture. It's the one in which Daniel is grinning from ear to ear; he's bare-chested and doing his utmost to accentuate his muscles, but in a silly, joking way. I recognize the Amish girl as Luane Raber.

I flip through all three photos, go back to the one in which Daniel is without a shirt. That's when I realize the thing that's bothering me is the birthmark on his abdomen. I've seen it before. But how is that possible? Where would I have seen something that's usually covered by clothing? I'd never met Daniel. . . .

The baby.

The memory strikes me like a blow. Ruth Petersheim's baby. The day Mona and I went to see her, little William had spit up. He'd been wearing a onesie and she'd changed his diaper, exposing the exact same mole on his abdomen. . . .

"My God," I whisper. "Is Daniel Gingerich the father?"

No wonder Ruth Petersheim had been so nervous, so standoffish. I'd assumed it was because she'd become pregnant out of wedlock. She fudged on the date and didn't want anyone to do the math. Having grown up Amish, I understand that. This is different, especially if she was pregnant by another man and passed off the child as her husband's.

In terms of motive, this could be a significant development and I find myself thinking about Mark Petersheim. If I'm right about the birthmark, does he know the baby isn't his? Did Ruth tell him? If Daniel is the baby's father, did he and Ruth have a consensual relationship? Or was it something else? If there was a sexual assault involved, does Mark Petersheim know about it? Does he know he's raising another man's child? Did he decide to do something about it?

The murder of Daniel Gingerich has been one of the most frustrating, twisty cases I've ever worked. Over the course of a few days, my victim has evolved from wholesome and much-loved Amish teenager to suspected sexual predator. Because of the nature of his alleged crimes—and the fact that his victims are Amish—none of the women came forward and none of them are willing to speak with me about it. I have no way of telling whether it's because they're trying to protect their privacy or the privacy of someone else—or because they, or a family member, are guilty of a horrific crime and attempting to cover their tracks.

Even the physical evidence is refusing to materialize. I'm not optimistic that the latents found on the key at the scene will be identified. We've received a handful of calls on the hotline; each was looked into, but so far nothing has panned out. That leaves me with a slew of suspects based solely on theory and guesswork, but none of it is compelling. All I can do at this point is continue talking to people in the hope someone will open up and level with me.

A glance at my computer tells me it's too late to pay Ruth Petersheim a visit tonight. Probably best to catch her when her husband is at work anyway; she'll be more apt to speak openly, especially if Mark Petersheim doesn't know the child he's raising as his own was fathered by Daniel Gingerich.

CHAPTER 14

It's not yet noon when I roll up to Ruth and Mark Petersheim's house and park curbside. I take the narrow sidewalk to the porch and knock. I hear shuffling on the other side of the door and I imagine Ruth looking out the peephole, trying to figure out a way to get rid of me. I'm about to knock a second time when the door opens a couple of inches. Ruth Petersheim peers out at me, eyes darting, a cat facing off with a junkyard dog.

"Hi, Ruth." Though we've already met, I show her my badge. "Do you have a minute to talk?"

Her eyes widen, then flick past me as if she's expecting to see an armada of cops, weapons drawn, cuffs at the ready. "Little William has a fever," she says quietly. "Maybe we could talk later?"

I smile, hoping to put her at ease. "I drove all the way from Painters Mill. I just have a few questions for you. I promise to keep it short."

A dozen excuses scroll across her face, but after a too-long moment she acquiesces.

The small house smells of bacon and coffee, with the

lingering redolence of dirty diapers. There's a can of furniture polish with a raggedy dishcloth on the end table.

The Amish woman stops in the center of the living room and turns to face me, blocking my way. "Like I said, I barely knew Daniel Gingerich."

"Your husband is at work?" I ask.

"Of course he is."

She doesn't invite me to sit. Doesn't want me venturing any more deeply into her refuge.

"I've heard a lot of things about Daniel Gingerich in the last few days," I begin. "Since I last spoke with you."

She stares at me, blinking, as if she doesn't know what to make of that or how to respond. She doesn't know where I'm going with this and she sure as hell doesn't want me to continue.

"I'm not sure he was the upstanding young man everyone seemed to think he was," I tell her.

No response.

I pull the baggie containing the photograph of Daniel Gingerich from my pocket, open it, and slide out the photo. It's the one in which he's without a shirt, smiling and carefree, showing off his muscles to his girlfriend. I hold it out so that Ruth can see it.

She stares at the photo as if it's a bloody, violent thing that's about to jump off the paper and tear her to shreds.

"The other day when I was here," I say, "I couldn't help but notice the birthmark on William's abdomen."

"He doesn't have a birthmark."

"I saw it," I say gently.

Her mouth opens. She raises her hand and steps back.

"I think you should go," she says in a strangled voice. "I don't want to talk to you anymore."

I hold my ground, hold her stare. "I did a little research on moles and birthmarks." I flick the photograph with my finger. "This type of mole is hereditary. It's passed down from parent to child." I wait, but she says nothing, doesn't respond, so I prod. "The mole on your son's abdomen is identical to Daniel's."

"*Sell is nix as baeffzes.*" That's nothing but trifling talk. She takes another step back. A quick glance left. If she'd had a place to run, she would have. But Ruth Petersheim knows there's no escape. This is a reality she must face. A truth that must be revealed.

"I need you to level with me about your relationship with Daniel Gingerich," I tell her.

She presses her hand to her mouth as if to suppress a cry, but she doesn't make a sound. She looks at me over her fingertips, her eyes filling with tears. "I can't talk about that."

"Did you have a relationship with Daniel?"

"No. Never."

"Is Daniel William's father?"

A brief hesitation and then, "No."

I say her name quietly, grappling with my own emotions, my patience, my conscience. "Ruth, I know this is difficult. I get that. I'll do my best to make sure that whatever you tell me today will go no farther than this room."

"I'm not going to tell you anything. There's nothing to tell."

"Did you have a sexual relationship with Daniel Gingerich?"

"*No.*" For the first time anger resonates in her voice. A flash of denial in her eyes. "What kind of question is that? How could you ask such a thing?"

I repeat the question, more firmly this time. "I need the truth and I need it right now. If you refuse to answer, I'll have no choice but to come back with a warrant and take you to the police station for formal questioning. If you force me to take that route, I can't guarantee I'll be able to keep this just between us."

The statement isn't exactly true. First of all, I'd need a judge to sign off on a warrant; this young woman isn't a viable suspect. Bringing her in for questioning on such a stretch would be a hard sell. Still, my questions are justified. If Daniel Gingerich is the father of her child, if the sexual encounter between them was not consensual, I have indisputable proof of what he was. I'm one step closer to establishing a motive for his murder. I also have another name to add to my growing list of suspects: Mark Petersheim.

"Tell me," I say quietly. "Please."

Ruth chokes out a sound and begins to cry. Raising both hands to her face, she swipes at the tears with shaking hands. "My husband doesn't know. No one knows. They cannot find out."

"What doesn't he know?"

"He doesn't know William is . . ." She closes her eyes as if uttering the words aloud is too painful, too shameful, to accomplish. "*Mark doesn't know.* Please don't tell him. He loves little William so much."

For a full minute, she stands there, head down, sobbing and shaking. Spotting a box of tissues on the coffee table, I tug one out and hand it to her. "Ruth, I'm not the enemy. I'm not trying to hurt you or your husband or that sweet little boy. But I need to know what happened. I can't walk away from this."

The statement seems to calm her, drive home the fact that I'm not going to go away, and she regains control of her emotions. Using the tissue, she takes a moment to wipe her eyes and blow her nose.

"Is Daniel Gingerich William's father?" I ask.

Closing her eyes against a fresh round of tears, she jerks her head. "Yes."

"You had a relationship with him?"

"No." She opens her eyes, looks at me. "Not a relationship. Never."

I wait.

As if resigning herself to physical torture, she sags, her shoulders coming forward, and she looks down at the floor. "I met him a few times over the last few years. You know how it is when you're Amish. Everyone knows everyone else. Daniel was . . . nice. Hardworking. All of the Amish thought highly of him." Her mouth twists. "He was handsome, too. All the girls liked him.

"I'd just met Mark and we'd gone out a few times, but we weren't that serious yet. We were of *Rumspringa* age, you know. Both of us were running around a little bit. And so when Danny asked me if I was going to be at the singing over to the Schwartz farm after worship, I told him I'd be there. I figured there'd be no harm in it. I knew most of the other Amish who would be there."

An Amish "singing" usually takes place on Sunday

evening, after worship and at the same farm where worship was held earlier in the day. It's an occasion in which Amish youths from different church districts can get together, sing hymns, and visit. It usually ends around ten or eleven P.M.

She shakes her head. "I know I'm not much to look at. I don't know why he chose me. But he was kind and interested, and I was . . . flattered. Too flattered, probably. So I asked Mamm and she said I could go."

A smile plays at the corners of her mouth, as if she's remembering what it had been like to be that young, carefree girl looking to have some innocent fun. But the twisting of her mouth is in direct conflict with the pain etched into her every feature.

"You have to understand, Chief Burkholder. Daniel was from a good family. He had a good job. Made good money, too. Those are important things when you're a seventeen-year-old Amish girl."

"You met him at the Schwartz farm for the singing?"

"I did, and he was a perfect gentleman. So funny. He announced several of the hymns that night. Afterward, he offered to drive me home. He had a car, you know, and the thought of riding in it was such a thrill. So I went."

She looks at me, eyes shimmering, and tilts her head. "We listened to the radio and it was . . . wonderful. He had a bottle of alcohol beneath the seat. I knew better than to drink. It's forbidden in our church district, you know. But it was . . . exciting, too. We parked and listened to music and drank tequila right out of the bottle."

Her mouth tightens. A flash of shame in her eyes. "It

was the first time I ever drank alcohol and I couldn't handle it. I drank too much. At first it was fun, but then . . . I told him I wanted to go home. I thought it was going to be okay. I thought . . .

"Chief Burkholder, something happened to him when we were parked out there on that back road." She says the words so quietly, I have to move closer to hear. "It was like he turned into another person," she whispers. "He . . . dragged me from the car, threw me on the ground, and he forced me." The words tumble out of her, a tangle of ugliness and cruelty and shame. "It was like . . . he turned into someone I didn't know. Someone I should have been afraid of all along but I was too stupid to see it."

"Did he rape you?"

She jerks her head. A single, devastating nod. A sob escapes her. Tears shimmer on her cheeks. Snot on her upper lip. She doesn't seem to notice. "It was my fault. I shouldn't have gone with him. I shouldn't have drank the alcohol. Worst of all, I was already seeing my husband. But that's what I get, isn't it?"

"It wasn't your fault," I tell her. "No one deserves that."

Her eyes go hard. "I'd never . . . you know. I mean, before that night. A few weeks later I knew I was *ime familye weg.*"

I stare at her, feeling more than is prudent. "What did you do?"

"I lied. To everyone. To Mark. To myself. I let Mark court me. I . . . you know, with him as quickly as I could manage." She closes her eyes, seems to struggle with something. "Mamm told me that those kinds of little white lies are okay as long as they're used to protect tender feelings."

"You told your mother what happened?"

Her gaze skitters away from mine. "She found the . . . blood from that night. You know . . . on my underwear." She takes a shuddery breath. "I told her nothing happened. That it was just my monthly. But I think she knew. She . . . was in an awful big hurry to get me married." She looks down at the floor.

I'm so drawn in to her story, the horrific nature of the assault, all of it without the support of her family or the Amish community, it takes me a moment to find the words for my next question. "Does your *datt* know what happened?"

"I don't think my *mamm* told him."

"Did you see Daniel or speak to him after that night?"

"No."

"Did you write to him? Or leave him a note or letter?"

"No." Her brows knit in confusion. "Why would I?"

"Did you ask him to meet you in the barn the night of the fire?"

"What?" She shakes her head. "Why would I do such a thing?"

"You tell me."

"Chief Burkholder, I haven't seen him since . . . that night. I couldn't face him. I can barely face myself. Some days I can't even look at my innocent little child."

Pain contorts her features and she begins to cry. "I don't mean that."

I let her cry, let the silence and the weight of the words that have passed between us ride.

"I've prayed for forgiveness," she tells me. "I've forgiven myself. I've forgiven *them*. I've moved on with my . . ."

I've forgiven them. . . .

The statement stops me cold, echoes in my ears like the report of a gunshot. "What did you say?"

She shoots me a blank look. "I said I've moved on—"

"You said 'them,'" I cut in. "Who are you talking about? Was there someone else there?"

Shame clouds her face. Something else she didn't want me to know. She looks away, anywhere but at me. "Daniel's friend was there. Milo Hershberger."

The ground shifts beneath my feet. "Milo was there the night Daniel assaulted you?"

"He needed a ride home after the singing. Daniel said he'd drive him. But instead of going to Milo's house, we started drinking. Ended up parking on that back road."

"Did Milo—"

"No." She shakes her head adamantly. "*No*. He got out of the car. I mean, he wasn't there . . . With all the alcohol, the night was so . . . confusing." Her visage turns sullen. "I do recall Milo being angry afterward. I mean, with Daniel. They had words."

"Daniel and Milo argued?" I ask.

"Milo was upset about what Daniel had done. He didn't like it at all."

"Did the argument become physical?"

Another shake of her head. "I don't know. I was so . . . ashamed and upset. My whole world just sort of fell apart that night."

The cry of a baby sounds from the bedroom at the rear of the house. Ruth looks over her shoulder, her eyes not meeting mine. Shame, I think, and I wish there were something I could say or do. But there isn't.

"Please, can you just go now? I've told you every-thing. I just want to forget it ever happened."

There are some topics that are so taboo among the Amish that they won't even acknowledge that they ex-ist. Sexual violence is one of them. Daniel Gingerich was a monster in disguise. The more I learn about him, the more I detest him. It's not a good mind-set for a cop who's been charged with solving his murder.

My exchange with Ruth Petersheim haunts me dur-ing the drive to Millersburg. I almost can't get my mind around the casual violence of it and the fact that the en-tire ordeal was swept under the rug. I think about my own history and the way my parents handled it. They did their best, but there are parallels I can't ignore. I warn myself not to get too caught up in the nature of the crime. Ruth, after all, could be lying. But I don't think that's the case.

I was wrong about Milo Hershberger. I'd liked him. I'd been taken with his boy-next-door charm and easy-going demeanor; I'd been moved by the fact that he'd been shunned by his Amish brethren, that he missed his family. I'd identified with him, believed him. Rookie mistakes all.

Parallels, that persistent little voice whispers.

I pull into the driveway of Hershberger's double-wide to find a hodgepodge of cars, a couple of pickup trucks, and two buggies parked haphazardly. A couple dozen young men mill about the front yard. Every single one of them is holding either a beer or a plastic cup full of some concoction that will likely kill a lot of brain cells by morning.

"Terrific," I mutter as I get out of the Explorer.

Pink Floyd's "Young Lust" rattles from two refrigerator-size speakers that have been set up on the porch.

My uniform draws plenty of stares; everyone gives me a wide berth as I make my way to the house. I catch a whiff of marijuana as I take the steps and cross to the door. I'm about to knock when the screen flies open and two young men stumble out, laughing.

Careful to keep his beer from spilling, one of them looks me up and down and grins. "Is that uniform for real or are you fucking around?" He shouts to be heard over the scream of music.

"I'm looking for Milo," I say.

"In the kitchen." He opens the door for me. "Beer's in the fridge. Purple Jesus in the pitcher. Help yourself and then come on out and enjoy the party."

The house smells of cigarette smoke and recently sprayed air freshener. I cross through a small living room. In the kitchen two young men help themselves to whatever's in the pitcher. Milo stands in the doorway, grinning. He jolts upon spotting me and then gives me a double take that might've been funny if my temper weren't lit.

"Hello, Milo," I say as I cross to him.

"Chief Burkholder?" He's wearing a DeKalb cap with the brim facing backward. He's smoking a cigarette, holding a can of beer in his left hand. His smile is lopsided.

"You must be missing your family something terrible this evening," I say.

He looks around as if anticipating I'll notice something he doesn't want me to see. "Uh, I didn't know you were coming over."

"Maybe I should have called." I look around. "You don't have any underage drinkers here, do you?"

"No, ma'am. Just a few friends." Never taking his eyes from mine, he goes to the table and sets down his beer.

"Is there someplace quiet we can talk?"

"We can go to the barn, if you want. Quieter there, probably."

Nodding, I turn and cross back through the living room. I hear Milo behind me, along with a few not-so-subtle comments aimed at me.

"Didn't know you were on a first-name basis with the cops, Milo!"

"Get her a beer, dude!"

"She going to cuff you?"

"If we don't hear from you in ten minutes, we'll come get you!"

Ignoring all of it, I head toward the barn. Midway

there Milo catches up with me and falls into step beside me. "What's going on?" he asks.

I don't respond. I'm too angry. This is going to be an important conversation; I need to calm down. Get it right. Get the answers I need. Good luck with that.

We reach the barn. He opens the door. The smell of horses and wood shavings greets me when I step inside. I walk midway down the aisle, then turn to face him. "Close the door behind you."

He blinks, then turns and goes back to the door, slides it shut. "What?"

"You lied to me," I tell him.

"About what?"

"Don't play dumb. You fucking lied to me, you phony little shit."

His puppy-dog eyes widen. "I don't know what you're talking about."

I stalk over to him, stop a foot away. My temper is pumping, so I yank it back. He's still got the cigarette in his mouth, so I slap it away. "Do you realize I've got cause to arrest you? Right here. Right now. In front of all your friends?"

He backs up, raises his hands. "Hey, wait a minute. I didn't do anything."

"No, you didn't, did you?"

Another blink. Mr. Innocent.

Easy, a little voice warns.

"Lying to the police is against the law," I tell him. "I could arrest you right now for the obstruction of official business and failure to report a crime."

"But . . . wait—"

"It may not stick once you get to court, but I would be within my rights to arrest you as an accomplice to sexual assault."

All that rejected-Amish-boy charm falls away. Something dark flashes in his eyes. Anger, I realize. *Careful,* that little voice warns. Even a friendly dog will become cross when cornered.

"I don't know what you're talking about," he says.

"I know about Ruth Petersheim. All of it."

His face pales. He stares at me, blinking, mouth open. Despite the alcohol, he's struggling to maintain his composure. I see the wheels spinning in his mind. Trying to come up with a lie, something that will excuse his behavior, exonerate him, but there's nothing there. Nothing he knows I will believe.

"You were there," I say, surprised because my teeth are clenched.

He starts to turn away, but I grasp his arm and stop him. He yanks it away. "Get your hands off me."

I let my hand slide off him, take a moment to pull myself back from a place I know better than to venture into. Once again, I remind myself this isn't about me. It's not about my feelings or my temper. It isn't even about Ruth Petersheim or Milo Hershberger. It's about establishing a motive that led to the death of Daniel Gingerich and finding the son of a bitch who murdered him.

He walks to the sliding door, but doesn't open it. Instead, he faces the wood, shoves his hands into his pockets, and then turns to face me.

"I didn't do anything wrong," he says.

"For God's sake, Milo. You witnessed a sexual assault. You didn't help her. Didn't stop it. Didn't report it."

"I didn't know!"

"You're a liar." Calmer now, I cross to him and stop a few feet away. "I'm in the midst of a murder investigation and you withheld information."

"I didn't have anything to do with what happened to Danny."

"You expect me to believe anything that comes out of your mouth now?"

He shakes his head angrily, looks away.

"Milo, I'm an inch away from arresting you for the sole reason that you are a lying, smug little son of a bitch. You had better start talking."

Without looking at me he walks over to where his still-lit cigarette is lying on the floor and snatches it up. He thinks about tossing it, but then seems to reconsider and puts it in his mouth.

"That fuckin' Danny," he says after a moment. "What a piece of work."

"Tell me something I don't already know."

He glares at me and then sucks hard on the cigarette. "Yeah, I was there."

"So start talking and don't you dare leave out a single word."

"Jesus." Scrubbing his hand over his face, he crosses the aisle to the nearest horse stall. The Appaloosa he was riding the other night sticks its head over the gate and nudges him. Milo leans into the animal, rubs behind its ears.

"I always knew there was something wrong with

him," he says. "Didn't figure out what it was until that night."

I wait, saying nothing.

"Danny was a charmer and boy did he love his women. I mean, it was like an addiction for him. They were his heroin. If we went out, drinking or whatever, and he found a chick he wanted to be with, he could really turn it on. Like laser focus. We're talking no holds barred. You know what's funny about that? Most of the time it worked. I mean, the girls were crazy about him. How ironic is that?

"But there were a few times when he got turned down and let me tell you, it pissed him off. He took it real personal. He was like Dr. Jekyll and Mr. Hyde."

"What happened with Ruth Petersheim?"

"Amish girls are a little different; they're not as wild, but then that didn't matter to Danny. He always said he liked a challenge. He said you're more likely to hit a cherry if the girl's Amish so they're the ones he went after."

I tamp down disgust; I won't give him the satisfaction of knowing he has the ability to do that to me. Make my skin crawl. Put my blood pressure into the red zone. I stare at him, saying nothing, giving him nothing.

"Danny knew Ruth was seeing the guy she eventually married. I think his name's Mark. Danny didn't care. In fact, it was like some kind of contest with him. He went after her. Turned on the charm and she fell for it hook, line, and sinker." He blows out a breath. "The night it happened . . . we went to a singing out to the Schwartz place. There were a bunch of us. A good group. Ruth was there with one of her friends. That Beachy chick that works over to The Mercantile."

"Neva Lambright?" In the back of my mind I wonder why Neva didn't mention it when I'd specifically asked about Daniel Gingerich.

"Yeah. Her. Anyway, Danny worked on Ruth all evening. And let me tell you, she was all smiles, like fucking putty in his hands. Around ten o'clock or so, Danny asked her if he could drive her home. She balked at first, you know like good girls do, but her friend told her to go ahead. 'Hey, he's fine—go for it!' So Ruth agreed, kind of reluctant like.

"All I needed was a ride home. Danny said he'd take me, so I went with them. I figured he'd drop me off first." Lowering his head, he rubs his eyes with his thumb and forefinger. "It was the three of us. I was sort of the third wheel, but Danny had the radio blasting. He broke out a bottle of tequila. We started passing it around, so we were all kind of fucked up. All the while I'm thinking three's a crowd, but it didn't stop Danny boy."

"What did he do?"

"We were on some back road. Everyone's shit-faced drunk. I got out to take a leak. When I get back in, Danny and Ruth are in the backseat, sort of . . . going at it. So I get out. I'm standing on the side of the road out in the middle of nowhere and I'm getting kind of pissed. Next thing I know the car door flies open and they just kind of spill out onto the asphalt. At first I think they're just goofing off." The muscles in his jaw flex. "They were . . . fighting. Danny was pissed. And Ruth was . . . crying. It was . . . ugly."

He turns his gaze on me. This time, his gaze is level and unwavering. "Look, I tried to intervene, but . . . I'd had too much to drink. I wasn't thinking straight. And Danny was . . ." He shrugs. "We came to blows right there in the middle of the road. He broke my fucking nose. It was pretty much the end of our friendship, and we'd been best friends since we were like six years old."

"What did you do?"

"I got the hell out of there. Ended up walking home. That was the end of it."

"So you just left her there with him?"

He looks away, but not before I see shame in his eyes, and I feel a small rise of satisfaction.

"I'm not proud of it," he says.

"You must have been angry."

"Yeah, I was pissed."

"Pissed enough to lure Daniel into the barn, lock him in that tack room, and start the fire?"

His smile is wry, but it's laced with bitterness. "Oh, I wanted to kill him plenty of times. Especially after I realized what he was. But I'm no killer. I didn't do it."

"So you say."

"So I say."

"Who else knows about what happened that night?"

"Far as I know, just me, Danny, and Ruth."

"What about Mark Petersheim?"

He hesitates, looks away. "I don't know."

"We can do this at the station if that will help your memory."

"Look, I don't know if she told him. What I can tell you is that . . . sometimes Danny would sort of hint around about things. I mean, about what he did. You know, he'd brag about his conquests or whatever. Thought he was some kind of fucking Romeo or something." He shrugs. "Word gets around."

"So it's possible Mark Petersheim knows?"

"I'm betting he probably knows *something* happened. I doubt if he knows how ugly it got. Let me tell you something about Mark. He may be Amish, but he's not the kind of guy who'd put up with any kind of infidelity."

"That wasn't infidelity," I snap.

"All I'm saying is he's not the kind of guy who'd swallow something like that happening behind his back. To his woman. If people were talking behind his back . . . he wouldn't like that either. He cares about what the Amish think."

I don't know if he's telling the truth, giving me some half-truth, or making it up as he goes. If he's lying, he's good at it. I find myself thinking about Ruth Petersheim and how an insecure husband might react to rumors that his wife had betrayed him or that his child belonged to another man. . . .

"Did Ruth's parents know?"

"You'll have to ask her about that."

"Were there other women he assaulted?" I ask.

He winces as if the question causes him physical pain. His cigarette has burned down to the filter, but he doesn't seem to notice. "I don't know. Danny was . . . you couldn't believe half of what he said. I mean, when it came to women. He was always hinting around that he'd been with someone."

"I need names."

"I don't have names. The only one that stands out now is this young Amish girl. I mean, really young. Like jailbait."

He has the audacity to blush. "I remember because Danny said she was, you know, cherry."

"What's her name?"

"I don't know. Danny just mentioned her in passing. Bragging. I'm not even sure he said her name. He was an asshole that way."

"Milo, you had better give me something."

He grimaces.

"He used to go up to that little shop in Charm all the time just to see those girls. Had his eye on all of them, I guess."

"The Mercantile?"

He nods. "It was like he was . . . stalking them. But after all that happened with Ruth, I cut ties with him. We stopped talking."

"Is it possible Daniel bragged about things that didn't really happen?" I ask.

"I'm sure he did. He was like that." His brows go together. "But I think something happened with the girl from The Mercantile. I don't know about any others."

I pull out my card, write my cell number on the back, and pass it to him. "I may want to talk to you again, so if you have to leave town, you need to let me know."

He takes the card, looks down at it. "All right."

"Stay away from Ruth Petersheim," I tell him. "If you try to make contact with her, I will come after you and I will make your life a living hell. Are we clear?"

"I got it." He shakes his head. "I tried to do the right thing that night, Chief Burkholder."

"Evidently, you didn't try hard enough." Turning away, I start toward the door.

"Chief Burkholder. Wait."

I don't stop until I reach the door; then I turn to him, fix him with a hard look.

"I should have stepped in that night. That I didn't . . . it kept me up nights. Still does." He blinks, looks down at the floor, then back at me. "If I could, I swear to God I'd make it right. I mean that."

"We don't get do-overs, Milo." Turning away, I slide open the door, and leave him standing in the aisle.

CHAPTER 15

My exchange with Milo Hershberger weighs on me the rest of the evening. Daniel Gingerich was a sexual predator and there's no doubt in my mind that someone killed him for it. I'm no proponent of street justice, especially the kind that entails murder. But I understand it. I've felt the dark pull of hatred. Fallen into the bottomless pit of shame. The questions foremost in my mind now are how many women did he rape and who knew about it?

It's after nine P.M. I'm in my office, the paperwork and photographs and various reports from the case spread out on my desk in front of me. I've been at it too long and the words have become a blur. Time to go home, Kate.

My cell phone chirps. Expecting Tomasetti, curbing a quick rise of guilt for still being here when I should have left hours ago, I check the display. My pulse jumps when DEPT OF COMM pops up in the window. I snatch up the phone.

"Hi Kate, it's Bob Schoening. I hope I'm not calling

too late. I figured you'd want to hear this as soon as possible."

"You have my undivided attention."

"A couple of things. First of all, the latent recovered from the key at the Gingerich fire? We ran it through AFIS and struck out."

"So they're not in the system."

"Correct. I also wanted to let you know that key you found at the home of Christopher Martino is, indeed, a match to the lock we recovered at the Gingerich fire."

I sit up straighter. "Were the mason jars the same as the jars found at the Gingerich place?"

"No way to tell. The only thing I *can* tell you is that they're made by the same manufacturer."

"Did you pick up any latents?"

"We got a single decent print off one of the mason jars. As with the key, we submitted to BCI via LiveScan and they're running it through AFIS now."

"Twenty-four hours?"

"Give or take."

I think about the key. "What about the key found at the Gingerich scene? The one with the print. Was it an original key? Or a duplicate?"

"The key recovered at the fire scene showed slight signs of wear. More than likely it's one of the original keys that came with the dead bolt Gideon Gingerich purchased at the Ace Hardware store in Millersburg a few months ago. The key found in Martino's shed was made by a different manufacturer and showed no discernible sign of wear, which means it's a duplicate."

I pause, my mind churning through the implications.

"Did Gideon Gingerich or anyone else in the family make a copy of the key?"

"He claims he did not."

"Is there any way I can get my hands on the duplicate key?"

"The lab guys have gone over it with a fine-tooth comb." He pauses. "You going to try and figure out where it was made and who made it?"

"You never know when you might get lucky." It'll take some time, and it's a long shot, but even with my limited manpower, I ought to be able to cover most of Holmes County.

"I'll have it couriered over to you first thing in the morning," he says. "One more thing of interest with regard to the keys. The dead bolt that Gingerich purchased came with two original keys, and so far no one has been able to locate the second one. Gideon Gingerich says he always left both keys on the hook in the barn."

"Tied together with a string," I say, recalling my conversation with him. "Lost in the fire maybe?"

"It's possible we missed it, but not likely. We took a metal detector to the place and my guys are thorough."

"Will you be taking another look?"

"I can send a technician out there tomorrow for another go-round." He doesn't sound optimistic about getting results. "Soon as I get all this written up, I'll put it in the report and send it your way."

I thank him and end the call. My mind is already jumping ahead to all the things I need to do. If I can get my hands on the key early tomorrow, I'll have Mona check area hardware stores. If we can find out where it was duplicated, we might be able to find out who had it made.

Now, however, I need to get home to Tomasetti and my life. I shut down the computer and head for the door. I'm in the process of locking my office behind me when Jodie calls out my name.

"You still back there, Chief?"

"Right here," I say as I enter reception.

"I know you're trying to get out of here, but I just took a call from a motorist out on Hogpath Road. Says he hit a deer and it busted his windshield. Vehicle's in the ditch."

My heart sinks. "Where's Skid?"

"He just responded to a fight call out at the Brass Rail. Reporting party said there was a knife involved, so he's going to be tied up for a while."

Thinking of Tomasetti, I sigh. "I'll take it. Give that motorist a call back and see if he needs medical attention or a wrecker."

"Will do."

"Where on Hogpath Road?"

"Just past the Painters Creek Bridge."

"Got it. See you tomorrow." I go through the door and into the night.

Hogpath Road is a narrow strip of asphalt banked by cornfields on both sides. The farms are both Amish and English, but they're large and some of the houses are more than a mile apart. The Painters Creek Bridge is about two miles south of Painters Mill. Deer like to graze along the floodplain where the grass is plentiful and they have the cover of the trees that flourish there. Occasionally they wander onto the road. Two years ago a woman from Portsmouth was killed after striking a deer, overcorrecting, and plowing into a tree.

I spot headlights in the distance as I approach the bridge. They cut through the dark at an odd angle, telling me the vehicle isn't level. Flipping on my emergency lights, I idle across the bridge and park on the shoulder, about thirty feet from where the vehicle faces me from its place in the ditch.

"I'm ten-twenty-three," I say into my lapel mike.

"Everyone okay out there, Chief?"

"Not sure just yet. No sign of the driver. I'm going to take a look." I slide my Maglite out of its pocket. "Did you ten-fifty-one?" I ask, referring to the dispatch of a wrecker.

"Wrecker's on the way."

"Roger that."

Leaving my headlights and emergency lights on, I get out and look around. The other vehicle's lights are blinding; I can't make out the make or model. The driver is nowhere in sight.

"Painters Mill Police Department!" I call out. "Everyone okay?"

"I hit a deer!" comes a male voice.

"Hang tight, sir," I tell him. "I'll be right there."

I'm well off the road, but it's fully dark and there's a blind curve behind me. The last thing I need is for some fool to fly across the bridge and plow into both of us, so I hit my fob, pop open the rear door, and grab four flares. I break open two and drop them well behind the Explorer. Two more in the middle of the lane out-side my driver's-side door.

Using my Maglite, I start toward the vehicle. I'd as-sumed the driver would have gotten out and walked over to me by now. "Sir, are you injured? Do you need an ambulance?"

"I'm okay. Just shook up."

I catch a glimpse of a silhouette. The driver is still behind the wheel, fiddling around with something on the seat. No passenger. "Could you step out here please?" I call out.

No response.

I shine my beam on the vehicle, getting my first good look. It's a pickup truck, not in the ditch, but parked at a steep angle a few feet off the shoulder. The truck is an extended-cab with a long bed. Dark blue or maybe black. That's when I notice the missing front license plate.

I stop walking and sweep the beam to where I'd last seen the driver, but he's gone.

"Sir? Can you step out here and talk to me?"

No answer.

The hairs at my nape stand up. Where the hell did he go?

I hit my shoulder mike. "Ten-seven-eight. Get Skid out here. Expedite."

Never taking my eyes from the vehicle, sweeping the beam left and right, I walk backward, toward my Ex-plorer. "Driver! Show yourself!"

My hand slides down to my service revolver. I thumb off the leather strap, tug it out. All the while I'm keenly aware that I have no cover. That I'm visible in the head-light beams.

The *crack* of a gunshot splits the air. I hear it ping into the Explorer behind me. Every nerve in my body jerks taut. A thousand alarms blast in my brain. A hot slash of adrenaline sears my belly.

"Shit. *Shit.*"

I turn, run headlong toward the Explorer. Vaguely I'm aware of my flashlight beam playing crazily against the trees ahead. Insects flying in the beams.

I hit my lapel mike. "Shots fired! Shots fired! Shots fired!"

I'm scant feet from my vehicle when a second gun-shot rings out. Then a third. I reach the Explorer, my hand against the hood. I'm midway to the rear when something slams into my left forearm. A sledgehammer sharpened to a razor point, swung by a four-hundred-pound sumo wrestler. Pain zings down my arm; my fin-gers go numb. My boots lose purchase on the gravel, and I go down hard, land on my left hip.

Pain registers like a blast furnace against my skin. I flop onto my belly. I lose my grip on the Maglite, make a wild grab for it, watch helplessly as it rolls out of reach.

I scramble to my hands and knees, clutching my .38, animal sounds tearing from my throat. I speed-crawl to the rear of the Explorer. Hunker down, my back against the bumper.

"Fuck!" I'm panting when I grapple for my mike. "Shots fired! Hogpath Road!" I scream. "Need assis-tance! Shots fired!"

I risk a look around the edge of the bumper. No

movement. No sign of the driver. I try to ascertain the make and model of the vehicle, but I'm blinded by the headlights. Sliding lower, I glance beneath the Explorer, spot my flashlight on the ground, a couple of feet from the left front tire. Too risky to reach. Traffic coming over my radio registers in my mind. Backup is on the way. All I have to do is stay put. . . .

Squeezing my eyes shut, I try to stay calm. But I'm vulnerable, especially if there's more than one shooter. I can't see shit because of the headlights. Worse, while the Explorer's engine or frame will stop a bullet, a round will go right through other parts of the vehicle. Pain pounds like a jackhammer in my forearm, keeping time with a pulse that's raging out of control. I lift it and look, try to gauge the damage. All I can see is the black glint of blood on my shirt, dripping into the gravel like gobs of tar.

I look beneath the vehicle again. No sign of anyone on the other side. No sound of footsteps. Maglite is still there, out of reach, pointing the wrong way.

Two more shots clang against the Explorer. My nerves jump like electrical wires. In the back of my mind, I wonder if the shooter has a rifle, if he's coming around to get me. I scramble to the passenger side of the Explorer, peer out. I see someone pass in front of the headlights of the truck. A male. Six feet tall. A hundred seventy-five pounds. Rifle in hand. Ten yards away. Too close. Raising my weapon, I fire two shots in quick succession.

"I'm a police officer!" I scream. "Drop your weapon! Do it now! *Drop it!*"

Vaguely, I'm aware of a dozen codes coming over my radio. I hear a car door slam. I scramble to the other side of the Explorer, keeping my vehicle between us. I'm on the ground, my back against the rear quarter panel. I peer around the bumper. No movement. No one there.

The truck's engine revs and I know the driver is coming for me.

I scuttle to the right front tire of the Explorer in time to see the vehicle lurch forward. The headlights play crazily against the trees as the tires bounce over rough ground. When the vehicle reaches the road, rubber barks against asphalt, then the tires grab. The truck jets backward—ten, twelve, fourteen yards—and skids to a halt. The driver cuts the wheel. Gears grind, then the vehicle leaps forward.

I fire two shots, but my aim is off. Panic hovers at the fringe of my brain. The kind of panic that can lead to deadly mistakes, and I struggle to keep my head, stay calm.

"Easy," I whisper. "Easy. Easy. Easy."

Engine screaming, the driver does an abrupt U-turn. Tires sliding, the vehicle spins, and I know he's going to run. Gravel flies, pings against the Explorer. Through the rise of dust, I see the red of taillights. Taking aim, I fire my last two rounds.

"You son of a bitch!" I grapple for my shoulder mike. "Suspect is eastbound on Hogpath Road! Pickup truck. Extended cab. Blue or black. Long bed. Male driver is armed!"

My radio is a cacophony of calls. Every cop within twenty miles and regardless of jurisdiction is on his way to assist. When a shots-fired call goes out, you drop everything and you haul your ass to the scene.

I hear sirens in the distance. Around me, the fields and woods seem unnaturally quiet. My Explorer is still running. Insects swarm in the headlights. I get up. Unsteady on my feet. I walk around to the driver's side, spot my Maglite on the ground, and pick it up.

Something dark hits the ground next to my boot. At first I think it's a bug, then realize my forearm is bleeding. I've yet to get a look at it. I don't think anything is broken. Still, it hurts plenty.

I need an ambulance, but I don't make the call. Instead, I lean against the Explorer's front fender. I holster my .38 and tug out my phone. I let gravity take me down to a squatting position. Using my uninjured hand, I reach for my lapel mike.

It's over.

CHAPTER 16

There's something about getting your ass shot off that conjures a whole new perspective. Not only about being a cop, but about life in general. It makes you think about the things that really matter.

Four hours have passed since I was hunkered down behind the Explorer while some crazy shit did his utmost to kill me. I spent the first hour or so sitting in the backseat of Skid's cruiser while officials from three different law enforcement agencies—the Holmes County Sheriff's Department, the State Highway Patrol, and of course BCI—took turns questioning me about what happened. No, I didn't get a good look at the shooter. Yes, he was male. I didn't see anyone else. I didn't get the make or model of the truck. I didn't get a plate number; evidently, he'd removed it beforehand. Basically, once I left my vehicle, someone opened fire and the situation went to shit. I think those were my exact words.

Tomasetti drove me to the Emergency Department of Pomerene Hospital, where my left forearm was X-rayed—no broken bones, thank God—and my "minor" gunshot wound was treated. I received a tetanus shot, four stitches, prescriptions for antibiotics and painkillers, and a dozen or so proclamations of how lucky I am.

So far, I've taken all of it on the chin. The cops who questioned me went to great lengths to let me feel like a cop. Like I hadn't screwed up or been careless. They let me know in no uncertain terms that they weren't going to let the crazy fucker get away with taking potshots at one of their own.

Law enforcement takes that sort of thing damn seriously. Every agency in this part of Ohio is on high alert and actively looking for the shooter. Even now, there's a part of me that wants to be out there with them, pissed off, pumped up, and on the hunt. Of course, none of that's going to happen.

It's one A.M. now, and I'm home safe and alive with the man I love. Tomasetti is saying and doing all the right things. He made me take one of the painkillers the doc prescribed. He's filling the silence with very un-Tomasetti-like small talk. He warmed a can of soup, got me into the shower and into bed. He gently reprimanded me for being out there in the middle of nowhere after dark. Of course, the words were tempered with the knowledge that it's what I do for a living. He even made me laugh because we decided I could use the shooting to my advantage to help convince the town council I need another full-time officer. One of a long list of things I love about John Tomasetti is his sense of humor.

I'm lying in our bed, propped against pillows with my arm elevated, my laptop open in front of me. Tucked beneath the pretty summer quilt my sister made me for my birthday last year, I'm wearing one of Tomasetti's old Cleveland Division of Police T-shirts. The pain in my forearm has faded to a dull ache. I wish the knot of foreboding that's taken up residence in the pit of my stomach could be so easily banished.

Someone nearly killed me tonight—and they're still out there. Is it about the Gingerich case? Was it a warning—some twisted effort to keep me from digging any deeper? A steady stream of names have cycled through my mind in the last hours. Mark Petersheim. Elam Schlabach. Milo Hershberger. Sam Miller. All of them had reason to want Daniel Gingerich dead. Are any of them desperate enough—cold-blooded enough— to murder a cop?

"You're still awake."

I look up from my laptop to see Tomasetti stride into the room. I watch as he crosses to the window and opens it. An orchestra of sound floats in on the cool night air. The frogs from the pond, crickets, and soft hoots from the family of owls that lives in the cottonwood tree at the water's edge. They are the sounds of my youth. Sounds we hear every night as we sleep. They're sounds that I appreciate now more than I ever have in my life.

"Any word on the shooter?" I ask.

"I talked to Rasmussen," he says. "Every agency in the four-county area is out in force. Nothing yet."

"Were they able to get tire tread impressions?" I ask. "Any brass?"

"They got brass." Tossing me a frown, he slides into bed beside me. "Not sure about impressions."

"They trace the call?"

"We got the tower. Still working on the rest."

"This wasn't random," I say after a moment.

His gaze meets mine and he scowls. I can tell by his expression he doesn't like the ramifications, but he doesn't disagree.

"This is about the Gingerich case," I say.

He sighs. "You got someone in mind?"

The names scroll through my brain again, but one doesn't stand out above the others. "No, but I know it circles back to Daniel Gingerich. It's the only thing that makes sense."

"So tell me about Gingerich."

"Everyone thought he was such a great guy. An innocent Amish kid. Hardworking. Charming." Disgust rings hard in my voice. "Tomasetti, that son of a bitch was the worst kind of predator. He preyed on young girls. *Amish* girls, for God's sake. Young women he knew would never tell a soul, not even their parents."

"How many women are we talking about?"

"At least two that I know of, probably more."

"The assaults were never reported?"

"All of it was swept under the rug so everyone could pretend it never happened. Except for those young women. They're forced to live with what happened to them. In some cases, they were blamed. Made to think it was their fault, that they did something wrong. And, of course, no one wants to talk about it."

"Evidently someone said *something*." He thinks about that a moment. "These young women that Gingerich preyed upon," he says. "They have boyfriends. Brothers. Fathers. Husbands." He shrugs. "The need to protect those you love can be a powerful motivator. It runs deep and it can transcend even religion."

"Two of the women became pregnant. One committed suicide. The other married. Her husband doesn't know. Both were still in their teens."

My voice shakes with the final word. I should leave it at that. Shut the hell up. Enough said. Blame that telltale quiver on the painkillers or the fact that I'm hurting and angry and repulsed. But it's as if some floodgate has been opened and a torrent of emotions whose existence I've refused to acknowledge rushes out.

"I know this isn't solely about them," I whisper. "But what happened to them is part of this."

"Motivation." Tomasetti holds my gaze, his expression contemplative and level. "You probably don't want to hear this, Kate, I think there are some parallels mixed up in all of this, too."

"Maybe. I don't want this to be about me or my past."

"For better or worse, our pasts are part of who we are. The things that have happened to us, good or bad, affect our perspectives, our outlook. They are our experience, and the tools we bring to the table. That's not always a negative."

"Duly noted." When he only continues to look at me, I add, "I can handle it."

"I know you can." His eyes probe mine. "So how did all of this culminate in someone taking a shot at you tonight?"

"Someone thinks I'm getting too close to the truth. Someone who has something to lose. Or else they're protecting someone."

"They want you to back off."

"Evidently, they don't know me very well."

"They have no idea," he mutters, and then reaches over, closes my laptop, and slides it onto the night table beside him. "Didn't the doc tell you to take the rest of the night off?"

I sense the tension coming off him. He's being kind. Patient. He's said and done all the right things since arriving at the scene on Hogpath Road a few hours ago. But I'll never forget the look on his face as he'd run to me. The way his eyes swept over me, as if looking for some catastrophic injury I wouldn't survive. I knew exactly the thoughts that were running through his mind. I'd hated doing that to him, and yet I don't know how to make it right.

We fall silent, thinking, listening to the night sounds outside the window. After a moment, I scooch higher on my pillow and turn slightly onto my side, facing him. "One more thing we need to cover."

"I'm not in trouble, am I?" The lightheartedness of the statement doesn't match the gravity in his eyes.

Still, I smile. "I want you to know . . . I'm careful when I'm on duty. I don't take chances. What happened tonight was . . . bad. But I'm good at what I do. I want you to understand . . . you don't have to worry about me."

Sliding down a bit, he turns to me, takes my uninjured hand in his, and kisses my knuckles. "That kind of comes with the territory."

I start to speak, but he presses two fingers against my lips and I realize there's something he needs to say, too. Something I need to hear that's important to both of us.

"I'm not going to lie to you. When I got the call . . . it scared the hell out of me. On the drive over, I was already making deals with God. The devil. Whoever happened to be listening. But, Kate, that fear was tempered by the knowledge that you're a good cop. I mean that."

I stare at him, wishing my head was clear, realizing that as usual he's one step ahead of me. That I've underestimated him.

Taking his time, he continues. "You're a small-town cop. We both know there are times when there's no one else. Times when you're on duty and a call comes in, and you take it regardless of the hour or location or nature of the call."

Of all the things he could have said, this is the most unexpected. The thing I didn't anticipate. I'd been trying to find a way to downplay the shooting. Or skirt the issue altogether if I could. Find a way to apologize for worrying him without shouldering the blame for doing so. I was going to promise to be more careful. Make some kind of compromise, even. But I'd also been prepared to do battle had he asked me to do something I didn't want to do.

"I don't know what to say," I tell him.

"You don't have to say anything. You don't have to

tiptoe around me. I'm a big boy, Kate. Good or bad or somewhere in between, I can handle it."

Because I don't trust my voice, I nod.

"Would I have said that two years ago? A year ago?" He shakes his head. "Probably not. Instead, we would have been lying here, arguing about your future as a cop. There was a time when I would have asked you to choose. You can be a cop or you can be with me but you can't do both."

"I know what you went through with your wife and kids," I say. "I understood it. I accepted it. And I knew we could work through it."

"A few months ago, none of those things would've stopped me from asking you to give up something you love. I would have forced the issue. Tried to manipulate you in whatever way I thought might work. That would have been incredibly selfish."

I start to speak, but he raises his hand and quiets me. "Someone tried to kill you tonight. They came pretty damn close to succeeding. And yet when you walked into our home with a bullet wound in your arm, your only thought was of me and *my* feelings. How screwed up is that?"

"No one said it's easy being married to a cop."

"I will never ask you to give that up."

I want to respond. Say something to let him know how much the words mean to me. But my throat is so tight, so clogged with emotion that I can't speak.

Reaching out, he cups the side of my face and caresses my cheek with the pad of his thumb. "Now you cry," he says dryly. "That's just like you, isn't it?"

I set my hand over his, find my voice. "I do have one small concern."

"Yeah?" He scoots closer to me. "Shoot."

I smack his shoulder for the poor word choice and then I nestle closer, lay my head on his shoulder. "I'm not sure how people will adjust to calling me Chief Tomasetti."

"It's got a nice ring."

"You think?"

"I think you don't have a thing to worry about."

I dream of Daniel Lapp. I'm fourteen years old and I still believe the world is a safe place where nothing bad could ever happen. I'm innocent and carefree and I have no concept of the violence that is about to shatter my sheltered and protected life.

I'm in my mamm's *sunny farmhouse kitchen, washing dishes and daydreaming about all the things I'm going to do with my life. The window is open and the curtains are blowing in the breeze, the little lead weights sewn into the hem tapping against the sill. Tap. Tap. Tap.*

The next thing I know Daniel Lapp is there, touching me, hurting me, and in that instant I understand that the world as I know it is about to change. I know it will never be the same. I'll never be the same.

I lie on the dusty floor as he rips at my clothes. My dress. My prayer kapp. *Shock and shame and numbing disbelief punching me as violently as any fist. His fingers dig into my throat, cutting off the blood flow to my head, and I feel as if I'm leaving my body, floating, watching the scene unfold from somewhere above.*

I can see his face, and he looks down at me the way a starving dog might look at a pile of meat. I writhe and scream and claw; I scream for help, but no one comes. No one comes. And the shame that follows makes me want to die. . . .

I wake gasping, my heart pounding. I sit up, my breaths shallow and fast. Pain streaks down my left forearm at the movement and I curse the son of a bitch who shot me.

I look around, realize I'm safe at home in my bed. Just a nightmare, I think, and the residual fear scampers back into its dark hole. It's early; the windows are gray with morning light, but Tomasetti is already gone.

The dream lingers, a stain, ugly and unwanted. I've spent years trying to erase that day from my memory. This morning, I open the gate and let myself remember. I think about Daniel Gingerich and all those parallels Tomasetti had mentioned, and it occurs to me that no matter how hard we try to forget, some emotions are indelibly branded onto our psyches. They become part of us. We wear the shame and the rage like invisible scars, unseen by others, but seared onto our souls, visible only to us, the damaged ones.

I consider taking the morning off, but there's too much going on, too much to do. Whoever ambushed me last night is still out there. Daniel Gingerich is still dead. And his killer is still on the loose.

Keeping those things in mind, I roll out of bed and head for the shower.

CHAPTER 17

Sexual assault is a hideous crime, one that wrecks lives and affects all the relationships in a victim's life. It shatters trust and destroys promising futures. It steals hope and changes the way a person views the world, the way they view others. The way they view themselves. Worst-case scenario, such as in the case of Emma Miller, it can kill.

It's the crime no one wants to talk about. The crime that too often goes unreported because of stigma, ignorance, self-blame or any combination of the above. When that happens, the perpetrators go free. Wash, rinse, repeat.

Despite my best efforts, it's ten A.M. by the time I hobble into the station. Lois is standing at the front desk, waving a handful of pink slips at me, when I walk in the door. As expected, I find Mona sitting cross-legged on the floor behind the desk, filing paperwork that could probably wait until her shift at midnight. They're both looking at me a little too closely and with a little too much concern.

"I'm fine," I say as I cross to the desk.

"Heard things got dicey out on Hogpath Road last night," Lois says as she hands me my messages. "Any word on the shooter?"

"Not yet," I tell her. "We'll get him."

Raising her brows, Mona rattles the bottle of ibuprofen she keeps on hand. I nod and she taps three tablets into my hand. "Thanks."

"Oh. Before I forget." Mona plucks a plain white envelope from my message slot and holds it out to me. "Someone left this for you."

I take the envelope, curious because the only thing written on it is my name. "Any idea who it's from?"

She shakes her head. "T.J. found it taped to the door when he brought in breakfast burritos at six A.M."

In my office, I flip on my computer, use my letter opener to slice open the envelope, and read.

Mark Petersheim killed Daniel Gingerich.

Rising, I leave my office and go back to reception. Both women watch in silence as I cross to the front door where the note was found, open it, and peer out across Main Street.

"Mona?" I say, without looking at her.

"Yeah?" She comes up beside me and we look across the street at the newest Amish tourist shop.

"*Dawdy Haus*" is *Deitsh* for "Grandfather's House." Owned by Janine Fourman, the shop is the first "gently used" Amish shop to grace downtown Painters Mill and

carries everything from bassinets and lanterns to post-
cards and homemade fudge. Like most downtown mer-
chants, Janine had been assigned five parking slots in
front of her rental space. She came to me a month ago,
complaining about the customers from Gordon's Five
and Dime next door commandeering her parking spaces.
The situation wasn't high priority; no one in my department wrote any citations, so in typical Janine Fourman
fashion, she took matters into her own hands and installed security cameras.

I motion toward Dawdy Haus, spot one of the cameras next to the striped awning that shades the sidewalk.
"If I'm not mistaken, that security camera will capture
the front of the police station."

Mona looks at me, her eyes widening. "The note."

"Might be worth a shot."

A few minutes later, Mona and I are in the small office at the rear of Dawdy Haus. The manager, Jenna
Fourman, is Janine's daughter. She's about twenty-five
years old and sitting at the computer, tapping keys.
"Heard what happened to you last night, Chief Burkholder. This have something to do with it?"

"I'm not sure yet," I say vaguely.

"Well, no one ever looks at these security-camera
tapes," she tells us. "I mean, except for Mom." She gives
me a knowing look. "She's kind of fanatical about the
whole parking thing."

I'm all too aware of Janine Fourman's petty obses-
sions and her heavy-handed tactics when it comes to
handling something she doesn't like. The owner of the

insurance-company office next door has complained about her take-no-prisoner tactics on more than one occasion.

I opt for diplomatic. "I understand."

The girl shoots me a grin that's part knowing, part apologetic; then her attention snaps back to the screen. "Oh, here we go." She presses the down-arrow key a dozen times; then her finger pauses. "This particular tape runs from six P.M. last night through six A.M. this morning."

"That's the time frame we're looking for." The last thing I want to do is sit through twelve hours of video of downtown Painters Mill overnight. "Is it possible to fast-forward through it?"

"Sure."

The buzzer on the outer door sounds, telling us a customer has arrived. Jenna glances at the door and rises. "I gotta get that." She motions toward the computer. "You guys can mouse through pretty quickly. Just drag that little blinking line from left to right."

"Got it." I motion Mona into her chair. "Thanks, Jenna."

She grins. "Just don't tell Mom I let you put your fingers on that keyboard."

I grin back. "Don't worry. I won't."

Mona sets to work mousing through twelve hours of video. There's not much action in downtown Painters Mill after hours. For twenty minutes, the only movement we see comes in the form of a stray cat and Mr. Wetzel out taking his midnight walk. At the 12:45 A.M.

mark, we both see the shadowed figure and lean closer to the monitor.

"It's a woman," Mona murmurs.

"Looks Amish," I say, squinting because the resolution is grainy and dark. The camera angle is bad. "Any idea how to enlarge that?"

"I can try. Probably lose resolution and it's not great to begin with." She hits the mouse roller and sure enough the image jumps and expands.

"Run it again."

The woman enters from the left, or south, side of the police station, walks directly up to the outer door, looks both ways, reaches into her pocket, and slaps the note onto the glass.

"Too dark to see her face," Mona comments.

"Or make out the details of her clothes. Definitely wearing a dress, though. Average build. Not too tall. She's sticking to the shadows."

"You think she knows about the camera?"

"Maybe." I reach over and usurp the mouse. Right-click and enlarge, but it's no help because the resolution deteriorates tenfold. I can't make out the details of her face. All I can see of her clothes is the silhouette of her dress and *kapp*.

Mona runs it again and sighs. "At least we know the culprit is a woman."

"And Amish. That's significant."

"What's next?"

"I thought we might borrow this tape and see if we can get some stills." Even as I say the words I'm not optimistic that an image will be helpful in terms of the case. Not only is the quality poor, but I have no idea if the note is even legitimate. I don't know the motive of the person who left it. Does she know what happened the night of the fire? Is she trying to influence the case? Or does she have some ax to grind against Petersheim? Some agenda? Still, it's *something;* it's more than I currently have, so I'm obliged to explore it further.

"Once we get the images," I say, "I want you to courier this tape up to BCI to see if they can enhance it."

"I'm on it."

"Thanks." I start toward the door. Midway there I stop and turn to her. "Did Bob Schoening with the fire marshal's office send that key over?"

"It came in this morning."

"On your way home I want you to hit the two hardware stores in Painters Mill to see if they can tell us if they made that duplicate key."

Mona looks after me, her face broadcasting how pleased she is to be part of this. "Anything else, Chief?"

"If it's not too difficult, you might want to squeeze in a few hours of sleep."

We grin at each other and then I turn and go through the door.

A lot of people had motive to want Daniel Gingerich dead. My mind always circles back to a single name: Emma Miller. Of all the people who were victimized by Gingerich, it was Emma who ended up dead. A sweet Amish girl forced into an agonizing situation. A girl whose parents blamed her. Whose church district would not support her if they found out she'd become pregnant out of wedlock. She took the only way out she could find.

It's a heartbreaking story, especially for the people who loved her. Her parents, Sam and Esther Miller, and her boyfriend, Elam Schlabach, all of whom now have a motive for murder.

By the time I get my hands on a decent image of the mysterious woman who left the note, the morning is gone. I'd been entertaining the notion of picking up Mark Petersheim and bringing him to the station. Push him a little to gauge his reaction. See if I can shake up his alibi or catch him in a lie. But I'm not convinced the note is legitimate. I opt instead to drive over to Charm to talk to the three Amish girls at The Mercantile.

According to Milo Hershberger, Neva Lambright was at the singing with Ruth Petersheim the night she was assaulted. Why didn't Neva mention it when I talked to her? Honest oversight? Was she simply trying to protect her friend's privacy? Or does she know more about what happened that night than she's letting on?

My forearm is pounding like a son of a bitch when I park in the gravel lot of The Mercantile and shut down the engine. I'm troubled by the growing pile of unanswered questions and grouchy because I'm in dire need of food and caffeine and a painkiller and not necessarily in that order.

I push through the antique door of The Mercantile. Half a dozen or so customers are standing in line at the cash register to pay for merchandise. A middle-aged Amish woman operates the register, laughing at something one of them is saying. The type and color of her dress tells me she's Beachy Amish and I wonder if she's Neva's mother, the owner of the shop.

I go to the aisle where the candles are displayed, select a pillar I'd spotted last time I was here, and take it to the register.

"That bergamot and sweet rosemary combination is a lovely scent," the woman says as she slides it across the counter and upends it to read the price sticker. "Is it a gift?"

She's about fifty years old with a stout build and a ruddy complexion that tells me she spends a good bit of her time out of doors. Dishwater blond hair just starting to go gray is tucked neatly into her *kapp*.

"It's my sister's birthday." I look around the store as she rings up the sale. "Is Neva around?"

"In the back, I think." Lifting a brow, she gives my uniform a once-over, her gaze landing on my bandaged forearm. "Anything I can help you with?"

I show her my badge and identify myself. "I'm looking into the death of Daniel Gingerich over in Painters Mill."

"I read about all that." Clucking, she assumes a somber expression. "Such a terrible thing losing a young one like that. Hard to believe anyone would do such a thing. Some of our men are going up there tomorrow to rebuild the barn for them, you know."

"The Gingerich family will appreciate that," I tell her in *Deitsh*.

If she's surprised by my fluency, she doesn't show it, but a smile touches the corners of her mouth. When she's finished with the sale, she offers her hand. "I'm Edna Lambright, by the way. My husband and I own the shop."

We shake over the counter. "You've done a nice job with the place."

"Always loved the idea of taking something old and forgotten, like this barn, and making something new out of it."

"I understand you're going to open a restaurant in the old round barn in the back."

She chuckles. "Well, it's a work in progress. Place is older than the hills and there are some structural issues according to our construction man. But God is smiling down on us. With Him leading the way, it'll get done."

Her eyes sharpen on mine. "What do you need to speak with my daughter about?"

"I know Emma Miller used to work here. I understand she knew Daniel Gingerich." I shrug, trying to keep my answers vague. "I'm hoping Neva might be able to answer some questions or at least offer some insights on their relationship."

"Well, the Amish are a tight-knit bunch. Everyone knows just about everyone else. Let me call her up here for you."

She picks up the phone and presses a button. "Neva, come to the front please," she says over the intercom system. "Would you like a gift box with that, Kate Burkholder?"

"I would. Thank you."

The sound of female chatter draws my attention. I turn to see Ina Yoder and Viola Stutzman coming down an aisle. They're deep in conversation, dresses swishing around their legs, arms loaded with what looks like this evening's projects. Ina is carrying a canvas bag with two rolls of fabric sticking out the top. Viola totes a wicker sewing kit in one hand, a bundle of what looks like crafting grapevine in the other.

"Hi, girls," I say.

Viola's stride falters. "Oh, hi, Chief Burkholder."

"Looks like you found another birthday gift for your sister." Ina's eyes flick to the bag in my hand. "Did you pick the bergamot and sweet rosemary?"

"I did." I look past her to see Neva Lambright striding toward us from the rear of the store. She looks harried, holding a large corrugated box in her arms, but there's a bounce in her step. She's wearing a lavender print dress and has a brown paper shopping bag sporting The Mercantile logo slung over her shoulder.

"You girls look as if you've got a busy afternoon ahead of you," I say.

"Always," Ina says.

"But we love it," Viola adds.

"Speak for yourself." Neva is still smiling when she crosses to Viola and hands her the shopping bag. "You forgot your yarn."

Viola takes the bag, peeks inside. "You're determined to keep me working, even when I'm off, aren't you?"

"I think she forgot it on purpose," Ina teases.

I watch the exchange, and I can't help but remember a time in my own life when everything was about friendship and fun and a future I couldn't wait to explore.

"I need a few minutes of your time," I tell them. "Is there a place where we can sit and chat?"

"We could sit at the café," Viola offers.

"Someplace private?" I say.

Edna Lambright looks up from the quarters she's counting. "You can use the break room in the back. Just leave it the way you found it."

"In the meantime." I pull out the photo of the woman who left the note on the police station door and set it on the counter. "Do any of you recognize her?"

Edna slides glasses onto her nose and looks down at the photo. Simultaneously, the three girls set their bags on the floor and gather around the counter.

"She's Amish," Edna says.

"Not a Beachy dress," Neva adds.

"Looks like gray fabric," Viola says to no one in particular.

"Do you have a better photo?" Ina asks.

"Just this one," I tell her.

As unobtrusively as possible, I watch the four women as they scrutinize the still. They're bent over the counter, expressions serious, brows knit.

"Can't really see her face," Ina says.

"Maybe if there was more light?" Neva adds.

"Angle isn't great, either." This, from Viola.

"Is there anything at all about her that's familiar?" I ask. "The shape of her silhouette? The dress? Shoes?"

Edna straightens, removes her glasses, drops them to the lanyard around her neck. "What did she do?"

"I'm not sure she did anything," I tell her. "At this point, I'm just trying to identify her."

"I'm sorry we can't be more helpful." Edna's eyes flick past me, to a customer who's approached with a shopping basket laden with an autumn wreath and kitchen towels. "*Zrikk zu verk,*" she mumbles to me. Back to work.

A few minutes later, Ina, Neva, Viola, and I are seated at a small oak table in a room that's not much bigger than a walk-in closet. There's a rustic butcher-block counter with a porcelain farmhouse sink, a microwave, and a coffeemaker. A mini refrigerator hums from its place in the corner. The table's centerpiece is a wicker basket containing several dozen candy bars with a small bowl with the words "Honor System" written in *Deitsh*.

The three girls sit stiffly at the table, trying not to look anxious. Probably wondering why I've come back a second time to speak with them. Viola can't seem to keep her eyes off the bandage on my forearm. "We heard what happened to you," she says solemnly.

"It must have been scary," Ina says. "Are you okay?"

"I'm fine," I tell them. I pause a moment before continuing. "You know I'm working on the Daniel Gingerich case," I say.

Three heads bob in unison.

I focus my attention on Neva. "I know you were close friends with Emma Miller and I understand your loyalty to her." I take a moment to get my thoughts, my words in order. "I know there may be certain things you don't want to talk about. Things that are private or painful or both. I'm not here to make you uncomfortable or pry into your personal business. Or Emma's. But I need you to be honest with me. Do you understand?"

Neva stares at me, eyes wide. Ina and Viola are looking down at the tabletop, not meeting my gaze.

They know where this is going, I think.

"I know what happened to Emma," I say, keeping it vague, hoping they'll fill in the blanks. "I need you to tell me what you know."

I wait, but no one speaks, so I add, "Emma deserves that. The truth. I think she'd want you to do the right thing."

I let the silence that follows work for a full minute. Just when I think no one is going to respond, Viola makes a sound. I glance over at her. Her head is bent forward. She's staring at the tabletop, crying.

"We have to tell her," the girl whispers.

"Viola," Neva snaps, a warning in her voice.

"Emma wouldn't want anyone to know," Ina says.

I give them another minute, then say, "You can trust me with the information. I'll do everything in my power to keep it confidential. You have my word."

None of the women meet my gaze. Neva stares down at her hands. Ina looks away, everywhere but at me. Viola covers her face with her hands. She doesn't make a sound, but I see tears on her chin.

After a moment, Neva raises her gaze to mine. "How did you find out?" she whispers.

"I can't tell you that," I say. "But I need to know exactly what happened. If you know something—anything—you need to tell me. Right now."

Another lengthy silence and then Ina raises her head

and glares at Viola. "Since you're so keen on telling the world what happened, why don't you just do it?" she snaps.

If an Amish girl could jump out of her skin and run, Viola would have done just that. I wait, expecting her to comply, but she sits frozen in place, unmoving, looking as if she's being led to her execution.

"Ina." Neva says her friend's name firmly, and then sets her hand over Viola's. "She's a police. It's okay."

"It's not okay," Ina hisses. "None of this is okay."

Viola snaps at her. "We have to tell."

"Tell me what?" I say.

After a moment, Neva squares her shoulders, raises her chin. "I'll do it then."

All eyes fall upon her. Neva maintains eye contact with me. It's so quiet in the small room, I can hear the air-conditioning rush through the vents, the hum of the refrigerator, the steady drip of water from the sink.

"We all noticed something different about her," Neva says. "She'd lost weight. Grown quiet. Pale." Her voice is little more than a whisper. "A few weeks before she died, she came to me after work. She was just . . . broken inside. Her heart torn to pieces."

The young Amish woman is putting on a brave front, but she's anxious and upset. Her foot is jiggling a hundred miles an hour, but she doesn't seem to notice. She's perched on the chair as if her legs are springs and she's ready to launch herself into a run at the first sign of danger, which is apparently very close.

When the silence goes on too long, I push. "What did Emma tell you?"

"It was about Daniel. When he was working for her parents. At first, she said he'd been . . . looking at her funny. I mean, she'd mentioned it before and we just kind of laughed it off, you know. But this was different. Serious. It had been happening the whole time he was there, working for her parents. Emma told her *mamm*, but Mrs. Miller . . . wouldn't listen. It hurt me to hear that. Emma was so sweet. Innocent. And in love with Elam. She didn't want anyone to know."

I pause, take a moment to make eye contact with each girl. Viola has stopped crying, but her eyes and nose are red. "Daniel raped her?" I ask.

Neva nods. "He trapped her out in the milk house. She was . . . so ashamed. Blamed herself. Thought she must have done something wrong. Her *mamm*—" She bites off the word, her eyes flashing anger.

"We told her it wasn't her fault," Viola whispers.

Neva shakes her head. "She didn't listen. It was incredibly sad."

"She'd been saving herself for Elam," Ina says, her voice shaking with anger. "All she wanted was to marry him and have children."

"She was . . . despondent," Neva says.

Looking miserable, Viola sniffs, keeps her eyes on the table. "It was like we couldn't . . . *reach* her."

None of what I've just heard is news; I'd already heard it from Esther Miller. But hearing it from these young women, seeing the anguish on their faces, adds yet another ugly layer to an already hideous story.

"Did Emma tell anyone else?" I ask.

Neva gives another shake of her head. "I don't think so."

"She didn't want anyone to know," Viola adds.

"Practically killed her to tell us," Ina puts in. "And we're her best friends."

"Do you think that's why Emma killed herself?" I ask.

Neva nods. "I do."

"She felt guilty about it even though she had no reason to blame herself," says Viola.

"And she couldn't get away from him," Ina adds.

I tamp down a rise of outrage. "Her parents didn't protect her?" I pose the question, but I already know.

Neva shakes her head. "They were . . . old-fashioned that way. I mean, about . . . you know, men and women."

No person or society is perfect. Far from it. I would never profess to be a fair judge of the Amish. I've got too much baggage to be impartial. There are elements about being Amish that I loved and to this day regret leaving behind. But there are also certain aspects of the community that I was born into that I detest. Generally speaking, the Amish are a patriarchal society. While most women certainly have a voice, a few do not. Growing up, I heard the whispered stories. It wasn't until I was an adult that I realized sometimes there's a fine line between coercion and force. Even when that line is crossed, some prefer to look the other way.

"Did Emma's *datt* know what had happened?" I ask.

Neva gives a minute shake of her head. "She never said."

"We didn't ask," Viola says.

"Maybe her *mamm* told him." Ina offers the words with a shrug. "I don't know."

"She wasn't that close to her *datt*," Neva says. "I mean, he was a good *datt* and all that, but to talk to a man about. . . . *that*. Emma wouldn't have."

Nodding, I move on. "Did Emma tell Elam Schlabach what happened? Did he know?"

Neva gives the question a good bit of thought and shakes her head. "She didn't say, but I don't think she would have told him."

"She wouldn't have risked hurting him," Viola adds.

Ina shakes her head as if the other girls' statements are naive. "Or else she was afraid he might—" She cuts the words off abruptly, as if realizing she'd been about to say something that shouldn't be said.

"That he might what?" I ask.

Ina's gaze skitters away from mine. "He might've blamed her, too," she mutters.

Neva sighs. "That would have destroyed her."

"Was Elam protective of Emma?" I ask.

The silence that follows goes on a beat too long. "Sometimes," Ina says.

"Does he have a temper?" I ask.

"He didn't . . . I mean, before Emma died," Neva says.

"And after she died?" I ask.

Neva slants a look toward the other two women and nods. "He . . . changed after he lost her. All that pain, I guess."

"Can't blame him," Viola says.

Ina squares her shoulders. "Anyone would change after something like that."

Neva looks me in the eye. "Elam Schlabach is one of the most decent young Amish men we know, Chief Burkholder. There's no way he would hurt anyone."

Viola wipes her nose with a tissue. "He would never commit such a sin. Not Elam."

Nodding, I rise. "I appreciate your answering my questions and talking about something so painful."

The three girls are subdued as they rise and push in their chairs. I take my time with my own chair, lingering as they shuffle from the room. I'm thinking about Ruth Petersheim now, and Neva is the girl I need to talk to. Alone.

"Neva?" I say as she goes through the door.

The Amish woman looks at me over her shoulder and raises her brows. "Yes?"

"One more thing." I walk to the doorway, motion toward the table and chairs. "Do you have a minute?"

Ina and Viola stop and turn toward us, start back into the room. I make eye contact with both of them. "Just Neva." I soften the words with a smile. "I won't keep her too long."

The two young women exchange looks, their expressions wary. They don't want to leave her.

Neva shrugs it off. "No problem." She sends a smile to her friends. "Go on. I'll be out in a sec."

I pull out one of the chairs. She returns to the break room and sinks into it. I wait by the door until Ina and

Viola start toward the front of the store and then I go back to the table.

"Why didn't you tell me you went to the singing with Ruth Petersheim the night she met up with Daniel Gingerich?" I ask as I take the chair opposite her.

Her shoulders stiffen. A subtle quiver moves through her body. If I hadn't been watching her for a reaction, I would have missed it. She tries to cover her discomfiture by choosing a candy bar from the wicker basket and dropping a dollar bill into the mix.

After a moment, she shrugs. "I didn't think it was important."

I let the statement hang. Both of us know it's not true. She's doing her best not to look uncomfortable, but she's not pulling it off.

"How well do you know Ruth?" I ask.

"I've known her since I was a kid, but we were never close."

"You rode together the night of the singing at the Schwartz place?"

"Yes."

"Did anything unusual happen that evening, Neva?"

She concentrates on the candy bar in her hands, takes a moment to peel off the wrapper. "Not that I know of."

"Who did Ruth ride home with?"

A too-long pause and then Neva raises her gaze to mine. "I think you already know the answer to that."

"Why did you lie to me?"

"I didn't lie, Chief Burkholder. I just didn't realize it was important."

"It's called lying by omission, Neva. I asked you specifically about Daniel Gingerich and you didn't see fit to tell me about that night?"

She narrows her eyes, cocks her head. "Did something happen to Ruthie?"

"You tell me."

She stares at me for a long time and then shakes her head. "If something happened to her, she never mentioned it. That's the truth."

"Did you hear any rumors? Anything like that?"

She shakes her head. "If I'd heard something, I would have told you. Especially after what happened to Emma. I've no reason to hold anything back."

I stare at her, looking for a lie or half truth, some sign of deception. I see none of those things.

"Is there anything else I need to know about?" I ask.

Her brows go together and she considers the question for the span of several heartbeats. Finally, as if she's come to some important conclusion, she gives a firm nod. "I think that's about it."

CHAPTER 18

After leaving The Mercantile, I head north toward Wilmot. I've just pulled onto the highway when my cell phone chimes. I glance at the display to see HOLMES CNTY SHERIFF and I snatch it up before the second ring.

"Kate, it's Mike Rasmussen. How's the arm?"

"An ID on the shooter would go a long way toward easing the pain," I tell him.

"Wish I could oblige. I figured you'd want an update, good or bad. I got a little of both."

"Lay it on me."

"We retrieved four cartridges at the scene."

"You get prints?"

"We did. A couple of good ones, in fact. Tomasetti expedited, got everything run through AFIS. Unfortunately, we didn't get a match."

"So he's not in the system." I sigh. "Apparently, that's the theme I'm keeping with the Gingerich case." I think about that a moment. "Caliber?"

"Caliber is three-oh-eight. Common hunting rifle."

"Bullet?"

"Too destroyed to get striations."

"Were you guys able to pick up tire tread imprints?"

"We got a partial. Lab's looking at it now."

"You're making my day with all this good news."

He doesn't laugh. "You still think it's related to the Gingerich thing?"

"I do."

A thoughtful silence and then, "Do me a favor and be careful out there, will you?"

"You got it."

I'm mulling my conversation with the sheriff when I drive by the Amish Door restaurant and pull around to the corner where Mark Petersheim was working last time I was here. But the fence is complete and there's no one there.

I continue into Wilmot proper, make a right on Milton, and park in front of the Petersheim house. I'm thinking about the note and the questions I need to ask as I take the narrow sidewalk to the front door. I knock and wait, but no one answers. I knock a second time, this time tapping with my key fob. When no one comes to the door, I go around to the back and knock on the screen door, but there's no reply.

Since the Petersheims don't have a phone, I tape a note to the door, asking Mark to call me as soon as possible. That's when I hear the baby crying. I stand on the porch, listening. The cries are definitely coming from inside. Not merely cries, but screaming. What the hell?

I knock again, this time using the heel of my hand.

"Mr. and Mrs. Petersheim? It's Kate Burkholder," I call out.

I wait but there's no response. No sound of footsteps. Just the continuous screaming of an unhappy infant. I remind myself Ruth could be in the shower or taking a nap. But there's something in the tone of that cry that's worrisome. Last time I was here Ruth was attentive and caring. I walk to the window that looks out over the front yard, but the curtains are drawn. I knock one more time and head back around to the rear of the house.

I take the narrow dirt path to the small garage in the alley. I tug open the door. Sure enough, the truck I'd seen at the Amish Door Village, where Mark Petersheim had been working on the fence, is parked inside. Leaving the door open, I cross to it, set my hand on the hood. Cold.

Turning, I leave the garage and jog to the back porch. I open the screen door and rap on the glass. "Mr. and Mrs. Petersheim! Kate Burkholder! Can you open the door please!"

I wait, but the only sound I hear is the howling cries of the child. Sheer yellow curtains cover the window. I look inside, see a small table and chairs, a refrigerator against the wall. A gas stove in the corner. On impulse, I try the knob, but the door is locked.

"Shit," I mutter.

There's a small window to my left. The curtains are parted; it's probably above the kitchen sink. I leave the porch and approach it, stand on my tiptoes to see inside. At first, all I see is a typical kitchen. There's a clay pot

on the sill where a basil plant flourishes. Yellow coun-
tertops. White cabinets. A doorway that leads to the
front of the house. No sign of anyone, but the baby continues to cry frantically.

Since I'm no longer in Holmes County, I tug out my
cell and dial 911. When the dispatcher answers, I quickly
identify myself as a police officer and explain the situation. "There may be an unattended infant inside the
home," I tell her. "I need a welfare check." I relay the
address.

Out of the corner of my eye, I see a cat in the window. A fat orange tabby, looking at me through the glass.
I don't pay much attention. Then the cat raises its paw
and leaves a red smear on the glass. The hairs on my
nape stand on end.

"I got blood," I tell the dispatcher. "I'm going to make
entry."

I hit END, scramble around to the porch. Grabbing a
terra-cotta pot from the step, I go to the door, avert my
face, and break the glass. I reach through the opening,
unlock the door, yank it open.

Then I'm in the kitchen. The first thing I notice is the
smell. A combination of dirty diapers and an unflushed
toilet. "Ruth Petersheim! Mark! Police!"

Sunlight spills in through the window. The scream
of the baby echoes throughout the house. In my peripheral vision I see the cat dart out the door. The counters
are mottled with . . . something. I look closer, realize
with burgeoning concern that the counters are covered
with bloody paw prints.

I go through the doorway, enter the same small living room where Mona and I spoke with Ruth Petersheim days ago. There's a sofa. Coffee table. Nothing out of place. I follow the sound of the baby's cries, down a dimly lit hall.

"Mark! Ruth! Are you okay? It's Kate Burkholder!"

The last thing any cop wants to do is walk into a house and surprise the homeowner. I always make it a point to shout out my location, and identify myself multiple times. Ever present in the back of my mind is the shooting last night, and that the shooter has yet to be apprehended.

I tug my .38 from my holster. Ahead, two doors stand open. A small bathroom. A bedroom. A third door is cracked open a few inches. The hardwood floors are mottled with bloody paw prints. The smell is worse here. Rotten eggs and sewage. It's a stench I've smelled before, one I don't want to identify, and I pray to God I'm wrong. All the while the baby screams. His little voice has gone hoarse. He screams with such ferocity that he's run out of breath.

"Mark? Ruth?" Pistol leading the way, I sidle to the end of the hall, push open the door with my left hand. The room is darkened. I see a window, curtains drawn. A closet door standing open. An oak headboard.

A gasp escapes me when I see them. Mark and Ruth Petersheim lie side by side atop a cream-colored quilt. I see pale faces and staring eyes. All of it surrounded by an ocean of blood, shocking and red. I know immediately they're dead.

Ruth lies prone, her head turned toward me. One eye closed, the other rolled back white. She's wearing a blue dress with a white apron, the bodice soaked with blood that's gone black in the center. She's still wearing her *kapp*. Tights. One shoe missing.

Next to her, Mark Petersheim lies supine. He's wearing dark trousers, a blue shirt, suspenders. Right arm slung over the side of the bed. His head is against the headboard, his neck bent at a severe angle. His mouth is a bloody, gaping hole. Copious amounts of blood and tissue and specks of bone spatter on the headboard. More blood on his shirt. A single tooth rests on his chest. There's a straw hat and a rifle on the floor next to the bed.

For a moment, my feet are cemented to the floor. I can't move. Can't speak. Can barely think. All sound leaches from the room. The light fades. My vision tunnels on the two bodies. It's as if the house has been submerged in water, and it's slowly sinking to the dark, cold depths of the ocean.

The crying of the baby snaps me back. I look to my left, see the crib. The infant inside is wriggling, little blanket tangled, tiny face red and wet with tears and spittle and a runny nose. He senses my gaze on his and falls silent. Mouth quivering, blue eyes watching, watching . . .

Giving myself a hard mental shake, I step away from the bed and go to the child. Something breaks loose inside of me at the sight of him. Hungry and dirty, frightened and alone. Dear God, the things he must have seen.

"Poor sweet baby." I hear the words, actually look around the room because it's as if they were spoken by someone else. There's no one there but me.

I go to the crib and scoop the child into my arms. He's wearing his little onesie. A T-shirt with Amish suspenders. I barely notice the smell of his dirty diaper as I lift him and pull him against me. I look down at his angel's face. I see tears in eyes the color of a summer sky and I want to cry for him.

"It's okay, little guy," I whisper. "I've got you now. I've got you. Everything's going to be okay."

Little William looks up at me and begins to wail.

It takes the Stark County sheriff's deputy six minutes to arrive on scene. While waiting, I called 911 again and let the sheriff's department know Mark and Ruth Petersheim are deceased. I let them know they need to notify a social worker from Children Services to care for William until a family member or foster parents can be located.

I'm standing next to my Explorer, holding William against me, when the first deputy rolls up. I show him my ID, tell him what happened, and he goes inside. Less than a minute later, he walks stiffly onto the porch, bends over, and throws up in the bushes. He goes back to his cruiser without speaking to me.

The next hours are a blur of questions from a flurry of law enforcement. I tell my story half a dozen times to several deputies. I spend most of that first hour trying to balance my need to know what happened to the Petersheims and caring for a hungry and dirty infant whose future has been forever altered.

I watch the Stark County Coroner's van arrive on scene. A fire truck with Wilmot Fire and Rescue. An ambulance from Stark County EMS. It takes an hour for the social worker from Children Services to arrive. A red Camry parks on the street two cars down from mine. A thirtysomething woman in a maroon suit and sensible heels gets out. She's watchful and harried, speaking into her phone as she starts toward me. I see her eyes taking in the scene. I know it the moment she spots me and William. Finishing her call, she starts toward us.

"Chief Burkholder?" She's walking fast, her heels clacking against the sidewalk. She's got brown hair and blue eyes, coiffed hair, and earrings the size of hen eggs dangling from her ears. "I'm Deb Cooke with Children Services."

"Hi." I cross to her and, shifting William, offer my hand.

We shake and then she reaches into her bag for her identification. I take my time, look at it closely. "Glad you're here," I tell her.

She looks at the baby sleeping in my arms, and her expression softens. "What a cutie."

"Yes, he is." I send a nod toward the house. "I think he's been alone for some time. I think he's hungry. Needs a clean diaper. His parents are inside, deceased."

Sighing, she shakes her head. "I've got a car seat in my car. No diaper or bottle, but I've been in contact with a foster family. They're a sweet couple, about fifteen minutes away."

"His parents were Amish," I tell her.

"We'll get it figured out, Chief. If we can place him with a family member, we will as quickly as possible." She pauses. "But for now . . ."

William's body is warm and soft against me as I carry him to the social worker's car. She strides ahead of me, opens the door to the backseat, prepares the car seat. When she turns to me, an awkward moment descends. She's waiting for me to hand off the baby. All I can think is that he's sleeping. I don't want to wake him. I don't like the idea of this poor little guy spending the night with strangers.

I think about Ruth and Mark Petersheim and I think, *How could you do this to your son?*

I press a kiss to the little boy's cheek and set him in her arms. "Take care of yourself, little William."

She lifts the child and, bending, places him in the car seat. I can tell by the way she buckles him in that she's competent and experienced. I can tell by the way she looks at him that she cares. None of those things make me feel any better about leaving him.

William wakes up and begins to cry.

"It won't be long now, sweetie," she says cheerfully.

Straightening, she looks at me, tilts her head, and digs into her bag for a card. "If you want to check on him later, give me a call."

"Thank you." After taking the card, I watch her get into the car and drive away. For a moment, I feel . . . bereft.

"Chief Burkholder?"

I turn to see a man striding toward me. He's about fifty years old with a receding hairline, wire-rimmed glasses, and the beginnings of a paunch. He's wearing khakis, a wrinkled white shirt, and a nicely coordinated tie. He's got cop written all over him.

"I'm Jim Hawkins with the investigations unit." He sticks out his hand and we shake. "Hell of a thing for you to walk into."

I nod. "What's your take?"

"Got all the hallmarks of a murder-suicide. Looks like there was somewhat of a struggle. He got her on the bed, shot her in the back. He got into the bed beside her, put the muzzle in his mouth and pulled the trigger with that rifle. Jesus Christ, I'm glad he didn't take that baby with him."

"Any idea how long they've been dead?" I ask.

"Coroner thinks eight to twelve hours. He'll be able to narrow it down once he gets the bodies to the morgue." His eyes narrow on mine. "Wilmot is a hike from Painters Mill. You know these people?"

I shake my head. "I talked to them a couple of times." I give him the condensed version of the Gingerich case.

"Heard about all that." But his mind is already poking into all those dark corners where cops' minds tend to go. "You think Mark Petersheim set that fire?"

"I think it's possible."

"If he did, it could be a precursor to all this." He motions toward the house and shrugs. "If he thought he was going to jail for what he did to Gingerich, he might've decided to just call it a day."

"Maybe."

Another look, sharp and assessing. "In light of your ongoing case, we'll take a real close look at this."

"I appreciate it." I hand him my card. "Let me know if I can help in any way."

"Will do."

* * *

It's fully dark by the time I arrive home. I'm thinking about little William as I let myself in through the back door. I can still smell his baby-powder scent on my clothes. I set my laptop case on the floor inside the kitchen doorway. I find Tomasetti standing at the counter, eating ice cream from the carton.

"You are so busted," I say as I cross to him.

He turns to me. "In that case I guess you're probably going to need your cuffs."

I pat the compartment on my belt and then go into his arms. "Sorry I'm late."

I'd called him from Wilmot and told him about the Petersheims. I tried to get my cop face on during the drive back to Painters Mill. I can tell by the way he's looking at me that I didn't quite succeed.

"You get that baby taken care of?" he asks.

"Handed him off to the social worker an hour ago."

"Tough break for the kid." He kisses the top of my head.

Over rum raisin, we discuss how the day's developments might affect the Gingerich case. "I'll get with Stark County and have them send Petersheim's fingerprints," he says. "We'll do a comp and see if they match anything we got from the Gingerich scene." His brows go together. "Petersheim had a rifle?"

My mind's eye flashes back to the rifle lying on the bedroom floor. Mark Petersheim's arm slung over the side of the bed. I'd been so shocked by the sight of the bodies, I didn't note the details of the long gun. But

I know where Tomasetti is going with this, and I realize I should have thought of it, too.

"You think he's the one who shot at me?" I ask.

"Gingerich raped his wife. Got her pregnant. She didn't tell Petersheim. She married him, and passed the baby off as his." He shrugs. "If he didn't want that coming to light . . ." His voice trails. "Sad as that is, it's the kind of scenario that fits."

"How long will the latent comps take?"

"Twenty-four hours. Thirty-six max. We'll get Petersheim's prints right away. We'll compare the latents picked up off the cartridges. Should be a pretty quick process."

I think about that a moment, trying to get a handle on what isn't settling in my gut. "I never figured Petersheim for killing Gingerich."

His eyes find mine. "The person who killed Gingerich may not be the person who took a shot at you last night."

I toss him a frown. "I thought of that."

"Who else are you looking at?"

"Elam Schlabach."

"The dead girl's boyfriend."

I nod. "And Milo Hershberger. The best friend."

"I don't have to tell you to keep those eyes in the back of your head open, do I?"

"Don't worry. I'm going to be looking over my shoulder for a long time."

I'm standing in the middle of a narrow and deserted road I don't recognize. It's nighttime. Somewhere in the distance, I hear a baby crying. Fog billows all around, and I get the sense that there's something unseen nearby, but I don't know what.

When I look down, I see blood on the asphalt. It's fresh. The night air is cold. Steam rises from the puddle and somehow I know this is the place where Ruth Petersheim was dragged from the car and raped.

God doesn't let things like that happen to good girls.

I glance over my shoulder to see a hideous version of Daniel Gingerich. Not the happy-go-lucky young man in the photos, but the monstrous thing lying on the gurney at the morgue. Black flesh. Hands burned off, bones protruding from the stumps. His arms are bent at the wrists and elbows into that terrible pugilistic posture. Though he's standing, his legs are severely bent at the knee.

"Who did that to you?" I ask.

Cloudy white eyes stare at me from within a charred face. The skin has burned away from his mouth and I can see his teeth.

"You did." He begins to chant. "You did. You did . . ."

"Kate. *Kate.*"

I open my eyes to see Tomasetti's face. Mussed hair. Concern sharp in his expression. Looking at me as if he isn't sure who I am.

I'm lying on the sofa in our living room. He's on his knees, leaning over me, hand on my shoulder, pressing me down. The dream lingers; the stench of burned flesh still in my nostrils, the sound of little William's screams ringing.

"I'm sorry." I try to sit up but he holds me down.

"It's okay," he says quickly. "Just . . . lie still a moment. Catch your breath."

I relax back into the cushions, but I'm shaking, my skin slicked with sweat. I know he can feel all of those things. I don't know why it embarrasses me. Why it makes me feel vulnerable in a way I detest.

"What are you doing out here on the sofa?" He growls the words—an attempt to divert my attention from the nightmare—and I appreciate it more than I can express.

"Arm was hurting. I couldn't sleep." I offer up a reproachful look. "Didn't want to wake you."

"Uh-huh." He's not buying it. I see him looking at the countless pages of notes and reports and photographs spread out on the coffee table. "Evidently, you do some of your best detecting after hours."

"I guess I'm found out." Setting my hand over his, I push myself to a sitting position. I'm wearing panties and one of his Cleveland Division of Police T-shirts. I catch him stealing a look at my bare legs and it makes me smile. "This is getting old, huh?"

"Nothing about you will ever get old."

I look away, a thought flashing that he deserves better than this, but I shove it away. "I didn't mean to wake you." I look around; the windows are still dark. "What time is it?"

"About five, I think."

I nod, look away.

He notices, tilts his head to snag my gaze: When I don't look at him, he reaches out, sets his hand beneath my chin, draws my face toward him. "What's this all about, Kate?"

"You mean the dream? Or the fact that I'm . . ." I don't know how to finish the sentence, so I let the words trail.

In typical Tomasetti fashion, he waits.

"All those parallels." I whisper the words, feeling stripped bare by them. "I don't like what's in my head. I don't want the past to get in the way."

"As much as we cops like to deny it, some of the cases we work *are* about us. Not in the way you think, but . . . It's about our experiences, good and bad, and everything we bring to the table."

"I guess I've brought a lot to the table with this case."

He sighs, letting me know in no uncertain terms that he's annoyed. "So use it," he says. "Use what you know. Put it to work. Use your insights. Maybe it's time you started thinking about this case with your whole brain and not just the part that fits your cop's sensibilities."

"Sometimes I'm afraid to look that deep," I say.

"That past can't hurt you now. If it's got something to tell you, listen to it."

"Tomasetti, the truth about what happened to me never came out. I was never punished for it."

"You killed a man in self-defense," he growls.

"Did I?"

His eyes narrow on mine.

"I never told you. Because I was ashamed. Because I hated myself. Tomasetti, I *wanted* his attention that summer. I was stupid and naive and—"

"Cut it out. You had no way of knowing what he was. You were a fourteen-year-old kid, for God's sake. You were Amish. Your parents didn't teach you about that kind of shit."

He's right, but somehow it doesn't make any of this any easier. "I thought I'd dealt with all of this. I thought I'd moved past it. But this case . . ." I shrug.

"Some things never go away, Kate. You know that. The key is learning to live with it in a way that doesn't tear you apart. If you're smart—and I know you are— you'll use it to your advantage."

He gives the words a moment to penetrate. "I know it's painful. But you have a unique perspective. You can think about this case like a cop. But you can also think about it from a victim's perspective. Use that. It'll make you a better cop."

"Or maybe my perspective is skewed."

"I don't buy that. You know right from wrong."

"And all those gray areas in between."

"You're going to have to explain that."

I close my eyes. "Is a homicide ever justified?" The words tumble around in my mind, the wrongness of them, that I'd had the audacity to say them aloud.

"Self-defense is justified," he says. "You have the right to protect yourself. You have the right to protect your family. Your children."

Our gazes lock. We stare at each other, unspoken words passing between us.

"There are a lot of motivations tangled up in this case," I say. "A lot of emotion. Rage. Shame. A need for revenge. Someone knew what Daniel Gingerich was. They knew he wouldn't stop so they took it upon themselves to stop him. Where does that fall?"

"Daniel Gingerich wasn't killed in self-defense," he says. "He wasn't killed by someone trying to protect themselves or their family. His murder was premeditated. It required forethought. Planning. Execution. Black and white."

He's got me thinking about the case in a slightly different light and I feel myself begin to calm down. The darkness and uncertainty that's been dogging me since the start loosens its grip.

Before I realize I'm going to move, I raise my hand and set it against his face. "Not bad for a BCI guy."

"Every now and then I get it right."

Nodding, I let my hand fall away from his face and take his hand in mine. "What time do you have to be at work?"

"Heading to the shower now."

"Want some company?"

CHAPTER 19

Aside from a loose-hog incident out at the Stutz farm in which Skid and I spent two hours chasing a three-hundred-pound boar down Dogleg Road, it's been an uneventful morning. I finished my report on the Petersheims. When I spoke with the chief deputy, he told me all indications pointed to a clear-cut case of murder-suicide. I also called the social worker to check on little William and learned he will be placed with family members later today. I'm a big fan of good news, especially in the face of tragedy.

Yesterday's events placed Mark Petersheim squarely at the top of my suspect list in the murder of Daniel Gingerich. If his prints or his wife's match the latents found on the mason jar, I'll close the case. Mark Petersheim had motive. He had means and opportunity. Chances are, he's also the person who tried to kill me. He owned a rifle, which was sent to the lab; he also drove a pickup truck. He knew he would be caught; he knew his darkest secrets would come pouring out, so he murdered his young wife and ended it.

So why aren't I convinced he's my killer?

"Because I don't think he did it," I whisper, glad there's no one around to hear me talking to myself.

I spent the last hour filling a legal pad with theories and motives and connections. So far none of it has panned out. As I page through the Gingerich file for the hundredth time, I can't help but recall the statistics Tomasetti laid out at the start of the case. *In the state of Ohio only about twenty-six percent of arson cases result in an arrest. . . .* The numbers are daunting and make for a frustrating and wearisome undertaking— with a prospective outcome that's worse than bleak.

I stare down at the autopsy photos of Daniel Gingerich, the blackened remains of what had once been an eighteen-year-old Amish boy with his own set of secrets. "Did Mark Petersheim do that to you?" I whisper.

"Chief?"

I look up to see Lois standing in the doorway of my office. "Everyone's here," she tells me.

"Thanks." I close the file, shift gears.

Just this morning the mayor came through, authorizing me to hire an additional patrol officer. I didn't waste any time; I called Mona into my office and promoted her on the spot. It's the first time I've seen her speechless. The first time I've seen her cry.

"You got the card?" I ask.

Lois presents a yellow envelope containing the congratulations card all of us signed for Mona. I take it out and scribble my name.

"I've never seen her this nervous," Lois says under her breath.

"In that case," I say as I rise, "let's not keep her waiting." Grabbing my notebook, I follow her to our meeting room.

One of the things I love most about my job as chief is the opportunity to work with such a great group of officers. In the years I've been here in Painters Mill, they've become my surrogate family when my own wouldn't speak to me. This small police department is the one place that has nothing to do with my being Amish or English. It's the place where I am a cop, the one place where I'm comfortable, and the one place I fit in without question.

I step into the meeting room to find my team already assembled. Glock sits at the head of the table, copying something from a notepad onto a form. Pickles sits across from him, talking to Glock, two cups of coffee from LaDonna's Diner in front of him. Skid is sprawled in a chair to my right, thumbing something into his phone. T.J. is in the midst of telling a tall tale to my second-shift dispatcher, Jodie, who's buying into every word and is unabashedly impressed. She has a lot to learn about cops.

I catch Lois's eye as I head toward the half podium. "Where's Mona?" I whisper.

"Restroom." She makes an exaggerated worried face. "Fourth time in twenty minutes."

I take my place behind the podium, clear my throat. "Skid, did you tell Stutz to get that fence repaired?"

"I told him next time we have to chase one of his stinkin' hogs, I'm going to cite him."

I give a thumbs-up. "Pickles, I understand a couple of kids were smoking cigarettes on school property yesterday afternoon."

"Willie Steele's boy, Chief. He's eleven and has the IQ of a two-year-old."

"Nut doesn't fall too far from the tree," Glock murmurs.

That conjures a round of laughter. I'm obliged to ignore it. "The parents called the mayor and complained," I tell him. "Said you were too rough on him."

"I confiscated the smokes, Chief. Kid wasn't happy about it."

"I'll let Auggie know. Keep up the good work."

Movement at the door draws my attention. I glance up to see Mona enter. Something goes soft in my chest at the sight of her. Navy jacket. Pale pink blouse. Pencil skirt that falls below her knees. I've seen her in everything from miniskirts to knee boots to burgundy-streaked hair. And I'm reminded that this is probably one of the most important days of her professional life.

"Glad you could join us," I say to her, using the same tone I'd use for Skid or Glock if they were late for a meeting.

"Sorry, Chief."

I pick up my mug and use my pen to ding it bell style. "As most of you know, our department is understaffed and has been for quite some time. I'm pleased to report Mayor Brock has increased our budget and as of this morning Mona Kurtz is Painters Mill's first female officer."

Some of the guys let fly with comments, so I raise my voice and speak over them. "Mona brings with her an associate's degree in criminal justice, over three years of dispatch experience, knowledge of our ten-code system, the Ohio Revised Code, and of course familiarity with Painters Mill."

Everyone in the room had already known about the promotion; they signed the card for her, after all. Still, the official announcement is a formality I felt was important.

"Mona will continue in her position as dispatcher until I can hire a replacement. During that time, I'll be asking her to ride with each of you on occasion."

I leave the podium and stride toward Mona, my hand extended. "Congratulations, Officer Kurtz."

We shake and I can't help but notice how incredibly happy she looks, despite the sheen of tears. "Thanks, Chief," she whispers, and then pulls me into an embrace.

Next to her, Skid rises and high-fives her. "Hell yeah!"

"About damn time," Pickles mutters.

From the door, Jodie squeals. "Oh my God! I'm so happy for you!" Joining hands, she and Lois dance in a circle.

Glock smacks Mona on the back before wrapping her in a bear hug. "Welcome aboard, rookie."

T.J. snaps a couple of photos with his phone and crosses to her. "I guess this means I'm off graveyard shift."

I pause at the doorway and watch the scene, taking it in, putting it to memory, knowing it's one of those moments that will stay with me.

* * *

It's nearly five P.M. when I get the call from Tomasetti. "What are you up to, Chief?"

"Chasing shadows mostly. How about you?"

"Chasing chickens."

I laugh, unduly pleased by the sound of his voice.

"The lab supervisor of the latent print unit just called. The latent on the casing left at the scene the night you were shot belongs to Mark Petersheim. He was your shooter."

I let out a breath. I hadn't realized until this moment how heavily the not knowing had been weighing on my shoulders. "Do his prints match the latent lifted off the key found at the Gingerich scene?"

"It's not a match," he tells me. "We've fingerprinted everyone in the Gingerich family. Those comps should be done soon."

"Okay."

"Interestingly, the latent on the mason jar found at Chris Martino's house doesn't belong to Petersheim either."

"So my arsonist is still out there."

"This is where the plot thickens. The print found on the key retrieved from the Gingerich scene *matches* the print found on the mason jar."

"So whoever handled the key at the Gingerich farm also handled the mason jars found in Martino's garage." The information swirls in my head, a leaf caught in an eddy. "What about the tire tread imprint?" I ask, refer-ring to the one taken the night of the shooting.

"Still working on the comp. Probably going to match

the tires on Petersheim's truck." He sighs. "Wish I had better news. I know you were hoping to close the case."

"At least the shooter was identified."

"One threat down." He pauses. "You coming home anytime soon?"

"I thought I might talk to Elam Schlabach before I call it a day."

"The Amish boyfriend of the girl who killed herself."

I give him my impressions of Schlabach. "He's twenty-three years old and newly married with a baby on the way. And yet the only emotion I got out of him when I talked to him is rage."

"Give me a call if you need anything."

"Bet on it."

It's nearly five P.M. when I swing by Buckeye Woodworks and Cabinetry on Fourth Street only to be told that Elam Schlabach has already left for the day. I drive out to his home on Dogleg Road. His wife tells me he's working late.

I stand in the driveway, my hands on my hips, and wonder. "Where the hell are you?"

In a small town like Painters Mill, that question isn't always difficult to answer, especially when there's a young male and a certain level of discontent involved. There are three drinking establishments in the area. The Brass Rail is too rowdy and too far away for Schlabach to reach via buggy. McNarie's is too . . . bikerish. That leaves Miller's Tavern. It's a dark, quiet drinking establishment that favors pop music over chain-saw rock and German beer over eighty-proof rotgut. There's an old-fashioned jukebox next to the bar, a decent menu replete with sliders and stuffed jalapeños, and ice cream soft-serve for the kids. Most of the patrons are local business owners and shopkeepers who stop in after hours for a beer or cocktail before calling it a day. Just the kind of place a young Amish man might frequent when he doesn't want to go home.

Back in the Explorer, I head toward town.

There are no buggies parked in front of Miller's Tavern, so I idle around to the alley at the rear. Sure enough, there's a nice-looking bay gelding hitched to a lone buggy, snoozing. I park next to it, take a moment to stroke the horse, and then enter the bar via the back door.

I take a narrow, dimly lit hall past the bathroom and janitor closet. I enter the main room to the Fixx blaring out "One Thing Leads to Another." Elam Schlabach sits in a booth, a mug of beer in front of him, watching me. A red plastic basket with the remnants of a burger and fries sits in the center of the table, next to an empty shot glass.

I hold his gaze as I make my way over to him.

"You come in through the back door, too, huh?" he says.

"Once or twice. Comes in handy."

"Especially when you're Amish."

"And the walls have eyes." I reach the booth. "Mind if I join you?"

"Do I have a choice?"

"Nope." I slide onto the seat opposite him.

For the span of a full minute, neither of us speaks. Schlabach appears to be perfectly at ease and fiddles with the paper lining the red basket. Fingers the condensation on the beer mug. Taps his fingers to the music against the tabletop.

He lifts his beer, takes a long pull. "So is this about Danny Gingerich or what?"

I pull out the photo of the woman who left the note on the police station door and set it on the table between us. "Do you recognize this woman?"

He sets down his beer, leans forward, takes a long look. "Not a very good picture." His eyes narrow. "She's Amish."

Leaning back in the booth, I give him a long, assessing look. "Did you have anything to do with the barn fire that killed Daniel Gingerich?"

"No. That's not to say I didn't think about it. I did. Fantasized about it. If anyone deserved it, that son of a bitch did. Hate to disappoint you, but I never mustered the grit."

"I know what he was," I say.

I can tell by the way he looks at me that he doesn't believe me. "I doubt it."

I hold his gaze. "I know what he did to Emma. And others."

"Look, Chief Burkholder, I know you think I killed Danny. But if you know what he was—that his soul belonged to the devil—then you've probably realized I'm not the only one who isn't exactly mourning his death."

"Do you have someone in mind?"

"Even if I did, I wouldn't say." He looks away, shrugs. "Far as I'm concerned, he did the world a favor."

The barmaid interrupts. I order coffee. Schlabach orders a shot of whiskey. I think about hassling him about drinking and driving, but he's talking so I let it go.

"How many other women did he rape?" I ask.

He shrugs. "I heard he did Mark Petersheim's wife." His expression distorts into something acerbic. "Heard what happened to him, too, by the way. They were a nice couple. Gingerich ruined the lives of a lot of good people."

"Yes, he did."

The barmaid returns with my coffee and a shot glass of amber liquid. I lay a ten-dollar bill in her hand. When she's gone, I ask, "What did you hear about Ruth Petersheim?"

"Just rumor is all." His mouth twists as if he's bitten into something bitter. "I guess rape and sodomy aren't exactly the kinds of things the Amish like to talk about though, are they?"

He's trying to shock me, or provoke me. When it doesn't work, he looks away, and I get the impression he's not sure how to react or what to do with all that rage.

The Fixx gives way to an old Badfinger tune. Schlabach throws back the whiskey, sets the glass on the tabletop with a little too much force.

"Who else had reason to want Gingerich dead?" I ask.

"Let me count the ways."

My temper spikes. This time I don't bother to curb it. I'm tired of his vague statements and riddles and bad attitude. "Look, if you want to play hardball, I will accommodate you, and I will one-up you. We can make this official and I can make it difficult. Do you get me?"

He ducks his head, looks away. "I got it," he mutters.

"Who else did Daniel Gingerich hurt?" I ask.

A full minute passes without an answer. I'm thinking about making good on my threat, hauling his ass down to the station if only for show, when he finally responds.

"I heard he done one of them other girls Emma used to hang with," he tells me. "The one worked with her at that shop in Charm."

I go still, my heart giving a single hard kick. All the while Milo Hershberger's words float through my mind. . . . *He used to go up to that little shop in Charm all the time just to see those girls. Had his eye on all of them . . .*

Milo hadn't given me a name. Is it possible Daniel had preyed upon one of the others, in addition to Emma Miller? Why didn't they tell me? But the question rings false, because I know. *I know.*

"I need a name," I say.

"I don't know." He shakes his head. "Look, if you want to know about Danny's escapades, I suggest you talk to Milo Hershberger. They were best friends. If Gingerich bragged about all that Amish pussy he was getting, I suspect Milo would be the moron he'd brag to."

"Are you and Milo friends?"

His laugh is bitter. "Not even close."

He looks away and for the first time I see a chink in his armor. A glimpse of the man he must have been before the woman he loved committed suicide. Before loss and bitterness turned him into something angry and lost, something he can't quite get a handle on.

"So are you going to arrest me or what?" he asks.

"You'll be the first to know." I pluck my card from a compartment on my belt as I rise and hold it out for him. "If you think of anything else, call me. And don't even think about leaving town."

He takes the card without looking at it and tosses it onto the tabletop.

I'm tempted to drive back to Charm tonight, but it's too late. The shop has been closed for hours. My injured forearm is making itself known in a big way. Besides, getting information out of any of those girls about something so devastating and personal is going to take forethought and finesse—something I don't think I can manage at the moment. Better to start fresh in the morning.

Dusk has fallen by the time I pull into the long lane of the farm where my sister and her husband live. Despite my best intentions, I missed her birthday. I've been carrying around the gift-wrapped candles and teas I bought for her at The Mercantile for a couple of days now.

I'm trying to remember the last time I saw her as I park adjacent to the chicken coop at the rear of the house. It's been a while. *Too long,* my conscience murmurs. I love my sister; I miss her, and I think of her often. Spending time with her shouldn't be so damn hard, but it is.

I look out across the driveway as I take the sidewalk to the back door. The barn door is open and I see her husband, William, inside grooming one of their Standardbreds. He's watching me, so I raise my hand in greeting. He waves back but the gesture is halfhearted. My brother-in-law doesn't approve of my leaving the fold; he doesn't approve of my lifestyle or the fact that I'm living in sin with Tomasetti. Unlike my sister, he makes no bones about letting me know.

The door opens. "Katie! What a nice surprise. Come in!"

Sarah is two years older than me. Blond and pretty with the kind of sweet smile I never quite mastered. She's wearing a light blue dress with a white apron and *kapp*. Sneakers. Ever-present dishcloth clutched in work-chapped hands.

Her eyes flick past me and I know she's looking for Tomasetti. "It's just me," I tell her.

"Well, he doesn't know what he's missing. I've got date pudding and mint tea. *Kumma inseid.*" Come inside.

Turning, she leads me into a big plain kitchen that smells of something toothsome and delicious. My little niece, Hannah, who has somehow grown into a toddler, is standing in the doorway, clutching an obese cat, watching me.

"Hi, Hannah," I say. "That's a pretty little *bussli* you've got there."

The little girl grins and hefts the cat. "Sammy!" she proclaims.

"*Er fett e faul.*" He's fat and lazy. My sister sends her child a sideways glance. "Say hello to Aunt Katie, Hannah."

The little girl obeys, but her expression lets me know in no uncertain terms that I'm a stranger to her, a fact that hurts more than I want it to.

"I'm just cooking up some of the *hembeer* for jam," Sarah says breezily, referring to raspberries. "*Schaptzsupp* for tomorrow." She goes to the stove, gives a pot a stir and then turns off the heat. "I heard about what happened to you. My goodness, are you okay?"

"I'm fine." I glance down at the bandage and shrug. "Just . . . at the wrong place at the wrong time."

Setting down the spoon, she looks at the bandage and shakes her head. "I have a boring life compared to yours."

"Boring is underrated." I take a chair at the table.

Smiling, she sits across from me. "I'm turning into a *bottelhinkel.*" It's the *Deitsh* word for a worn-out old hen that's ready for the stewpot. Our *mamm* used to say it (usually in reference to herself) and the memory takes me back to a time when my relationship with my sister was a lot simpler.

"Happy birthday." I set the bag containing the gifts on the table and slide it toward her. "Sorry it's late."

Eyeing me, she rattles the bag. "I'm just glad you're here. You don't come over enough, you know."

She delivers the admonition in her usual gentle way, which somehow makes the sting all the more powerful.

"I got tied up in the Gingerich thing," I tell her. "Still trying to figure things out."

"You work too much," she chides. "And you're always doing things that are too dangerous for a woman."

"Or a man."

She snorts. "That's my Katie. Taking on the world all by herself."

I don't argue. I came here to spend a few minutes with my sister. Give her the birthday gift. Remind my sweet little niece she has an aunt. Try to hang on to something precious before it slips away. Despite all the years that have passed and everything that's happened, there's still a small part of me that craves the approval of my family. Maybe even the Amish community as a whole.

"I have news." She sets her hand protectively over her abdomen. I know what she's going to say before she utters the words. "I'm *ime familye weg*."

Emotion surges and then I'm out of the chair, bending to her, hugging her close. "You just one-upped my birthday present."

She chuckles. "It's such a blessing. I just hope . . ."

I don't let her finish. Before my niece was born, Sarah lost several pregnancies. It took a heavy toll on her and William. She's wanted a big family since she was a little girl. "I'm sure everything will be fine."

For an instant, I think about telling her that Tomasetti and I have set a date for our wedding, but the timing doesn't seem right. This is her moment. I'll fill her in next time I see her.

I motion toward the gift. "It's not going to open it-self."

Grinning, she digs in, tearing the paper with the rel-ish of a kid at Christmas. I know it's for my benefit, to put me at ease, and we both enjoy the moment.

"Something smells heavenly." She says the words as she reaches inside and the tissue paper falls away. "Oh! A candle! From The Mercantile! Katie, that's my favor-ite store these days. *Danki*!"

"It's bergamot and sweet rosemary."

"They make the best candles."

"Best everything." I glance at the gift bag. "There's more."

"Well, my goodness, Katie." She digs around the bot-tom of the bag with gusto, pulls out the soaps and tin of tea. "Oh and just look at that pretty tin! The little soaps are nice. They smell almost as good as that candle." My sister hugs them to her. "Did those sweet Amish girls make all of this?"

"They made the candles. I think the owner made the soap."

"Edna," she says.

"You know them?"

"William helped out with the plumbing right before they opened the store. Those girls were the sweetest things. Made his lunch every day and wouldn't let him pay a penny." She shakes her head. "I was just there last week. Had all the keys made for the new gates."

"Keys?"

"*Ja*. Someone opened the gate in that back pasture

last week. Let all of our goats out. One of the ewes was hit by a car and killed. William says it was probably teenagers, but it gave us a start. We're keeping all the gates locked now. William wanted extra keys so I had duplicates made."

"You had keys made at The Mercantile?"

"Edna made them." Smiling conspiratorially, she leans close. "William thinks I'm quite the dutiful wife. Little did he know the only reason I went there was for the shopping."

CHAPTER 20

It's eight A.M. and I've been sitting in the parking lot of
The Mercantile for half an hour, watching the construction crew work on the old round barn, thinking about
things I shouldn't be thinking about. I didn't sleep much
last night. My conversation with Elam Schlabach kept
running through my head.

*I heard he done one of them other girls Emma used
to hang with. . . .*

Is it possible? I've spoken with the three girls on several occasions and not once did they give me any indication that something had happened.

*I guess rape and sodomy aren't exactly the kinds of
things the Amish like to talk about though, are they?*

I'm so caught up in my thoughts I don't spot the
buggy until it stops outside the big antique door. I watch
Ina Yoder and Viola Stutzman climb down. Both girls
are animated and chatting with the driver as they gather
their things—several brown paper bags and two large
trays heaped with what looks like individually wrapped
pastries. Viola turns and waves to the driver as the buggy

drives away. Ina pulls a wad of keys from her pocket and starts toward the door.

I reach them as Ina unlocks the door. *"Guder mariye."*

Viola startles upon hearing my voice. "Oh, Chief Burkholder! Didn't hear you drive up. *Guder mariye* to you, too."

Ina pushes open the door and ushers us inside. "We're not quite open yet, but you're welcome to coffee while we get the register up and running."

"I appreciate that."

The aromas of jasmine and peppermint and fresh-brewed coffee greet me as we clamber inside. Ina locks the door behind us.

"Is Neva here yet?" I ask.

"She always gets here early to make coffee," Viola tells me.

"She drives a car, so the drive doesn't take her quite as long," Ina says with a hint of petulance.

"I heard that."

The three of us look ahead to see Neva ·standing next to the customer service counter, hands on her hips, staring at us. She's wearing a dusty pink dress with her Beachy *kapp* and a pair of Keds that are a little too stylish for most Amish. She makes eye contact with me. "Is everything all right, Chief Burkholder?"

"Everything's fine," I tell her. "I just need to speak with the three of you if you can spare a few minutes."

Ina looks at me and nods. "We don't open until nine, so we have some time."

"Coffee's made," Neva says. "Would you like to sit?"

Viola hefts the tray of pastries. "We could sample these cranberry-orange scones."

"Sampling pastries is not a hardship," Ina says. "I'm starved."

Neva motions toward the café. "As long as we don't make a mess."

"Famous last words," Ina mutters.

A few minutes later, the four of us are seated in the café. It's a small area with a smattering of tables, an antique sofa table that's been transformed into a coffee station, and a buffet where Viola has arranged scones on paper doilies.

I pull the key from the plastic bag and slide it over to the center of the table. "Can any of you tell me if this duplicate key was made here at The Mercantile?"

The three girls stare at the key.

"I don't know if there's any way to tell." Neva starts to reach for the key, but hesitates. "Can I look?"

"Sure."

She picks it up, turns it over in her hand, and glances at Ina. "Is this one of ours?"

Ina shakes her head. "I don't even know how to run the machine."

Viola leans close for a better look. "I told Mrs. Lambright I want to learn how to make the keys. She promised to show me, but she hasn't yet."

"Probably need to check with Mamm on that," Neva tells me.

"I will." I take the key and drop it into the bag.

I look from face to face. "You heard about Ruth Petersheim?" I ask.

Neva drops her gaze to the tabletop and nods. The other two don't meet my gaze.

"We heard," Ina mumbles.

"Mrs. Fisher came in late yesterday and told Mamm," Neva says. "Poor Ruthie."

"I heard little William is going to live with his *grossmudder*," Viola says, referring to the baby's grandmother.

"*Ruth's* grossmudder," Neva says.

Ina waits a beat and then whispers, "Word is Mark may not have been the baby's father."

"If not Mark, then who?" I ask.

"That's just cruel gossip if you ask me," Viola snaps. "Especially with both of them being gone."

"Well, people are talking," Neva points out.

Viola's gaze finds mine. "Do you think what happened to them has something to do with Daniel Gingerich?" Her voice has dropped to a whisper.

"I do." I take a sip of coffee, watching, aware of a new tension zinging among us. "I know Daniel used to come in here on occasion."

Neva shoots me a look over the rim of her cup. "Lots of people come in here."

I don't respond, don't even look at her. "Did it cross your minds that maybe that information was important?"

"I think he only came in a few times," Neva says dismissively.

Viola slurps hot chocolate. "It was a long time ago."

They're downplaying it. I can't tell if they're covering for each other or if they simply don't want to discuss it.

The girls begin to chatter among themselves, so I

smack my hand down on the tabletop hard enough to get their attention. "Stop lying to me."

Startled looks are exchanged. Neva sets down her cup. Ina looks away. Viola pretends her chair isn't situated just right and scoots it closer to the table.

"I'm not the enemy here," I say softly.

"We know that," Neva says.

"I just need information," I say. "The truth."

"We haven't lied to you," Ina says.

"If I hadn't pushed, you wouldn't have told me about Emma," I say. "You didn't tell me that Daniel used to come in here, bothering the three of you."

"He didn't," Neva blurts.

I give her a look that lets her know in no uncertain terms I'm not happy with the answers I'm getting. "I think he did a lot more than bother you." I look from girl to girl. "What else haven't you told me?"

"I think he came here to see Emma," Ina says after a moment. "That's all."

"Who else did he come here to see?"

I watch them closely, their body language, facial expressions. Of the three, Neva looks the most apprehensive. I turn my full attention to her. "Neva?"

She blinks rapidly, a prey animal being approached by a predator. "No one."

"Are you sure about that?" I ask.

"Why are you being so pushy?" Ina snaps.

"Because I think you know more than you're telling me," I snap back.

Neva jumps into the fray. "You don't know us. You don't know anything about us."

"I know more than you think," I tell her.

"Like what?" she shoots back, defiant.

"I know what it's like to keep secrets," I say quietly. "I know what it's like to make a bad decision." I look from girl to girl. "I know that sometimes we're not who we think we are. We're not who we want to be. We're not the person others see when they look at us."

The three young women stare at me, eyes wide, expressions taken aback and wary.

I don't know if I'm getting through to them. If I'm helping or hindering my quest for information.

"Daniel came into The Mercantile a few times," Neva says quietly. "He'd always pretend that he was looking for something, some merchandise he seemed to need help with, but it wasn't about the merchandise. It was about us." She trades looks with the other girls. "All of us."

"Thank you," I say.

I'm debating the wisdom of pushing for more when the tinkle of keys draws my attention. I glance over to see Edna Lambright approach the café. I hadn't heard her come in. She's carrying a quilted tote bag on her shoulder. Two pies stacked one on top of the other in her hands.

"Looks like you girls are having a productive morning." She reaches the railing. Narrowed eyes flick from Neva to me and back to Neva. She holds out the two pies. "These custards need to be sliced, put on plates, and wrapped."

Neva rises so quickly, her chair screeches across the floor. I'm in the process of getting to my feet when she rushes to her mother and takes the pies. "Put them in the cooler?" she asks.

"*Ja.*"

"Thank you for the coffee," I say to the girls.

Chairs clatter as the girls rise. Quickly, they push in their chairs and scatter.

Viola slants a look my way as she heads toward the rear of the store. "You're welcome," she mutters.

And then they're gone.

Edna Lambright is standing at the railing, taking it all in, watching me. "What brings you here this morning?" she asks.

"I'm trying to find out where this duplicate key was made." I pull the key from the bag as I leave the café area. "Any chance it was made here at The Mercantile?"

She lifts the reading glasses on the lanyard around her neck and shoves them onto her nose. "Looks brand-new," she says as she squints at the key. "It's possible we made it here, but there's really no way to tell for sure." She lowers the key. "Is that what you were talking to the girls about?"

I take my time answering. "I was told Daniel Gingerich used to come in here."

"Lots of people come in here." She looks down her nose at me. "All kinds of boys skulking around to get a look at those girls. They don't think too much about it."

I stare at her, wondering how much she knows about Emma Miller. "Are you sure?"

"I'm quite sure." Her eyes latch onto mine. "We're close, you know. All of us. My daughter tells me everything. Everything." She hands me the key. "Sorry we couldn't be more help."

I drop the key into the bag.

Cocking her head, she looks at me over the top of her glasses. "This have something to do with the fire?"

"Yes, it does."

"How does that key play into all that?"

"I'm not sure, but I think I'm going to get it figured out soon." I stuff the bag into my pocket. "Thanks again for the coffee."

The police station is quiet on a weeknight at seven P.M. Skid left for patrol a couple hours ago and everyone except Jodie and me has gone home for the day. I'm sitting at my desk, photos and reports and notes from the Gingerich file spread out in front of me like some macabre collage.

The thing that bothers me most about the case—aside from my victim being a violent sexual predator—is that it wasn't some panicked response to danger or threat or physical harm, but a premeditated act of homicide. Whoever killed Gingerich conceived the idea. They thought it through. Prepared for it. Planned the timeline. Came up with contingency plans. And then they cold-bloodedly carried out an agonizing and gruesome execution.

It's still relatively early in the game, but the thought of this heinous crime going unsolved grates on my cop's sensibilities. All I can do at this point is keep plugging away at it in the hope that something will break.

I'm in the process of sliding my laptop into its case when my cell phone vibrates against my desk blotter. Expecting Tomasetti because I'm late—again—I snatch it up. "Hey."

"Chief Burkholder? It's Edna Lambright." Her tone

is frantic and rushed, the words coming too fast. "It's Neva. She's . . . gone. I can't find her. She left a . . . note."

"She's missing?"

"Yes. She was . . . upset . . . all afternoon. She was quiet. Too quiet. Please. There's something wrong." Her voice is breathless, every syllable tumbling out in disarray.

"How long has she been missing?" I ask.

"I haven't seen her since five or so. I found the note half an hour ago."

"What does the note say?"

A brief hesitation and then: "It says she doesn't want to be on this earth anymore." She makes a sound, the squeak of some small animal with its leg caught in a trap. "I'm afraid she's going to hurt herself."

"Have you searched for her?"

"Isaac checked the barn. He walked our whole property. I looked in the house, even the attic and root cellar. She's not here."

"Is there some place she might've gone? A friend's maybe?"

"She's close with Ina Yoder, of course. Little Viola. I'm in the car, on my way to the Yoders' now."

"Is there any place else you can think of that she might've gone?"

"Isaac is on his way to the Stutzman place. If I don't find her at the Yoders' . . . I don't know. She might've gone to the shop." She makes a strangled sound. "I'm scared, Chief Burkholder. She's never done anything like this before. Neva is a . . . sensible girl. A *good* girl."

"Do you know what she's upset about?" I ask.

"I don't know. She barely said a word all day."

I pause, wondering if it has anything to do with my visit earlier, and ask, "Edna, do you think Neva is suicidal?"

I hear a quick intake of breath on the other end and then a sob. "I don't know. I just . . . the note scared me. Why would she write something like that?"

"Do the Yoders have a phone?"

"They're not Beachy, so no. I'm just a few minutes from their farm."

"How long will it take Isaac to reach the Stutzmans' place?"

"Fifteen minutes in the buggy."

"I'll send one of my officers over there now, save some time."

"Thank you. I'm so upset I can't even think straight."

"Does Neva have a car, Edna? Or is she on foot?"

"She has that old car Isaac gave her. I just can't see her driving on a night like this. Raining cats and dogs . . ." A sob cuts her words short. "I just want to find her. Make sure she's okay."

"What's the make and model of the car?"

"It's white. A Ford Taurus. Old. Two thousand five, I think."

I'm not inordinately alarmed about Neva. Yet. She hasn't been missing long—just a couple of hours. She isn't a minor. But the note is worrisome.

. . . she doesn't want to be on this earth anymore . . .

"Chief Burkholder, would you mind driving over to The Mercantile to see if she's there?"

"I can be there in fifteen minutes."

"Oh, thank you. I'll meet you there as soon as I talk to the Yoders. They're only ten minutes from the shop."

"Don't worry. We'll find her."

I hang up and call Skid with a quick summary of the situation. "She's eighteen years old and might be on her way to the Yoder farm out on County Road Twenty-Four."

"I know the place," he says. "I'll swing by, do a welfare check."

"Thanks. I'm on my way over to The Mercantile. Keep me posted."

"You, too."

CHAPTER 21

I let Jodie know where I'm going as I go through reception, and then I dash into the deluge. I run the Explorer twenty miles an hour over the speed limit and make it to The Mercantile in twelve minutes. As I pull into the front lot, my headlights play over the building's facade, glint off the darkened windows. There are no cars in the lot. No lights inside.

I pick up my radio. "I'm ten-twenty-three," I say, to let Skid and dispatch know I've arrived on scene.

"You got eyes on her?" comes Skid's voice.

"Negative." I have to raise my voice to be heard above the rain pounding the roof of my vehicle. "Are you at the Stutzmans'?"

"ETA two minutes."

"Roger that."

I rack my mike and scan the front of the shop. The place is homey and inviting during the day, with hanging baskets and half whiskey barrels full of fall mums, pansies, and asparagus ferns. Tonight, surrounded by impenetrable darkness and the rain pouring down, it possesses a postapocalyptic feel.

"Come on, Neva," I whisper. "You're too smart to do something like this. Where the hell are you?"

Flipping the switch for my spotlight, I reach for the handle and shine it along the front of the building. I idle past, watching the shadows, keeping my eye on the doors and windows for movement or light. I reach the end of the building and peer into the side lot.

Lightning flashes with blinding intensity. An instant later thunder cracks like cannon shot. I pull around to the side and creep toward the rear, where the old round barn is being renovated. The lot is vacant, ghostlike fingers of steam rising from the gravel.

Hitting my high beams, I crank the wipers up a notch, lean forward, and squint to see through the rain-streaked windshield. The round barn is a huge structure, half of which is surrounded by scaffolding. It had once been white, but decades of weather extremes have stripped the paint and turned the tin roof shingles to rust. There's a massive cupola at the peak. A small square window stares down at me like a dead, blank eye. It's an interesting building, and even in the dark and through the driving rain, I can see the vision Edna Lambright and her husband must have for the place.

The structure is built into a hillside. An orange skid loader lurks in the shadows where some of the foundation has crumbled. My beams illuminate a Dumpster full of refuse. A couple of five-gallon buckets stacked against the exterior wall. The place is deserted. No sign of Neva.

I'm in the process of turning around to wait for Edna Lambright when I see a flicker of light near the front door. I run my spotlight over the facade, but there's no one there; the door is closed. No light in the window. There's no vehicle. No buggy. Still, I'm certain I saw a light. So where the hell did it come from?

"Only one way to find out."

Resigned to getting wet, I shut down the engine, grab my Maglite, and hightail it to the door. My clothes are soaked when I reach for the knob. I'm half expecting to find it locked, but when I twist, the door creaks open. The interior is dark as a cave. The rain pounding the roof is deafening. The smells of wood and plaster waft out on a draft of damp air.

"Hello?" I call out. "Neva? Are you here? It's Kate Burkholder."

I listen, but no response comes. Stepping inside, I shine the beam around the interior. It's a large area with a wood plank floor. The remnants of a dilapidated silo stand in the center. Several stanchions on a raised concrete slab are still recognizable. Two full-size stalls to my right. Curved stairs run along the wall to a second-level loft and down to the ground level. To my left I see a scaffolding set up against the wall where workers have been shoring up the overhead beams.

"Neva Lambright!" I call out her name and identify myself again. "Can you come talk to me please!"

I walk to the center of the space, run my beam along the floor. "Neva!"

Ducking between the stall rails, I cross to the stanchions, and peer into the silo. The air smells of damp earth and rotting wood. The dirt floor is ten feet down. In the yellow beam of light, I see an antique milk can lying on its side. An old cot without a mattress. I startle when something darts across the floor. A field mouse.

"Great," I say on a sigh.

Dust motes fly in the sphere of the beam when I shift the light, point it toward the stairs. They're made of stone and oak planks. Original to the building, but they look solid enough to support my weight.

I'm midway to the stairs when I notice a faint dome of light coming from a niche ahead. Moving quickly, I start toward it. My beam illuminates a small battery-powered lantern atop a wood crate. There's a spiral-bound notebook next to a can of Diet Coke. A pen. A cell phone. A brown prescription bottle.

. . . *she doesn't want to be on this earth anymore* . . .

"Oh, no," I mutter, and then, "Neva! It's Kate Burkholder! Come out here and talk to me."

The floor is covered with a drop cloth or tarp. The kind a painter might use. I'm midway to the alcove when a loud *crack!* sounds. The floor gives way beneath my feet. Then I'm falling into space.

I land hard, feet first, dust and debris flying. My knees buckle on impact. The ground isn't level and I pitch left. Something sharp gouges my thigh. The tarp tangles around my legs. I fall sideways, land on my side, my shoulder and head slamming against the ground.

I brown out for a second, unable to move, my brain

like a cold engine, trying to fire. The breath has been knocked out of me, and I'm gasping like an asthmatic. I hear myself spit, realize my mouth is full of dirt. Pain in my right ankle. Searing heat in my thigh.

Groaning, I roll onto my back, blink dust from my eyes. Darkness all around. Flashlight nowhere in sight. Rain pounding the roof above in a deafening roar.

"Shit." I choke out the word and spit again.

Bad move, Burkholder, a little voice chides.

I make an undignified sound that's part curse word, part moan. I lie still, wait for my head to clear, taking physical stock, shifting my legs. Pain in my back, but not too bad. Aside from some scrapes and bruises, I think I'm okay.

"Chief Burkholder?"

Relief sweeps through me at the sound of Edna Lambright's voice. I push myself to a sitting position. Dizziness swirls, but levels off. "Down here," I call out.

"I heard the ruckus. You've taken quite a fall. Are you all right?"

A flashlight beam appears to my left. I glance over to see the Amish woman making her way down rickety steps. "Guess I should have taken the stairs," I say, trying not to feel foolish.

"I should have warned you about that floor. We're having it replaced, you know. Are you hurt?" she asks as she reaches the ground level.

"I'm fine." Setting my hands on the ground, I get my legs under me, make it to my knees. "Any sign of Neva?"

"No." She blinds me with the flashlight beam. "She's never done anything like this before."

I'm still shaken, my head reeling. "Can you get that light off me?" I say.

"Sorry." She reaches me and stops. "Let me help you."

Her light shifts. I can see the outline of her dress. Thick ankles, feet clad in sneakers that are muddy and wet. The bulk of her body. She's fiddling with something in her right hand. I hear the rip-tear of Velcro. She bends toward me. Something hard is jabbed against my back.

"What are you doing?" I bring up my right leg, set my foot against the ground, start to get up.

A loud *crack!* snaps through the air. Pain explodes through my body. Every muscle contracts into a single, massive cramp. I stiffen. My balance leaves me. I fall sideways. Pain grinds throughout my body, seems to go on forever.

The next thing I know I'm laid out on the ground. For an instant I think I've been shot. But I know that sound. *Stun gun.* Lingering tremors ripple through my muscles.

Edna Lambright stands over me, looking down at me. No emotion on her face. Squatting, she reaches for me, yanks my radio from my belt. I try to stop her, but she hits my arm with the stunner, and another jolt zips from my shoulder to my fingers. My arm flops ineffectually to my side. I try to roll away, end up folding into a fetal position. She reaches for me again. I brace, but she flicks off the thumb snap, slides my .38 from its nest. I try to speak, but no words come. Instead, I do a quarter roll, flail uselessly.

Shit. Shit. Shit.

"Where's that phone of yours?" she mutters.

"What the hell are you doing?" I rasp.

She sets her hands on me, digs into my pockets, grapples for my phone and yanks it out. "Danny Gingerich was a devil in disguise," the Amish woman says. "Looked like some mama's boy. Let me tell you something, he was a monster."

I don't know if she's speaking to me or talking to herself. The one thing I do know is that I'm in trouble.

"That boy hurt everyone he came into contact with," Edna tells me. "Man like him has no place on this earth. God struck him down is what He did. I just helped Him get the job done."

I just helped Him get the job done.

I flop onto my side. Cold earth against my cheek. Dirt on my lips. Grit in my mouth. But my coordination coming back. My brain beginning to clear.

"Where's Neva?" I ask.

"Don't worry about her."

The shaft of light moves toward me. I try to get up, but my arms and legs fail. I get my first good look at the stun gun as she thrusts it at me. I roll, make it to my belly. "Don't!" I shout.

The electrodes snap. She stabs it hard against my back. Agony streaks up my spine, burns like a lit fuse down my limbs. A grand-mal seizure of pain that leaves me twitching and helpless.

"You know what he was," she says. "You should've looked the other way. Let it be so we could all be done with it."

She blinds me with the flashlight. I catch a glimpse

of her face. Her expression is chillingly serene, her eyes alight with intent.

My brain is misfiring. I try to sit up, end up wallowing in the dirt. "People know where I am," I manage.

"Nothing I can do about that."

She starts toward the stairs. I'm aware of the hiss and bark of my radio as she carries it away. Skid trying to get me on the horn. I think of him walking into this. She's armed with my .38. No one is suspicious of her.

"You would have gotten away with it, Edna. Why do this now?"

She stops, turns to me, blinds me with the flashlight. "I did what I had to do. There was no pleasure in it. But it had to be done. He had to be stopped."

I try another tactic. "You're right about Daniel. Let me go, and I won't say a word."

The Amish woman crosses to me, squats a safe distance away, keeps the light in my eyes. "I don't believe you. I know your kind."

"You have my word," I say.

"Too late for that now, Kate Burkholder." She rises. "That's all I've got to say."

For an instant, I think she's going to level the .38 and empty the cylinder into my body. Instead, she lowers the flashlight and starts toward the stairs.

I struggle to my hands and knees, scramble to my feet. She's midway up the stairs; there's no way I can catch her. "I'm a cop, Edna. You can't lock me in this barn and hope I'll go away. People know where I am. They'll be looking for me."

I stumble toward her, teeter right, careen off a beam. But my coordination is returning. I dash to the base of the stairs, look up to see her go through the door at the top. I clamber up the steps, using my hands, as fast as I can manage. I'm halfway there when the door slams. The lock snicks into place.

"Edna!" I reach the door, grab the knob and twist, but it's locked. "Open the door!" I shout. "Open it! Now!"

Nothing.

Setting my ear against the wood, I listen, hear her drop the barricade lock into place. I yank the knob, rattle the door. "Open it!" I listen, but I can't hear anything over the din of rain overhead. What the hell could she possibly be thinking? Skid knows where I am, as does Dispatch. When they can't raise me on the radio, he'll drive over straightaway.

Frustrated, I slap my hands against the door. "Open it!"

Out of habit, I touch the place where my radio would have been. My weapon. Cell phone. All of them gone.

Turning, I face the darkness, wonder if there's another way out. I feel my way down the stairs, carefully because there's very little light. Just a jagged circle of gray seeping in through the hole in the ceiling where I fell through.

Reaching the base of the stairs, I take a moment to get my bearings. I'd had my flashlight in my hand when I fell. Did it come down with me? Or did Edna take it? It had been on; I should be able to see the beam.

I make my way over to the place I landed and kick away some of the wood and debris. Sure enough, I spot the beam and I snatch up the flashlight. I get my first good look at my dungeon. The space is about thirty feet wide with a low ceiling comprised of wood support beams and planks, all of it held up by massive columns resting on concrete piers. The floor is dirt. The exterior wall is a mosaic of wood siding set atop an ancient stone foundation. There are no windows on this level. Just the staircase to my left.

I point the beam upward and look at the hole from which I fell. No dangling boards or wiring; nothing I can use to pull myself up with. Probably safer to stay put until Skid arrives.

The good news is that I now know Edna Lambright is either guilty of—or at the very least involved in—the death of Daniel Gingerich. I think about Neva and I wonder if her going missing was a ruse, or if she's somehow involved, too.

A noise from above quiets my thoughts. Flipping off the flashlight, I look up, listening. I hear footsteps, movement, something being dragged across the floor. Through the opening, I see the shifting of shadows.

"Edna, you need to open that door and let me out of here. One of my officers is on the way. It's over."

I wait but there's no response.

"It's not too late to stop this, Edna. Think of your family. They need you. Talk to me and we'll work through this together."

Nothing.

The rain is still coming down, but not as hard and I can hear her moving around. What the hell is she doing?

"Talk to me, Edna," I say. "Come on, work with me."

The next thing I know, something heavy lands a few feet away from me. Flicking on the light, I realize she tossed a wood pallet through the opening. Dust flies in the cone of light. I shift the beam upward in time to see a wooden crate tumble down, nearly striking me. A second crate follows, busting on impact. What the hell?

I'm about to call out to her when I discern the unmistakable smell of gasoline. Fear lands a punch squarely in my chest. If this woman was capable of locking Daniel Gingerich in that tack room and setting the barn on fire, who's to say she won't do the same to me?

"Edna!" I shout. "Don't do anything foolish. Unlock that door and let me out!"

Several more boards fly down through the hole. The smell of gasoline intensifies and I realize she's dousing all that old wood with gas.

I try to appeal to her. *"Mer sot em sei eegne net verlosse; Gott verlosst die seine nicht."* One should not abandon one's own; God does not abandon His own.

Another board clatters atop the others.

"Edna!" I shout. "Don't do this! The police are on the way!"

Silence.

Spinning, I shine the beam around the room, looking for an escape, windows, doors, loose siding or even a loose stone in the foundation. Seeing nothing, I hasten to the staircase, take the steps two at a time to the top. I try the knob again. No go. I check for hinges, thinking I might be able to tap out the pins, but they're on the other side of the door.

Without hesitation, I step back, raise my right leg and kick the wood next to the knob hard enough to jolt my bones. Once. Twice. Three times. I look around for something heavy with which to ram it. But there's nothing. Getting a running start, I thrust my shoulder and hip into the door, putting as much body weight as I can behind it. The door holds solid.

"Edna! Don't do anything stupid." Grinding out the words between gritted teeth, I take the steps back down to ground level.

My eyes scan the area, looking for something I can use to bust down the door. A cinder block. A length of wood. A stone from the foundation. All the while I'm aware of the shuffling of feet above. Someone moving around. Something scraping against the floor. I spot a T-post, rush to it. I'm bending to pick it up when I hear a tremendous *whoosh!* A fireball the size of a car flares above and then plummets downward.

A gust of intense heat shoves me backward. Turning away, I sprint to the stairs. At the base, I glance over my shoulder to see the pile of wood ignite. For an instant, I consider trying to douse the flames, but the fire is too large, there's too much gas, and I don't have the means.

"Edna!" I scream. "Open the door!"

Panic jabs my solar plexus hard enough to take my breath. Smoke rises and expands along the ceiling, pouring out through the opening from which I fell.

I dart to the T-post I saw earlier, snatch it up. I run to the fire, poke at it with the post, hoping to disperse the fuel source, weaken the flames. Within seconds the heat and smoke drive me back. Steel post in hand, I rush back to the stairs, take them two at a time to the top. Using the post like a battering ram, I slam it into the door as hard as I can. The impact jars my body, scrapes my palms. But the door holds.

All the while smoke billows all around, a noxious cloud reaching for me with black, toxic fingers. I ram the post against the lock. Once. Twice. Three times.

"Help me!"

In the back of my mind I wonder where Skid is. If he's tried to raise me on the radio. If he's on his way. Images of Daniel Gingerich's burned body flash in my mind's eye. I see the contracted tendons and charred, split flesh, his face blackened beyond recognition. I wonder if his last minutes were like this. If he'd thought up until the end that he was going to survive. It's a terrifying thought that pushes me to the edge of panic.

Setting down the T-post, I snatch the flashlight from my waistband and descend the stairs. Another layer of fear tears through me when I see that the fire has doubled in size. A bellowing monster spewing smoke and heat and snatching all the air.

I stand there, heat singeing my face, smoke burning my lungs. I look up at the hole in the ceiling. No one there. I scream out her name anyway. "Edna! Open the door!"

Heat sends me backward. Coughing, I look around. I'm not strong enough, heavy enough, to break down the door. There are no windows. No other doors. No escape.

"*Help me!*" I scream.

Smoke scorches my throat. My shirt is still damp from the rain. Not bothering with the buttons, I tear it open, rip it off my shoulders. Setting down the flashlight, I use my teeth to tear off one of the sleeves, wrap it around my head, cover my nose and mouth, and tie it at my nape. I put what's left of my shirt back on and jog to the wall farthest from the fire. The stone and concrete foundation is a couple of feet high. I run my hands over the wood siding, looking for loose or rotting boards, but there's nothing.

Turning, I rush the stairs, snap up the T-post I left on the landing and I clatter back down. Once again at the farthest point from the fire, I draw back the T-post and smash it against the siding. I ram it again and again; I swing it like a bat, but the wood holds firm.

The fire has transformed into a living thing. A merciless, bellowing monster bent on devouring everything in its path.

"Help me!" I try to scream the words, but I break into coughing. The smoke is choking and so thick I can barely see. It's acrid and caustic. The heat is unbearable. I can feel it scorching my shirt, smell it singeing the fabric.

Dropping the T-post, I go to my knees, hacking and retching. I think about Tomasetti and a scream of outrage pours from my throat. I don't want to do this to him. I don't want him to suffer the unbearable pain of losing another loved one.

I don't want to die.

I drop to the ground, set my face against the dirt. The air is marginally cleaner. I scoot closer to the stone foundation. Still hot, but cooler. I want to go back to the stairs, try the door again. It's my only hope. My last hope. I'm not sure I can make it.

Disbelief swamps me. I can't believe my life is going to end this way. I think of the people I'll leave behind. My brother and sister. My team of officers. The Amish community that has shunned me, yet that I still love.

But it's John Tomasetti that dominates my thoughts. Even in the throes of a chaotic and mindless horror, it's he who lights the darkness. The intensity of my love for him. Even if I die here today, I know that will live on.

A crash shakes the building. In my peripheral vision I see sparks raining down, and I know the ceiling is starting to cave. If I don't get out now, I'll either be crushed to death or burned alive.

"Tomasetti . . ."

I scoot closer to the foundation. Nowhere else to go. No air to breathe. Just fire and heat and smoke.

Dear God.

A cool puff hits my face. At first, I think my mind is playing tricks. Then I smell rain. The flashlight is still in my right hand. Groaning, I drag it up. The beam illuminates nothing but dirt and stone, all of it obscured by smoke. Then I spot the gap where the mortar has crumbled. Water seeping in from the outside.

The urge to run back and grab the T-post again is powerful, but there's too much smoke, too much heat; I might not make it back. Instead, I roll onto my back, set my feet against the stone foundation, and I stomp as hard as I can. Hope leaps when the stones shift. I kick again, this time with so much force that my body slides away. I reposition myself, mule kick with all my might.

Another surge of hope when I feel movement. The stone is smaller than a cinder block; even if I manage to dislodge it, I won't fit through the hole. But I'll be in a better position to kick out a second one.

Lifting both legs, I stomp the stone, again and again. It slides a couple of inches. Finger-size chunks of mortar fall toward me. I scream and kick and choke in a frenzy of panic and resolve and the will to survive. All the while the fire rages. Debris crashes down from above. I ignore all of it and kick, kick, kick.

The stone gives way. The one above it shifts down. Mortar crumbles. Sobbing, lungs burning, I kick it. Once. Twice. And it's gone.

Twisting, I sit up, set my face against the rush of cool, clean air. I thrust my hands and arms and head through the hole. Digging my toes into the dirt, I shove my torso and hips through. Drizzle and cool night air greet me. I'm still coughing and sobbing. I grab handfuls of weeds and grass and mud, and pull myself free of the hole. I hear someone laughing maniacally, realize it's me.

Then I'm outside, gulping fresh air, coughing. Rain cools my heated skin. I roll onto my back, look up at the night sky. For an instant I can't move. I don't know whether to laugh or cry.

A crash from inside the barn snaps me from my stupor. I sit up, struggle to my feet. The flashlight is lying in the weeds, so I bend and pick it up. The fire lights up the entire area. I back away from the barn. I'm on the downhill side of the structure. Unseen from the parking lot. I'd been so focused on escape, I hadn't considered the possibility that Edna Lambright is still around. That she's got my .38. Starting up the hill, I make my way toward the Explorer to radio for help.

CHAPTER 22

I'm midway to the Explorer when I hear tires on gravel. I'm about to take cover when I see the flash of emergency lights against the treetops. Skid's cruiser pulls up next to my Explorer.

The driver's-side door flies open. Skid jumps out and jogs toward me. "Chief!"

I break into a run. "Edna Lambright is armed!" I call out. "She locked me in the barn. Set it on fire."

He flicks the thumb strap off his sidearm and pulls it. Simultaneously, he speaks into his lapel mike. "Ten-thirty-five," he says, putting out the code for a major crime alert.

"I think she's in a 2005 Taurus," I tell him. "We need to stop her." I reach him, aware that he's staring at me with concern as he relays the information into his mike.

"You okay, Chief? You need an ambulance?"

I yank open the passenger door of his cruiser. "I'm fine. Let's go get her."

I slide into the seat. Gravel flies from beneath the

tires as he turns around and starts toward the road. "She's probably on her way to her farm."

He makes a right. The engine groans when he floors the accelerator and cranks the speedometer to seventy.

"Skid, she's got my gun," I tell him. "You got an extra?"

"Just that shotgun in the trunk."

"That'll do."

The radio lights up with activity as the alert goes out to dispatch and the Holmes County Sheriff's Department. Most days Skid is Mr. Laid-Back Practical Joker. Tonight, he's all business. He's driving fast, eyes scanning left and right as he passes dark country roads, fields, and lanes obscured by trees.

Taillights appear ahead. "There," I say.

"Looks like our vehicle."

I pick up the mike. "Ten-thirty-eight," I say, letting our counterparts know we're about to stop a suspicious vehicle. "That's her," I tell Skid.

Hitting his bright lights, he pulls up close behind the car, keeping slightly left. We're moving at about forty miles per hour; she's not slowing quickly enough, so he pulses the siren three times.

For a second, I think she's going to run. Then the turn signal flicks on; she pulls onto the shoulder and stops. Skid sticks with her, keeping left, and stops. He jams the shifter into park, glances my way. "I'm going to get her out."

"Armed driver protocol," I say. "Pop the trunk."

"Yep." He draws his weapon.

The trunk mechanism clicks.

Opening his door, he grabs the mike for his loud-speaker. "Driver! Turn off the engine! Roll down your window and let me see your hands!"

Never taking my eyes from the Taurus, I open my door and, staying low, slink around to the trunk. Ever aware that a .38 round will penetrate everything but the engine, I lift the trunk and unseat the Remington 870 from its mount.

"Driver!" Skid's out of the car now, his weapon trained on the vehicle. "Show me your hands now!"

The Taurus's engine goes silent. Headlights still on. Brake lights glowing. I watch, waiting, holding my breath. All the while, my heart pounds adrenaline to every muscle in my body. I can hear myself breathing heavily, the rush of blood through my veins.

Two hands appear through the driver's-side window.

"Open your door and step out of the vehicle! Keep your back to me."

The driver's-side door opens. The Amish woman sets her feet on the ground and slides out of the vehicle.

"Get your hands up! Turn away from me! Face the other way!"

I raise the shotgun, praying I don't have to use it.

Edna Lambright stands quietly with her back to us, her hands raised to shoulder level. She's shaking. It's a surreal scene. Because she's Amish. A woman. A mother. The last kind of person anyone would expect to be involved in a situation like this.

"Walk backward!" Skid shouts the command twice.

When she's a few yards away, he orders her to stop. "Get down on your knees! Keep your hands up."

She turns her head to look at him, but he shouts her down. "Do not look at me! Face forward! Get on your knees!"

Skid's .38 is aimed at the woman, center mass. I move forward, round the front right quarter panel, shotgun at the ready.

"Do not move!" he tells her. "Do you understand? *Do not move!*"

In the light of his headlights, I see him remove the handcuffs from his belt. Cautiously, he approaches her. I stay slightly behind and to the right of them. Shotgun level, my finger inside the guard.

"Where's the gun?" he asks.

"I don't know," she cries. "I dropped it. In the car."

He's a few feet away from her. The cuffs are in his left hand. He's reaching out to cuff her left wrist when her right hand drops.

Skid sees it at the same time I do. "Get your hand up!" he shouts. "Get it fucking up!"

As if in slow motion, Edna Lambright turns, still on her knees. In the glare of the headlights I see a black weapon in her right hand. Coming up. Her eyes on Skid.

"Drop it!" I scream. "Drop the weapon! Drop it!"

Skid is too close to her for me to fire the shotgun. I see his gun hand move upward.

"Drop it!" he shouts.

The gunshot freezes everything in place. I see a tremor pass through Skid. The Amish woman on her knees, twisting around, facing him. Face contorted. Her right arm straight, the weapon pointed at him.

Two more shots in quick succession are like an explosion in my brain. Edna Lambright pitches forward, falls facedown on the asphalt.

"Skid! *Skid!*" I lower the shotgun, dart over to him.

He backs up a couple of steps, nearly runs into me. I set my hand on his shoulder. "Are you hit?"

"No." He shakes his head. "I don't think so."

"Are you sure? Check, damn it." But my eyes are already moving to Edna Lambright.

"I'm okay." He takes another step back, lets out a sigh that shudders. "Might've crapped my pants, though."

I don't have my radio, so I look at Skid. "Ten-fifty-two."

He's already making the call and giving our location.

I kneel next to Edna Lambright. She's lying prone with her head turned. She's alive, her eyes open and blinking. She's not moving, but I can see the rise and fall of her back as she breathes. There's blood on her dress. A hole in the fabric where the bullet struck her.

I touch her shoulder. "An ambulance is on the way, Edna. Just stay calm for me. You're going to be all right."

"Neva," she whispers.

"Neva will be fine," I say. "You, too. Just hang on."

She closes her eyes. "I set the fire."

"I know. We'll deal with that later."

"No. The Gingerich fire. I set it. I did it."

I look at Skid. He heard it, too. I look down at her, but the Amish woman is gone.

* * *

Never doubt in the dark what God has shown you in the light.

The words were one of my *mamm*'s favorite sayings, especially in the face of tragedy, and I heard it often growing up. When my *grossmudder* passed away. When a neighbor was killed in a buggy accident. The day I was attacked by Daniel Lapp. The axiom reflects the Amish tenet of maintaining faith in times of heartbreak. One of many reasons I never fit in.

Edna Lambright was pronounced dead at the scene a little after ten P.M. It took the fire department an hour to extinguish the blaze. Because the incident included an officer-involved shooting, I called Tomasetti. Somehow, he made the thirty-minute drive from Wooster in under twenty. At that point, BCI assumed control of the scene. Sheriff Mike Rasmussen showed up a short time later along with the BCI crime scene unit truck, and the technician set to work, photographing, videotaping, and collecting evidence. Later, Bob Schoening with the fire marshal's office arrived and I spent another half an hour or so answering questions.

I stuck with Skid throughout. He's my officer and, at the moment, my number-one priority. We stayed on scene until the coroner pulled up. That's when Tomasetti offered us a ride to the police station. We accepted the offer. Of course neither of us had a choice.

Once we arrived at the station we were separated. Tomasetti interviewed Skid. He collected Skid's revolver, which will be tested and, later—once Skid is off administrative leave—returned to him. I gave my statement to one of the other BCI agents. He was professional and straightforward; he was decent enough to do a welfare check on Neva Lambright, who was safe at home and hadn't left the house all evening. He even brought me coffee. But he was excruciatingly thorough. None of the Painters Mill police vehicles have dash cams—it's not in the budget—and so the initial officer interview is extremely important.

As chief, one of the responsibilities I take very seriously is the death notification to the deceased's next of kin. I disliked the idea of sending T.J. to break the horrific news to Edna's husband, Isaac, and Neva. But because I was personally involved in the shooting, I couldn't do it myself.

"Go to Bishop Troyer's house first," I told him as he headed out. Even though the Lambrights are Beachy Amish, the bishop will be a comfort to them. "Tell him what happened and ask him to go with you."

"You got it, Chief."

I know T.J. will be the consummate professional. He'll be kind, but straightforward. Still, it's a difficult assignment and I hated to put it on his shoulders.

It's now two A.M. I'm sitting at my desk, a cold cup of coffee in front of me. I'm trying not to notice the smell of smoke and singed hair that clings to me. I'm wondering if Tomasetti is still around—if they're finished with me for the night—when Skid walks in. Something shakes loose inside me at the sight of him. He's the one member of my team I don't worry about; he's got a resilient personality. He doesn't lose sleep over things he can't control. He's a natural-born smartass with a wicked sense of humor and no sense for political correctness. Tonight, he looks as troubled and vulnerable as I feel.

"You're looking a little worse for wear," I say.

"You, too."

"Figured." I motion to the chair opposite my desk. "They done with you?"

"I think so." He looks down at his uniform. "I feel kind of naked without my gun."

"I'm glad you're not naked." It's a lame joke, but we both smile. "You'll get it back in a week or so."

He takes the chair, and an uncomfortable silence ensues. Though the last hours have been busy, my mind keeps taking me back to the moment when Edna Lambright reached for that weapon and Skid reacted—rightfully—with deadly force. It was a nightmare scenario that no cop ever wants to face. It's a scene both of us are going to be reliving for a very long time.

"So are you okay?" I ask.

"Me?" He forces a laugh. "I'm fine."

Another silence. Longer. He's not fine. No one is fine after killing another person, justified or not.

Finally, he meets my gaze and grimaces. "Chief, an Amish woman? For God's sake . . . why the hell did she pull that gun? I mean, we had her. It was done. For her to do something like that . . . she had to have known it wouldn't end well. For any of us."

I think about that fateful moment and I shake my head. "You heard her last words, right?"

"Yep."

"You put that in your statement?"

"I put everything in there exactly the way it happened."

"Good," I tell him. "I did the same."

"You think that's why she did it?" he asks. "Why she pulled the gun? She figured her life was over anyway and she decided to go fucking death by cop?"

There's a bitterness to his voice I don't like. "Maybe. I don't know. Skid, the most important thing for you to remember right now is that we get to walk away from this. Because you did your job. You stuck to your training. You did everything right."

"I killed a fucking Amish woman." He leans forward, sets his elbows on his knees, scrubs his hands over his face. "That's so nuts I can't even get my head around it."

"I know. Me, too. She didn't leave you any choice."

A soft tap at the door draws my attention. I look up to see Glock and Pickles standing in the doorway, peering in tentatively. Mona stands behind them, craning her neck to see over Pickles's shoulder, listening for the phone.

"I hope we're not interrupting," Glock says.

I stand, drawing their attention, giving Skid a moment to shore up. "I probably don't have to point out it's after two o'clock in the morning."

"Bladder keeps me up half the night anyway," Pickles grumbles. "Always keep an ear on the scanner. Heard what went down."

"That's a little TMI about your bladder, dude," says Glock.

The old man mutters something appropriately rude beneath his breath.

Skid looks over his shoulder at them. "There goes the neighborhood." But he's off-kilter; the words lack his usual cockiness.

Glock and Pickles shuffle in. I make eye contact with Mona and, with a nod, she heads back out to reception.

That's one of the things I love about my team. Not only are they good cops, but they're good people. When one of their own is in trouble, they drop everything and show up in force to support them. Skid might be resilient, but he doesn't have family here in Painters Mill. Last I heard, he doesn't even have a girlfriend. Tonight, he shouldn't be alone.

I notice the brown paper bag Glock's holding at his side and I shake my head. "You sure you want to break the seal on that tonight?" I'm not kidding.

"When the shit hits the fan, Jack Daniel's comes to the rescue," Pickles says.

"He's in good hands," Glock assures me.

"We're professionals, Chief," Pickles adds.

I nod, trying not to notice that Skid has his elbows on his knees, staring at the floor.

Glock jabs a thumb toward reception. "Those suits out there done with this guy?"

"I think so." I turn my attention to Skid. "You're off for a few days, Skidmore. Protocol for an officer-involved shooting. I'll keep you posted on how things are going, and let you know if we need anything."

"Great." He runs his palms over the thighs of his uniform pants and rises. "Appreciate it, Chief."

Glock cocks his head at me. "You want to come with us, Chief?"

I shake my head. "Jack and I are sort of on the outs."

He chuckles. "Gotcha."

I let my gaze connect with Glock's and then Pickles's. "If it's not too much to ask, stay out of trouble."

"We got this, Chief," Pickles says, and they usher Skid through the door.

CHAPTER 23

It's not until I'm home that I realize what an absolute wreck I am. I put on a fresh shirt at the station, but I reek of smoke and sweat and singed hair. The bathroom mirror reveals a face and neck that are smudged with soot and dirt. Hair that's singed on one side. My left palm is blistered, but I haven't the slightest idea how it happened. I've got a dozen or so pockmarks on my right cheek, small burns more than likely caused by sparks or flying ash.

Tomasetti was with another BCI agent when I left. I caught his eye as I headed toward the door. I could tell by his expression he didn't want me to leave without him. But I needed to get out of there. On the drive to the farm, I called T.J. to see how it went with the Lambright family. In typical Amish fashion, they'd taken news of Edna's death—and the circumstances of it—quietly. He'd spent twenty minutes with them, answering questions. Bishop Troyer stayed on, saying he would get a ride home later.

It's only when I'm in the shower that I examine my

own emotions—and relive the horrific moments I was locked inside the barn. The ordeal lasted only a few minutes, but it seemed like an eternity. The sense of being trapped. The terrifying thought of being burned alive. The all-encompassing panic and disbelief.

When I close my eyes, I see Edna Lambright as she lay dying on the ground. I see the blood on her dress. The hole in the fabric where the bullet entered her body. The resolve on her face when she'd spoken her final words.

The Gingerich fire. I set it. . . .

I rush through the shower, scrubbing myself clean, my hair and face and hands, wishing I could scrub away the images. I don't want them in my head.

I'm sitting at the kitchen table in my old sweatpants and a T-shirt from my police academy days when Tomasetti comes in the back door. I can tell by his expression that he's concerned.

"I couldn't get away," he tells me as he closes the door behind him.

I smile. "Kind of hard to carry on a relationship with a bunch of nosy cops around."

"Probably not much of a secret these days." He crosses to me, sets his hands on my shoulders, and kisses the top of my head. "You're shaking."

"I'm okay. Hair didn't fare so well."

Spotting the tumbler of whiskey in front of me, he growls low in his throat. "You hate whiskey."

"It'll do in a pinch." I look over at him. "Want one?"

"I have no such aversion." I start to get up, but he stops me. "I got it."

He pours two fingers of eighty-proof into a glass. He's still wearing the suit he put on this morning. The tie I bought him for his birthday last September. He's rumpled, with a five-o'clock shadow. He wears all of those things very well.

"Tomasetti, you are an extraordinarily nice-looking man," I say.

He arches a brow. "How many of those whiskeys have you had?"

I smile, and it makes me feel almost normal.

He takes the chair across from me, sets the glass on the table, and reaches for my hands. "You scared the hell out of me."

"I know. I'm sorry. I—"

"Don't apologize. It's okay. I just . . . when I got the call . . ." He turns my hands over in his, looks down at the smattering of blisters on my palm, and frowns. "You're burned."

"I don't think they're bad."

"Uh-huh." He leaves the kitchen and returns with the first-aid kit. After washing his hands at the sink, he sits and pops the lid. "Let's have a look."

Taking my hands in his, he studies the blisters and reaches for the burn gel. "Blisters are broken, so I'm going to bandage your hand, okay?"

Neither of us speaks as he tears open a roll of sterile gauze, wraps it loosely around my hand, and tapes it.

"You've got great hands, Tomasetti."

"That's what all the female chiefs of police tell me."

"I bet."

"How does it feel?"

"Hurts."

"You planning on milking this thing or what?"

"To the max."

He's trying to distract me. I'm not sure if it's working just yet, but I like it.

"How's Skid?" he asks.

"Not sure. I'm going to keep an eye on him."

"Tough thing for anyone to deal with."

"I think what makes this even worse is that she was Amish. And a woman . . ." I shrug. "Glock and Pickles showed up with a bottle of Jack Daniel's to take him home."

"What could possibly go wrong?" He tucks the remaining gauze and gel back into the first-aid kit and closes the lid.

For a moment, he doesn't say anything. Just sits there, staring at the kit. Then he raises his gaze to mine. "Kate." He takes both my hands in his and squeezes my uninjured one. "Look, this isn't official yet, but I thought you should know. The crime scene technician found several rounds in the console and on the floor of Edna Lambright's car. When he checked your thirty-eight . . . the cylinder was empty."

"*What?* But . . . that doesn't make sense. She drew her weapon." My thoughts fragment, part of my brain trying to figure out why she would have done that, the other half jumping ahead to how the news will affect Skid.

"It looks like she emptied the cylinder," he says.

"Why would she do that?"

He shakes his head. "I don't know."

I pick up the glass and sip. "You know she confessed to setting the fire that killed Daniel Gingerich."

"I read your statement." He looks down at the glass in his hands, swirls the whiskey. "Hard to figure."

I shake my head. "Tomasetti, suicide by cop?"

"We've seen crazier things." He shrugs. "With her being Amish, maybe the guilt was too much."

"She knew what Gingerich was."

"Even so." He shrugs. "Maybe she couldn't handle what she'd done and decided to end her life without having to do the dirty work herself."

It's a solid theory. But Edna Lambright was so far removed from the profile of someone who would do something so desperate, I can't accept it. "Was there a note?"

"Not in the vehicle," he tells me. "Or on her person. Agent talked to the family earlier and there's nothing there."

"It doesn't make sense."

Even as I say the words, I realize it does, but in a way that's so twisted, so perverse, I'm not sure I'll ever be able to get my head around it.

They say criminals always return to the scene of the crime. Sometimes cops do, too. For different reasons, of course. Closure being one of them. Not that I believe in that sort of thing. When you're a cop, believing in something as trite as closure—or even justice, for that matter—is sort of like believing in the tooth fairy. Life isn't that neat.

Drizzle falls from a Teflon-gray sky when I pull into

the parking lot of The Mercantile. For five days I've debated whether to come back. I want to think it's for a final look at the place where I nearly lost my life. Maybe thumb my nose at the Grim Reaper. But this pilgrimage isn't about coming to terms with either of those things. I haven't been able to stop thinking about the three young Amish women whose lives intersected with mine in the course of the Gingerich case. Viola Stutzman. Ina Yoder. And Neva Lambright. Especially Neva.

Instead of parking near the front entrance, where a dozen or so vehicles and half as many buggies are lined up outside the door, I idle around to the rear, where the skeletal remains of the round barn stand in dark testament to the tragedy that occurred here just five days ago. The only things left are the blackened bones of the wood frame, the rafters, and the stone foundation. I wonder if it's been slated for demolition.

Shutting down the engine, I get out, barely noticing the drizzle or the breeze that's kicked up from the east. A lone piece of yellow caution tape demarks what had once been the crime scene. I think about Skid and I wonder if he's been back to the scene where Edna Lambright died.

It wasn't easy telling him he shot and killed an unarmed woman. She brandished the weapon; we had no way of knowing the gun was unloaded. There's no doubt he had just cause for deadly force. Still, there are some who will argue the point. Skid put on a brave front after receiving the news; he cracked a couple of inappropriate jokes. We laughed when we probably shouldn't have. He cursed the woman who'd used him in such a cruel, life-altering way. Despite his efforts to convince me otherwise, I'm pretty sure I left him in worse condition than when I arrived.

I've talked to him every day since it happened. Twice he was drunk and alone—a bad combination for a cop dealing with killing an unarmed citizen. But he's trying. BCI is handling the investigation. I fully expect him to be exonerated of any wrongdoing. Once that happens, I'll put him back on duty. I'm hoping his old routine— and being around people who care about him—will help get him back on track.

I stroll over to the barn. The stone foundation looks like rows of rotting and missing teeth. Inside, the ground is littered with charred debris of indiscernible origin, burned chunks of wood, blackened rock. I make my way down the hill and around to the back. The two rocks I dislodged to escape are still there, lying in the weeds and mud, forgotten.

"What the hell were you thinking, Edna?" I whisper.

The only answer is the solitary whistle of a cardinal from the row of trees at the edge of the parking lot.

Back in the Explorer, I drive around to the front of The Mercantile and head inside. Today is the first day the shop has been open for business since Edna Lambright's death. The community—Amish and English alike—have come out in force to support the Lambright family, and the place is a beehive of activity.

Inside, a handful of customers stand in line at the cash register, which is being manned by a somber-looking Ina Yoder. A family of four, out-of-town tourists probably, is checking out the greeting card display. I wave to Ina when I walk in, but she doesn't notice. I start toward the rear of the store.

I'm midway through the candle section when I spot Viola Stutzman in the next row. She's with two customers, but spots me. Her eyes jump with a quick flash of recognition, but I can't read her expression. I'm not sure how my being here will be received, since I was there the night Edna Lambright was killed.

I start toward Viola, pausing a few feet away, giving her time to finish with her customers. She's been crying at some point. Her eyes are puffy; the tip of her nose is red and chapped. Her face is paler than usual. If I'm not mistaken, she's lost a couple of pounds since I last saw her. Despite her evident sadness, she's doing a decent sales pitch for the pretty knitted afghan draped over her arm.

"My *grossmudder* made this one," she tells them. "It's my favorite and I'm sure your aunt would love it, especially on those cold winter nights up there in Cleveland."

Sold, the couple thanks her and takes the afghan to the cash register.

"You're a natural," I tell her.

There's no hostility in her eyes when she looks at me, no blame. Just a thinly veiled sadness and the same kind of discomfort I feel in the pit of my stomach.

"Chief Burkholder. I'm . . . I'm glad you're okay."

"I hope you're all right with my being here. If you're not, I can take off."

"I'm okay with it. I just . . ." She lets the words trail as if she isn't quite sure how to finish the sentence. "What a terrible . . . tragedy."

"I'm sorry about Edna," I tell her.

Pain flashes across her face. "Thank you."

For an instant I think she's going to burst into tears, but she holds on to her composure. "I don't think it's sunk in yet. I mean, that she's gone. I still can't believe it." She looks out across the shop. "I keep thinking she's going to barrel around the corner, shoes stomping, face stern like always, and she's going to have some chore or errand for me that I don't want to do."

"How are you holding up?"

"I'm okay. Sad for Neva mostly. She took it hard."

I glance around the shop. "How is she?"

"Her heart is broken. First Emma and now her *mamm*." She shakes her head. "I told her not to come in today. It's too soon. I caught her crying back in the break room twice now. I don't think she's going to be able to stay."

I nod. "I'd like to offer my condolences. Do you think she'd talk to me?"

Her eyes fill, but she doesn't let the tears fall. "She doesn't blame you for what happened, Chief Burkholder. I talked to her earlier, and she's just . . . sad and confused. If you want to see her, she's in the break room."

"Thank you." I reach out and squeeze her hand. "I won't keep her long."

I make my way to the rear of the store, where the break room is located. I find Neva sitting at the table, unmoving, staring blankly at the tabletop. She doesn't look up when I enter. I'm not even sure she heard me. For an instant, I consider turning around and leaving.

Then she raises her head. Her eyes meet mine and widen. Surprise flashes, but it's overshadowed by the grief I see etched into her every feature. "Chief Burkholder."

"Hi, Neva."

She starts to rise. "I didn't think you'd—"

"Don't get up," I tell her. "I can't stay. I just wanted to . . . see you. See how you're doing."

She lowers herself back into the chair. "I'm okay."

We both know the words couldn't be farther from the truth. Her eyes have a dull sheen. Her nose is red from crying. Her lips are dry and chapped.

"I'm sorry about your *mamm*," I say quietly.

Bowing her head, she chokes out a sob and begins to cry.

I'm not much of a hugger, but this girl looks so sad, so broken, so utterly lost. I vacillate a moment, then go to her, put my arms around her shoulders, give a brief but heartfelt embrace.

"If you want me to leave, I'll understand," I say quietly.

Pulling away slightly, she raises her head, pulls a well-used tissue from her apron pocket, and blots her face. "Don't go." She blows her nose. "I know it wasn't your fault."

I tug out the chair next to her and sit. "I didn't think you'd be back at work so soon."

"Everyone thinks I'm nuts." She chokes out a laugh

that sounds more like a sob. "I probably am. But I couldn't stay away. Mamm loved this place so much. I know it sounds weird, but I feel closer to her here. I mean, everything you see on the shelves? Chances are, she put it there. She touched it with her own hands. The candles. The quilts. The afghans."

"Sometimes work is good therapy," I tell her. "And it helps to be around people who love you."

"I don't know how I'd have gotten through the last few days without Ina and Viola. They've been so good. Even the customers have been sweet."

I take a moment to get my words in order and say what I've wanted to say for days now. "I know what happened is painful and confusing for you and your family. I want you know . . . if you have questions or want to talk about it, I'm here for you. If you prefer not to talk about it, that's okay, too."

She gives me a grateful look, but there's caution in her eyes, as well, right next to the pain and every bit as large. "I can't believe the things people are saying about her. The things I've read in the newspaper."

She's referring to a piece that ran in *The Budget,* the newspaper that serves most of Ohio's Amish population. Other publications ran stories, too. The *Plain Dealer* out of Cleveland. *The Columbus Dispatch.* Stories that elucidated the circumstances of Edna Lambright's death, including her confession to the murder of Daniel Gingerich.

Absently, Neva rubs away the tears that have begun to fall. "I don't know what could have compelled her to do such things. To Daniel Gingerich. To *you.*" She chokes out a sound of pure anguish. "She was kind, and she loved God. . . ." Lowering her head, she puts her fingers to her temples. "It hurts to think of how all of it must have weighed on her conscience."

She raises her gaze to mine, tears shimmering, torment etched into her every feature. "What could she possibly have been thinking?"

Those are the questions I've struggled with for five days now. Questions I still don't know how to answer. "We may never know for sure."

"How could she do that to us?" she whispers.

I think about the final minutes I spent with Edna Lambright in the barn. The things she said. The things she knew.

Danny Gingerich was a devil in disguise. . . .

"Your *mamm* knew what Daniel Gingerich was," I tell her. "She knew what he did to Emma Miller. I think she knew he wouldn't stop. That he would continue to hurt people." I shrug. "Maybe she handled it the only way she knew how."

She stares at me, blinking, looking so fragile I'm almost afraid she's going to shatter right before my eyes. "Mamm loved Emma like a daughter."

I nod, wishing there was something I could say or do to ease her pain, but there's nothing.

"None of that explains what she did to you." Her whisper is hoarse, her words barely audible.

"I was a threat." I shrug. "We'll probably never know all of it."

She struggles for a moment, then raises shimmering

eyes to mine. "I'm sorry for what she did. To you. To Daniel, even. I don't know how to make any of it right. I'm so . . . ashamed."

"It wasn't your fault."

She shakes her head, tears spilling over her lashes. "I love her. I'll always love her. And I miss her desperately. But I'm *angry* with her, too."

Pulling the shredded tissue from the pocket of her apron, she wipes her eyes. We fall silent and for the first time she looks uncomfortable. I feel that same discomfort. Time to go, I realize. Let this be. Let all of it go and move on.

"I've got to get back to the station," I tell her as I rise. "I just wanted to stop in and see how you were doing."

She wipes her eyes with the tissue, takes a deep breath, and composes herself. "It must have been hard for you. Thank you."

Before I can respond, she rises abruptly, rushes to me, throws her arms around me, and buries her face against my shoulder. "I'm glad you're okay."

Pulling away, she gives me a quick, sad smile and then she's gone.

I stand there a moment, hands in my pockets, feeling uncharacteristically melancholy. "Bye, Neva."

Letting out a long sigh, I leave the break room and start toward the front of the store. I'd wanted to see Ina, too, but I'm too raw. Better to leave things as they are and get on with my life.

I'm nearly to the door when I walk past the old-fashioned bulletin board affixed to a column. A piece of card stock tacked to the cork catches my eye. I almost don't stop, but a prickly sensation on the back of my neck prompts me to turn around and go back.

I scan the board, trying to figure out what had snagged my attention. My eyes are drawn to a handwritten announcement.

> *Candle making class! Tuesday evening 6:30 to 7:30 PM. Just $15. Open to the public. Sign up at the customer service desk.* ☺

The advertisement is written on a five-by-eight-inch index card in purple ink, and pinned to the cork with a lime-green tack. Someone has drawn in a smiley face in the lower right-hand corner. There's nothing particularly unusual about it. Nothing that should have given me pause. And yet . . .

Around me, the sounds of the shop—conversation, the ding of the cash register, and the clatter of merchandise being handled—fade to babble. My vision tunnels on the handwriting. It's cursive embellished with ornate swirls and curlicues. There are five "i"s; each one is dotted with a little heart.

I snatch the card from the board and take it to the customer service desk, where a Mennonite woman is helping a customer with a return. I show her the card. "Do you know who wrote this?"

She frowns at me, letting me know I'm being rude for butting in line, but she glances at the card. "That's Viola's handwriting," she says. "I can sign you up for the class, but you'll need to get in line and wait your turn."

For an instant I stand there, feeling as if I've been sucker punched. I'm aware of the Amish woman staring at me, wondering what's wrong with me.

Sliding the card into the back pocket of my trousers, I back away from her and head for the door.

CHAPTER 24

Twenty minutes later, I pull into the parking lot of Quality Implement and park in the fire lane a few feet from the front door. Hoping I'm wrong, I tug out the card as I walk inside and look at it again. The handwriting stares back at me in indisputable black and white.

"What did you do?" I whisper.

Then I'm through the door and striding directly to the tire, battery, and auto department. I find Ralph Baker sitting on the top rung of a stepladder in the windshield wiper aisle, jotting SKU numbers onto a clipboard.

"Mr. Baker?"

He glances up. "Oh, hi, Chief Burkholder." Smiling, he rises. "What can I help you with today?"

I show him the card. "Do you recognize this handwriting?"

"Huh? Well . . . let me see." Lowering reading glasses from his crown, he tilts his head back to look at it through his bifocals and squints. "What am I looking at here, exactly? I mean, what is this?"

I rephrase my question. "Is there anything about this handwriting that's familiar to you?"

Again, he lowers the glasses and looks at the handwriting. "I don't know that I've ever seen it before. But I'm not exactly sure where you're coming from here."

The last thing I want to do is ask a leading question. A question posed in such a way that it could influence his answer. "Mr. Baker, when you came to me about the note Daniel Gingerich received shortly before his death, you described it as a 'girlie' style of handwriting. You mentioned little hearts over the i's. Is that correct?"

"Oh! By golly, I did. I'd forgotten all about that. Sheesh." He makes a "crazy" gesture with his hand, then takes another look at the index card and frowns. "Gosh, Chief, I only saw that note for a second, but this sure looks like the same writing. Same little hearts over the i's, just like what's on that card there. Same color ink, too."

"Do you think it's the same handwriting?"

"Well, I can't say for sure, but it sure looks like it."

Questions bombard me as I walk back to the Explorer. Is it possible Viola Stutzman wrote the note that lured Daniel Gingerich to the barn the night he was killed? Was she somehow involved? Or did she simply write the note for Edna Lambright? If that's the case, why didn't she mention it when I talked to her about it?

By the time I climb into the Explorer, I've got a knot in my gut. My hands are shaking when I set them on the steering wheel. I sit there a moment, trying to make sense of it, and what it could mean in terms of the case.

Thoughts racing, I pick up the phone and call Tomasetti. "Do the latent prints on the key found at the scene of the Gingerich fire belong to Edna Lambright?" I hear the high-wire tension in my voice. I'm pretty sure Tomasetti hears it, too, because he takes his time responding.

"I thought you were about to close the case."

"I thought so, too." I tell him about finding the card at The Mercantile and my conversation with Ralph Baker.

"He thinks it's the same handwriting?"

"He only got a glimpse, but he remembers the little hearts above the i's and the purple ink."

"Viola Stutzman probably isn't the only teenaged girl who writes that way or uses colored ink."

"I know. And I know it's a tenuous connection."

"That's not to mention you don't have the note for comparison purposes."

"The note was never found. I assumed it was destroyed in the fire." I take a breath, blow it out. "Tomasetti, I don't think I can ignore this."

I hear computer keys clicking on the other end of the line and I know he's accessing the information on the latents. He makes a sound low in his throat, telling me he found what he was looking for—and he doesn't like what he sees.

"Because of the cause and manner of Edna Lambright's death, fingerprints were obtained at the time of autopsy." A few more clicks sound, and then, "That comparative analysis was never done because Edna Lambright confessed."

"Can you get that for me?"

"Let me make some calls." But he pauses. "Look, Kate, one thing we need to keep in mind is that Edna Lambright confessed. She tried to murder you. We can't ignore that either."

"Tomasetti, what if she was trying to protect someone?"

A too-long pause ensues, and then, "Viola Stutzman? Were they that close?"

Mamm loved Emma like a daughter.

"I don't know. She's close to the girls . . ."

The next thought that strikes me fills me with such repugnance that it makes me nauseous. Sweat breaks out on my forehead, and I shift the air-conditioning vent to my face, crank it up.

"Tomasetti," I whisper. "I don't like where this is going."

"And where is that?"

I close my eyes. "Look, if you could check on those latents for me. I need to check a couple of things on my end."

"What are you going to do?"

"I'm going to go back to The Mercantile."

It's nearly six P.M.—a few minutes before closing at The Mercantile. The lavender hues of evening settle over air fragrant with the smells of burning leaves and a backyard barbecue somewhere nearby. I'm sitting in my Explorer in the side parking lot. My police radio is turned down low. I'm listening to an old Alan Parsons Project tune, feeling more than is prudent, wishing I could walk away from this. Like so many other times, I can't.

I didn't hear back from Tomasetti until nearly four
P.M. The news wasn't what I wanted to hear. The latent
prints found on the mason jar that was discovered in
Chris Martino's garage, and the prints lifted from the
key found at the scene of the Gingerich barn fire, did
not belong to Edna Lambright. He also took the time to
have the latent-print expert compare the prints to those
of the Gingerich family members, including the children. Again, there were no matches.

I get out of the Explorer and walk into the shop. The
now-familiar aromas of vanilla, citrus, and bergamot
greet me. Neva Lambright stands at the cash register,
ringing up a sale for a Mennonite couple. I head toward
the back of the shop. I'm not sure exactly what I'm looking for until I find myself in an aisle jam-packed with
kitchen décor: glass pitchers, vases, votives, and other
appealing items that draw tourists from as far away as
Pennsylvania.

I grab four votives. They're about two inches tall and
made of smoked glass. Unusual-looking, but pretty, just
like everything else in The Mercantile. I tug a tissue
from my pocket, take a moment to wipe each of the votives clean, and start toward the front of the store.

Neva Lambright stands at the cash register, listless,
a ghost of her former self. Her shoulders are slumped.
Her complexion is pale and mottled. Her nose glows
pink, as if the skin is chafed from blowing. She gives
me a double take on spotting me, and offers a poor im-
itation of a smile. "You're back."

"I forgot to buy these when I stopped in earlier." I set

three of the votives on the counter, hand the remaining one to her.

She takes the votive, turns it over in her hand. "I love these." Her smile is sad. "For your sister?"

"These are for me." I watch as she upends the votive, looks at the price sticker and enters the SKU number and amount into the cash register.

"You're becoming one of our best customers, Chief Burkholder."

"I know a good thing when I see it." My smile feels plastic on my face. I'm keenly aware of how she's handling the votive.

"Would you like a gift box?"

"Yes, I would. Thank you."

She tugs tissue paper from a box, sets it on the counter, and carefully wraps each of the votives.

"Are Ina and Viola around?" I ask.

"You missed them by about twenty minutes. Left early today." She sighs. "Datt's going to help me close up."

I'd been hoping to catch the other girls, too. I'm going to have to settle for what I've got—and hope to hell I'm wrong.

"Thanks." Making eye contact with her, I reach across the counter and touch her arm. "Take care of yourself," I tell her, and head for the door.

Once I'm in the Explorer, I call Tomasetti. "Where are you?"

"I'm standing in our kitchen, trying to decide on the

Brie or Manchego, and letting this nice Spanish Rioja breathe."

"Will it keep?" I ask.

"That depends. What do you have?"

"Fingerprints. I need to process them for a comparison with the latents found on the mason jars and the key."

"You've been busy."

I hesitate and then say, "Tomasetti, I don't want to be right about this."

"You mean about Viola Stutzman?"

"I mean about any of them."

He sighs. "I know the lab supervisor in the latent print unit in Richfield. Let me give her a call. Can you meet me up there?"

"I'm on my way," I tell him, and disconnect.

When I was a teenager, my *mamm* told me that it was usually a *bang gvissa* or "worried conscience" that kept people up nights. I think she may have been trying to goad me—or guilt me—into behaving myself. It didn't work, of course. I've been an insomniac long enough to know that while conscience can play a role, it's those other troubles piled on top of it that wreak havoc on a person's peace of mind.

After leaving The Mercantile, I met Tomasetti at the BCI field office in Richfield, where he works. He got me through security and we met with the supervisor of the latent print section of the lab. Margaret Brooks is a certified latent print examiner. I don't know how Tomasetti did it, but she agreed to process and extract the prints from the votives, do the comparison, and get back to us.

It's nearly five A.M. now. I'd planned on grabbing a few hours of sleep, but after two hours of tossing and turning I gave up on the idea. *Bang gvissa,* a little voice whispers, and I find myself thinking of my *mamm.*

I'm sitting at the table in my big farmhouse kitchen, a cold cup of coffee in front of me. I actually considered breaking out the bottle of whiskey we keep above the fridge, but I have a sinking feeling I'm facing a busy morning. I'm going to need to keep my wits about me, because I also know that none of it's going to be pleasant. In fact, if my hunch is correct, it's going to break my heart.

The window above the sink is open and I can hear the cacophony of the bullfrogs from the pond. The hoot of an owl on the hunt. The occasional squawk of a goose that overnighted in the pond. They're comforting sounds I've grown to cherish in the past months. Tonight, they don't quite penetrate the darkness surrounding my heart.

"Kate."

I look toward the door to see Tomasetti come through and squint at me. Despite my mood, the sight of him conjures a smile. Mussed hair. Scruffy whiskers. Sweatpants and a faded police academy T-shirt. He's not a morning guy and he's not shy about letting me know. This morning, he's mindful of my presentiment, so he does his best to be civil.

"You get any sleep?" he asks.

"A little."

"Uh-huh." He knows better.

I motion toward the coffeemaker on the counter. "It's fresh. Milk in the fridge."

He pads to the counter and pours.

"I figured Margaret would have called by now," I say.

"If anything, Margaret Brooks is thorough and a perfectionist to boot," he says. "But you can rest assured that when she calls, there will be no question."

"She must have owed you a big favor."

"She did." He carries his cup to the table and sits across from me. "Now I owe her."

One of many benefits of living with John Tomasetti, who's been with BCI for several years now, is that when I need help—whether it be on a personal or professional level—he's there for me. He's good at what he does, he has a lot of connections, and he has no qualms about putting them to work for me.

I look at the clock on the wall for the hundredth time. My cell phone on the table next to my cup. Leaning forward, I set my hand over Tomasetti's. "Thank you."

He meets my gaze and a shadow of a smile touches his mouth. "Lovers with benefits."

I try to smile, but don't quite manage. We sit in silence for a few minutes. I sip cold coffee and make an effort to keep my eyes off my cell.

"Daniel Gingerich was a serial sexual predator." I say the words without looking up from my cup. "He ruined countless lives. He indirectly caused the death of at least one young Amish woman and her unborn child. Maybe the Petersheims. Tomasetti, if I'm right about this, if I follow through, where is the justice?"

He sets down his cup. "You and I have been around the block enough times to know that Lady Justice doesn't always get it right. We make the hard choices. We do the best we can. We pick up the pieces and we move the fuck on."

"Those girls are barely out of their teens. They've got their entire lives ahead of them."

"They should have thought of that before they locked that son of a bitch in the barn and burned him to death."

The words make me wince despite my resolve to remain detached. "They knew what he was. They knew he wouldn't stop."

"In the eyes of the law, that is not a justifiable homicide."

"Gingerich was a threat. If he'd escalated—"

"He was not an imminent threat." He gives me a hard, assessing look. "There are a lot of ways to look at what might've happened. Maybe Daniel Gingerich got what he deserved. Those girls—*if* they did it—served up a little street justice, Amish style. We don't get to judge, Kate. We enforce the law. The rest is up to the courts."

"I hate this."

Tomasetti scowls at me, unmoved.

I rub my hands over my face, realizing I'm too tired to think clearly, and too mired in my own history to maintain any semblance of distance.

After a moment, he reaches for my hand, waits until I make eye contact with him. "Look, if you're right and all of this plays out, if it goes to court and those girls are put in front of a jury . . ." He shrugs. "I'm not a lawyer, but I've been involved in enough trials to know there's such a thing as extenuating circumstances. If other women—other victims—come forward." Another shrug. "Furthermore, even if those girls are convicted, they may not draw long sentences. They may not do time. We don't know."

I jump when my cell phone chirps. I hesitate, let it ring two more times, and snatch it up. "Burkholder."

"Kate, hi. It's Margaret Brooks. I didn't wake you, did I?"

"No. I've been expecting your call."

"Figured as much." She sighs. "Look, since we were dealing with a nonporous surface, I did a straightforward cyanoacrylate process in the chamber, which netted damn near perfect prints. I photographed everything and lifted the most complete prints with tape. It took some extra time, but I know this is important so I did dual comparisons. One with the computer. And a side-by-side visual comparison using the ACE-V method. It is my determination that those prints came from the same source. Of course I'll still need to have my findings verified by another . . ."

I don't hear the rest of the sentence. I look at Tomasetti. He's watching me intently.

It is my determination that those prints came from the same source.

"Chief Burkholder? Are you there?"

"I'm here," I hear myself say. "Margaret, thank you so much for doing this. For staying up all night. I appreciate it."

"Yeah, well, you're welcome, Kate. Just tell that Tomasetti character he owes me big-time."

"Will do."

I end the call. I don't look at Tomasetti as I drop the phone into my pocket. I take that moment to shore up, slip back into my cop persona. I rise and look at him. "The prints on the key and the mason jar belong to Neva Lambright."

"It's enough." He rises, too. "You got her."

I look at the clock on the wall. Not yet six A.M. "I'm going to grab a shower and head that way."

I start to turn, but he reaches out and stops me. "You want me to go with you? Or meet you there?"

I think about that a moment. "I'll call you."

"You know where to find me."

CHAPTER 25

The Mercantile doesn't open until nine A.M., but when I roll into the parking lot a little after eight, I spot Neva Lambright's car parked between the burned-out shell of the round barn and the shop. I pull up behind her car and call Tomasetti.

He picks up on the first ring. "You there?" he asks.

"Yup."

"I'm twenty minutes away."

"See you then."

I disconnect and sit there a moment, trying to get a handle on my emotions, not quite succeeding. It's not until I get out of the Explorer that I spot Viola inside the barn. She's standing next to the foundation with her back to me. As I draw closer, I see the other two girls standing together on what's left of the steps. Neva has lowered her face into her hands. Ina stands next to her as if she's at a complete loss on how to help or comfort her.

Sighing, I step into the building. "Good morning," I say as I enter.

Viola and Ina spin toward me, their expressions surprised. Neva raises her face from her hands, blinks upon recognizing me, and swipes at the tears with her fingertips.

"Hi, Chief Burkholder," says Ina.

"Didn't expect to see you here this morning," Viola adds.

I stand just inside the building and look from girl to girl, my gaze lingering on Neva. Her face is blotchy and red, her eyes anguished. There's so much misery there. But there's guilt, too. *Bang gvissa,* I think, and I feel that same grief and guilt pressing down on me, expanding in my chest.

"You're not here to buy something else for your sister, are you?" Viola asks.

"Actually, I'm here to see the three of you." I make my way more deeply into the barn and look around. The stink of charred wood and wet earth hovers. The girls stand about ten feet away. They've fallen quiet, watching me, wondering why I'm here.

"This place looks different with all that sunlight streaming in," I say.

"Datt says it's not a complete loss," Neva says solemnly. "He talked to the contractor yesterday. Mr. Graber says he can shore up the roof and the walls. It's going to take some work. Probably cost a pretty penny, too. But we're not going to lose it."

"That's good news," I say.

"Mr. Lambright told us the café is still a go," Ina proclaims.

Neva clasps her hands in front of her and looks down

at the ground. "We're going to call it Edna's. After Mamm."

"She would have liked that." I walk the perimeter of the room, taking in the damage, thinking too much, feeling so much more. Most of the roof is gone. The siding will need to be replaced. The foundation will have to be repaired.

The girls watch me. I sense their curiosity and apprehension. Still, I take the time to circle the room. I stop when I reach them. "I think the café is going to have to wait awhile."

Looks are exchanged, but no one speaks. It's so quiet I can hear the traffic on the road in front of the shop. The moan of the wind as it eases through the rafters above.

"So much of life is about the decisions we make." I say the words to no one in particular, struggling to find my way through the tangled jungle of emotion I don't want to feel. "I've made my share of bad ones. I live with them every day. What do you do when there's no way to make it right?"

Viola takes a step back, presses her hand against her stomach. *She knows,* I think. Ina stares at me, eyes wide, her mouth partially open. Neva raises her gaze to mine. In the depths of her eyes I see all the things I don't want to see. Realization. Comprehension. A sense of betrayal. And fear.

"I need to talk to you about Daniel Gingerich," I tell them.

"We've already talked to you about him," Neva says.

"We don't know anything." This, from Viola.

"I always wondered," I say slowly. "What kind of killer lets the livestock out of the barn to keep them safe?"

Ina's smile falters. Something unsettling flickers in her eyes. Alarm and the initial, cold fingers of panic. "We have no idea what you're talking about."

I don't relent. "I know what you did. I know what all of you did. I have the fingerprints to prove it."

My gaze settles on Neva. Her face is colorless now. She stares back, unmoving, her eyes wide, darting, searching.

"Your fingerprints were on the mason jar you planted at Chris Martino's house," I tell her.

"But . . . that's not possible," she says. "I didn't go there. It's not mine. It can't be."

Looking sick to her stomach, Viola sets her hand on a crossbeam and leans. "We didn't do anything wrong." But her voice has gone hoarse.

"Where does it end?" I ask.

A sob bursts from Neva's throat. "My *mamm* put those jars there!" she cries. "I must have . . . touched them or something when they were in the cellar. That's all."

"I only mentioned one jar. How did you know there were two?"

Her eyes dart to her friends, begging for help, for backup. "I don't know what you're talking about. Jar. Jars. What does it matter?"

"Your fingerprints are also on the key we found in

the Gingerich barn." I divide my attention among the three of them, so they don't know which of them I'm addressing. "You were there and you lied to me."

"We have no reason to lie about anything." This, from Ina. But her eyes flit left and right, seeking some logical explanation that isn't there.

"The Amish community is a small one, Chief Burkholder," Viola tells me. "Maybe we made the key for him. Maybe—"

"Stop lying to me," I snap. "Just . . . stop."

The girls fall silent.

I look at the three of them. Young women with their entire lives ahead and I'm filled with an impotent mix of regret and anger and what I can only describe as grief. "Hate and shame are powerful emotions. The kind that can make good people do bad things."

"We didn't do anything wrong," Viola whispers.

"You should have gone to the police after what he did to Emma," I say. "Instead, you took things into your own hands. You made a bad decision, and look where you are now."

"We did nothing," Ina says.

"Which of you did he rape?" When no one answers, I focus my attention on Neva. "Was it you?"

She raises her hands, sets them against her face. Bending, she lets out a wail so filled with agony that I feel it echo all the way to my bones. "Stop saying that! You've no right to say it!"

Ina rushes forward, grasps her friend's shoulders, sets her hand against her back; then she raises her gaze to mine. "You're wrong, Chief Burkholder. She didn't do anything. None of us did."

I push harder. "He raped Emma. He got her pregnant. And she committed suicide. Then it was Neva. The three of you knew what he was, and you knew he wouldn't stop. So you put your heads together and came up with a plan." I look at Viola. "You wrote the note. Purple ink. Little hearts and swirls." I look at the other two. "Then you lured him to the barn, locked him in the tack room, and you set the place on fire."

Viola launches herself off the wall where she'd been leaning. Her face is contorted and red. "He was a monster! He was . . . *da Deivel!*" The Devil. "I hated him. *Hated him!*"

I face her, step back, keeping a safe distance between us. "That doesn't give you the right to murder him."

Viola opens her mouth as if to say something, but no words come. Holding her hand up as if to stop me, she takes a step back, stumbles over some debris, nearly falls, keeps backing away. "I thought you cared about us. How could you do this? How could you betray us like this?"

"Because I don't have a choice," I tell her. "Because life isn't fair. Because you didn't do the right thing, and I have a job to do."

Neva straightens, raises her face from her hands. "I thought you were our friend."

"Right now I am the best friend you have," I tell her. "I will help you, but you have to tell the truth. All of it. Do you understand?"

"Don't do this," Ina cries. "Please don't make us—"

I cut her off. "I know he was a monster. I know what he did. And I know Emma and her unborn child weren't his only victims." I can hear myself breathing. I stop speaking, rein in my emotions. "You can't do what you did. You can't do that. *Even if he deserved it.*"

My own damning words echo within the confines of the barn. For a full minute no one speaks. I'm aware that Neva is crying openly, choking back sobs. Ina is standing next to Neva; she's shaking so violently, I see her dress quivering.

"Please don't tell," Viola whispers.

"I do not have a choice. It's over." I look at each of them. "You should have done the right thing. You should have gone to the police."

Neva sobs hysterically, her entire body quaking. "Emma would have been shamed. She was *ime familye weg.*" Pregnant. "Everyone would have assumed she'd given in to Elam. The bishop would have put her under the *bann.*" Her voice is strangled, the words running together. "She didn't do anything wrong. Daniel did that to her. He treated her like an animal. Made her want to die!" She screams the last sentence at the top of her lungs.

I struggle for calm, reach for it, grab it hard and snatch it back. "Which one of you lured Daniel to the barn that night?" When no one answers, I turn to Neva. "Was it you?" I turn my attention to Ina. "I know you used the guise of a meet-up to get him into the tack room. Then all you had to do was lock the door and set the fire."

"I did it," Neva cries, slanting a look at her friends. "It was me. Just me. They had no part."

Viola shoots her a warning look. "I wrote the note. I gave it to him, told him I wanted to meet him in the barn. That I was . . . ready."

"He was so stupid and predictable," Ina hisses. "We knew he would come. He couldn't stop himself. He deserved what he got!"

I divide my attention among them. "Who was in the barn with him the night he was killed?"

"All of us," Ina says, her eyes flicking to Neva, her voice breathless and shaking.

"Who set the fire?" I ask.

"I bought the gas." Viola looks from girl to girl.

"I closed the door, locked it." This from Neva. "Then I poured from the can."

"We piled some things against the door," Ina adds. "All of us. The cinder blocks. That old wheelbarrow and hay."

"I threw the matches," Ina tells me.

Viola starts to cry. "He was pounding on the door."

"We wanted to let him out." Neva sobs the words. "But the fire got too big, too fast. And then we couldn't."

"So we just . . . ran," Ina finishes.

I stare at them, feeling as if I should be pondering the question of how they could do something so monstrous. But I already know.

"What about Edna?" I ask. "How much did she know?"

Neva looks at me as if I just thrust a knife into her

belly. She's sobbing, her face red and tear-streaked. "My *mamm* was only trying to protect us."

Ina puts her arm around her friend's shoulders. "Edna knew what he was."

"We didn't tell her," Viola puts in. "She just sort of figured things out."

"She was smart that way," Ina adds.

"And the night she was killed?" I ask.

"She did it for us," Neva tells me. "For Emma. For all of us."

The Amish believe that every day is a gift from God. It's the Amish way. Be thankful for what you have, even in the face of adversity. Especially in the face of adversity. It's one of many Amish tenets I could never quite subscribe to. There are certain days I wish I could erase from my life. Today is one of them.

It's dusk now, and I'm at the farm, sitting on the dock, looking out across the pond. Around me, the frogs are just getting warmed up. The blue jays in the woods are arguing about something of consequence. It's a beautiful night, warm and humid with a barely discernible breeze from the south that carries with it the aromas of fresh-cut grass and Mr. Cline's meat smoker from a quarter mile away. I've got my jeans rolled up to my knees, my feet in the water, and a cold bottle of Killian's Red beside me.

"I thought I might find you out here."

I look over my shoulder to see Tomasetti approaching from the house. He's already changed into faded jeans and a T-shirt that has a hole the size of my thumb in the shoulder. He's holding a Killian's Red in his right hand. "You found the Killian's."

"Balm for a troubled cop's soul," I tell him.

He reaches the dock, sets down his beer, toes off his sneakers, and proceeds to roll up his pants. "How's the water?"

"Not too bad for October."

He sits down beside me and lowers his feet into the water. For the span of several minutes, neither of us speaks. Instead, we sit in companionable silence, listening to the sounds of early evening.

"Rasmussen booked the three girls into the county jail," he tells me. "They'll be arraigned and formally charged in the morning."

I close my eyes against an unexpected rush of heat. A tangle of emotions I don't want to feel. Remorse. Guilt. The loss of something that had seemed innocent and good.

Tomasetti had been there for the arrest, along with a female deputy with the Holmes County Sheriff's Department. It was an intense and emotionally wrenching event. Ina had been stoic. Neva and Viola had cried throughout. I'd done my utmost to keep them calm and explain to them what would be happening in the coming hours and days and weeks. I don't think it was much help.

"Their lives are ruined," I say.

"Changed to be sure." He shrugs. "Maybe not ruined entirely."

"I talked to the prosecutor," I tell him.

He sends me a sideways look, arches a brow. "And?"

"He's talking about second-degree homicide."

"That could change."

I slant him a look.

"Neva Lambright told Rasmussen that Mark Petersheim had been threatening her."

"Did she explain why?"

"According to her, he blamed her for his wife getting into the car with Gingerich the night she was raped. Blamed her for all of it. He was afraid Neva was going to talk about it and the Amish community would find out. He didn't want that to happen."

"Jesus."

"Look, there's no doubt those girls are in serious trouble, but there are extenuating circumstances. There was a certain level of intimidation occurring." He shrugs. "Prosecutor might be a little more willing to cut a deal."

"Tomasetti, what they did was wrong on every level. I mean that. But I don't think they're . . ." I almost say "criminals" but that wouldn't be true. The fact of the matter is they *are* criminals. "They're not sociopaths. I don't believe they're a danger to society."

"If you want to help them, I suggest you get the other women who were victimized by Gingerich to come forward."

I find myself thinking about Milo Hershberger and our final conversation. *If I could, I swear to God I'd make it right.* . . . He isn't the only person with regrets. Emma Miller's mother remained silent and her daughter died because of it. I don't think she'll make the same mistake twice.

"I've got a couple of people in mind who'll step up," I tell him.

Leaning closer, he puts his arm around my shoulders and presses a kiss to my temple. "Is there anything I can do?"

I rest my head on his shoulder. "Just be you."

"Now, there's a scary thought."

I laugh and it feels good; it releases some of the melancholy that's been plaguing me. It reminds me that life goes on. That it's good. That I'm a lucky woman with a lot to be thankful for.

"What do you say we swing by the barn on our way back inside?" he says. "Check on those chicks?"

"I'm game." I get to my feet, brush dust from the seat of my pants. Tomasetti rises, too, and we take the time to roll down our cuffs and step into our shoes. For a moment we stand there, looking out over the water.

I hear the bawling of a cow somewhere in the distance. I think of the man standing beside me and I acknowledge how far we've come in the short years we've known each other. How much we have to look forward to in the future.

"That water looks nice," he says after a moment.

I nod. "Nice on the feet."

"You know what we haven't done yet?"

I slant him a look. "Had dinner?"

He grins. "Christen the pond."

I grin, step away from him. "You wouldn't."

"You know I would."

"John Tomasetti, you're *so* not going to—"

He reaches for my hands, pulls me against him,

crushes his mouth to mine. The next thing I know we're falling. His body is solid and warm against mine, then the quick slap of cold as the water envelops me. The smells of fish and earth and living things in my nostrils.

The water isn't deep, about four feet. We come up sputtering, facing each other. His hair is sticking up on one side. He's got moss on his forehead.

We burst into laughter.

"I thought that might cheer you up," he says after a moment.

"That speck of moss above your eyebrow helped."

"Small sacrifices and all that."

Leaning into him, I put my arms around him. "Seeing those chicks probably would have done the job."

"Now you tell me," he says with a laugh.

Hand in hand, we wade to the bank and then start toward the barn.

Read on for an excerpt from

SHAMED—

the next electrifying Kate Burkholder novel,
coming soon in hardcover from Linda Castillo
and Minotaur Books!

No one went to the old Schattenbaum place anymore. No one had lived there since the flood back in 1974 washed away the crops and swept the outhouse and one of the barns into Painters Creek. Rumor had it Mr. Schattenbaum's 1960 Chevy Corvair was still sitting in the gully where the water left it.

The place had never been grand. Even in its heyday, the house had been run-down. The roof shingles were rusty and curled. Mr. Schattenbaum had talked about painting the house, but he'd never gotten around to it. Sometimes, he didn't even cut the grass. Despite its dilapidated state, once upon a time the Schattenbaum house had been the center of Mary Yoder's world, filled with laughter, love, and life.

The Schattenbaums had six kids, and even though they weren't Amish, Mary's *mamm* had let her visit—and Mary did just that every chance she got. The Schattenbaums had four spotted ponies, after all; they had baby pigs, a slew of donkeys, a big tom turkey, and too many goats to count. Mary had been ten years old that last summer, and she'd had the time of her life.

It was hard for her to believe fifty years had passed; she was a grandmother now, a widow, and had seen her sixtieth birthday just last week. Every time she drove the buggy past the old farm, the years melted away and she always thought: If a place could speak, the stories it would tell.

Mary still lived in her childhood home, with her daughter and son-in-law now, half a mile down the road. She made it a point to walk this way when the opportunity presented itself. In spring, she cut the irises that still bloomed in the flower bed at the back of the house. In summer, she came for the peonies. In fall, it was all about the walnuts. According to Mr. Schattenbaum, his grandfather had planted a dozen or so black walnut trees. They were a hundred years old now and flourished where the backyard had once been. Every fall, the trees dropped thousands of nuts that kept Mary baking throughout the year—and her eight grandchildren well supplied with walnut layer cake.

The house looked much the same as it did all those years ago. The barn where Mary had spent so many afternoons cooing over those ponies had collapsed in a windstorm a few years back. The rafters and siding were slowly being reclaimed by a jungle of vines, overgrowth, and waist-high grass.

"Grossmammi! Do you want me to open the gate?"

Mary looked over at the girl on the seat beside her, and her heart soared. She'd brought her granddaughters with her to help pick up walnuts. Annie was five and the picture of her *mamm* at that age: Blond hair that easily tangled. Blue eyes that cried a little too readily. A thoughtful child already talking about teaching in the two-room schoolhouse down the road.

At seven, Elsie was a sweet, effervescent girl. She was one of the special ones, curious and affectionate, with a plump little body and round eyeglasses with lenses as thick as a pop bottle. She was a true gift from God, and Mary loved her all the more because of her differences.

"Might be a good idea for me to stop the buggy first, don't you think?" Tugging the reins, Mary slowed the horse to a walk and made the turn into the weed-riddled gravel lane. "Whoa."

She could just make out the blazing orange canopies of the trees behind the house, and she felt that familiar tug of homecoming, of nostalgia.

"Hop on down now," she told the girls. "Open that gate. Watch out for that barbed wire, you hear?"

Both children clambered from the buggy. Their skirts swished around their legs as they ran to the rusted steel gate, their hands making short work of the chain.

Mary drove the horse through, then stopped to wait for the girls. "Come on, little ones! Leave the gate open. I hear all those pretty walnuts calling for us!"

Giggling, the girls climbed into the buggy.

"Get your bags ready," Mary told them as she drove past the house. "I think we're going to harvest enough this afternoon to fill all those baskets we brought."

She smiled as the two little ones gathered their bags. Mary had made them from burlap last year for just this occasion. The bags were large, with double handles easily looped over a small shoulder. She'd embroidered green walnut leaves on the front of Elsie's bag. On Annie's she'd stitched a brown walnut that had been cracked open, exposing all that deliciousness inside.

Mary drove the buggy around to the back of the house, where the yard had once been. A smile whispered across her mouth when she saw that the old tire swing was still there. She stopped the horse in the shade of a hackberry tree where the grass was tall enough for the mare to nibble, and she drew in the sight, felt that familiar swell in her chest. Picking up their gloves and her own bag, Mary climbed down. For a moment, she stood there and listened to the place. The chirp of a cardinal from the tallest tree. The whisper of wind through the treetops.

"Girls, I think we've chosen the perfect day to harvest walnuts," she said.

Bag draped over her shoulder, Elsie followed suit. Annie was still a little thing, so Mary reached for her and set her on the ground. She handed the two girls their tiny leather gloves.

"I don't want to see any stained fingers," she told them.

"You, too, Grossmammi."

Chuckling, Mary walked with them to the stand of trees, where the sun dappled the ground at her feet.

"Look how big that tree is, Grossmammi!" Annie exclaimed.

"That's my favorite," Mary replied.

"Look at all the walnuts!" Elsie said with an exuberance only a seven-year-old could manage.

"God blessed us with a good crop this year," Mary replied.

"Are we going to make cakes, Grossmammi?"

"Of course we are," Mary assured her.

"Walnut layer cake!" Annie put in.

"And pumpkin bread!" Elsie added.

"If you girls picked as much as you talked, we'd be done by now." She tempered the admonition with a smile.

Stepping beneath the canopy of the tree, Mary knelt and scooped up a few walnuts, looking closely at the husks. They were green, mottled with black, but solid and mold free. It was best to gather them by October, but they were already into November. "Firm ones only, girls. They've been on the ground awhile. We're late to harvest this year."

Out of the corner of her eye, she saw little Annie squat and drop a walnut into her bag. Ten yards away, Elsie was already at the next tree, leather gloves on her little hands. Such a sweet, obedient child.

They worked in silence for half an hour. The girls chattered. Mary pretended not to notice when they tossed walnuts at each other. Before she knew it, her bag was full. Hefting it onto her shoulder, she walked to the buggy, and dumped her spoils into the bushel basket.

She was on her way to join the girls when something in the house snagged her attention. Movement in the window? She didn't think so; no one ever came here, after all. Probably just the branches swaying in the breeze and reflecting off the glass. But as Mary started toward the girls, she saw it again. She was sure of it this time. A shadow in the kitchen window.

Making sure the girls were embroiled in their work, she set her bag on the ground. A crow cawed from atop the roof as she made her way to the back of the house and stepped onto the rickety porch. The door stood open a few inches, so she called out. "Hello?"

"Who are you talking to, Grossmammi?"

She glanced over her shoulder to see Annie watching her from her place beneath the tree, hands on her hips. Behind her, Elsie was making a valiant effort to juggle walnuts and not having very much luck.

"You just mind those walnuts," she told them. "I'm taking a quick peek at Mrs. Schattenbaum's kitchen."

"Can we come?"

"I'll only be a minute. You girls get back to work or we'll be here till dark."

Mary waited until the girls resumed their task and then crossed the porch, set her hand against the door. The hinges groaned when she pushed it open. "Hello? Is someone there?"

Memories assailed her as she stepped inside. She recalled peanut-butter-and-jelly sandwiches at the big kitchen table. Mrs. Schattenbaum stirring a pot of something that smelled heavenly on the stove. Sneaking chocolate-chip cookies from the jar in the cupboard. The old Formica counters were still intact. The pitted porcelain sink. The stove was gone; all that remained was a gas line and rust stains on the floor. Rat droppings everywhere. Some of the linoleum had been chewed away.

Mary was about to go to the cabinet, to see if that old cookie jar was still in its place, when a sound from the next room stopped her. Something—or someone—was definitely in there. Probably whatever had chewed up that flooring, she thought. A raccoon or possum. Or a rat. Mary wasn't squeamish about animals; she'd grown up on a farm, after all. But she'd never liked rats. . . .

She glanced out the window above the sink. Annie was pitching walnuts baseball style. Elsie was using a stick as a bat. Shaking her head, Mary chuckled. Probably best not to leave them alone too long. . . .

Turning, she went to the doorway that opened to the living room. It was a dimly lit space filled with shadows. The smells of mildew and rotting wood laced the air. The plank floors were badly warped. Water stains on the ceiling. Wallpaper hung off the walls like sunburned skin. Curtains going to rot.

"Who's there?" she said quietly.

A sound to her right startled a gasp from her. She saw movement from the shadows. Heard the shuffle of shoes against the floor. Someone rushing toward her . . .

The first blow landed against her chest, hard enough to take her breath. She reeled backward, arms flailing. A shock of pain registered behind her ribs, hot and deep. The knowledge that she was injured. All of it followed by an explosion of terror.

Something glinted in the periphery of her vision. A silhouette coming at her fast. She saw the pale oval of a face. She raised her hands. A scream ripped from her throat.

The second blow came from above. Slashed her right hand. Slammed into her shoulder and went deep. Pain zinged; then her arm went numb. It wasn't until she saw the shiny black of blood that she realized she'd been cut. That it was bad.

Mewling, she stumbled into the kitchen, trying to put some distance between her and her attacker. He followed, aggressive and intent. The light hit his face and recognition kicked. Another layer of fear swamped her and she thought: *This can't be happening.*

"You!" she cried.

The knife went up again, came down hard, hit her clavicle. Pain arced, like a lightning strike in her brain. The shocking red of blood, warm and wet on her arms, her hands, streaming down the front of her dress, splattering the floor.

And in that instant she knew. Why he'd come. What came next. The realization filled her with such horror that for an instant, she couldn't move, couldn't speak. Then she turned, flung herself toward the door, tried to run. But her shoe slipped in the blood; her foot went out from under her, and she fell to her knees.

She twisted to face him, looked up at her assailant. "Leave her alone!" she screamed. "In the name of God *leave her alone!*"

The knife went up. She lunged at him, grabbed his trousers, fisting the fabric, yanking and slapping. Hope leapt when he staggered sideways. The knife slammed into her back like a hammer blow. A starburst of pain as the blade careened off bone. Her vision dimmed. No breath left. No time.

Her attacker raised the knife. Lips peeled back. Teeth clenched and grinding.

She scrambled to her feet, threw herself toward the window above the sink, and smashed her hand through the glass. Caught a glimpse of the girls.

"Run!" she screamed. "*Da Deivel!*" The Devil. "Run! *Run!*"

Footfalls sounded behind her. She looked over her shoulder. A flash of silver as the knife came down, slammed into her back like an ax. White-hot pain streaked up her spine. Her knees buckled and she went down. Her face hit the floor. Above, her attacker bellowed like a beast.

Da Deivel.

He knelt, muttering ungodly words in a voice like gravel. Another knife blow jolted her body, but she couldn't move. No pain this time. A rivulet of blood on the linoleum. More in her mouth. Breaths gurgling. Too weak to spit, so she opened her lips and let it run. Using the last of her strength, she looked up at her attacker.

Run, sweet child, she thought. *Run for your life.*

The knife arced, the impact as violent as a bare-fisted punch, hot as fire. The blow rocked her body. Once. Twice. No more fight left. She couldn't get away, couldn't move.

She was aware of the linoleum cold and gritty against her cheek. The sunlight streaming in through the window. The crow cawing somewhere outside. Finally, the sound of his footfalls as he walked to the door.